GENERATION GONE VOL.1

Originally published as Generation Gone #1–5

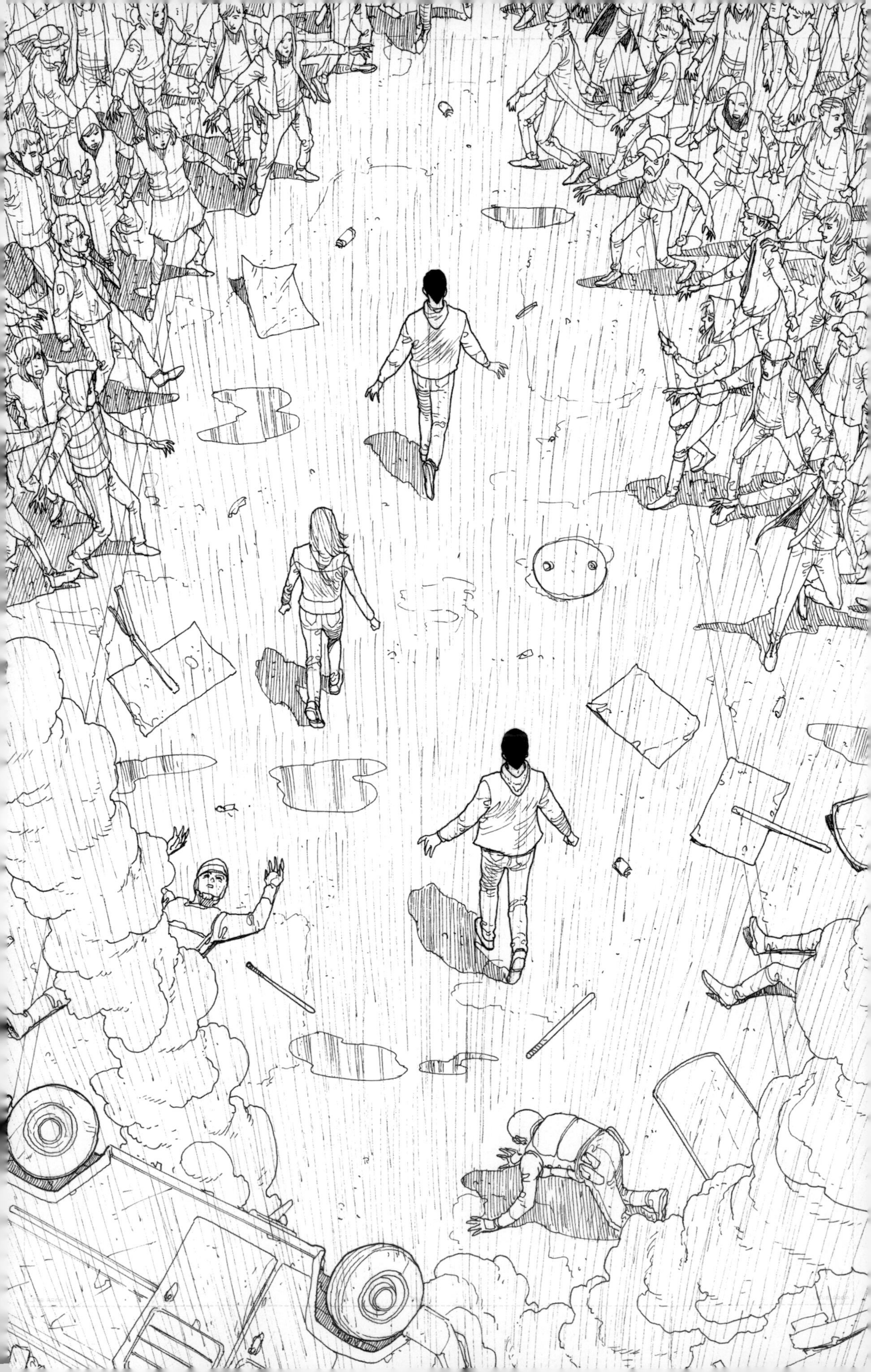

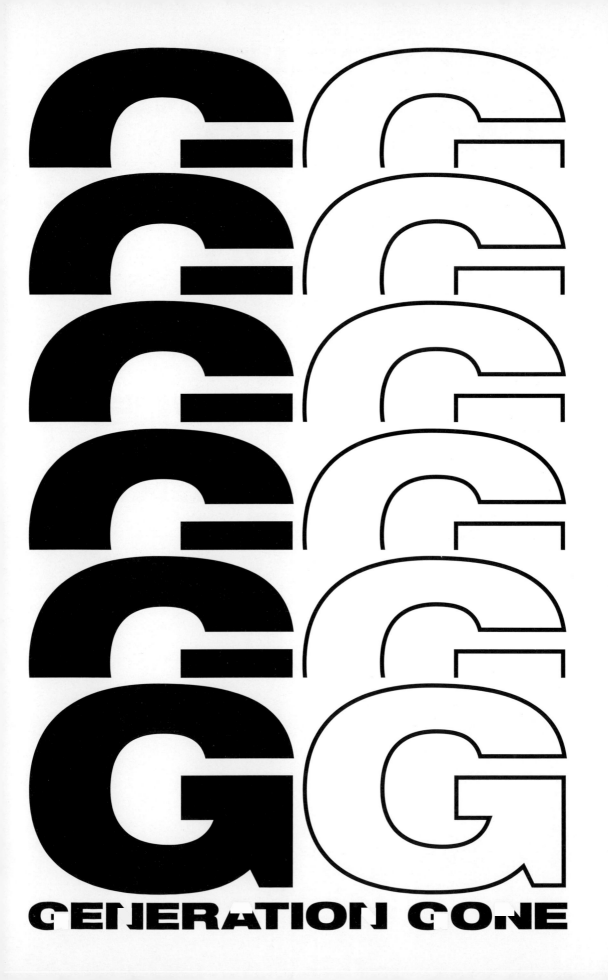

GENERATION GONE

STORYTELLERS: ALEŠ KOT & ANDRÉ LIMA ARAÚJO

WRITTEN BY ALEŠ KOT **ART BY ANDRÉ LIMA ARAÚJO**

COLORING: CHRIS O'HALLORAN

LETTERING: CLAYTON COWLES

DESIGN: TOM MULLER **EDITOR: LIZZIE KAYE**

CHAPTER ONE

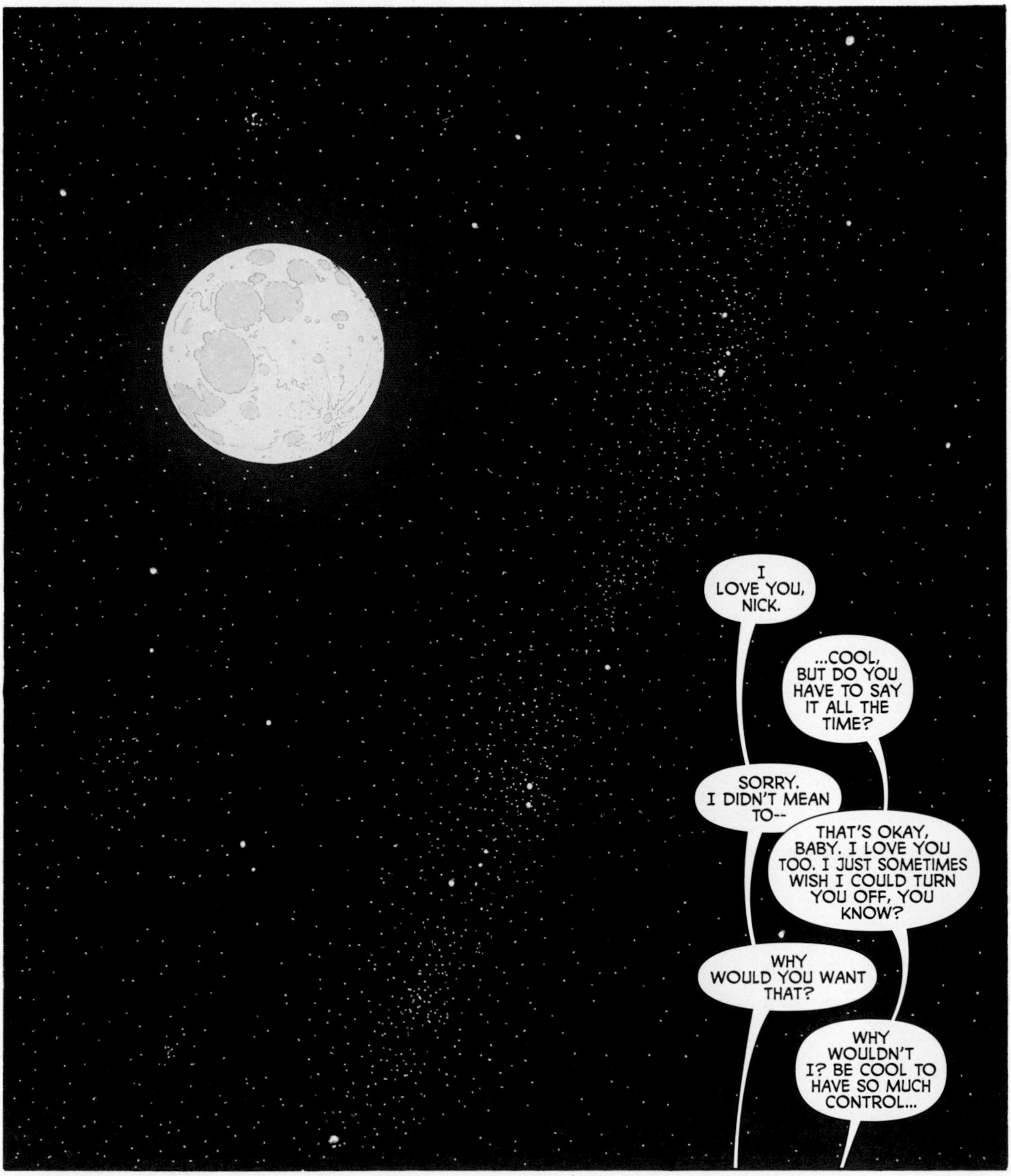
I LOVE YOU, NICK.
...COOL, BUT DO YOU HAVE TO SAY IT ALL THE TIME?
SORRY. I DIDN'T MEAN TO--
THAT'S OKAY, BABY. I LOVE YOU TOO. I JUST SOMETIMES WISH I COULD TURN YOU OFF, YOU KNOW?
WHY WOULD YOU WANT THAT?
WHY WOULDN'T I? BE COOL TO HAVE SO MUCH CONTROL...

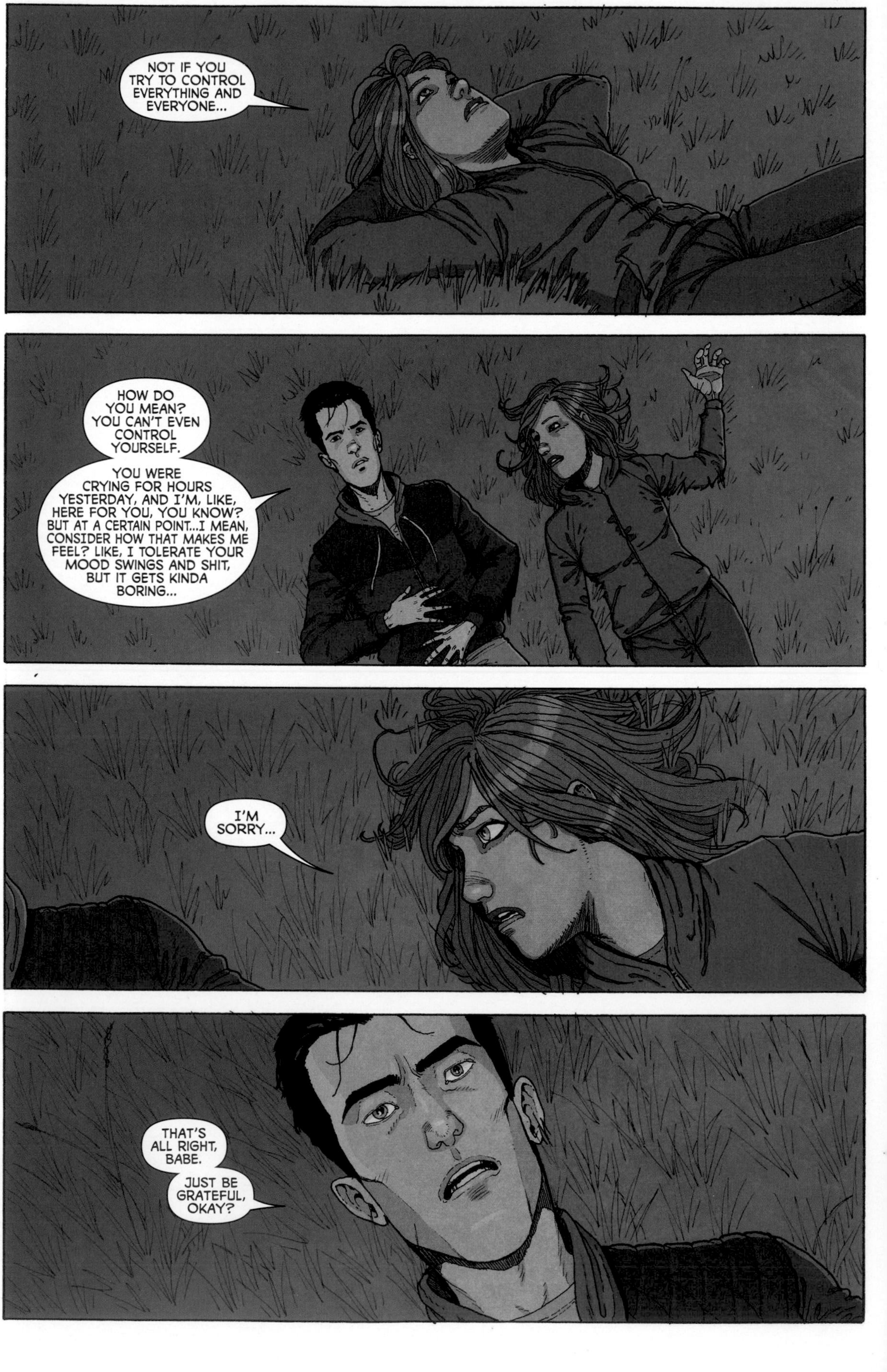
NOT IF YOU TRY TO CONTROL EVERYTHING AND EVERYONE...
HOW DO YOU MEAN? YOU CAN'T EVEN CONTROL YOURSELF.
YOU WERE CRYING FOR HOURS YESTERDAY, AND I'M, LIKE, HERE FOR YOU, YOU KNOW? BUT AT A CERTAIN POINT...I MEAN, CONSIDER HOW THAT MAKES ME FEEL? LIKE, I TOLERATE YOUR MOOD SWINGS AND SHIT, BUT IT GETS KINDA BORING...
I'M SORRY...
THAT'S ALL RIGHT, BABE.
JUST BE GRATEFUL, OKAY?

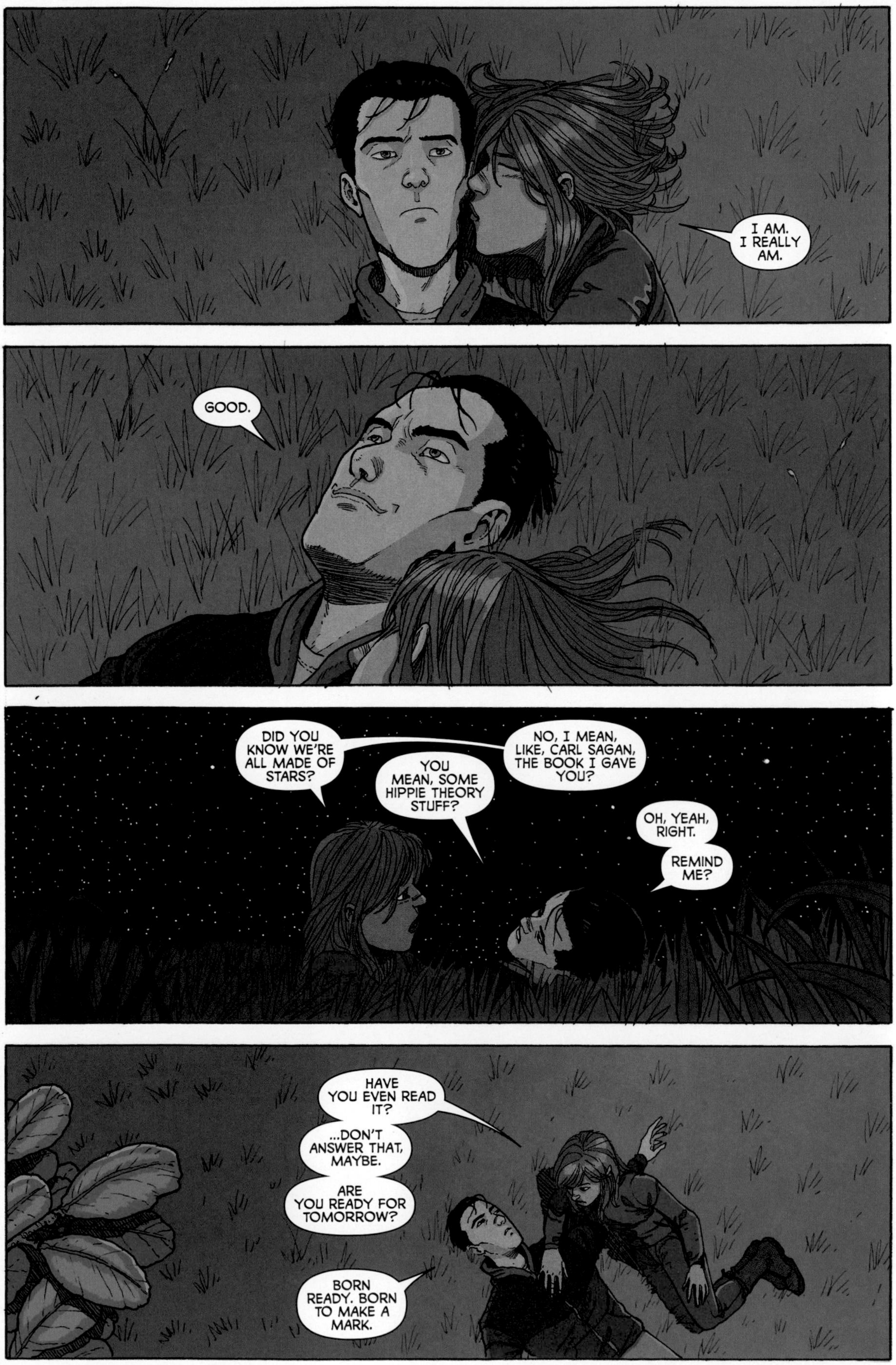
I AM. I REALLY AM.
GOOD.
DID YOU KNOW WE'RE ALL MADE OF STARS?
YOU MEAN, SOME HIPPIE THEORY STUFF?
NO, I MEAN, LIKE, CARL SAGAN, THE BOOK I GAVE YOU?
OH, YEAH, RIGHT.
REMIND ME?
HAVE YOU EVEN READ IT?
...DON'T ANSWER THAT, MAYBE.
ARE YOU READY FOR TOMORROW?
BORN READY. BORN TO MAKE A MARK.

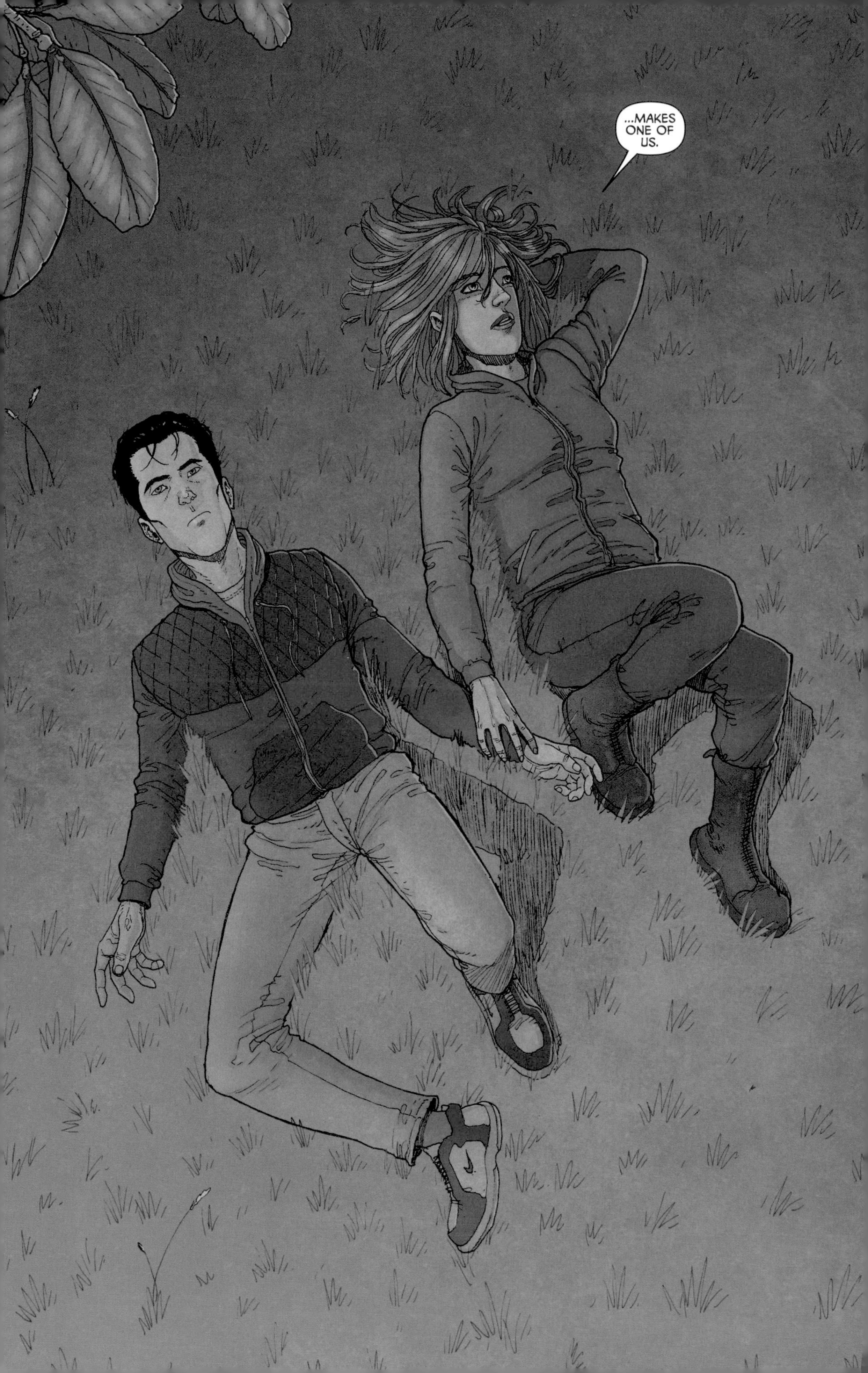
...MAKES ONE OF US.

WE HAVE TO AIM HIGHER.

I AM NOT GOING TO PRETEND I DON'T KNOW WHAT WE ARE DOING HERE. REGARDLESS OF MY OWN INTENTIONS, S.T.A.R. IS STILL A SUBSECTION OF D.A.R.P.A.--

--AND THUS WE BUILD IDEAS, CODES, AND MACHINES YOU ALL CAN USE TO CONTINUE RE-ESTABLISHING THE GLOBAL DOMINANCE OF THE UNITED STATES OF AMERICA WHICH HAS BEEN ERODING...

...AT AN INCREASINGLY RAPID RATE SINCE THE 1970s.

PERHAPS I AM TOO DIRECT FOR YOU.

I ALSO MADE IT CLEAR WHEN YOU HIRED ME THAT I WAS INTERESTED IN MORE THAN THE MILITARY-INDUSTRIAL COMPLEX APPLICATION OF MY IDEAS.

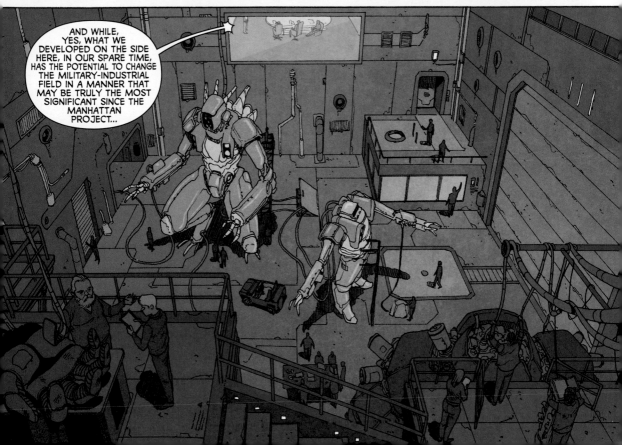

AND WHILE, YES, WHAT WE DEVELOPED ON THE SIDE HERE, IN OUR SPARE TIME, HAS THE POTENTIAL TO CHANGE THE MILITARY-INDUSTRIAL FIELD IN A MANNER THAT MAY BE TRULY THE MOST SIGNIFICANT SINCE THE MANHATTAN PROJECT...

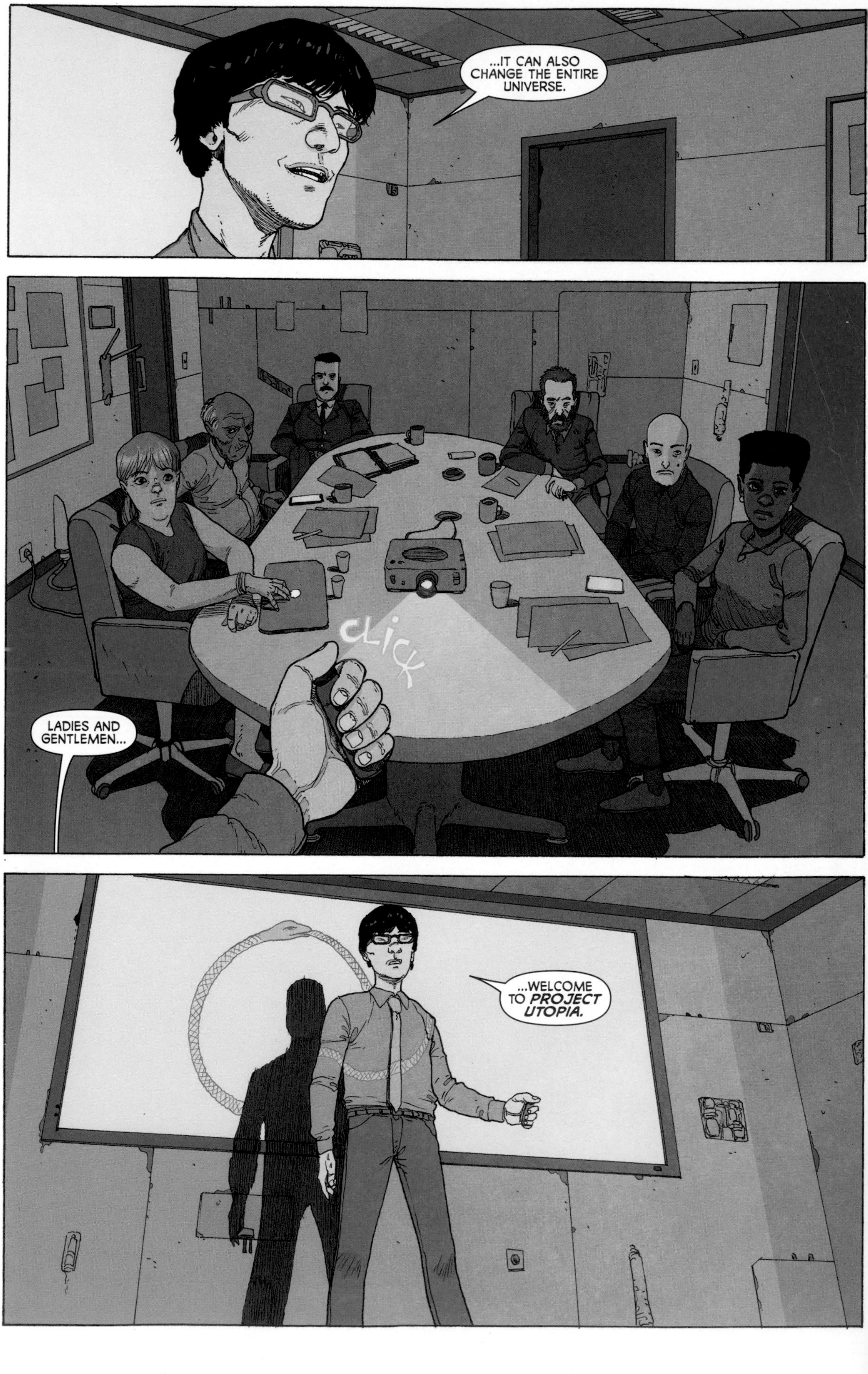
...IT CAN ALSO CHANGE THE ENTIRE UNIVERSE.
LADIES AND GENTLEMEN...
CLICK
...WELCOME TO *PROJECT UTOPIA.*

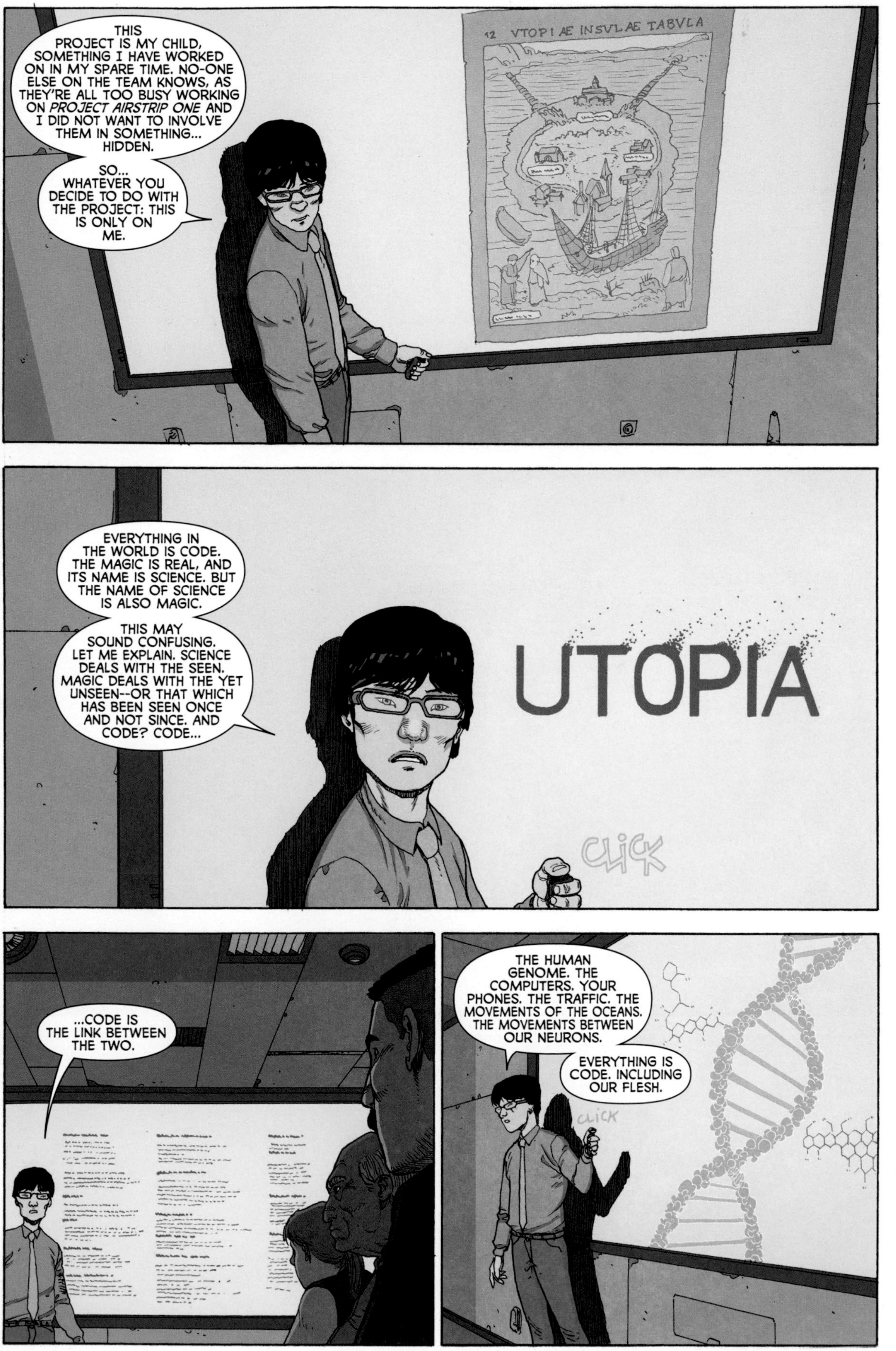
THIS PROJECT IS MY CHILD, SOMETHING I HAVE WORKED ON IN MY SPARE TIME. NO-ONE ELSE ON THE TEAM KNOWS, AS THEY'RE ALL TOO BUSY WORKING ON *PROJECT AIRSTRIP ONE* AND I DID NOT WANT TO INVOLVE THEM IN SOMETHING... HIDDEN.
SO... WHATEVER YOU DECIDE TO DO WITH THE PROJECT: THIS IS ONLY ON ME.
12 VTOPI AE INSVLAE TABVLA
EVERYTHING IN THE WORLD IS CODE. THE MAGIC IS REAL, AND ITS NAME IS SCIENCE. BUT THE NAME OF SCIENCE IS ALSO MAGIC.
THIS MAY SOUND CONFUSING. LET ME EXPLAIN. SCIENCE DEALS WITH THE SEEN. MAGIC DEALS WITH THE YET UNSEEN--OR THAT WHICH HAS BEEN SEEN ONCE AND NOT SINCE. AND CODE? CODE...
UTOPIA
CLICK
...CODE IS THE LINK BETWEEN THE TWO.
THE HUMAN GENOME. THE COMPUTERS. YOUR PHONES. THE TRAFFIC. THE MOVEMENTS OF THE OCEANS. THE MOVEMENTS BETWEEN OUR NEURONS.
EVERYTHING IS CODE. INCLUDING OUR FLESH.
CLICK

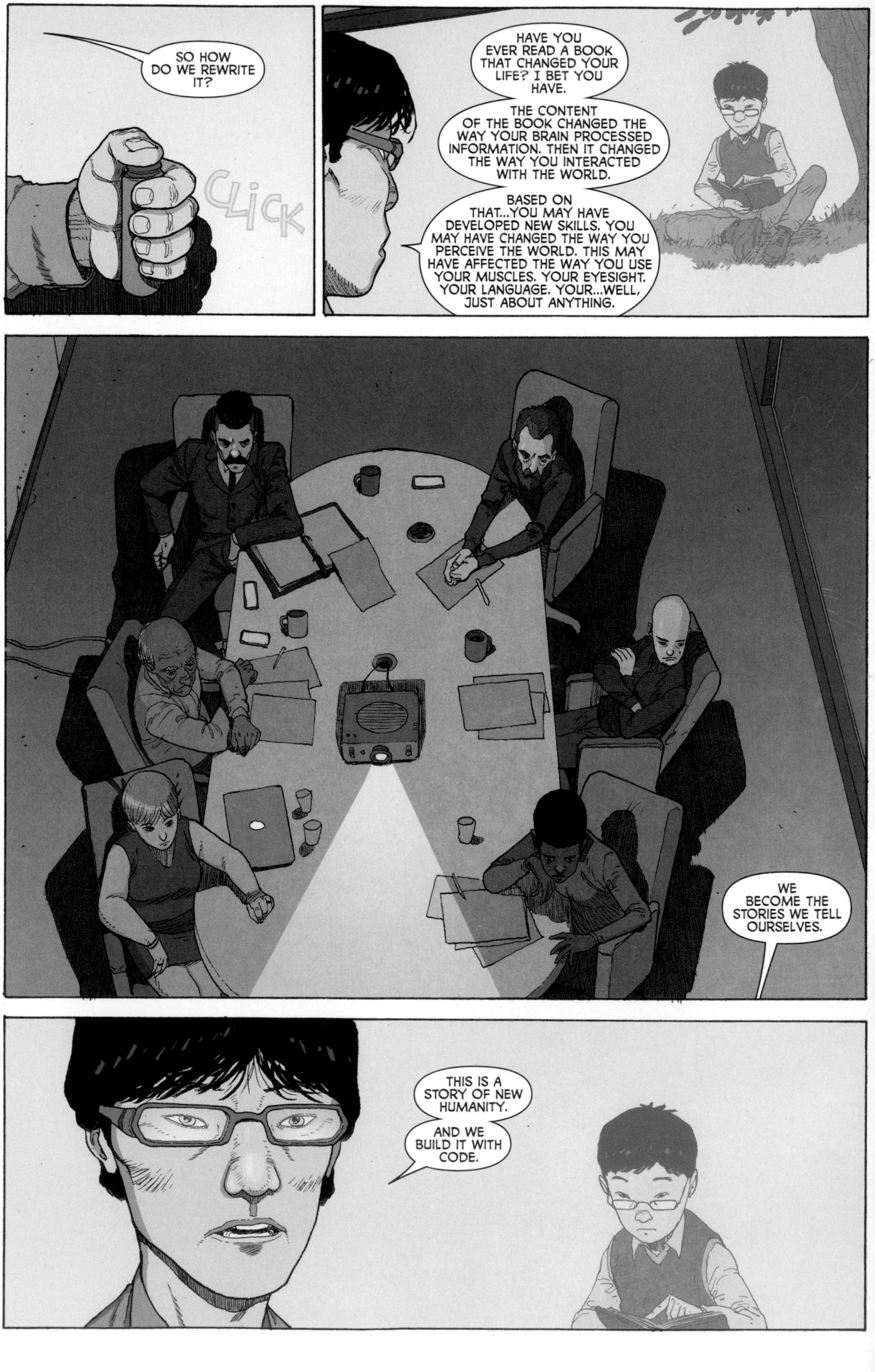
SO HOW DO WE REWRITE IT?
CLICK
HAVE YOU EVER READ A BOOK THAT CHANGED YOUR LIFE? I BET YOU HAVE.
THE CONTENT OF THE BOOK CHANGED THE WAY YOUR BRAIN PROCESSED INFORMATION. THEN IT CHANGED THE WAY YOU INTERACTED WITH THE WORLD.
BASED ON THAT...YOU MAY HAVE DEVELOPED NEW SKILLS. YOU MAY HAVE CHANGED THE WAY YOU PERCEIVE THE WORLD. THIS MAY HAVE AFFECTED THE WAY YOU USE YOUR MUSCLES. YOUR EYESIGHT. YOUR LANGUAGE. YOUR...WELL, JUST ABOUT ANYTHING.
WE BECOME THE STORIES WE TELL OURSELVES.
THIS IS A STORY OF NEW HUMANITY.
AND WE BUILD IT WITH CODE.

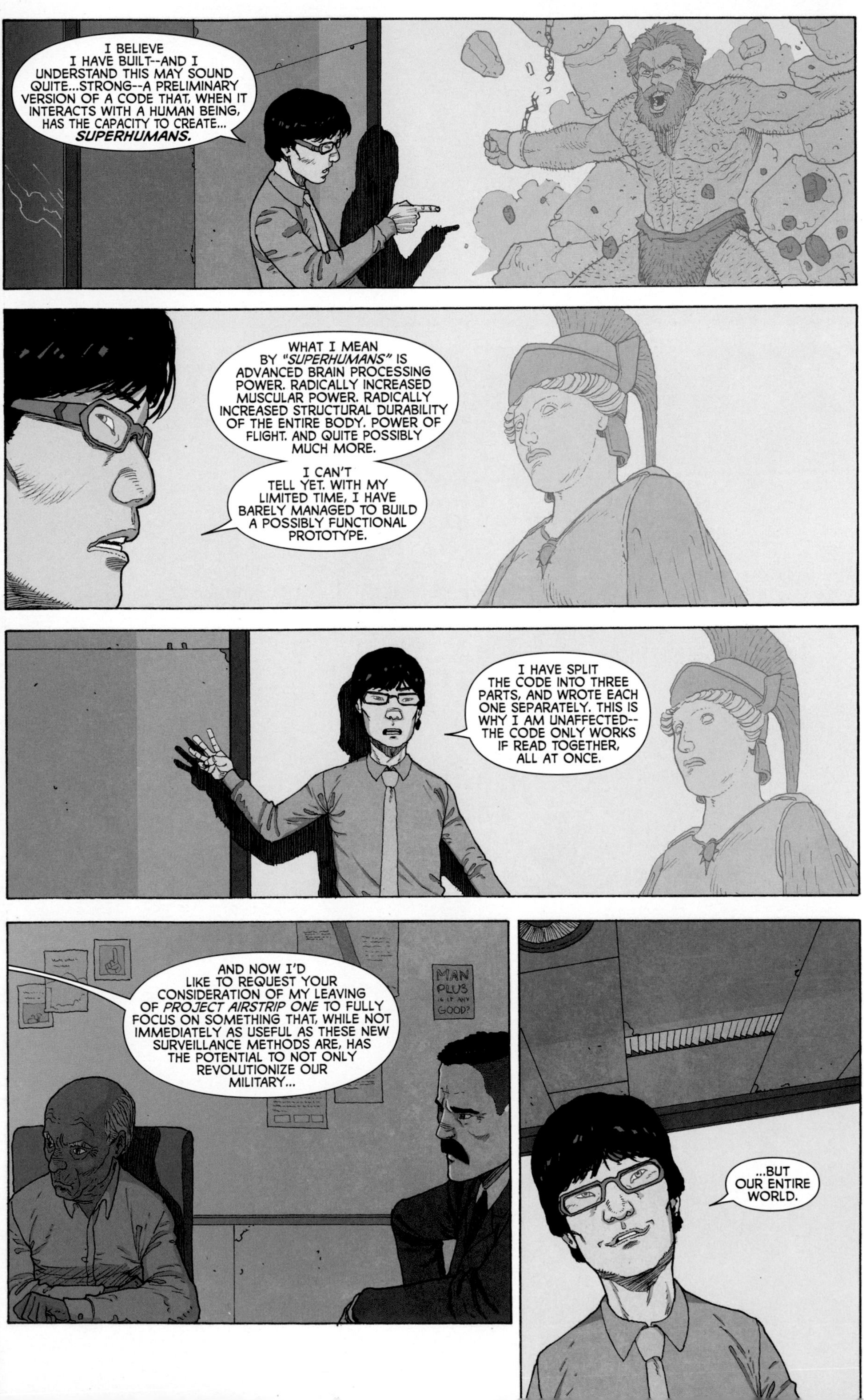
I BELIEVE I HAVE BUILT--AND I UNDERSTAND THIS MAY SOUND QUITE...STRONG--A PRELIMINARY VERSION OF A CODE THAT, WHEN IT INTERACTS WITH A HUMAN BEING, HAS THE CAPACITY TO CREATE... *SUPERHUMANS.*
WHAT I MEAN BY "*SUPERHUMANS*" IS ADVANCED BRAIN PROCESSING POWER. RADICALLY INCREASED MUSCULAR POWER. RADICALLY INCREASED STRUCTURAL DURABILITY OF THE ENTIRE BODY. POWER OF FLIGHT. AND QUITE POSSIBLY MUCH MORE.
I CAN'T TELL YET. WITH MY LIMITED TIME, I HAVE BARELY MANAGED TO BUILD A POSSIBLY FUNCTIONAL PROTOTYPE.
I HAVE SPLIT THE CODE INTO THREE PARTS, AND WROTE EACH ONE SEPARATELY. THIS IS WHY I AM UNAFFECTED-- THE CODE ONLY WORKS IF READ TOGETHER, ALL AT ONCE.
MAN PLUS IS IT ANY GOOD?
AND NOW I'D LIKE TO REQUEST YOUR CONSIDERATION OF MY LEAVING OF *PROJECT AIRSTRIP ONE* TO FULLY FOCUS ON SOMETHING THAT, WHILE NOT IMMEDIATELY AS USEFUL AS THESE NEW SURVEILLANCE METHODS ARE, HAS THE POTENTIAL TO NOT ONLY REVOLUTIONIZE OUR MILITARY...
...BUT OUR ENTIRE WORLD.

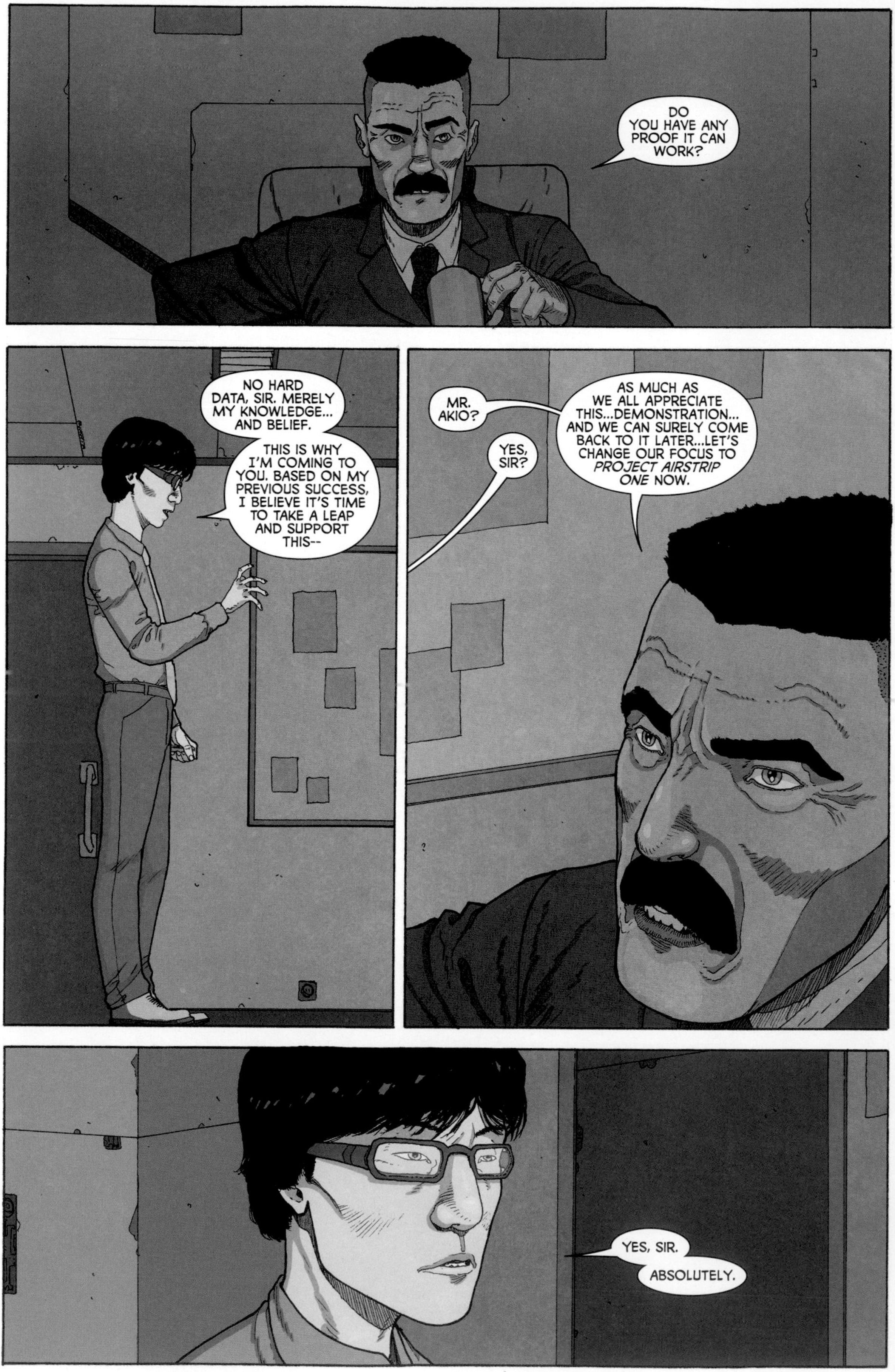
DO YOU HAVE ANY PROOF IT CAN WORK?
NO HARD DATA, SIR. MERELY MY KNOWLEDGE... AND BELIEF.
THIS IS WHY I'M COMING TO YOU. BASED ON MY PREVIOUS SUCCESS, I BELIEVE IT'S TIME TO TAKE A LEAP AND SUPPORT THIS--
MR. AKIO?
YES, SIR?
AS MUCH AS WE ALL APPRECIATE THIS...DEMONSTRATION... AND WE CAN SURELY COME BACK TO IT LATER...LET'S CHANGE OUR FOCUS TO *PROJECT AIRSTRIP ONE* NOW.
YES, SIR.
ABSOLUTELY.

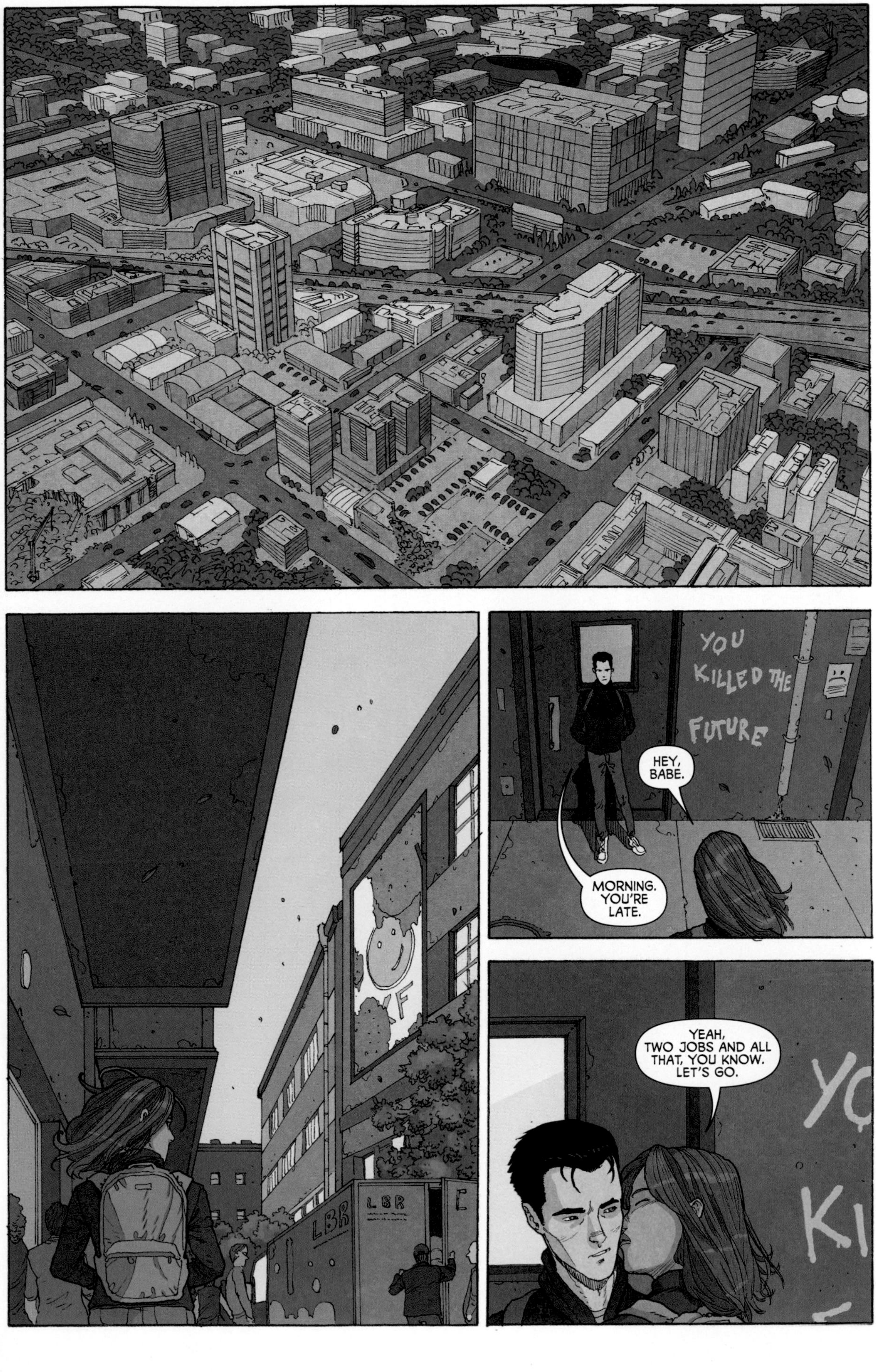
YOU KILLED THE FUTURE
HEY, BABE.
MORNING. YOU'RE LATE.
YEAH, TWO JOBS AND ALL THAT, YOU KNOW. LET'S GO.

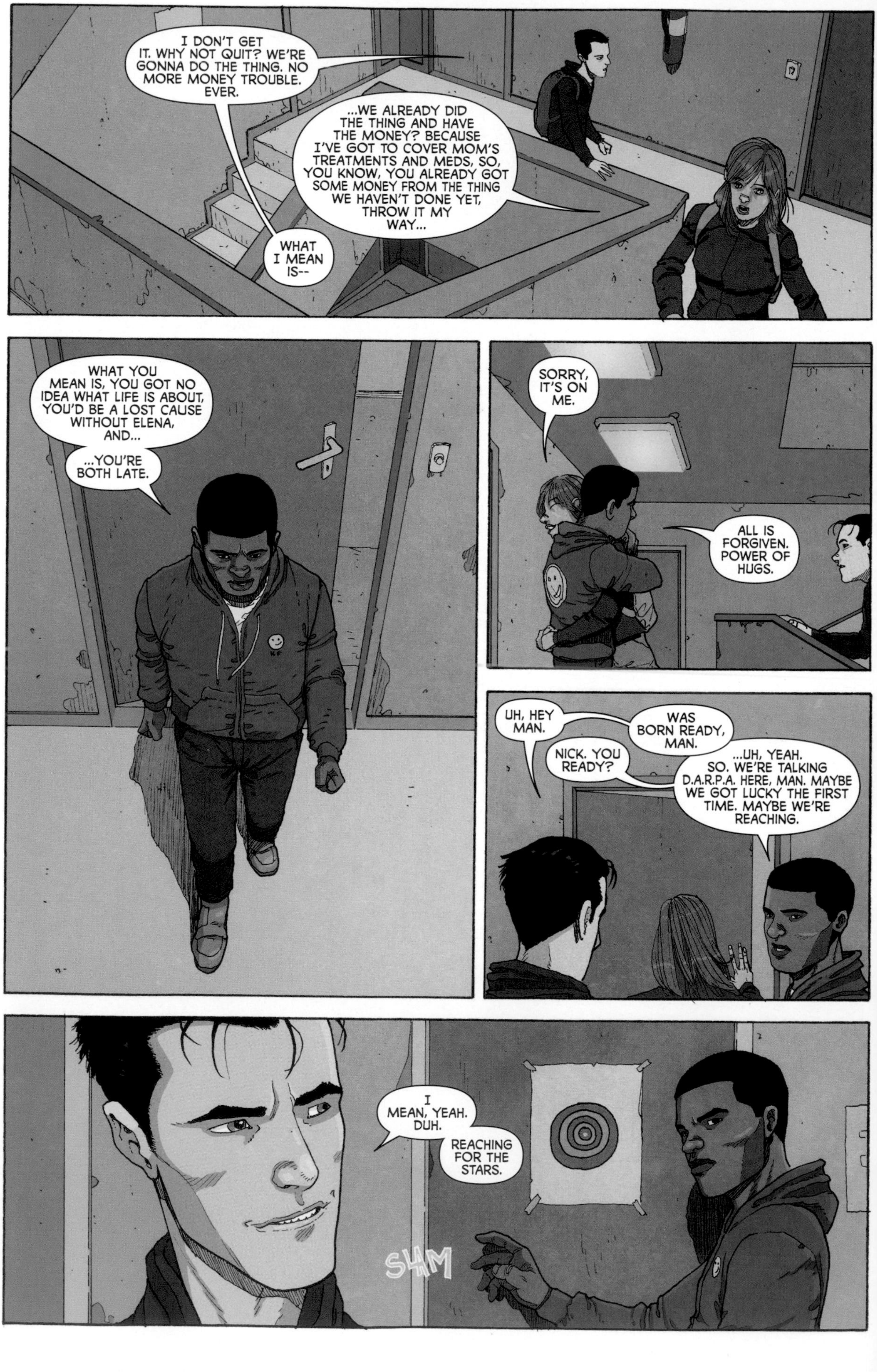
I DON'T GET IT. WHY NOT QUIT? WE'RE GONNA DO THE THING. NO MORE MONEY TROUBLE. EVER.
...WE ALREADY DID THE THING AND HAVE THE MONEY? BECAUSE I'VE GOT TO COVER MOM'S TREATMENTS AND MEDS, SO, YOU KNOW, YOU ALREADY GOT SOME MONEY FROM THE THING WE HAVEN'T DONE YET, THROW IT MY WAY...
WHAT I MEAN IS--
WHAT YOU MEAN IS, YOU GOT NO IDEA WHAT LIFE IS ABOUT, YOU'D BE A LOST CAUSE WITHOUT ELENA, AND...
...YOU'RE BOTH LATE.
SORRY, IT'S ON ME.
ALL IS FORGIVEN. POWER OF HUGS.
UH, HEY MAN.
WAS BORN READY, MAN.
NICK. YOU READY?
...UH, YEAH. SO. WE'RE TALKING D.A.R.P.A. HERE, MAN. MAYBE WE GOT LUCKY THE FIRST TIME. MAYBE WE'RE REACHING.
I MEAN, YEAH. DUH.
REACHING FOR THE STARS.
SHM

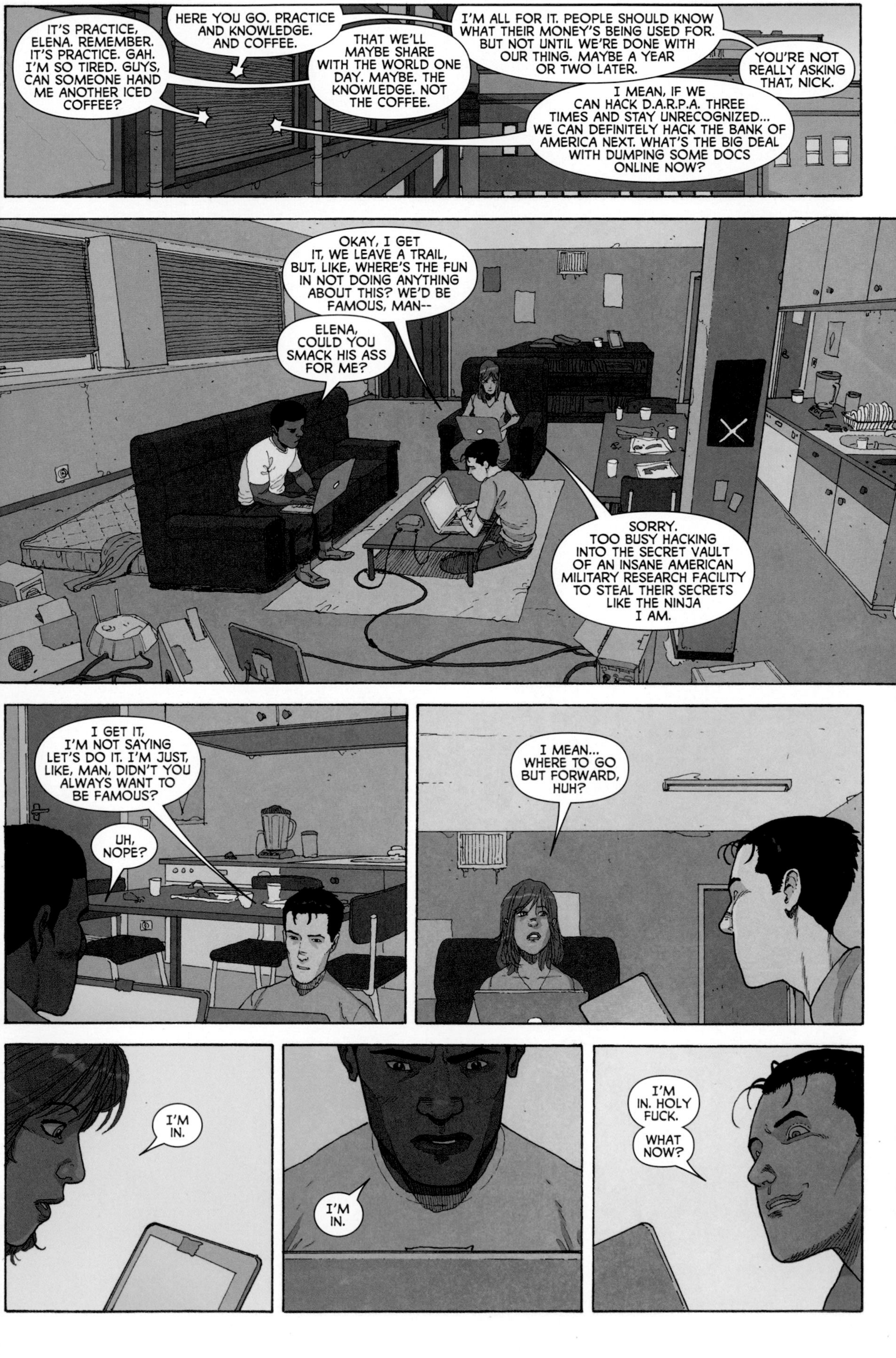
IT'S PRACTICE, ELENA. REMEMBER. IT'S PRACTICE. GAH. I'M SO TIRED. GUYS, CAN SOMEONE HAND ME ANOTHER ICED COFFEE?
HERE YOU GO. PRACTICE AND KNOWLEDGE. AND COFFEE.
THAT WE'LL MAYBE SHARE WITH THE WORLD ONE DAY. MAYBE. THE KNOWLEDGE. NOT THE COFFEE.
I'M ALL FOR IT. PEOPLE SHOULD KNOW WHAT THEIR MONEY'S BEING USED FOR. BUT NOT UNTIL WE'RE DONE WITH OUR THING. MAYBE A YEAR OR TWO LATER.
YOU'RE NOT REALLY ASKING THAT, NICK.
I MEAN, IF WE CAN HACK D.A.R.P.A. THREE TIMES AND STAY UNRECOGNIZED... WE CAN DEFINITELY HACK THE BANK OF AMERICA NEXT. WHAT'S THE BIG DEAL WITH DUMPING SOME DOCS ONLINE NOW?
OKAY, I GET IT, WE LEAVE A TRAIL, BUT, LIKE, WHERE'S THE FUN IN NOT DOING ANYTHING ABOUT THIS? WE'D BE FAMOUS, MAN--
ELENA, COULD YOU SMACK HIS ASS FOR ME?
SORRY. TOO BUSY HACKING INTO THE SECRET VAULT OF AN INSANE AMERICAN MILITARY RESEARCH FACILITY TO STEAL THEIR SECRETS LIKE THE NINJA I AM.
I GET IT, I'M NOT SAYING LET'S DO IT. I'M JUST, LIKE, MAN, DIDN'T YOU ALWAYS WANT TO BE FAMOUS?
UH, NOPE?
I MEAN... WHERE TO GO BUT FORWARD, HUH?
I'M IN.
I'M IN.
I'M IN. HOLY FUCK.
WHAT NOW?

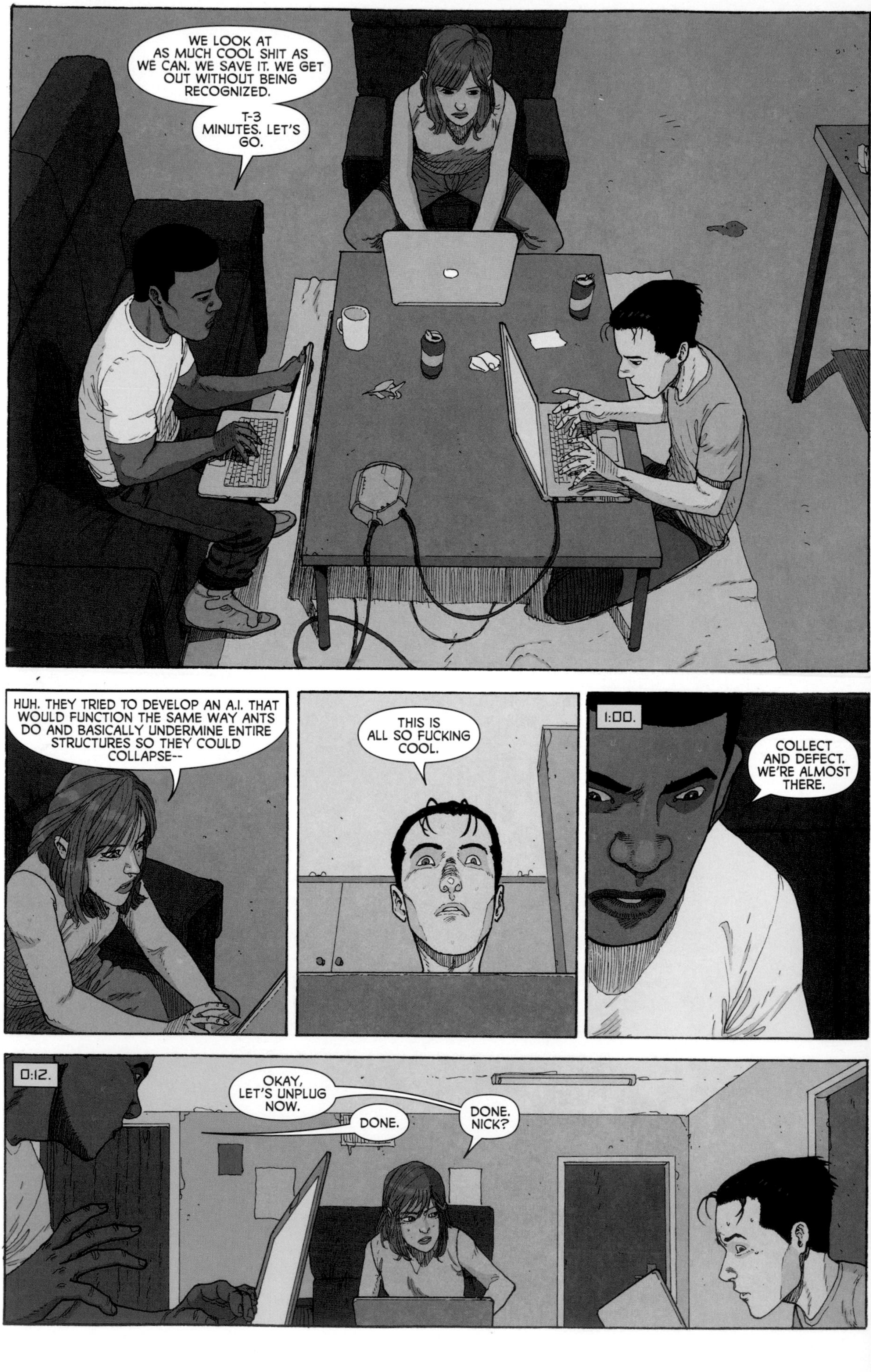
WE LOOK AT AS MUCH COOL SHIT AS WE CAN. WE SAVE IT. WE GET OUT WITHOUT BEING RECOGNIZED.
T-3 MINUTES. LET'S GO.
HUH. THEY TRIED TO DEVELOP AN A.I. THAT WOULD FUNCTION THE SAME WAY ANTS DO AND BASICALLY UNDERMINE ENTIRE STRUCTURES SO THEY COULD COLLAPSE--
THIS IS ALL SO FUCKING COOL.
1:00.
COLLECT AND DEFECT. WE'RE ALMOST THERE.
0:12.
OKAY, LET'S UNPLUG NOW.
DONE.
DONE. NICK?

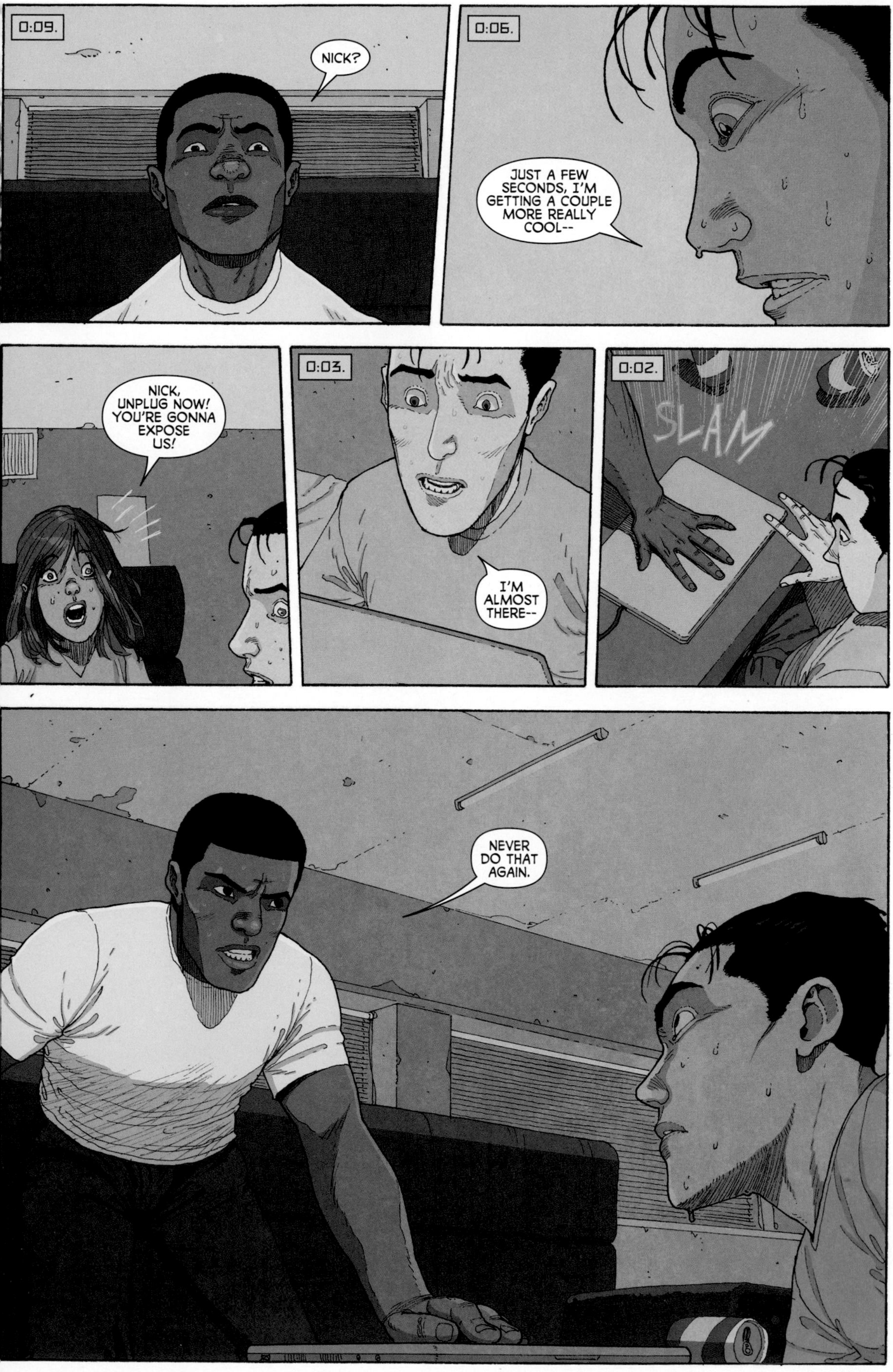
0:09.
NICK?
0:06.
JUST A FEW SECONDS, I'M GETTING A COUPLE MORE REALLY COOL--
NICK, UNPLUG NOW! YOU'RE GONNA EXPOSE US!
0:03.
I'M ALMOST THERE--
0:02.
SLAM
NEVER DO THAT AGAIN.

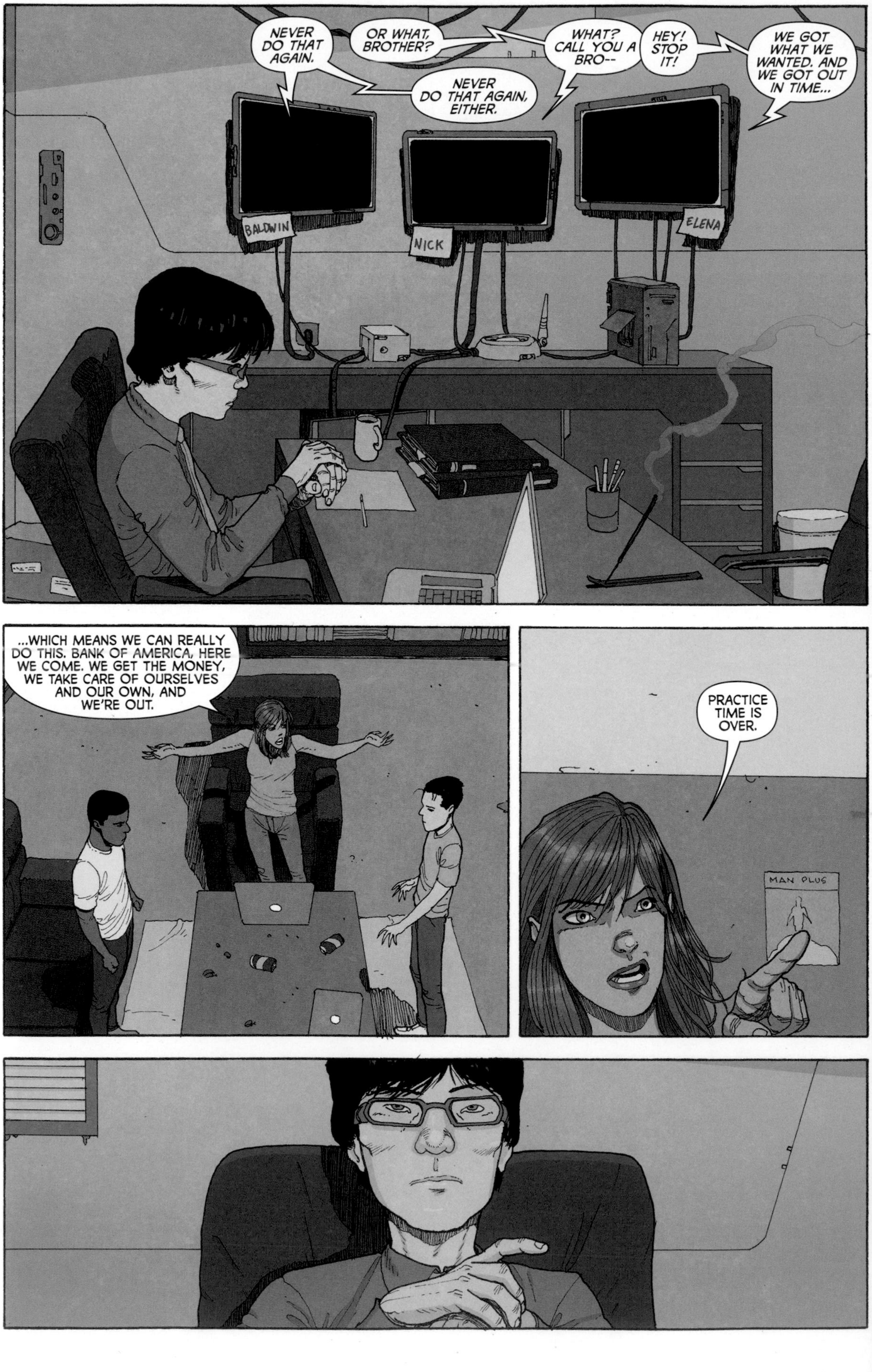
NEVER DO THAT AGAIN.
OR WHAT, BROTHER?
NEVER DO THAT AGAIN, EITHER.
WHAT? CALL YOU A BRO--
HEY! STOP IT!
WE GOT WHAT WE WANTED. AND WE GOT OUT IN TIME...
BALDWIN
NICK
ELENA
...WHICH MEANS WE CAN REALLY DO THIS. BANK OF AMERICA, HERE WE COME. WE GET THE MONEY, WE TAKE CARE OF OURSELVES AND OUR OWN, AND WE'RE OUT.
PRACTICE TIME IS OVER.
MAN PLUS

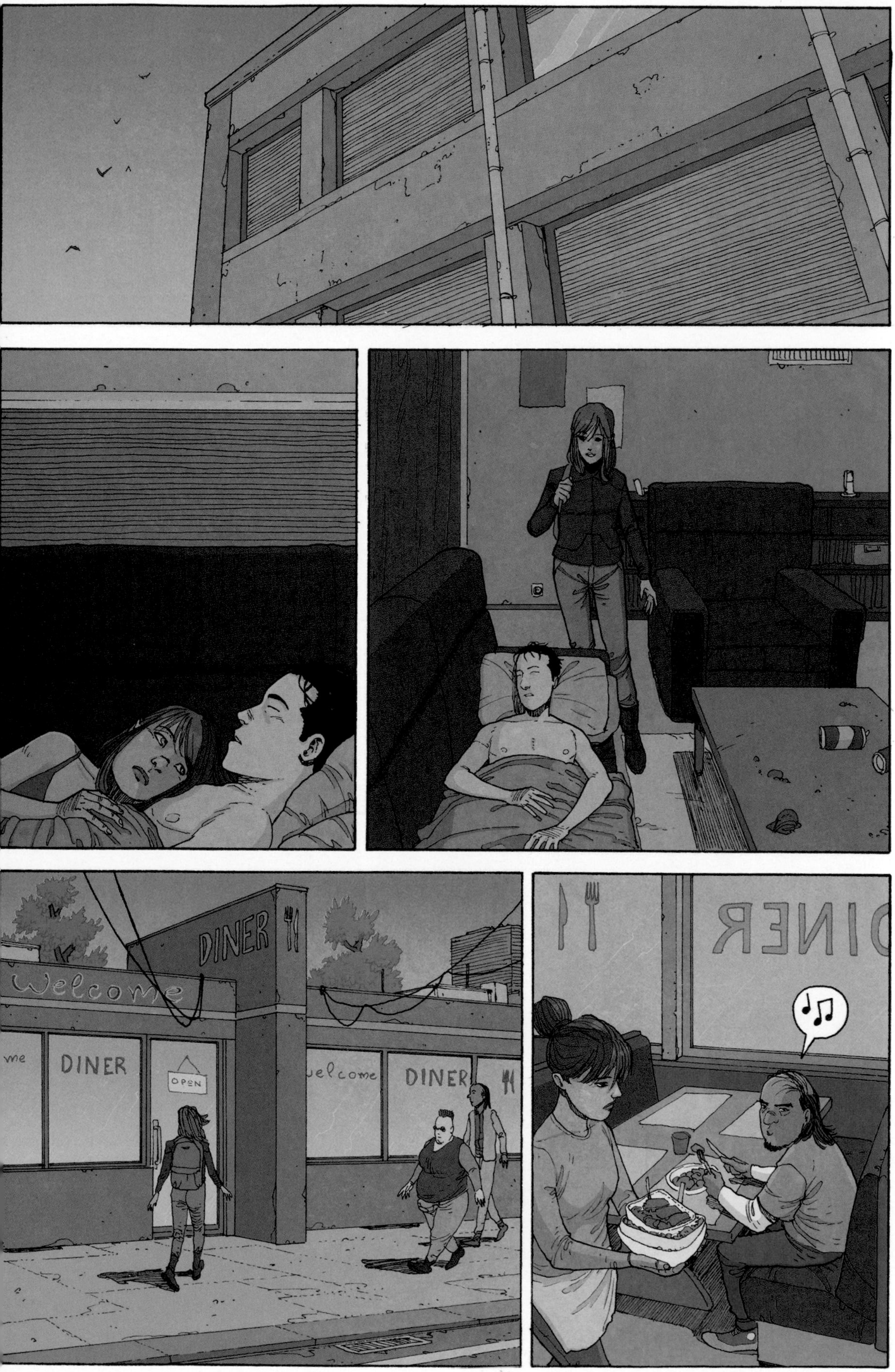
DINER
Welcome
DINER
OPEN
welcome
DINER

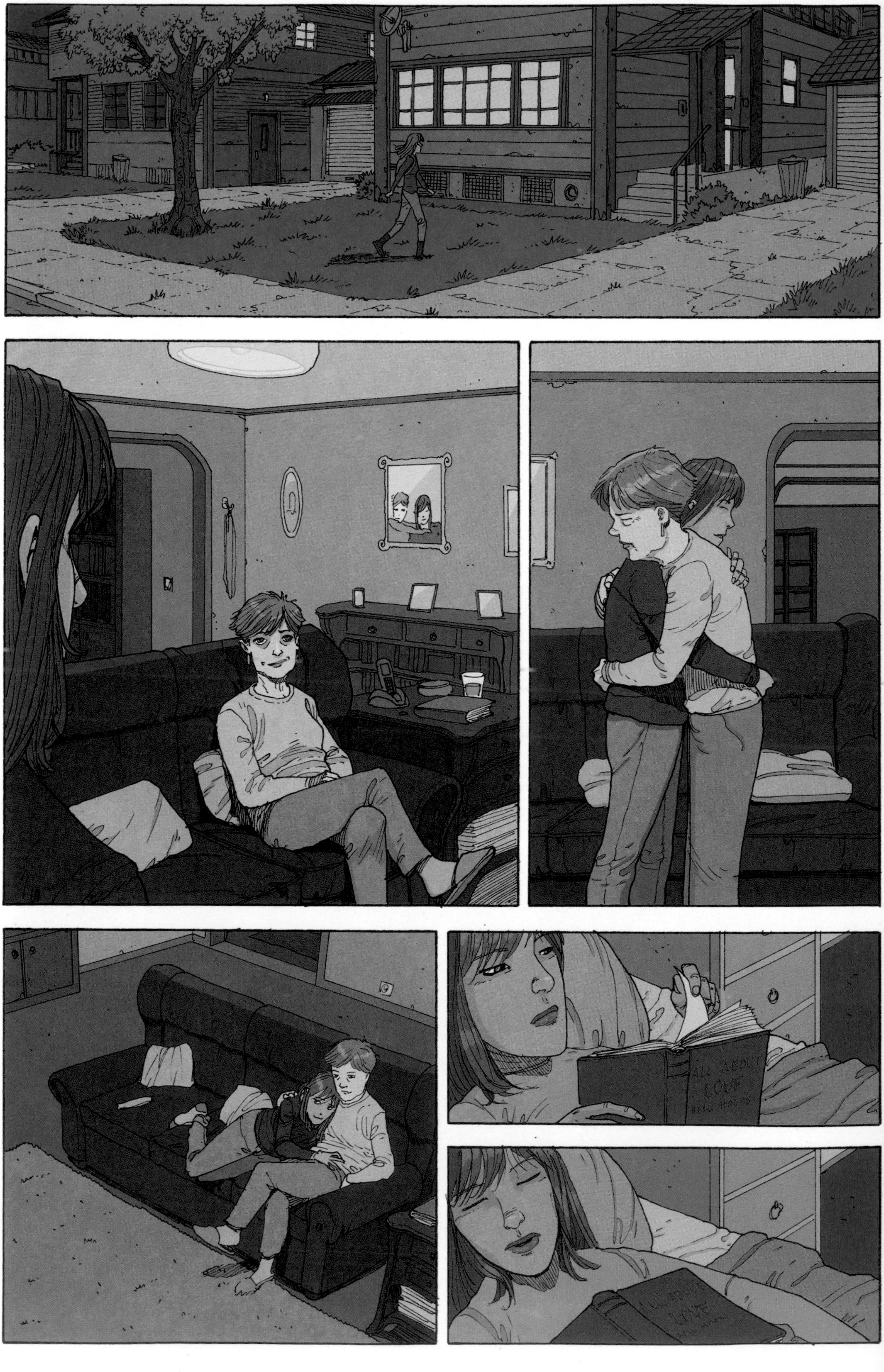
ALL ABOUT LOVE

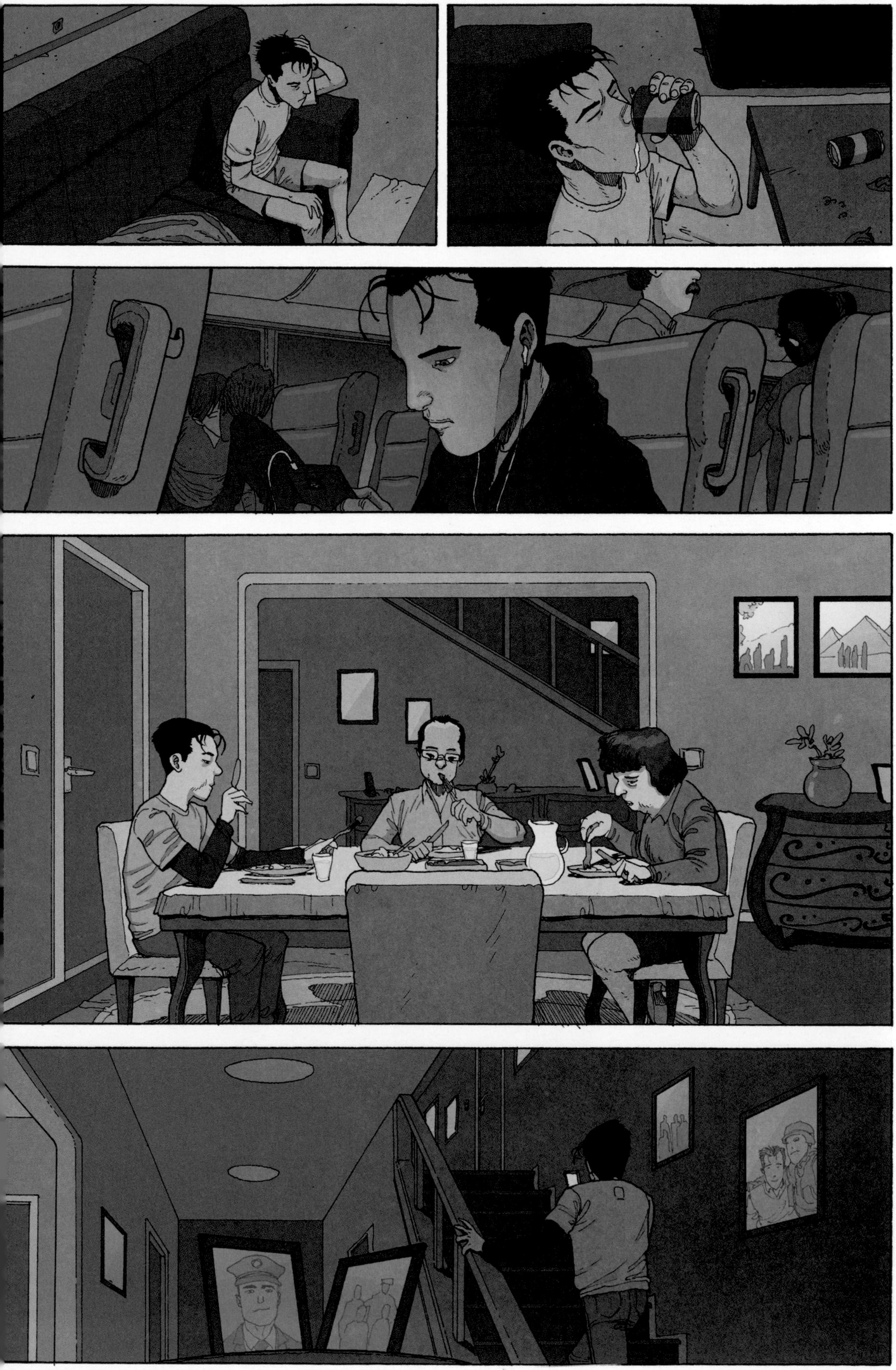

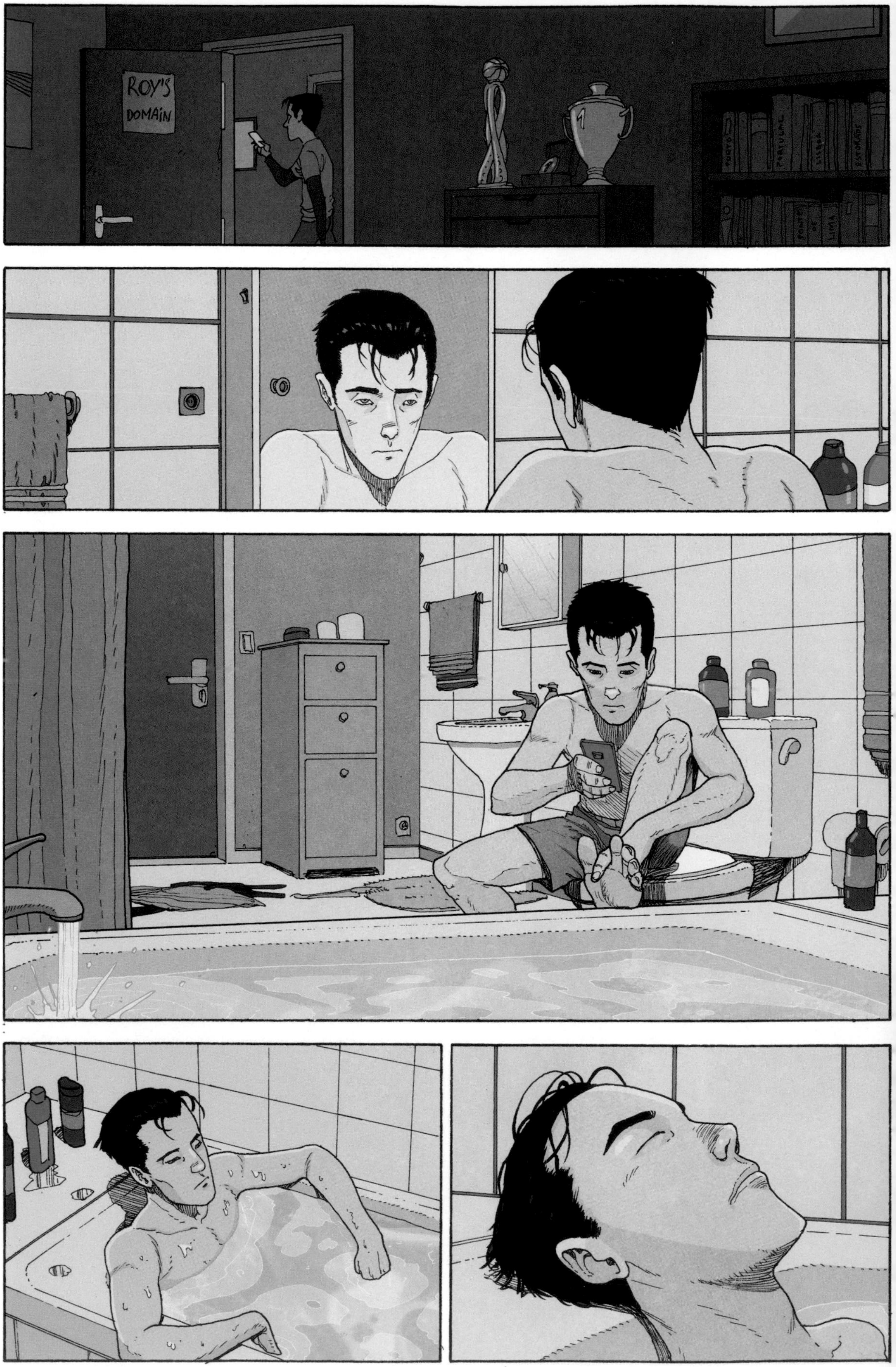
ROY'S DOMAIN

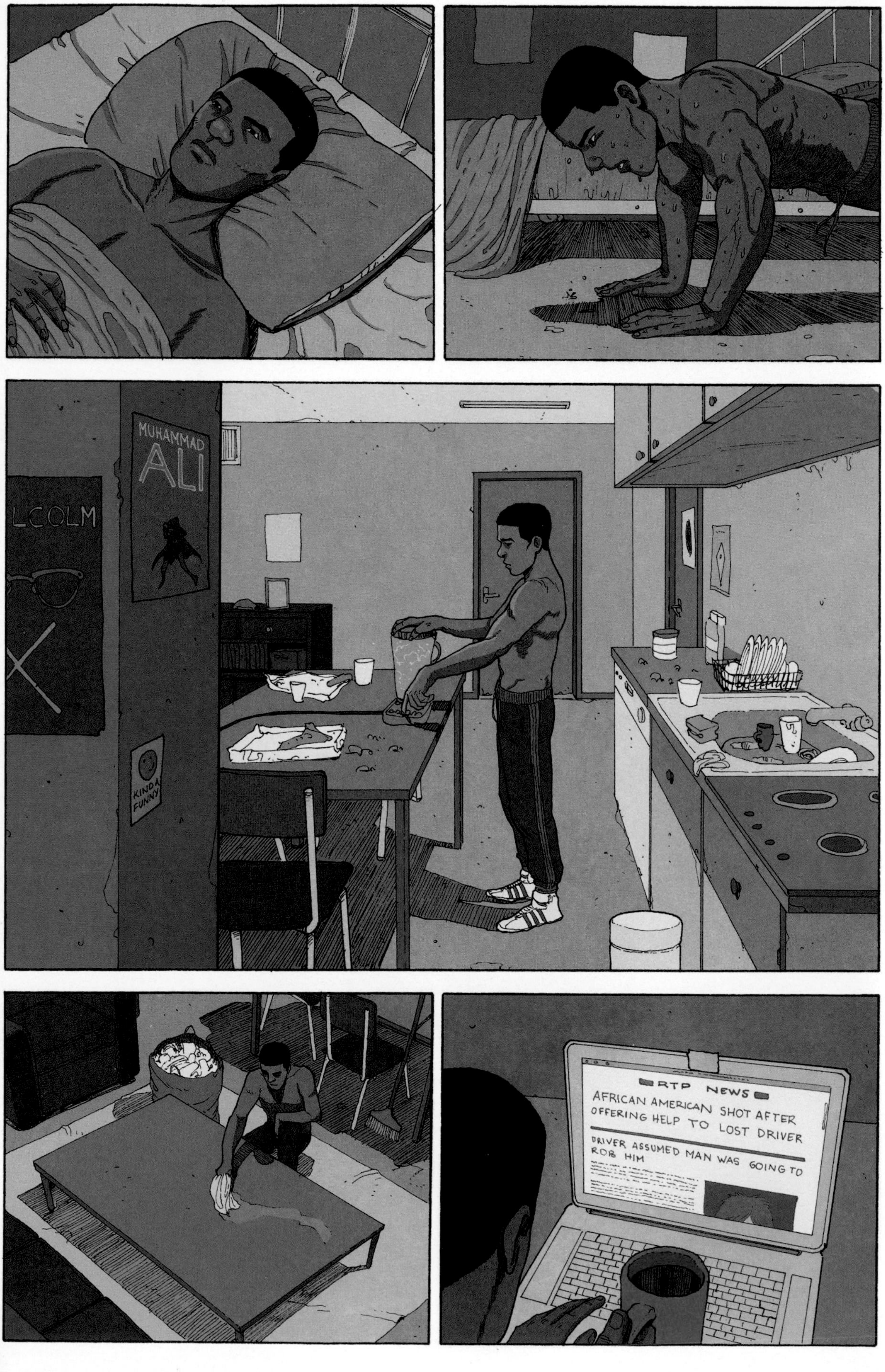
MUHAMMAD ALI
KINDA FUNNY
RTP NEWS
AFRICAN AMERICAN SHOT AFTER OFFERING HELP TO LOST DRIVER
DRIVER ASSUMED MAN WAS GOING TO ROB HIM

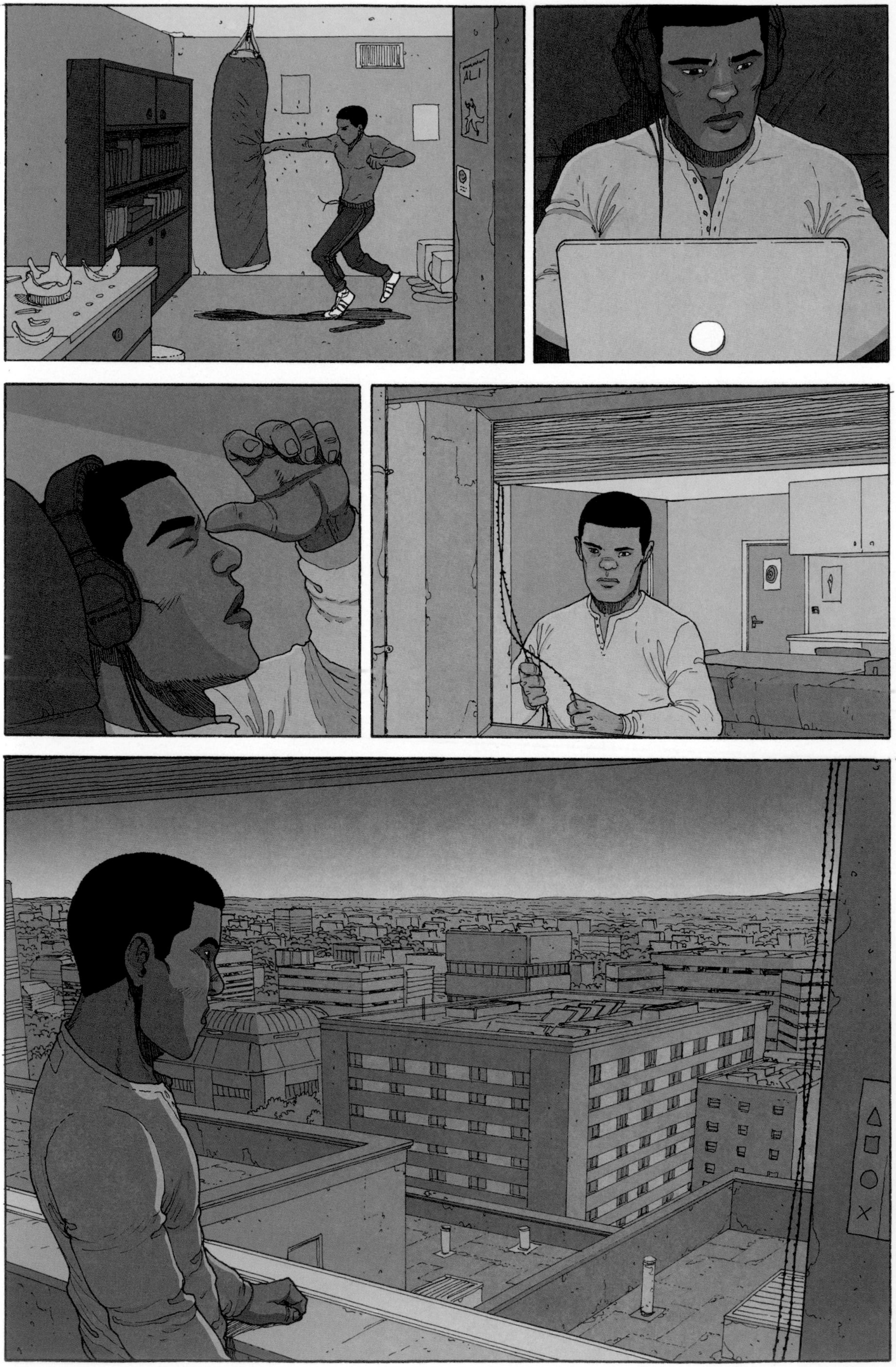
ALI

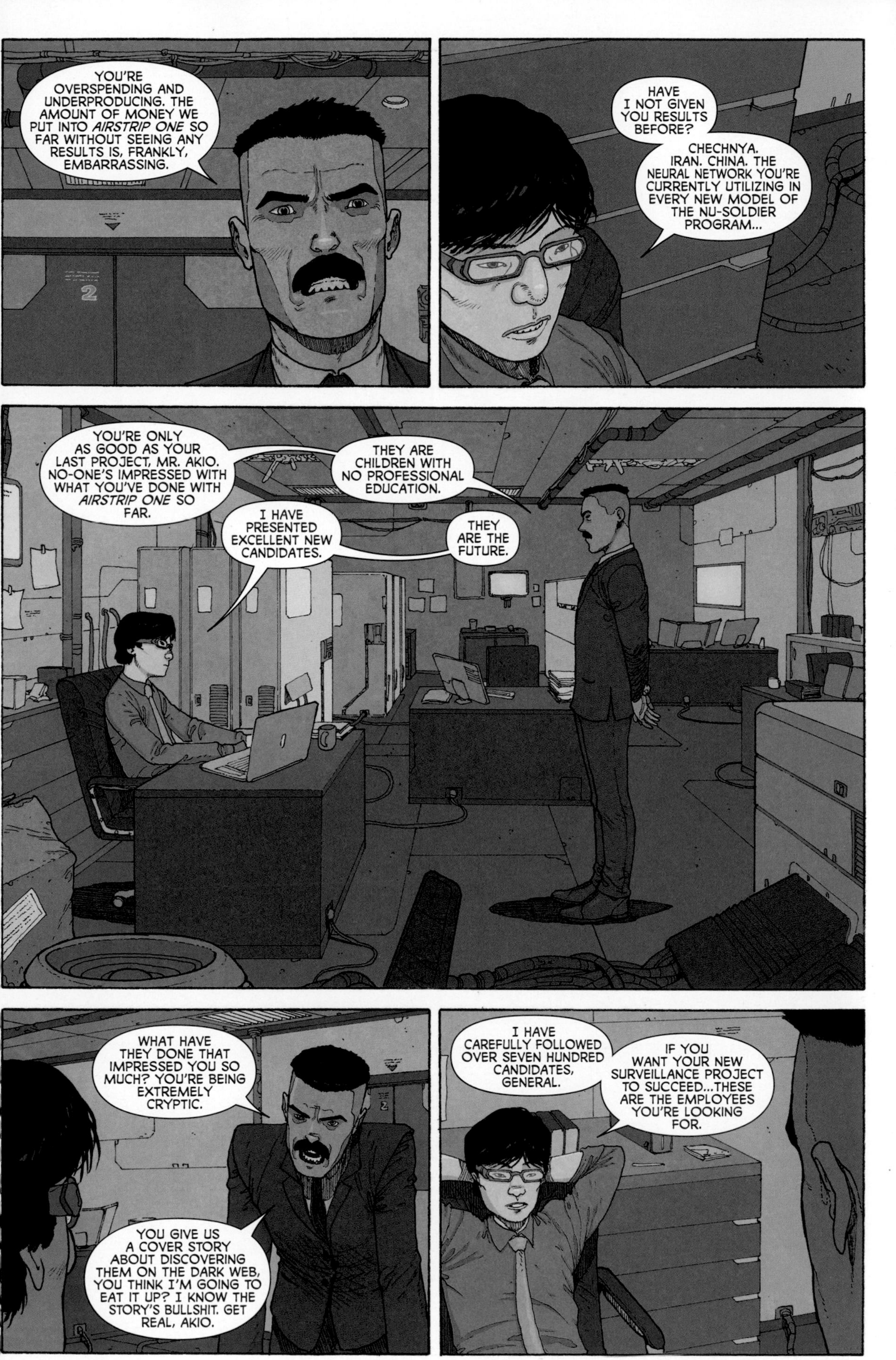
YOU'RE OVERSPENDING AND UNDERPRODUCING. THE AMOUNT OF MONEY WE PUT INTO *AIRSTRIP ONE* SO FAR WITHOUT SEEING ANY RESULTS IS, FRANKLY, EMBARRASSING.
HAVE I NOT GIVEN YOU RESULTS BEFORE?
CHECHNYA. IRAN. CHINA. THE NEURAL NETWORK YOU'RE CURRENTLY UTILIZING IN EVERY NEW MODEL OF THE NU-SOLDIER PROGRAM...
YOU'RE ONLY AS GOOD AS YOUR LAST PROJECT, MR. AKIO. NO-ONE'S IMPRESSED WITH WHAT YOU'VE DONE WITH *AIRSTRIP ONE* SO FAR.
THEY ARE CHILDREN WITH NO PROFESSIONAL EDUCATION.
I HAVE PRESENTED EXCELLENT NEW CANDIDATES.
THEY ARE THE FUTURE.
WHAT HAVE THEY DONE THAT IMPRESSED YOU SO MUCH? YOU'RE BEING EXTREMELY CRYPTIC.
YOU GIVE US A COVER STORY ABOUT DISCOVERING THEM ON THE DARK WEB, YOU THINK I'M GOING TO EAT IT UP? I KNOW THE STORY'S BULLSHIT. GET REAL, AKIO.
I HAVE CAREFULLY FOLLOWED OVER SEVEN HUNDRED CANDIDATES, GENERAL.
IF YOU WANT YOUR NEW SURVEILLANCE PROJECT TO SUCCEED...THESE ARE THE EMPLOYEES YOU'RE LOOKING FOR.

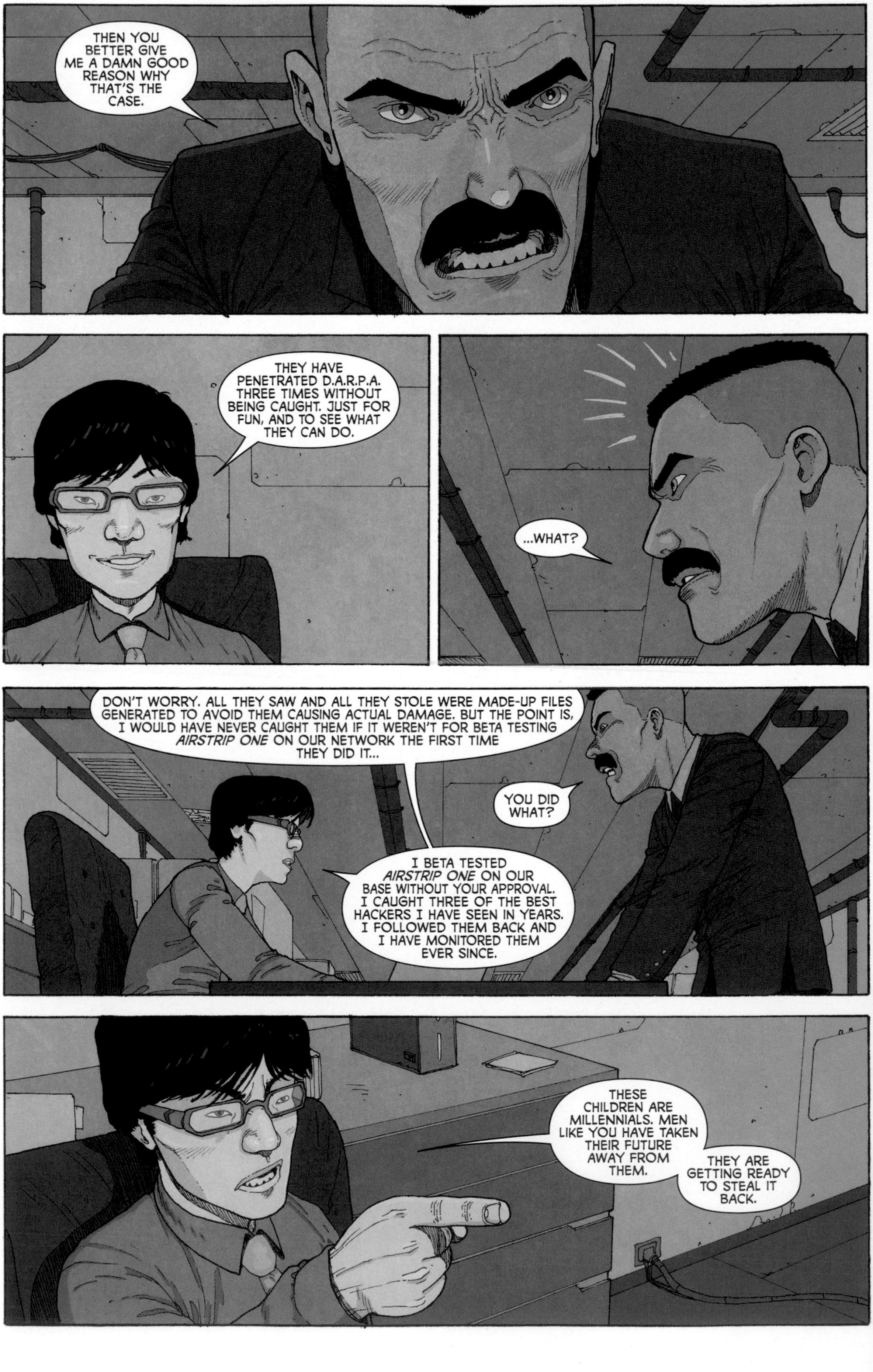
THEN YOU BETTER GIVE ME A DAMN GOOD REASON WHY THAT'S THE CASE.
THEY HAVE PENETRATED D.A.R.P.A. THREE TIMES WITHOUT BEING CAUGHT. JUST FOR FUN, AND TO SEE WHAT THEY CAN DO.
...WHAT?
DON'T WORRY. ALL THEY SAW AND ALL THEY STOLE WERE MADE-UP FILES GENERATED TO AVOID THEM CAUSING ACTUAL DAMAGE. BUT THE POINT IS, I WOULD HAVE NEVER CAUGHT THEM IF IT WEREN'T FOR BETA TESTING *AIRSTRIP ONE* ON OUR NETWORK THE FIRST TIME THEY DID IT...
YOU DID WHAT?
I BETA TESTED *AIRSTRIP ONE* ON OUR BASE WITHOUT YOUR APPROVAL. I CAUGHT THREE OF THE BEST HACKERS I HAVE SEEN IN YEARS. I FOLLOWED THEM BACK AND I HAVE MONITORED THEM EVER SINCE.
THESE CHILDREN ARE MILLENNIALS. MEN LIKE YOU HAVE TAKEN THEIR FUTURE AWAY FROM THEM.
THEY ARE GETTING READY TO STEAL IT BACK.

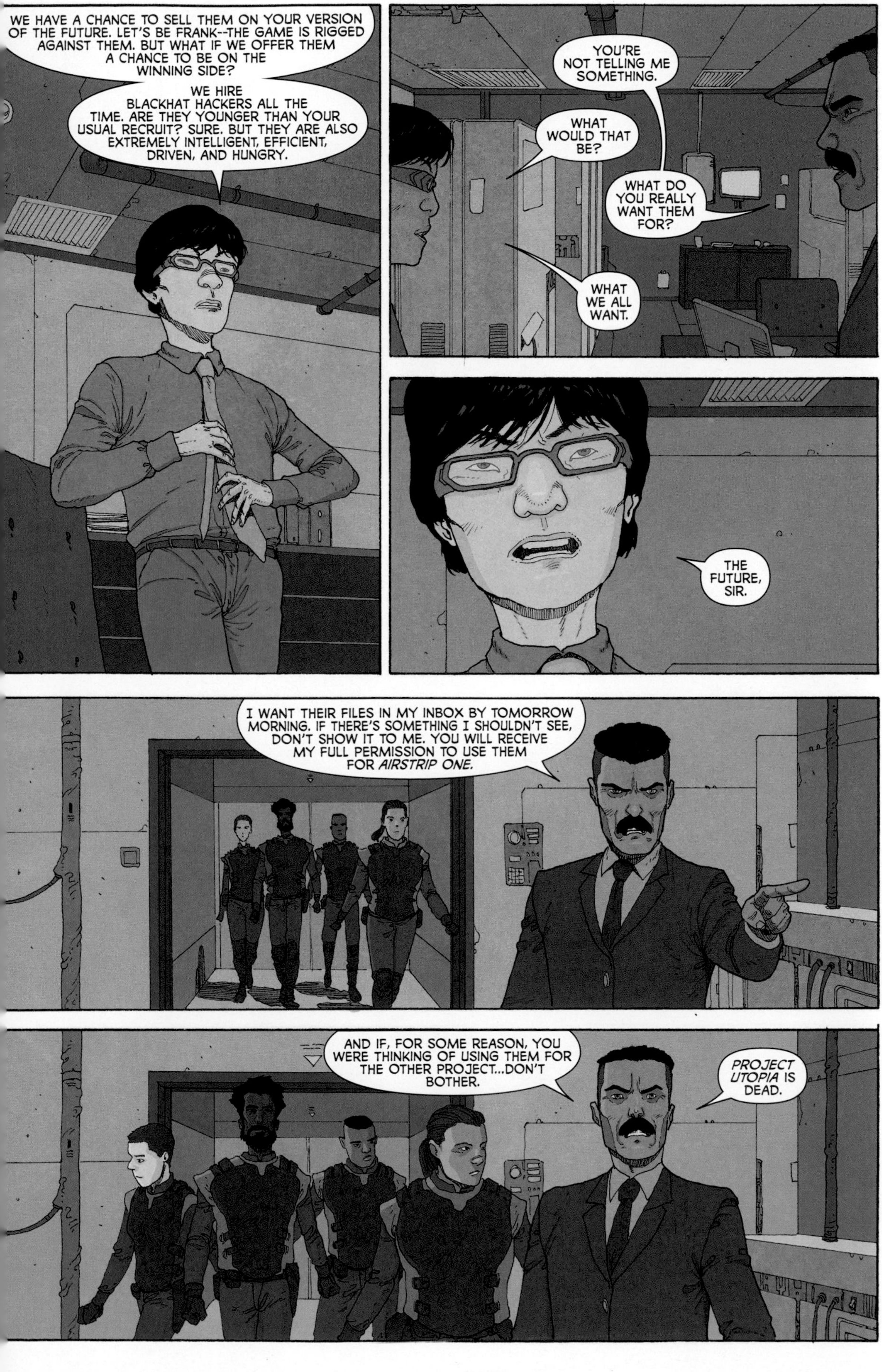
WE HAVE A CHANCE TO SELL THEM ON YOUR VERSION OF THE FUTURE. LET'S BE FRANK--THE GAME IS RIGGED AGAINST THEM. BUT WHAT IF WE OFFER THEM A CHANCE TO BE ON THE WINNING SIDE?
WE HIRE BLACKHAT HACKERS ALL THE TIME. ARE THEY YOUNGER THAN YOUR USUAL RECRUIT? SURE. BUT THEY ARE ALSO EXTREMELY INTELLIGENT, EFFICIENT, DRIVEN, AND HUNGRY.
YOU'RE NOT TELLING ME SOMETHING.
WHAT WOULD THAT BE?
WHAT DO YOU REALLY WANT THEM FOR?
WHAT WE ALL WANT.
THE FUTURE, SIR.
I WANT THEIR FILES IN MY INBOX BY TOMORROW MORNING. IF THERE'S SOMETHING I SHOULDN'T SEE, DON'T SHOW IT TO ME. YOU WILL RECEIVE MY FULL PERMISSION TO USE THEM FOR AIRSTRIP ONE.
AND IF, FOR SOME REASON, YOU WERE THINKING OF USING THEM FOR THE OTHER PROJECT...DON'T BOTHER.
PROJECT UTOPIA IS DEAD.

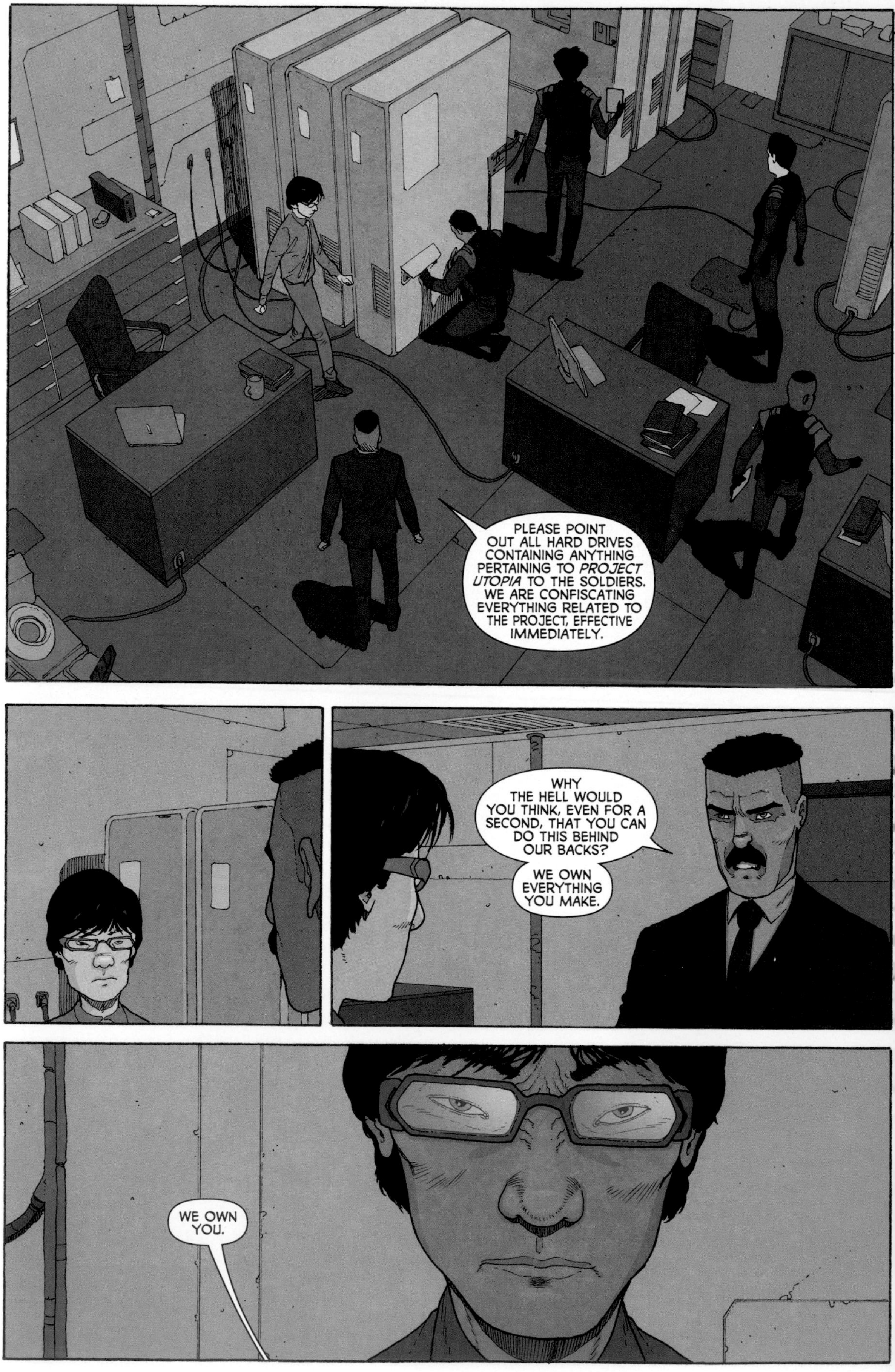
PLEASE POINT OUT ALL HARD DRIVES CONTAINING ANYTHING PERTAINING TO *PROJECT UTOPIA* TO THE SOLDIERS. WE ARE CONFISCATING EVERYTHING RELATED TO THE PROJECT, EFFECTIVE IMMEDIATELY.
WHY THE HELL WOULD YOU THINK, EVEN FOR A SECOND, THAT YOU CAN DO THIS BEHIND OUR BACKS?
WE OWN EVERYTHING YOU MAKE.
WE OWN YOU.

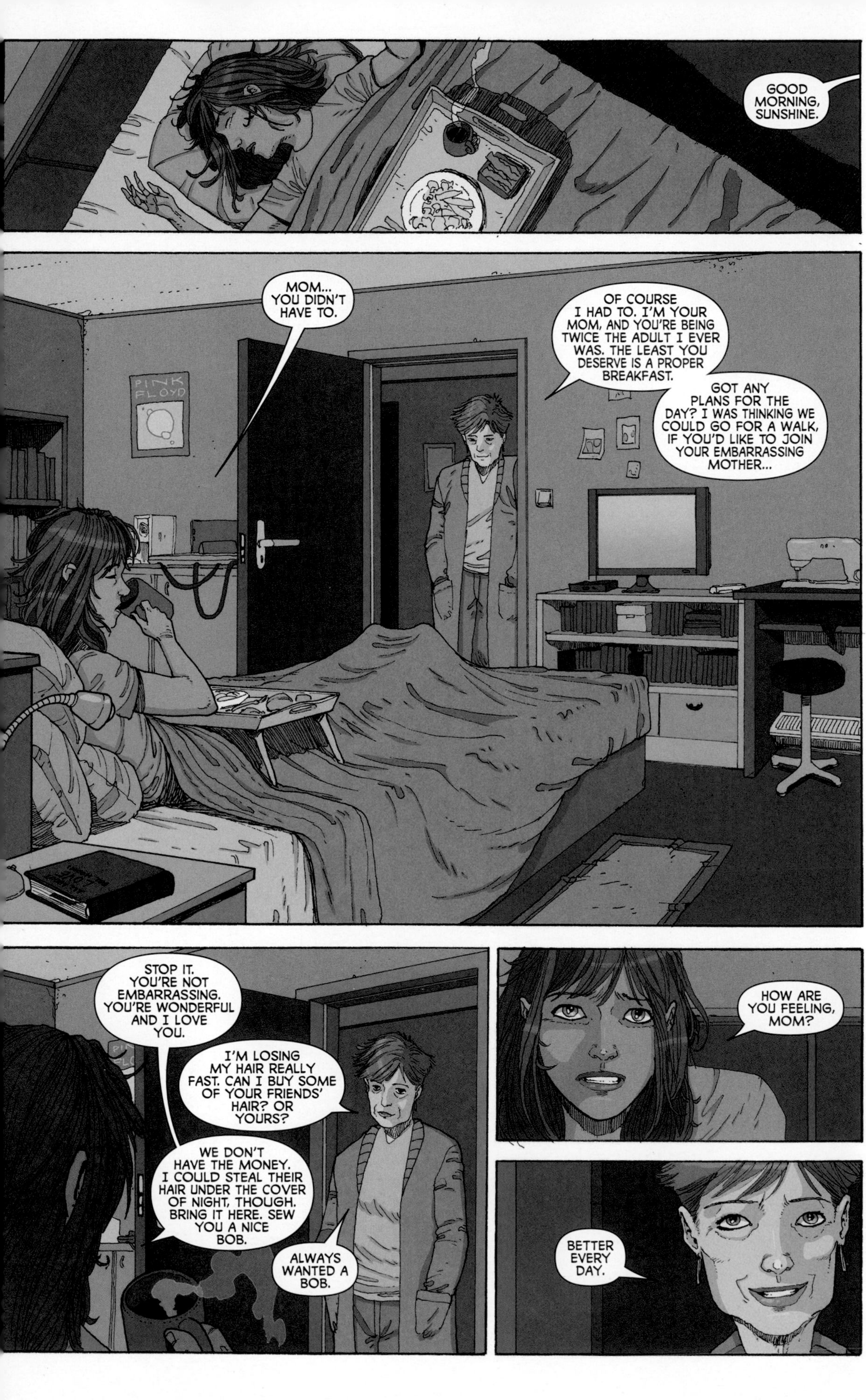
GOOD MORNING, SUNSHINE.
MOM... YOU DIDN'T HAVE TO.
OF COURSE I HAD TO. I'M YOUR MOM, AND YOU'RE BEING TWICE THE ADULT I EVER WAS. THE LEAST YOU DESERVE IS A PROPER BREAKFAST.
GOT ANY PLANS FOR THE DAY? I WAS THINKING WE COULD GO FOR A WALK, IF YOU'D LIKE TO JOIN YOUR EMBARRASSING MOTHER...
PINK FLOYD
STOP IT. YOU'RE NOT EMBARRASSING. YOU'RE WONDERFUL AND I LOVE YOU.
I'M LOSING MY HAIR REALLY FAST. CAN I BUY SOME OF YOUR FRIENDS' HAIR? OR YOURS?
WE DON'T HAVE THE MONEY. I COULD STEAL THEIR HAIR UNDER THE COVER OF NIGHT, THOUGH. BRING IT HERE. SEW YOU A NICE BOB.
ALWAYS WANTED A BOB.
HOW ARE YOU FEELING, MOM?
BETTER EVERY DAY.

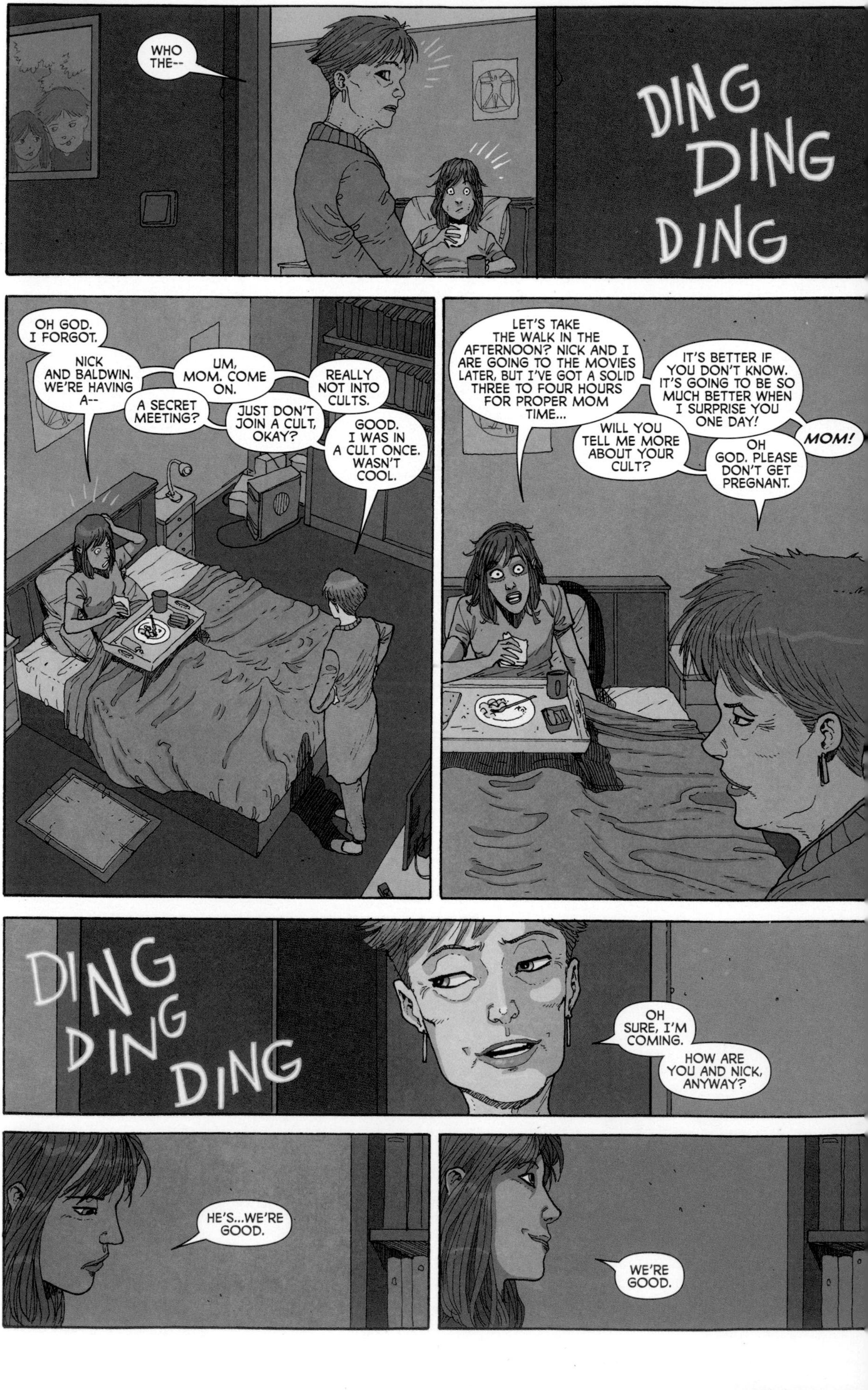
WHO THE--
DING DING DING
OH GOD. I FORGOT.
NICK AND BALDWIN. WE'RE HAVING A--
A SECRET MEETING?
UM, MOM. COME ON.
JUST DON'T JOIN A CULT, OKAY?
REALLY NOT INTO CULTS.
GOOD. I WAS IN A CULT ONCE. WASN'T COOL.
LET'S TAKE THE WALK IN THE AFTERNOON? NICK AND I ARE GOING TO THE MOVIES LATER, BUT I'VE GOT A SOLID THREE TO FOUR HOURS FOR PROPER MOM TIME...
WILL YOU TELL ME MORE ABOUT YOUR CULT?
IT'S BETTER IF YOU DON'T KNOW. IT'S GOING TO BE SO MUCH BETTER WHEN I SURPRISE YOU ONE DAY!
OH GOD. PLEASE DON'T GET PREGNANT.
MOM!
DING DING DING
OH SURE, I'M COMING.
HOW ARE YOU AND NICK, ANYWAY?
HE'S...WE'RE GOOD.
WE'RE GOOD.

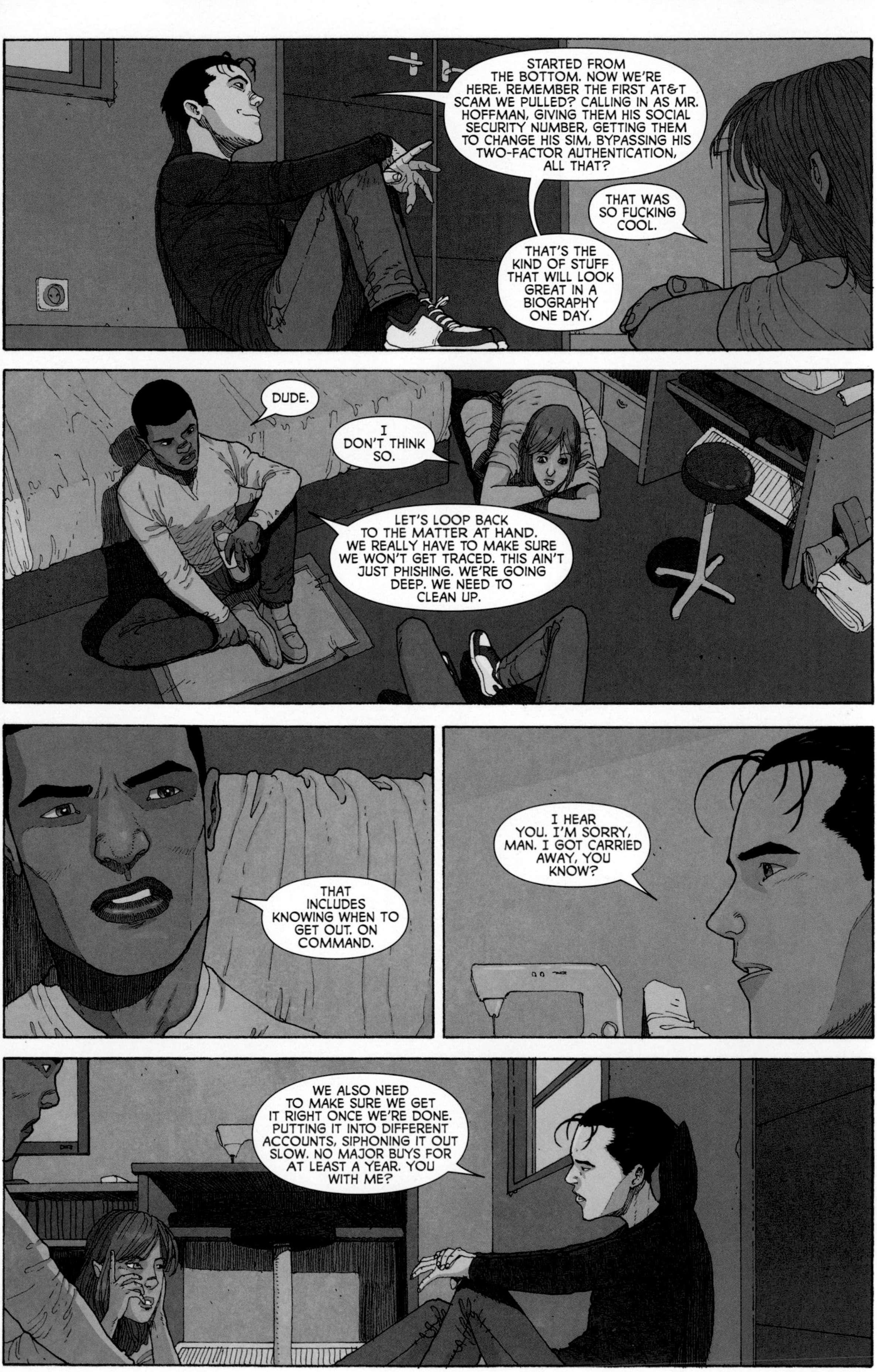
STARTED FROM THE BOTTOM. NOW WE'RE HERE. REMEMBER THE FIRST AT&T SCAM WE PULLED? CALLING IN AS MR. HOFFMAN, GIVING THEM HIS SOCIAL SECURITY NUMBER, GETTING THEM TO CHANGE HIS SIM, BYPASSING HIS TWO-FACTOR AUTHENTICATION, ALL THAT?
THAT WAS SO FUCKING COOL.
THAT'S THE KIND OF STUFF THAT WILL LOOK GREAT IN A BIOGRAPHY ONE DAY.
DUDE.
I DON'T THINK SO.
LET'S LOOP BACK TO THE MATTER AT HAND. WE REALLY HAVE TO MAKE SURE WE WON'T GET TRACED. THIS AIN'T JUST PHISHING. WE'RE GOING DEEP. WE NEED TO CLEAN UP.
THAT INCLUDES KNOWING WHEN TO GET OUT. ON COMMAND.
I HEAR YOU. I'M SORRY, MAN. I GOT CARRIED AWAY, YOU KNOW?
WE ALSO NEED TO MAKE SURE WE GET IT RIGHT ONCE WE'RE DONE. PUTTING IT INTO DIFFERENT ACCOUNTS, SIPHONING IT OUT SLOW. NO MAJOR BUYS FOR AT LEAST A YEAR. YOU WITH ME?

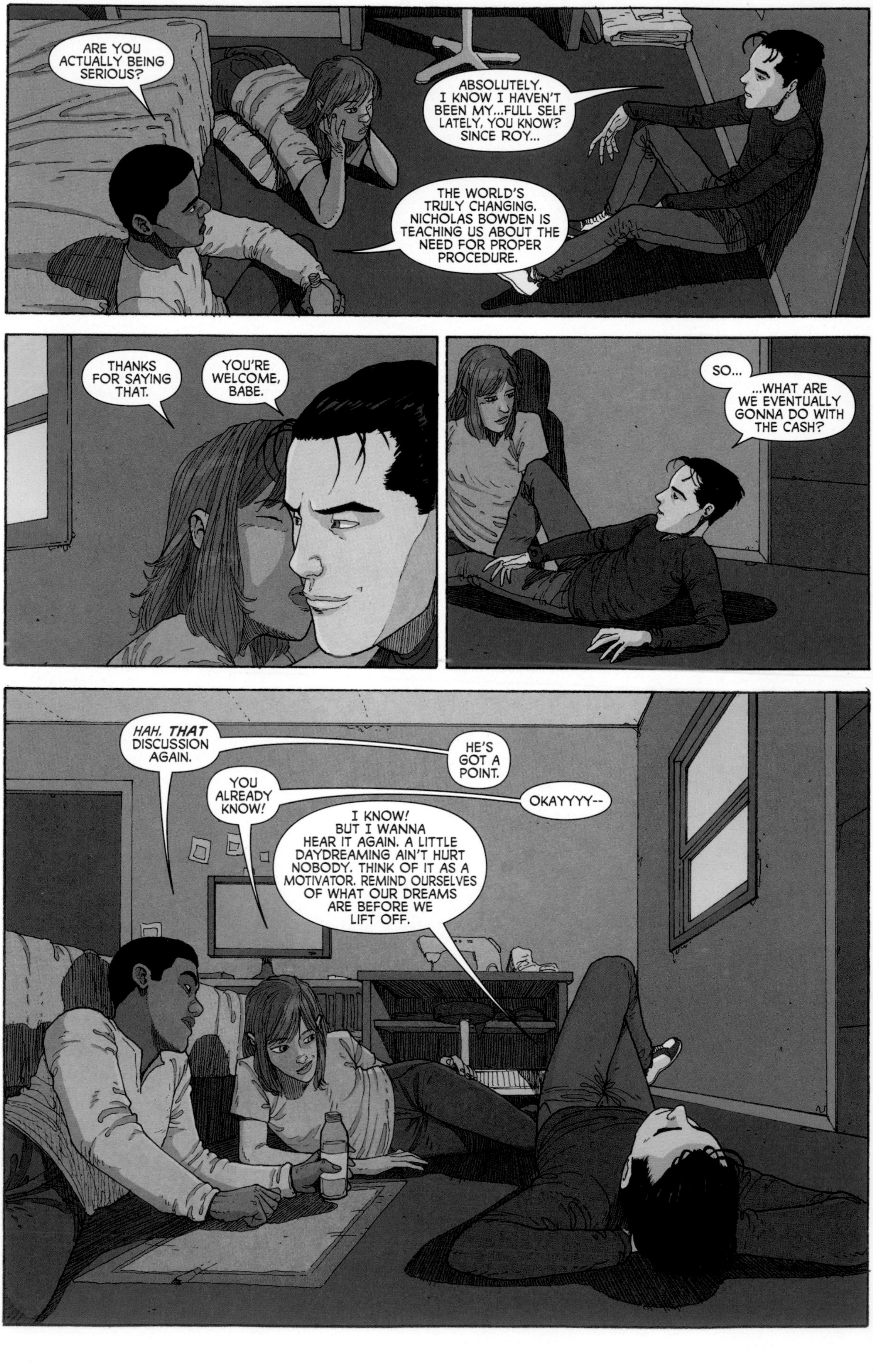
ARE YOU ACTUALLY BEING SERIOUS?
ABSOLUTELY. I KNOW I HAVEN'T BEEN MY...FULL SELF LATELY, YOU KNOW? SINCE ROY...
THE WORLD'S TRULY CHANGING. NICHOLAS BOWDEN IS TEACHING US ABOUT THE NEED FOR PROPER PROCEDURE.
THANKS FOR SAYING THAT.
YOU'RE WELCOME, BABE.
SO...
...WHAT ARE WE EVENTUALLY GONNA DO WITH THE CASH?
HAH. **THAT** DISCUSSION AGAIN.
HE'S GOT A POINT.
YOU ALREADY KNOW!
OKAYYYY--
I KNOW! BUT I WANNA HEAR IT AGAIN. A LITTLE DAYDREAMING AIN'T HURT NOBODY. THINK OF IT AS A MOTIVATOR. REMIND OURSELVES OF WHAT OUR DREAMS ARE BEFORE WE LIFT OFF.

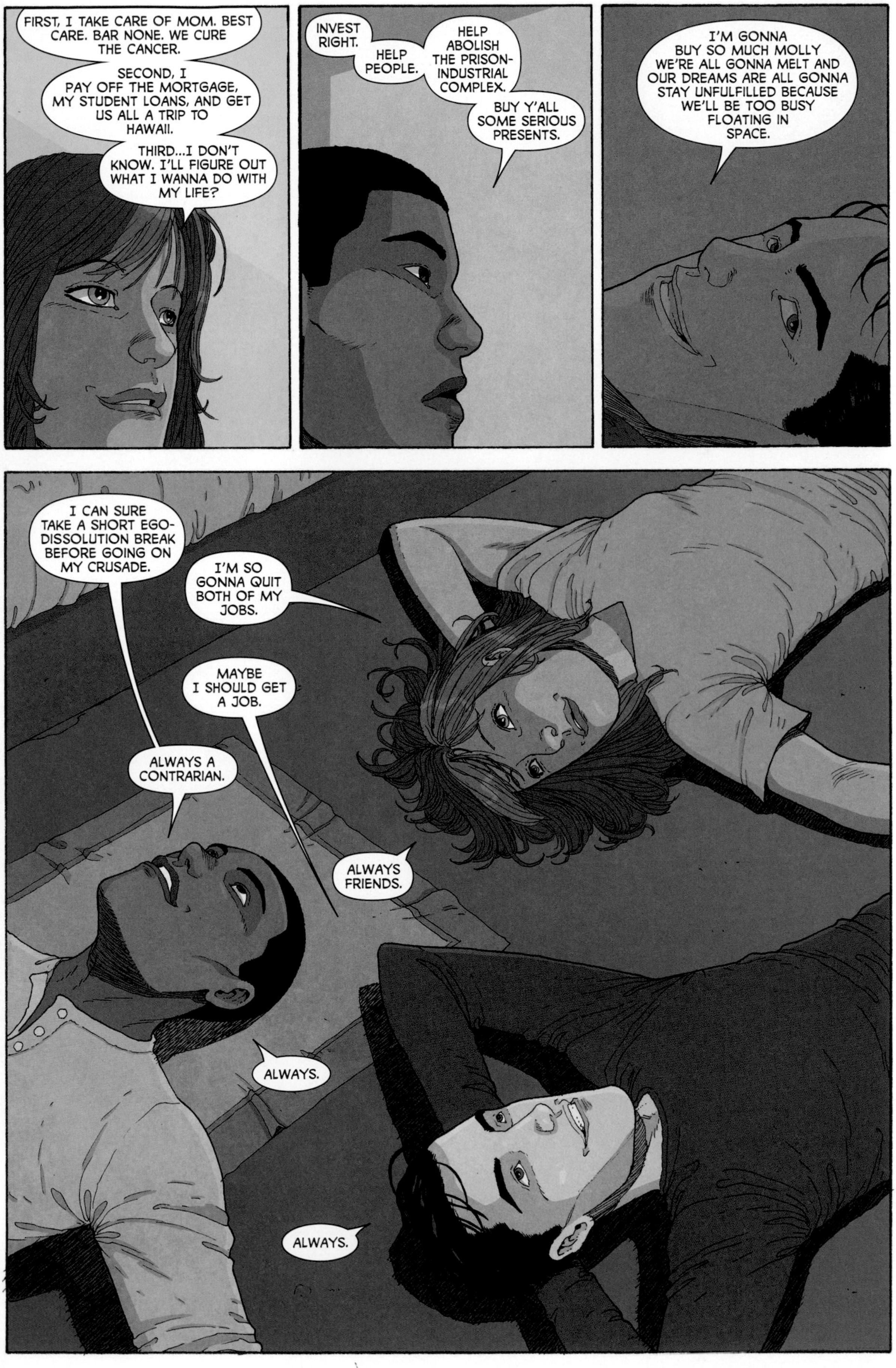
FIRST, I TAKE CARE OF MOM. BEST CARE. BAR NONE. WE CURE THE CANCER.
SECOND, I PAY OFF THE MORTGAGE, MY STUDENT LOANS, AND GET US ALL A TRIP TO HAWAII.
THIRD...I DON'T KNOW. I'LL FIGURE OUT WHAT I WANNA DO WITH MY LIFE?
INVEST RIGHT.
HELP PEOPLE.
HELP ABOLISH THE PRISON-INDUSTRIAL COMPLEX.
BUY Y'ALL SOME SERIOUS PRESENTS.
I'M GONNA BUY SO MUCH MOLLY WE'RE ALL GONNA MELT AND OUR DREAMS ARE ALL GONNA STAY UNFULFILLED BECAUSE WE'LL BE TOO BUSY FLOATING IN SPACE.
I CAN SURE TAKE A SHORT EGO-DISSOLUTION BREAK BEFORE GOING ON MY CRUSADE.
I'M SO GONNA QUIT BOTH OF MY JOBS.
MAYBE I SHOULD GET A JOB.
ALWAYS A CONTRARIAN.
ALWAYS FRIENDS.
ALWAYS.
ALWAYS.

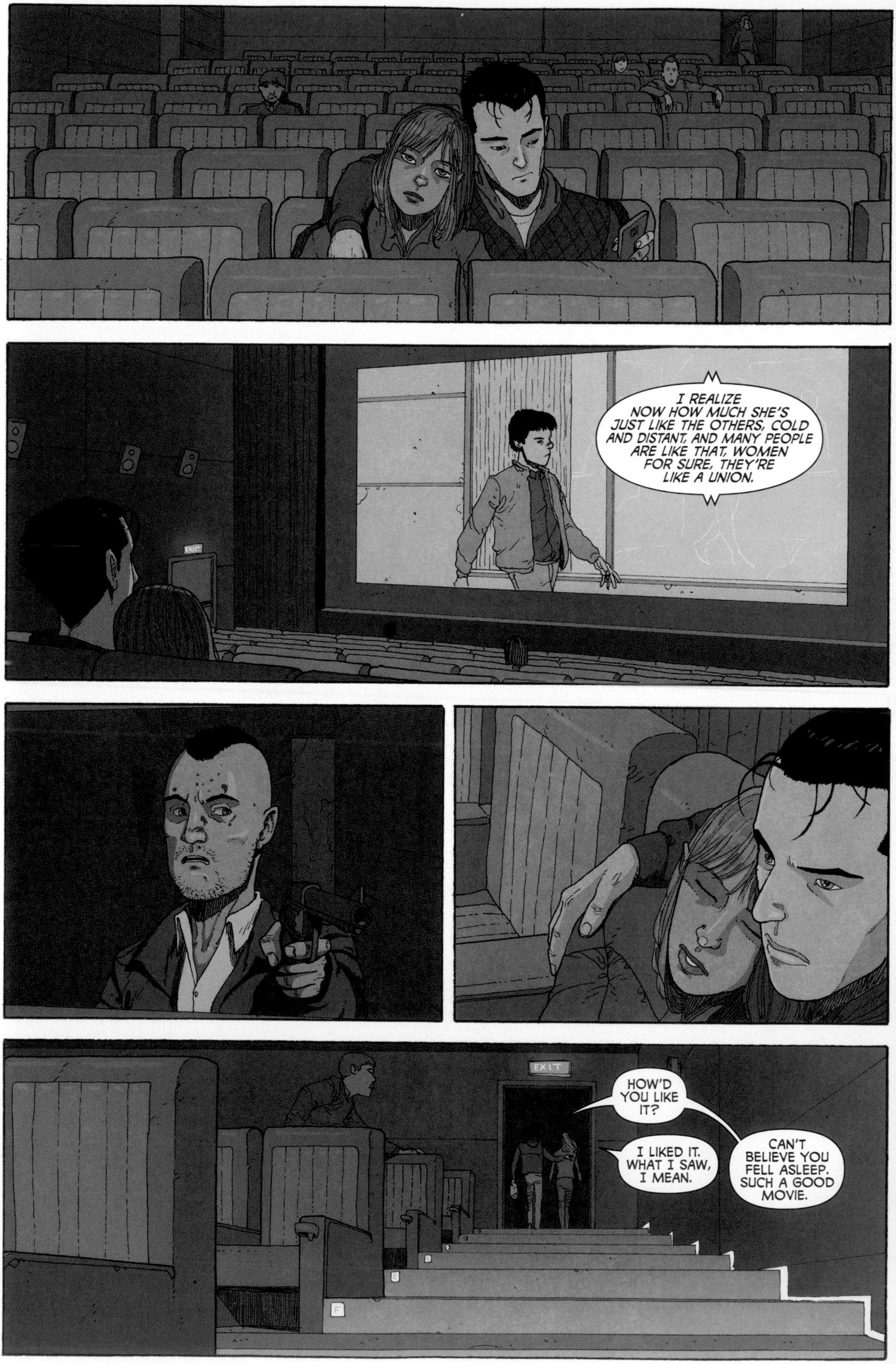
I REALIZE NOW HOW MUCH SHE'S JUST LIKE THE OTHERS, COLD AND DISTANT, AND MANY PEOPLE ARE LIKE THAT, WOMEN FOR SURE, THEY'RE LIKE A UNION.
EXIT
EXIT
HOW'D YOU LIKE IT?
I LIKED IT. WHAT I SAW, I MEAN.
CAN'T BELIEVE YOU FELL ASLEEP. SUCH A GOOD MOVIE.

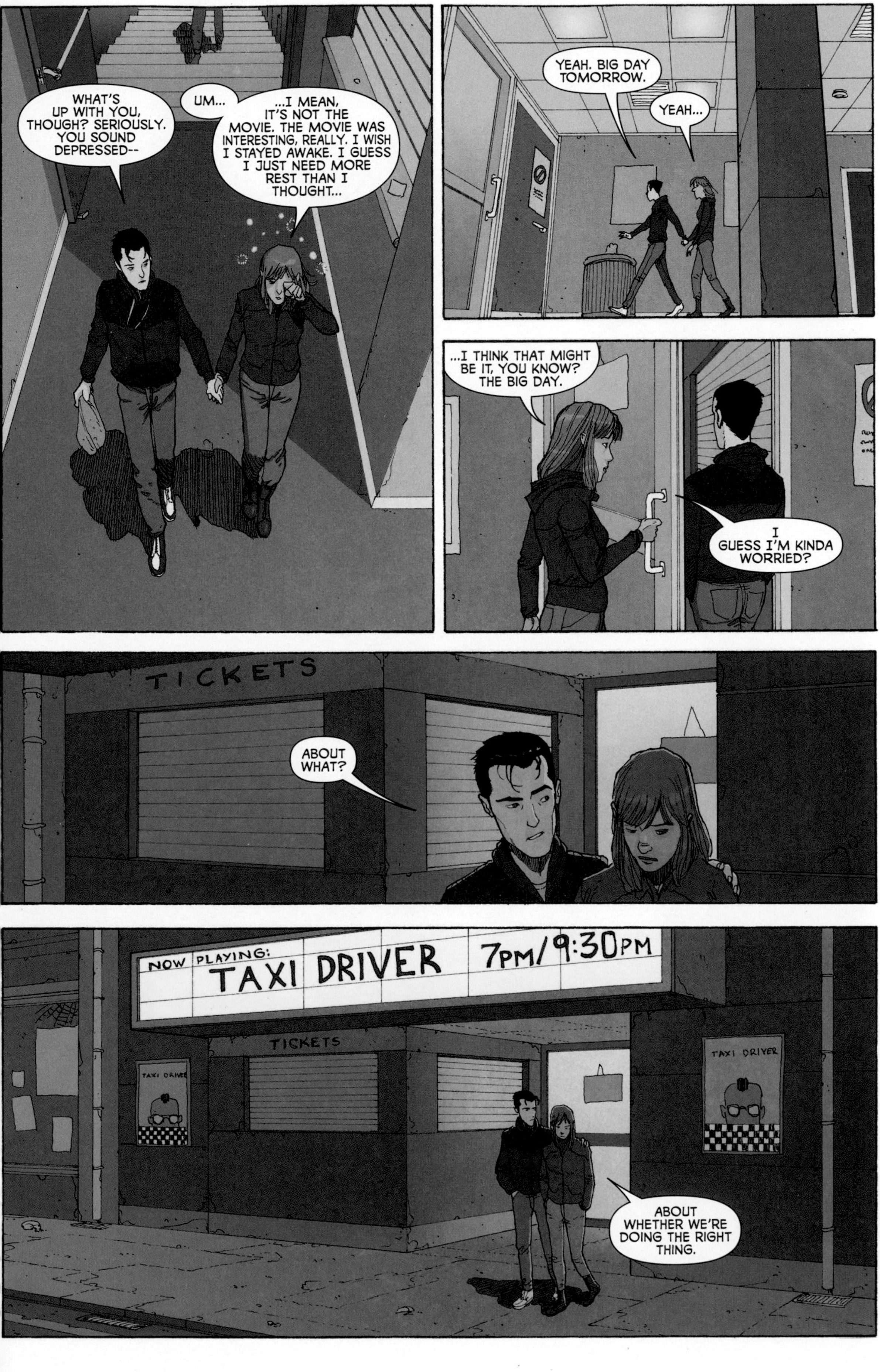
WHAT'S UP WITH YOU, THOUGH? SERIOUSLY. YOU SOUND DEPRESSED--
UM...
...I MEAN, IT'S NOT THE MOVIE. THE MOVIE WAS INTERESTING, REALLY. I WISH I STAYED AWAKE. I GUESS I JUST NEED MORE REST THAN I THOUGHT...
YEAH. BIG DAY TOMORROW.
YEAH...
...I THINK THAT MIGHT BE IT, YOU KNOW? THE BIG DAY.
I GUESS I'M KINDA WORRIED?
TICKETS
ABOUT WHAT?
NOW PLAYING: TAXI DRIVER 7PM/9:30PM
TICKETS
TAXI DRIVER
TAXI DRIVER
ABOUT WHETHER WE'RE DOING THE RIGHT THING.

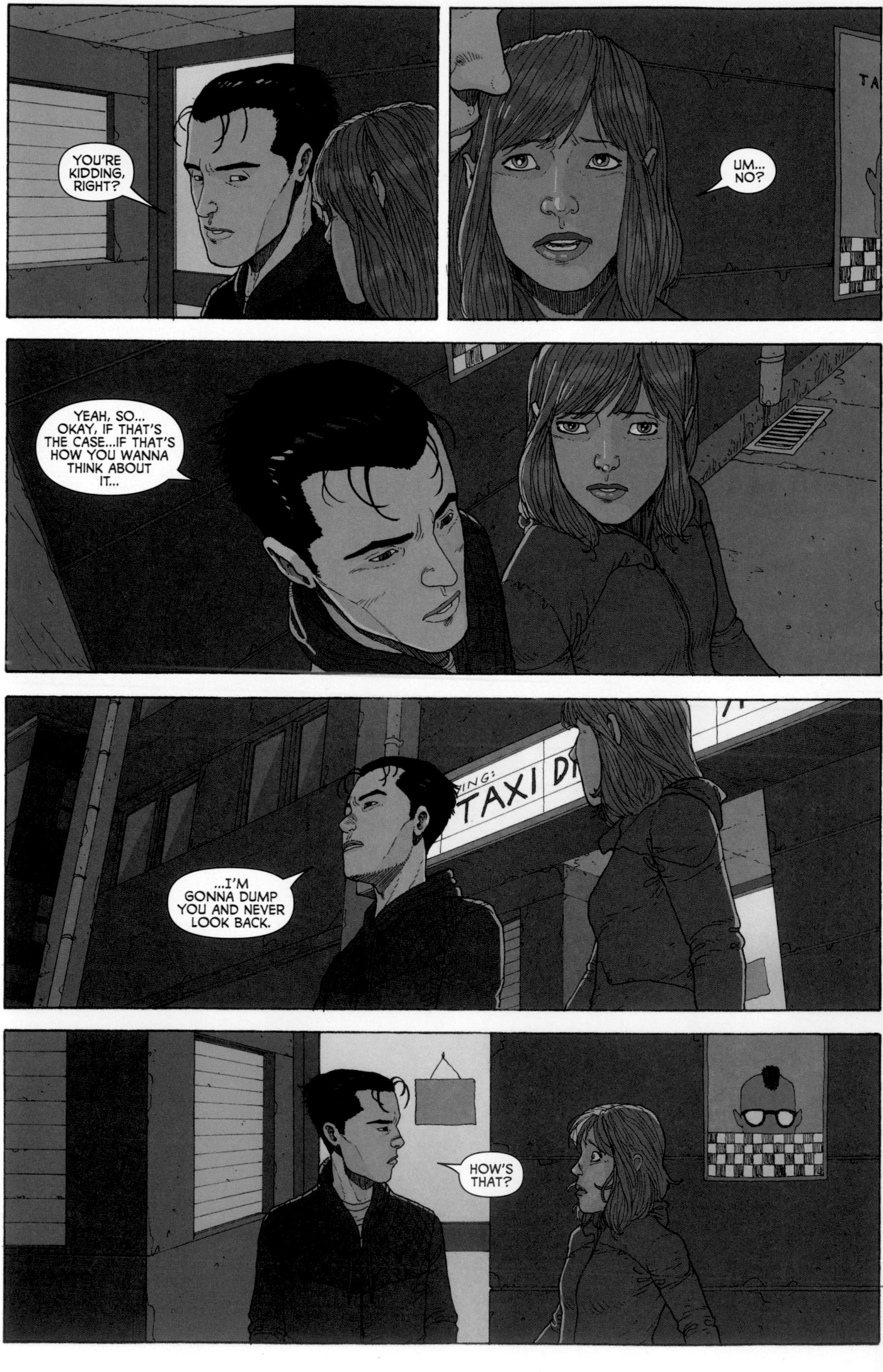
YOU'RE KIDDING, RIGHT?
UM... NO?
YEAH, SO... OKAY, IF THAT'S THE CASE...IF THAT'S HOW YOU WANNA THINK ABOUT IT...
TAXI D
...I'M GONNA DUMP YOU AND NEVER LOOK BACK.
HOW'S THAT?

SEE YOU
TOMORROW.

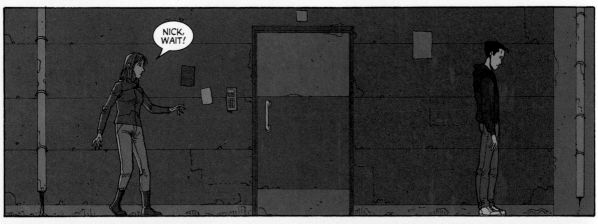

NICK,
WAIT!

I'M GONNA DO
IT.

I'M JUST
SCARED.

DRIVER

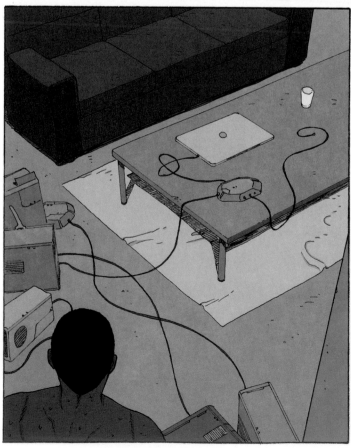

DAMN.

TODAY BE THE DAY.

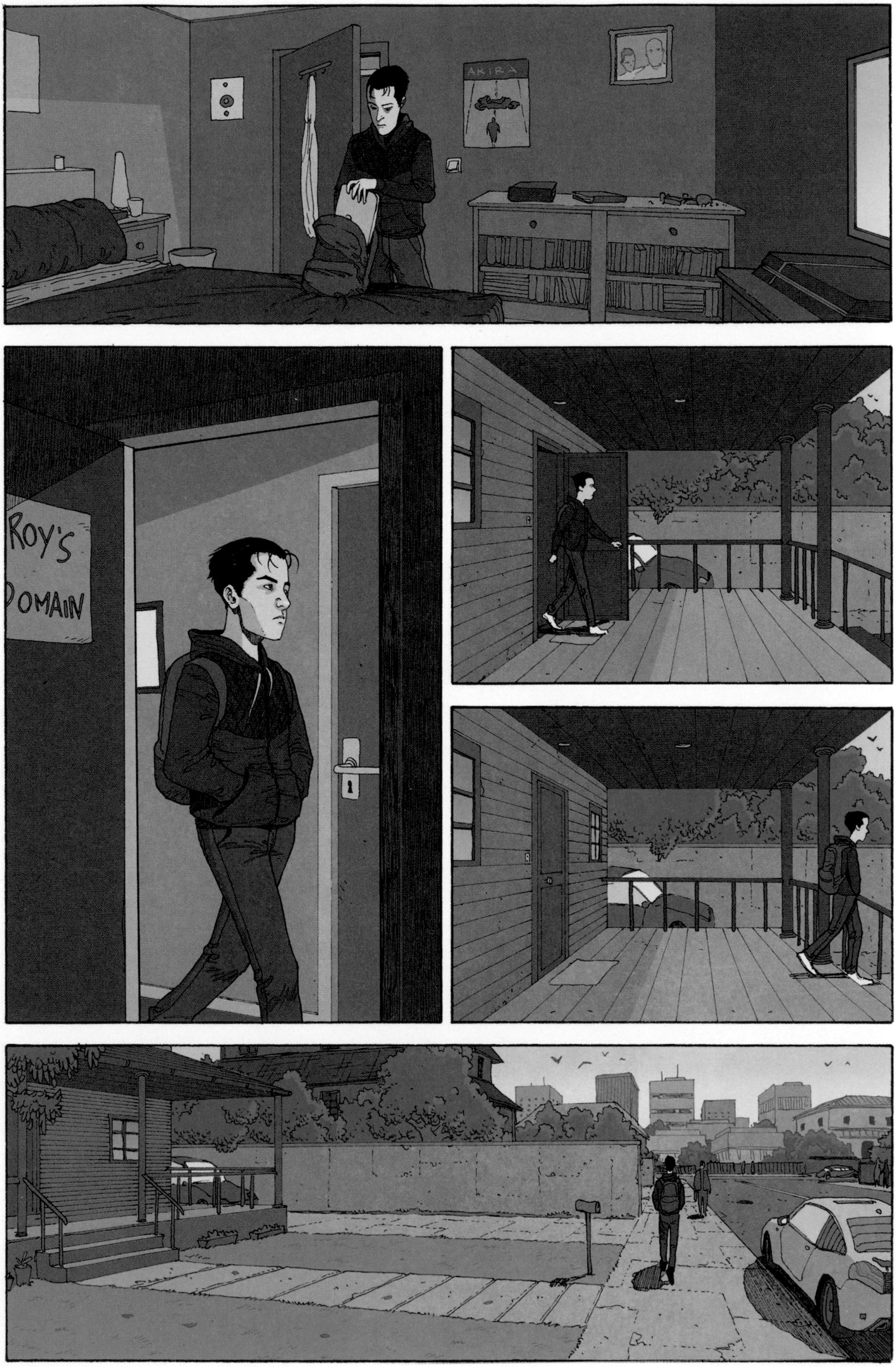
AKIRA
ROY'S
DOMAIN

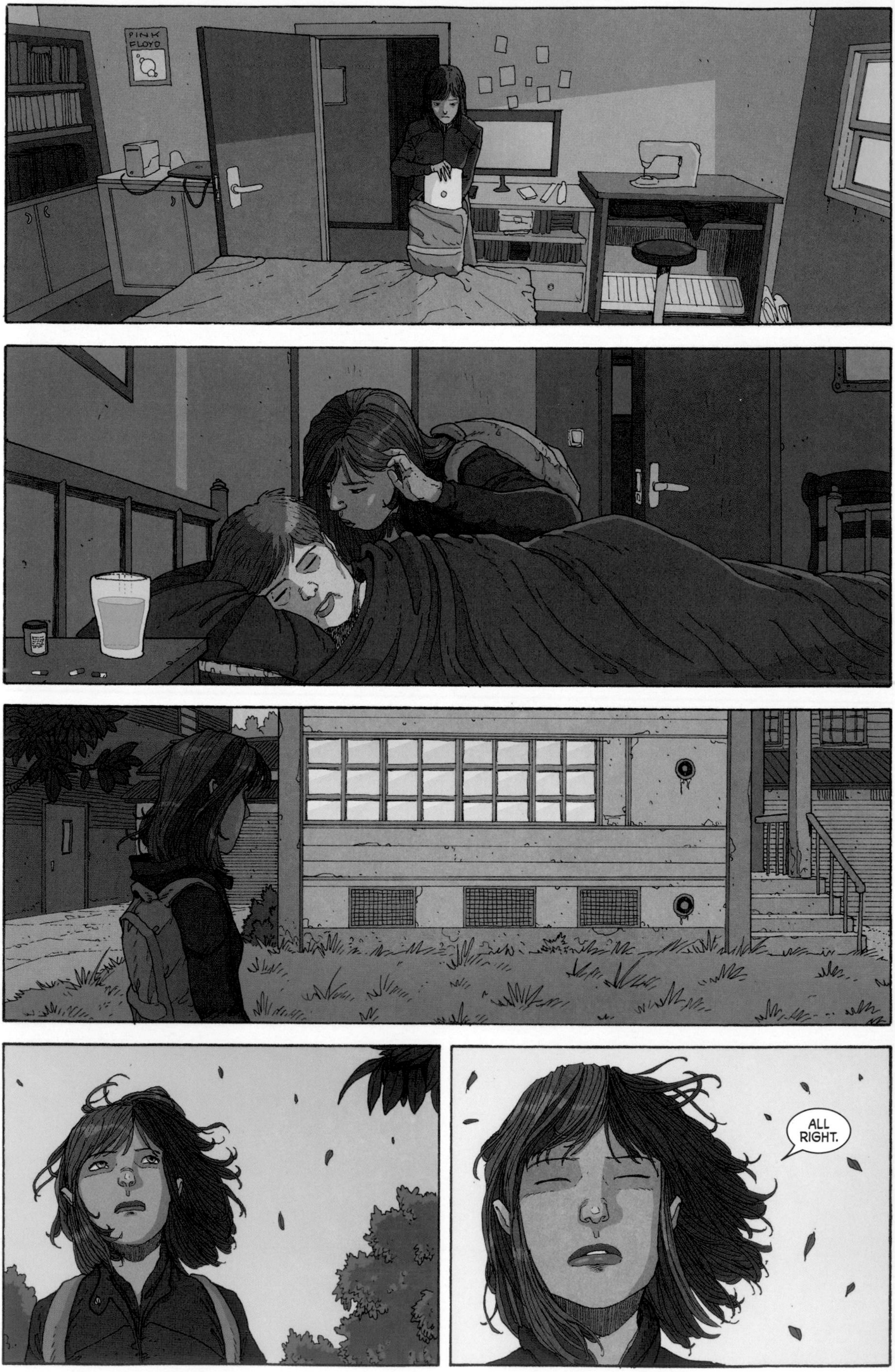
PINK FLOYD
ALL RIGHT.

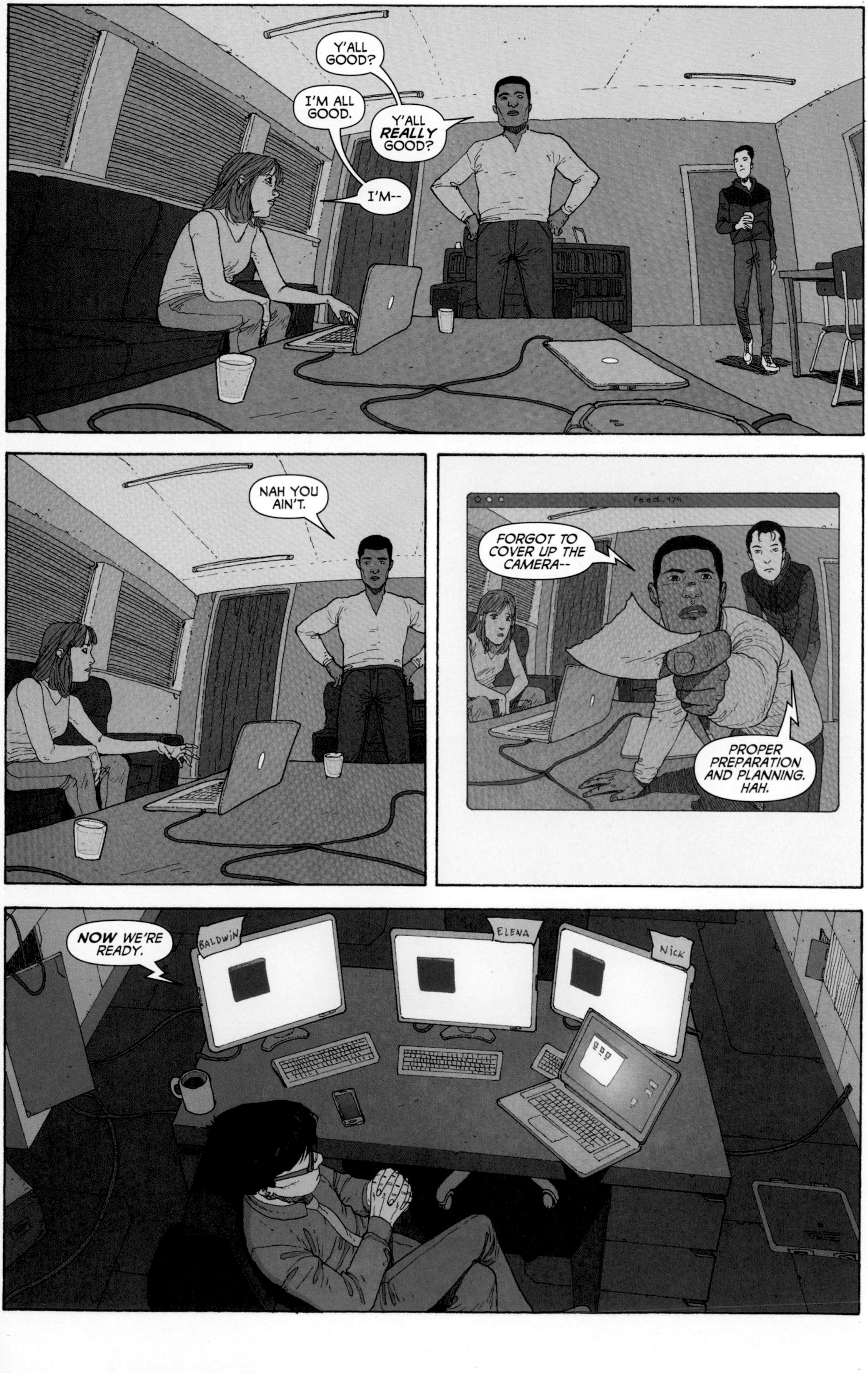
Y'ALL GOOD?
I'M ALL GOOD.
Y'ALL *REALLY* GOOD?
I'M--
NAH YOU AIN'T.
feed.174
FORGOT TO COVER UP THE CAMERA--
PROPER PREPARATION AND PLANNING. HAH.
NOW WE'RE READY.
BALDWIN
ELENA
Nick

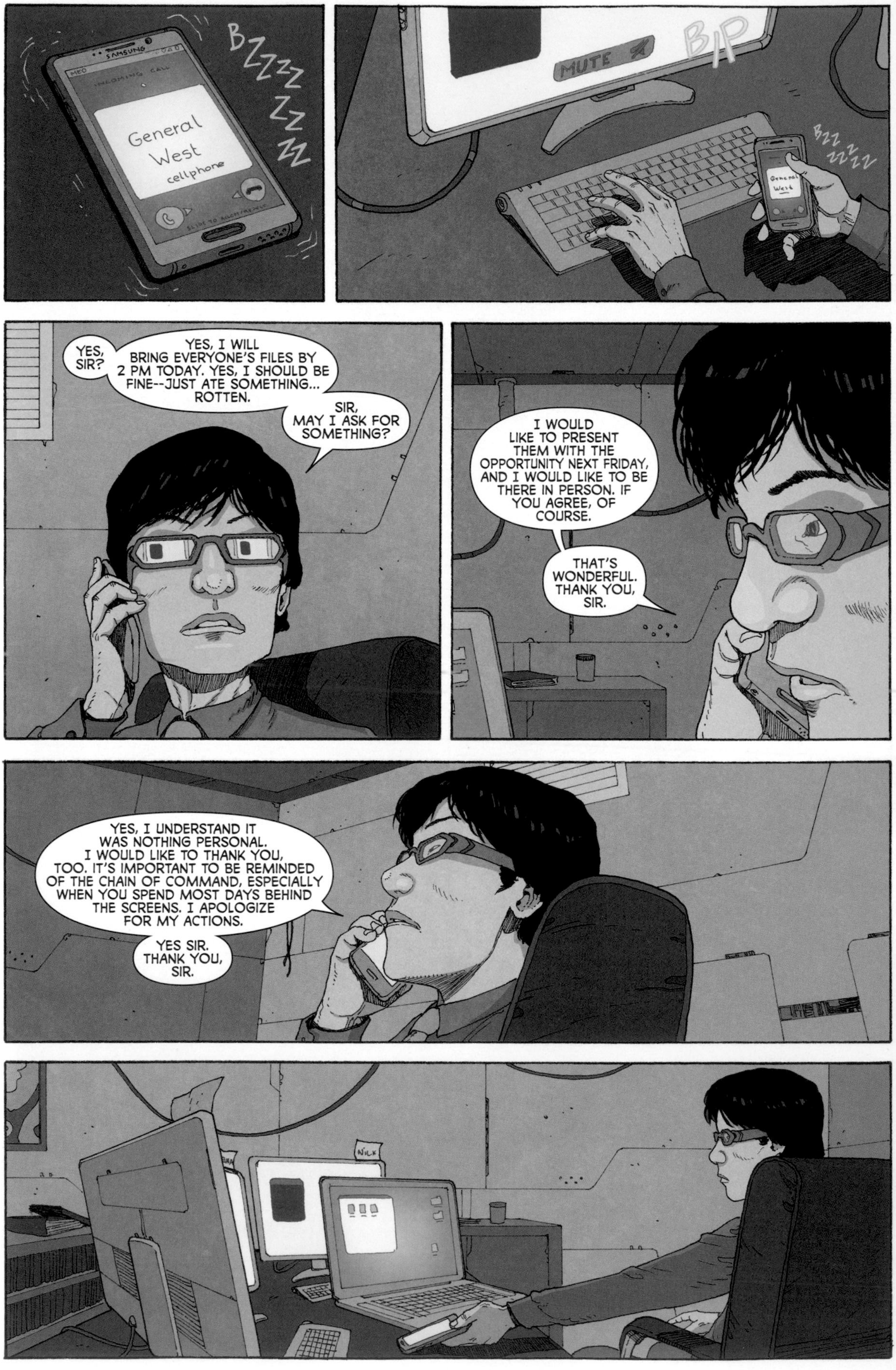
BZZZZ ZZ ZZ
General West cellphone
MUTE
BIP
BZZ ZZZZ
General West
YES, SIR?
YES, I WILL BRING EVERYONE'S FILES BY 2 PM TODAY. YES, I SHOULD BE FINE--JUST ATE SOMETHING... ROTTEN.
SIR, MAY I ASK FOR SOMETHING?
I WOULD LIKE TO PRESENT THEM WITH THE OPPORTUNITY NEXT FRIDAY, AND I WOULD LIKE TO BE THERE IN PERSON. IF YOU AGREE, OF COURSE.
THAT'S WONDERFUL. THANK YOU, SIR.
YES, I UNDERSTAND IT WAS NOTHING PERSONAL. I WOULD LIKE TO THANK YOU, TOO. IT'S IMPORTANT TO BE REMINDED OF THE CHAIN OF COMMAND, ESPECIALLY WHEN YOU SPEND MOST DAYS BEHIND THE SCREENS. I APOLOGIZE FOR MY ACTIONS.
YES SIR. THANK YOU, SIR.

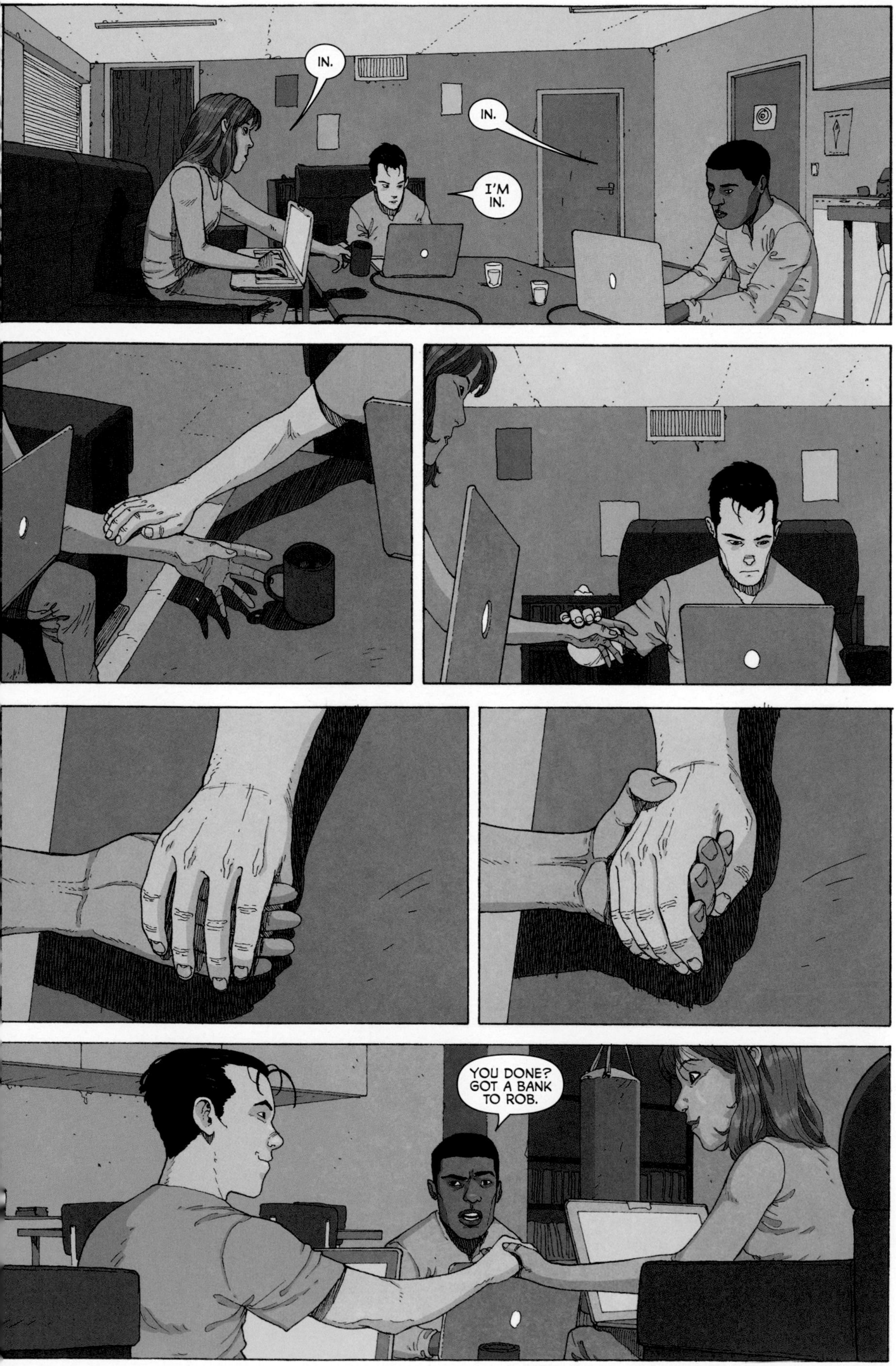
IN.
IN.
I'M IN.
YOU DONE? GOT A BANK TO ROB.

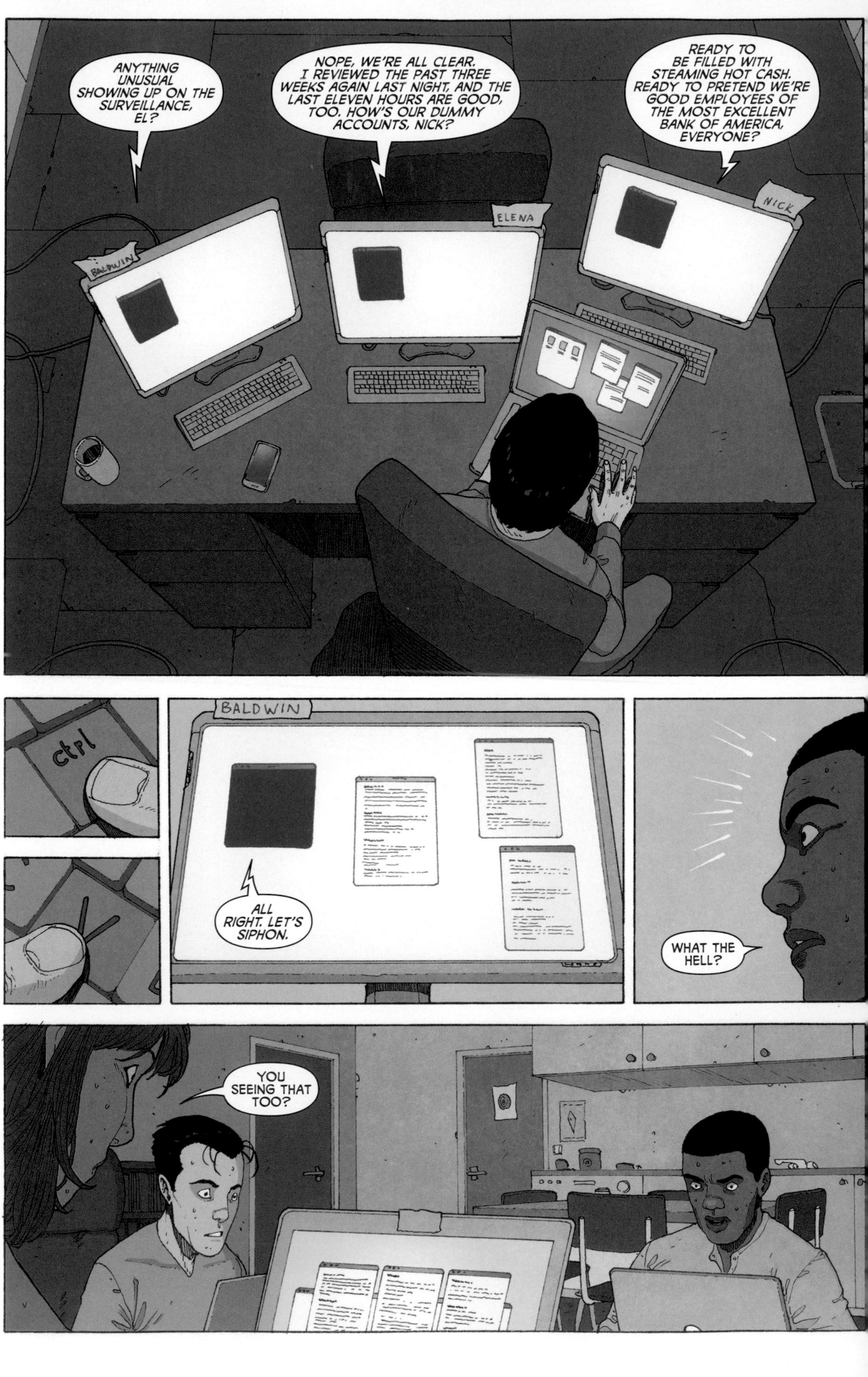
ANYTHING UNUSUAL SHOWING UP ON THE SURVEILLANCE, EL?
NOPE, WE'RE ALL CLEAR. I REVIEWED THE PAST THREE WEEKS AGAIN LAST NIGHT, AND THE LAST ELEVEN HOURS ARE GOOD, TOO. HOW'S OUR DUMMY ACCOUNTS, NICK?
READY TO BE FILLED WITH STEAMING HOT CASH. READY TO PRETEND WE'RE GOOD EMPLOYEES OF THE MOST EXCELLENT BANK OF AMERICA, EVERYONE?
BALDWIN
ELENA
NICK
ctrl
BALDWIN
ALL RIGHT. LET'S SIPHON.
WHAT THE HELL?
YOU SEEING THAT TOO?

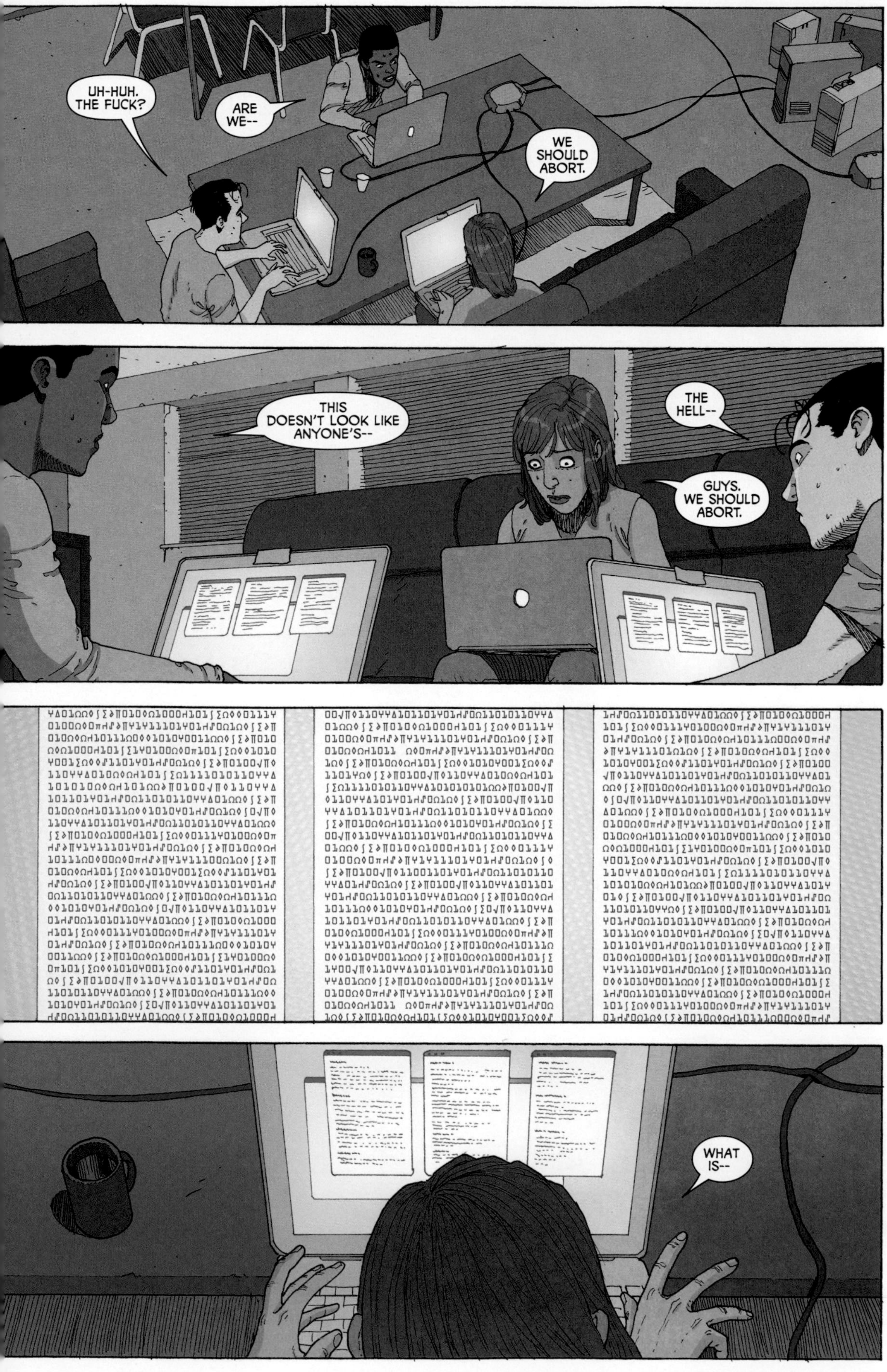
UH-HUH. THE FUCK?
ARE WE--
WE SHOULD ABORT.
THIS DOESN'T LOOK LIKE ANYONE'S--
THE HELL--
GUYS. WE SHOULD ABORT.
WHAT IS--

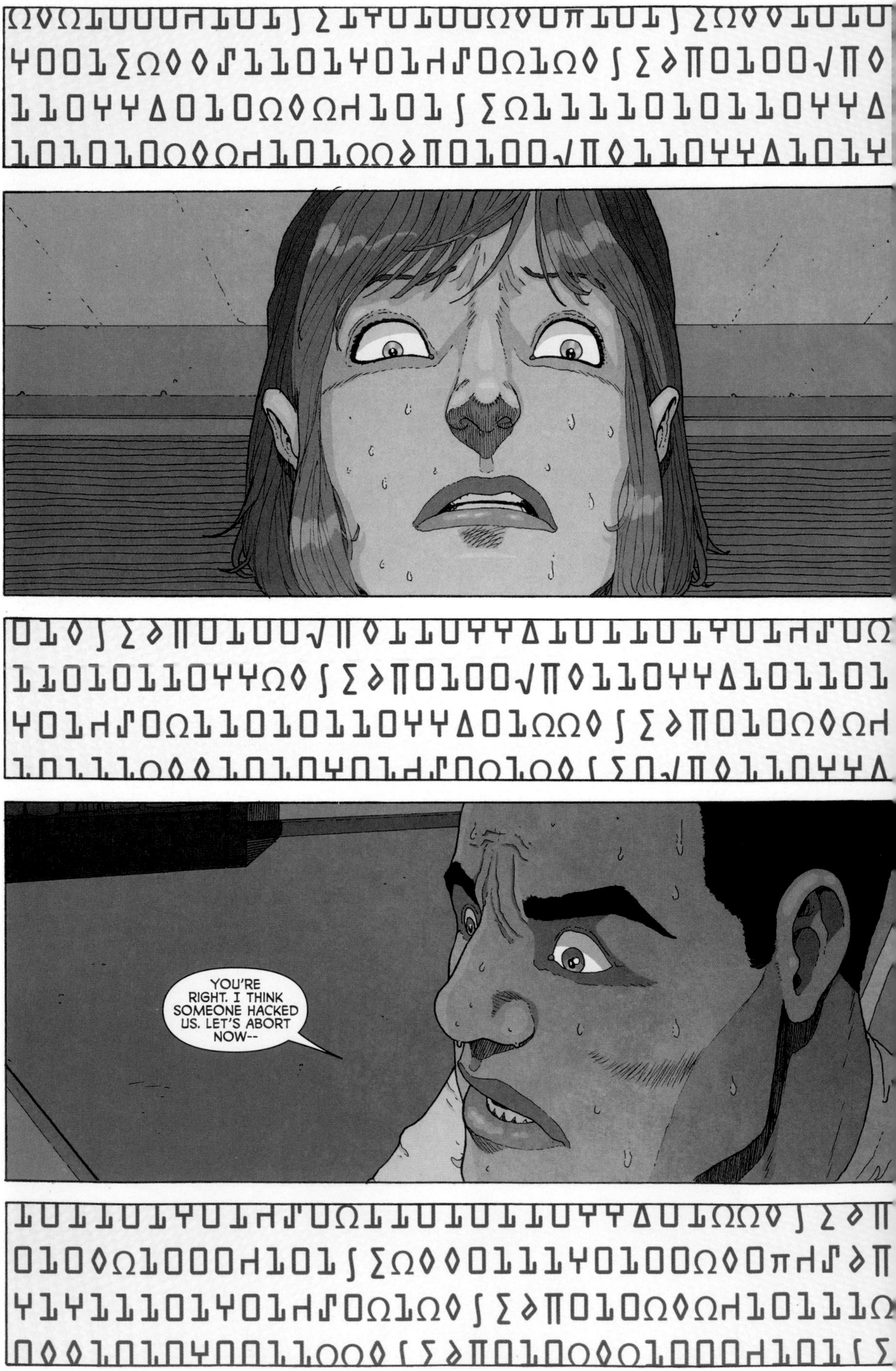
YOU'RE RIGHT. I THINK SOMEONE HACKED US. LET'S ABORT NOW--

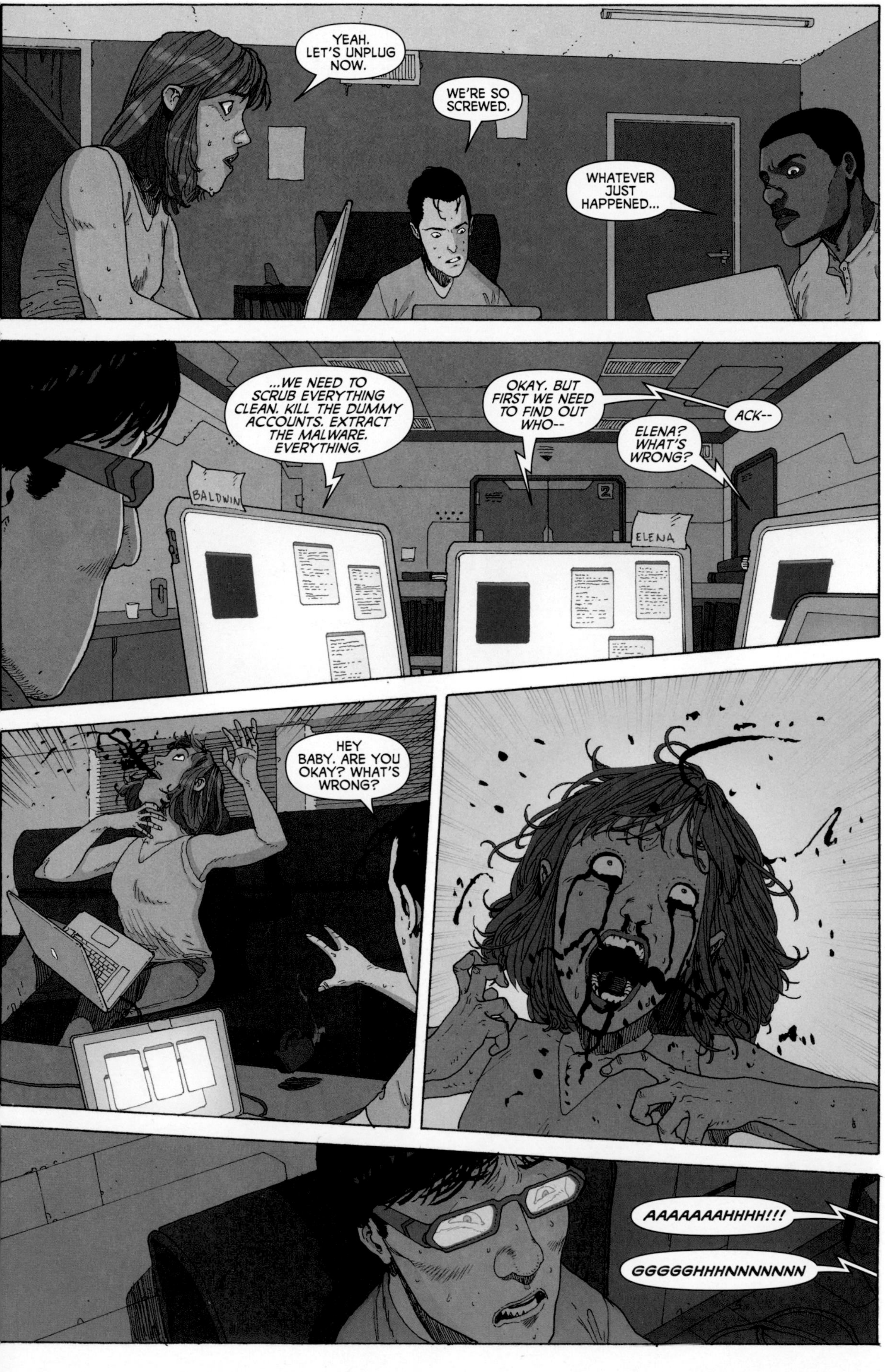
YEAH. LET'S UNPLUG NOW.
WE'RE SO SCREWED.
WHATEVER JUST HAPPENED...
...WE NEED TO SCRUB EVERYTHING CLEAN. KILL THE DUMMY ACCOUNTS. EXTRACT THE MALWARE. EVERYTHING.
OKAY. BUT FIRST WE NEED TO FIND OUT WHO--
ACK--
ELENA? WHAT'S WRONG?
BALDWIN
ELENA
HEY BABY. ARE YOU OKAY? WHAT'S WRONG?
AAAAAAAHHHH!!!
GGGGGHHHNNNNNNN

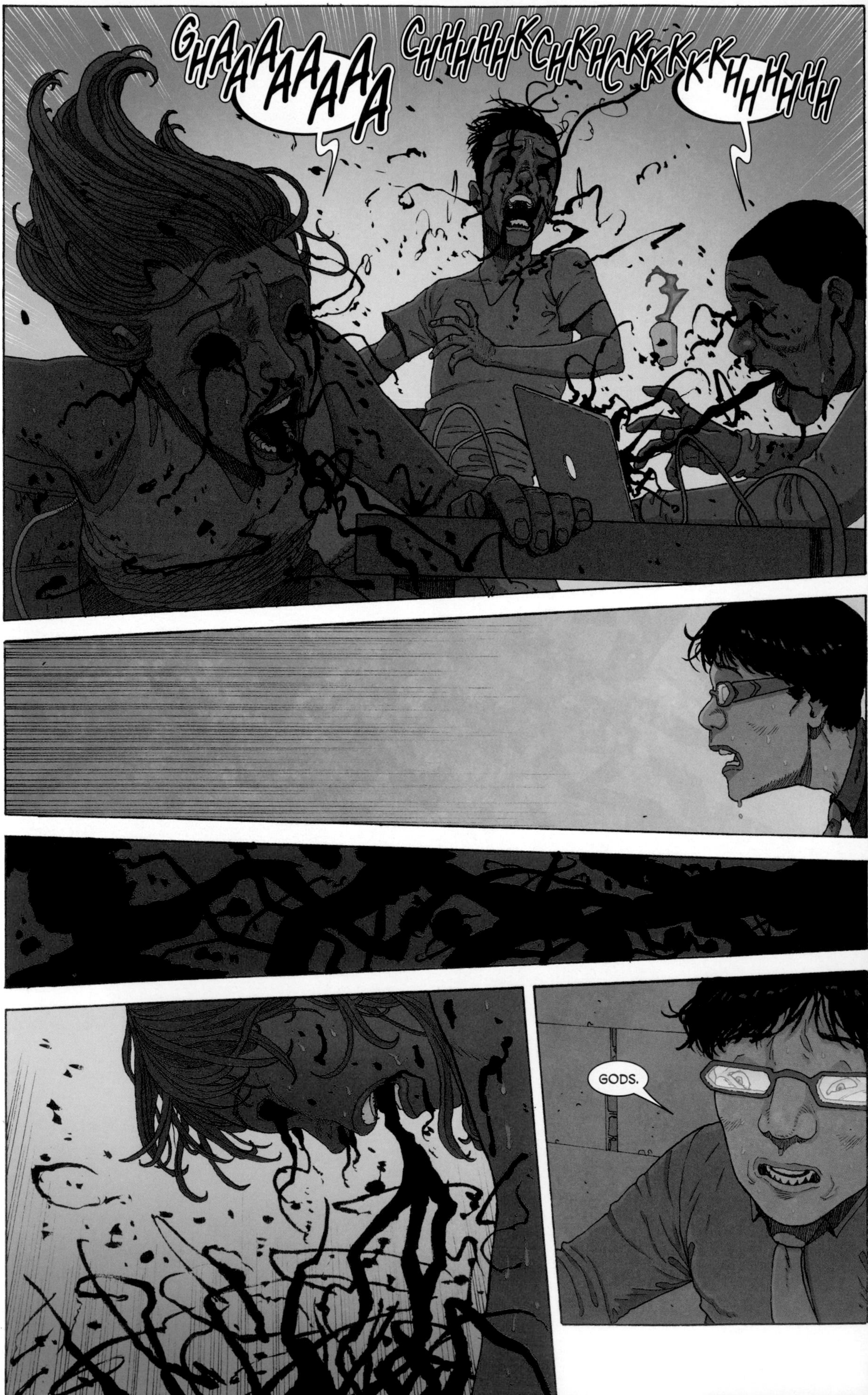
GHAAAAAAAAA
CHHHHHKCHKHCKKKKHHHHHH
GODS.

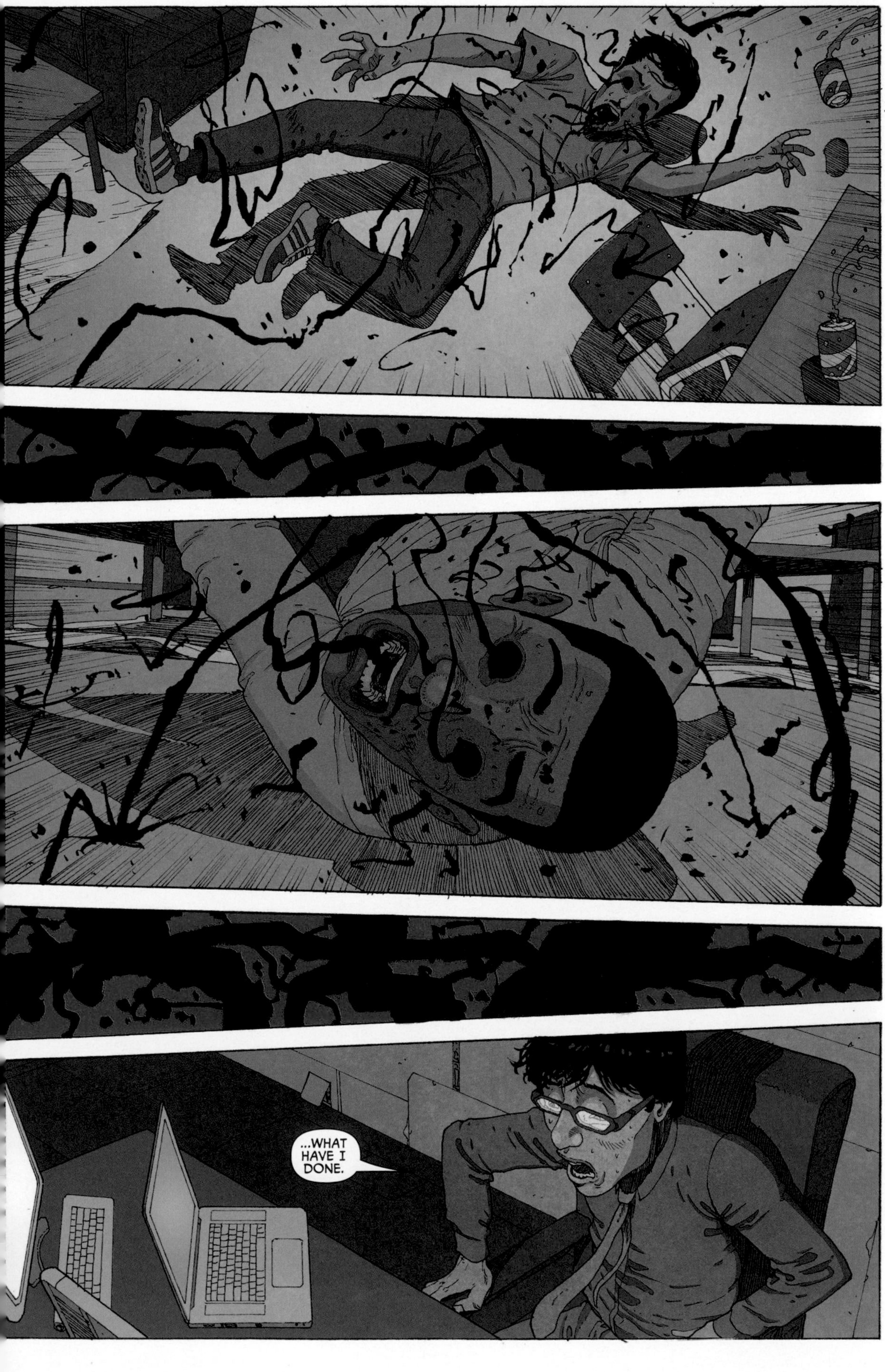
...WHAT HAVE I DONE.

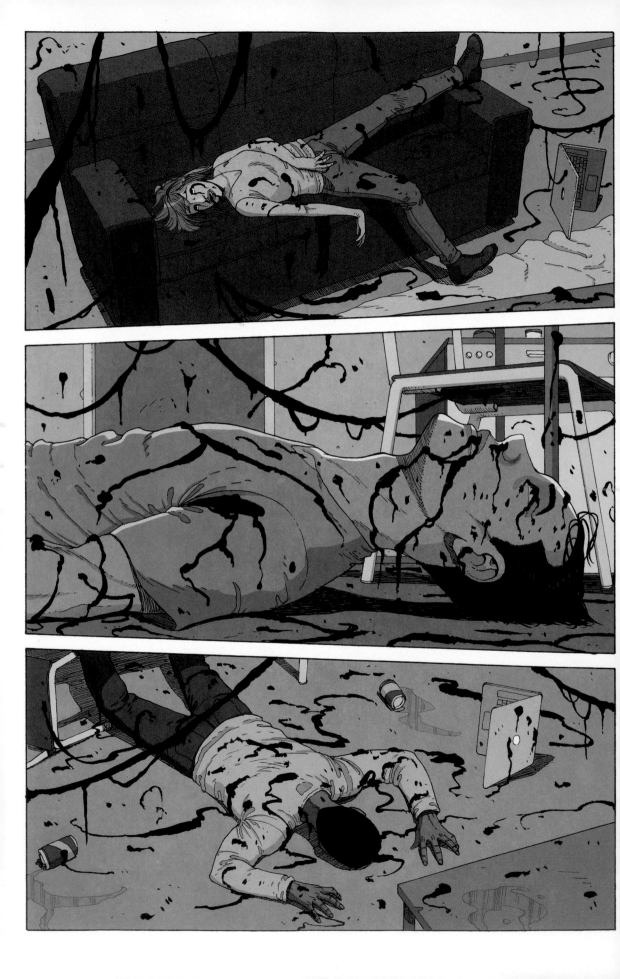

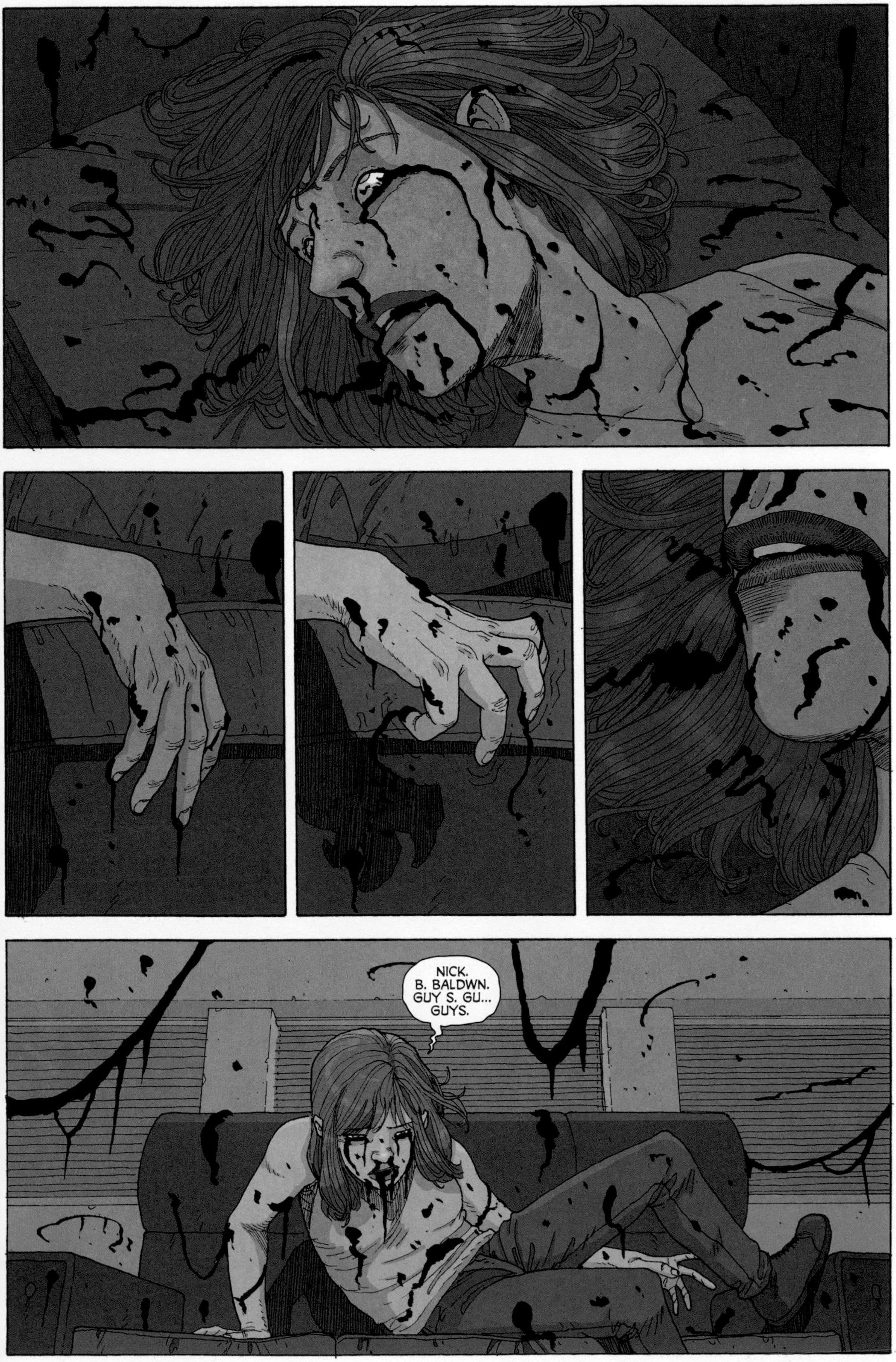
NICK. B. BALDWN. GUY S. GU... GUYS.

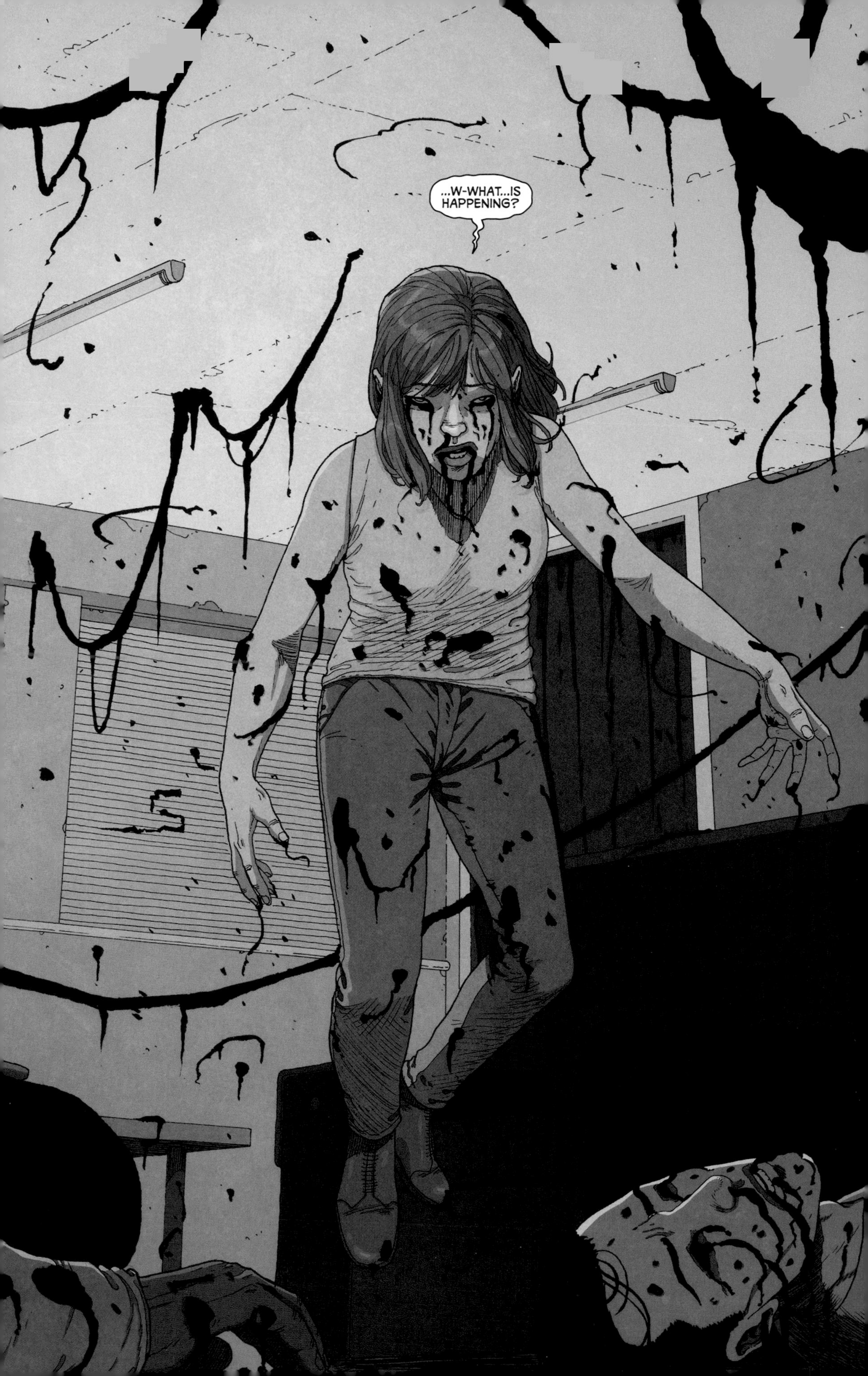
...W-WHAT...IS HAPPENING?

CHAPTER TWO

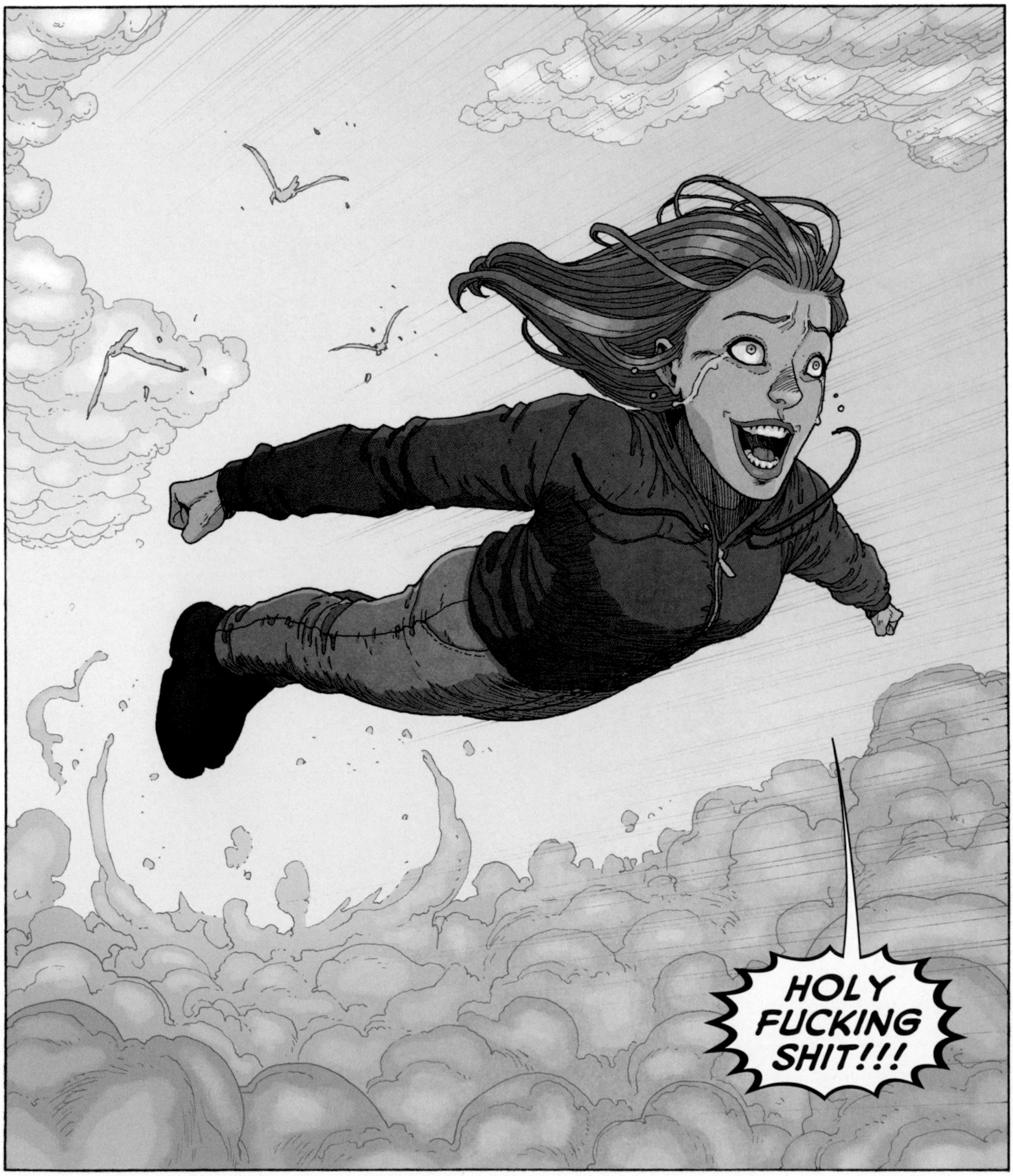
HOLY FUCKING SHIT!!!

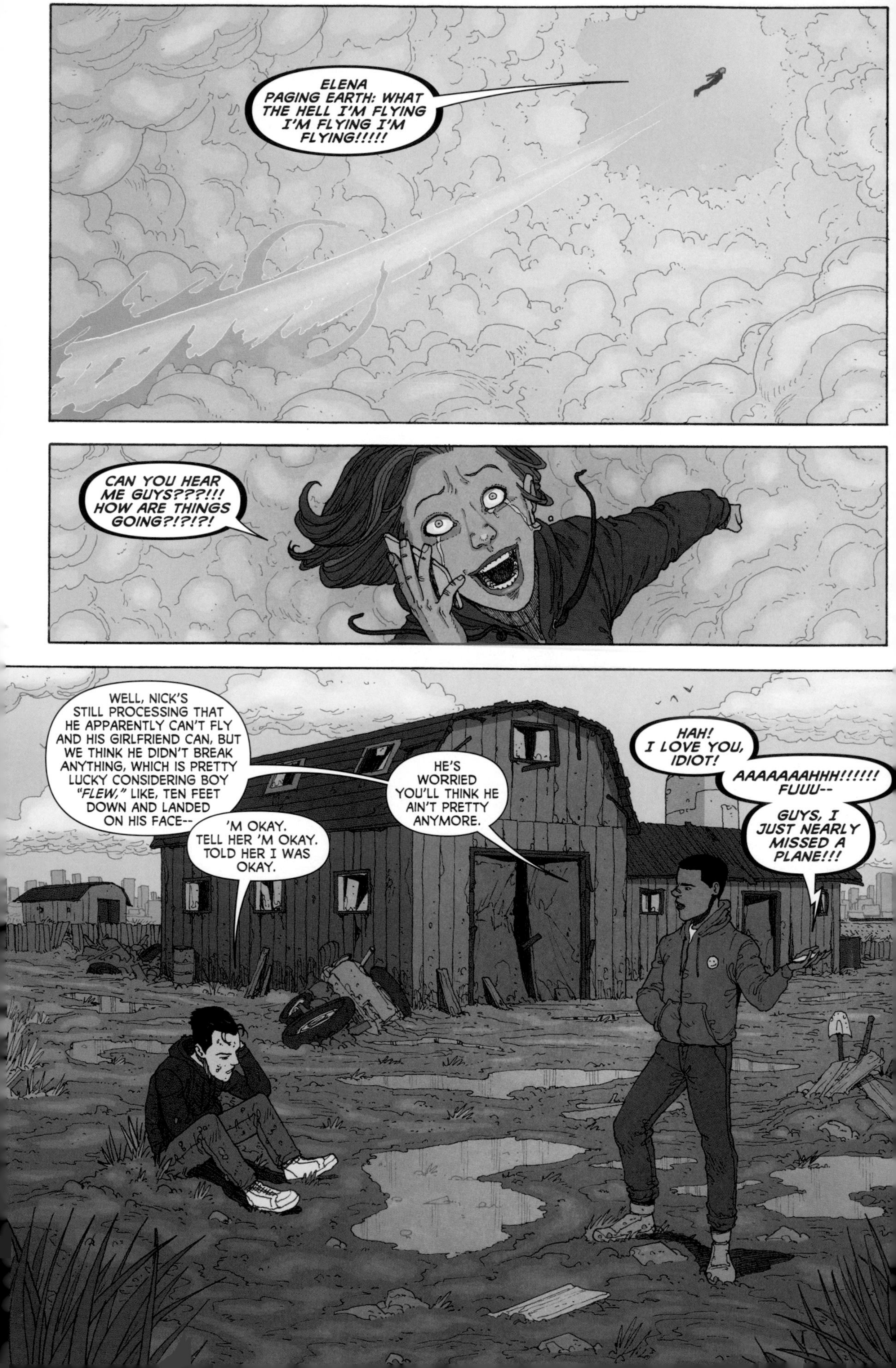
ELENA PAGING EARTH: WHAT THE HELL I'M FLYING I'M FLYING I'M FLYING!!!!!
CAN YOU HEAR ME GUYS???!!! HOW ARE THINGS GOING?!?!?!
WELL, NICK'S STILL PROCESSING THAT HE APPARENTLY CAN'T FLY AND HIS GIRLFRIEND CAN, BUT WE THINK HE DIDN'T BREAK ANYTHING, WHICH IS PRETTY LUCKY CONSIDERING BOY "FLEW," LIKE, TEN FEET DOWN AND LANDED ON HIS FACE--
'M OKAY. TELL HER 'M OKAY. TOLD HER I WAS OKAY.
HE'S WORRIED YOU'LL THINK HE AIN'T PRETTY ANYMORE.
HAH! I LOVE YOU, IDIOT!
AAAAAAAHHH!!!!!! FUUU--
GUYS, I JUST NEARLY MISSED A PLANE!!!

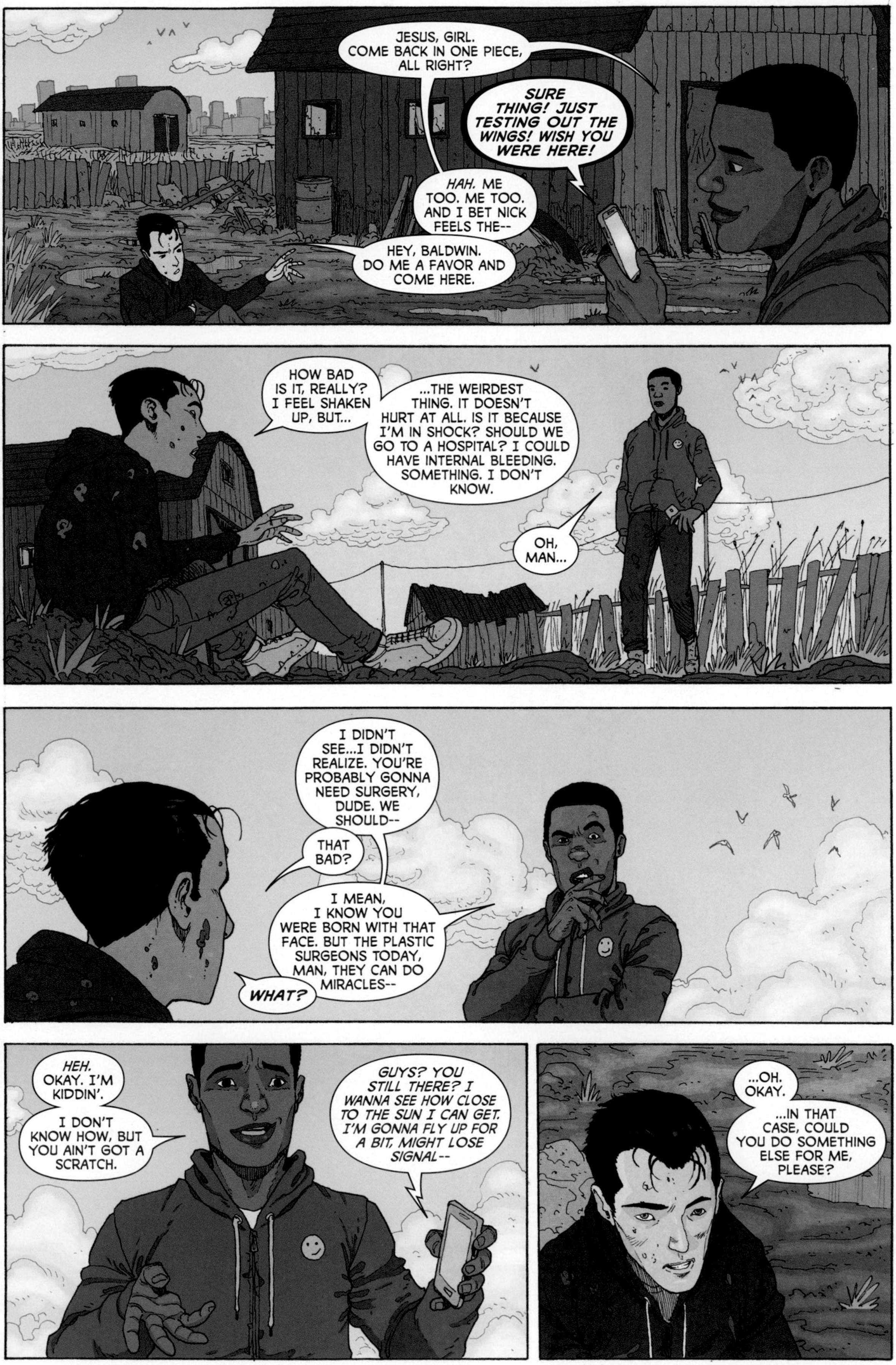
JESUS, GIRL. COME BACK IN ONE PIECE, ALL RIGHT?
SURE THING! JUST TESTING OUT THE WINGS! WISH YOU WERE HERE!
HAH. ME TOO. ME TOO. AND I BET NICK FEELS THE--
HEY, BALDWIN. DO ME A FAVOR AND COME HERE.
HOW BAD IS IT, REALLY? I FEEL SHAKEN UP, BUT...
...THE WEIRDEST THING. IT DOESN'T HURT AT ALL. IS IT BECAUSE I'M IN SHOCK? SHOULD WE GO TO A HOSPITAL? I COULD HAVE INTERNAL BLEEDING. SOMETHING. I DON'T KNOW.
OH, MAN...
I DIDN'T SEE...I DIDN'T REALIZE. YOU'RE PROBABLY GONNA NEED SURGERY, DUDE. WE SHOULD--
THAT BAD?
I MEAN, I KNOW YOU WERE BORN WITH THAT FACE. BUT THE PLASTIC SURGEONS TODAY, MAN, THEY CAN DO MIRACLES--
WHAT?
HEH. OKAY. I'M KIDDIN'.
I DON'T KNOW HOW, BUT YOU AIN'T GOT A SCRATCH.
GUYS? YOU STILL THERE? I WANNA SEE HOW CLOSE TO THE SUN I CAN GET. I'M GONNA FLY UP FOR A BIT, MIGHT LOSE SIGNAL--
...OH. OKAY.
...IN THAT CASE, COULD YOU DO SOMETHING ELSE FOR ME, PLEASE?

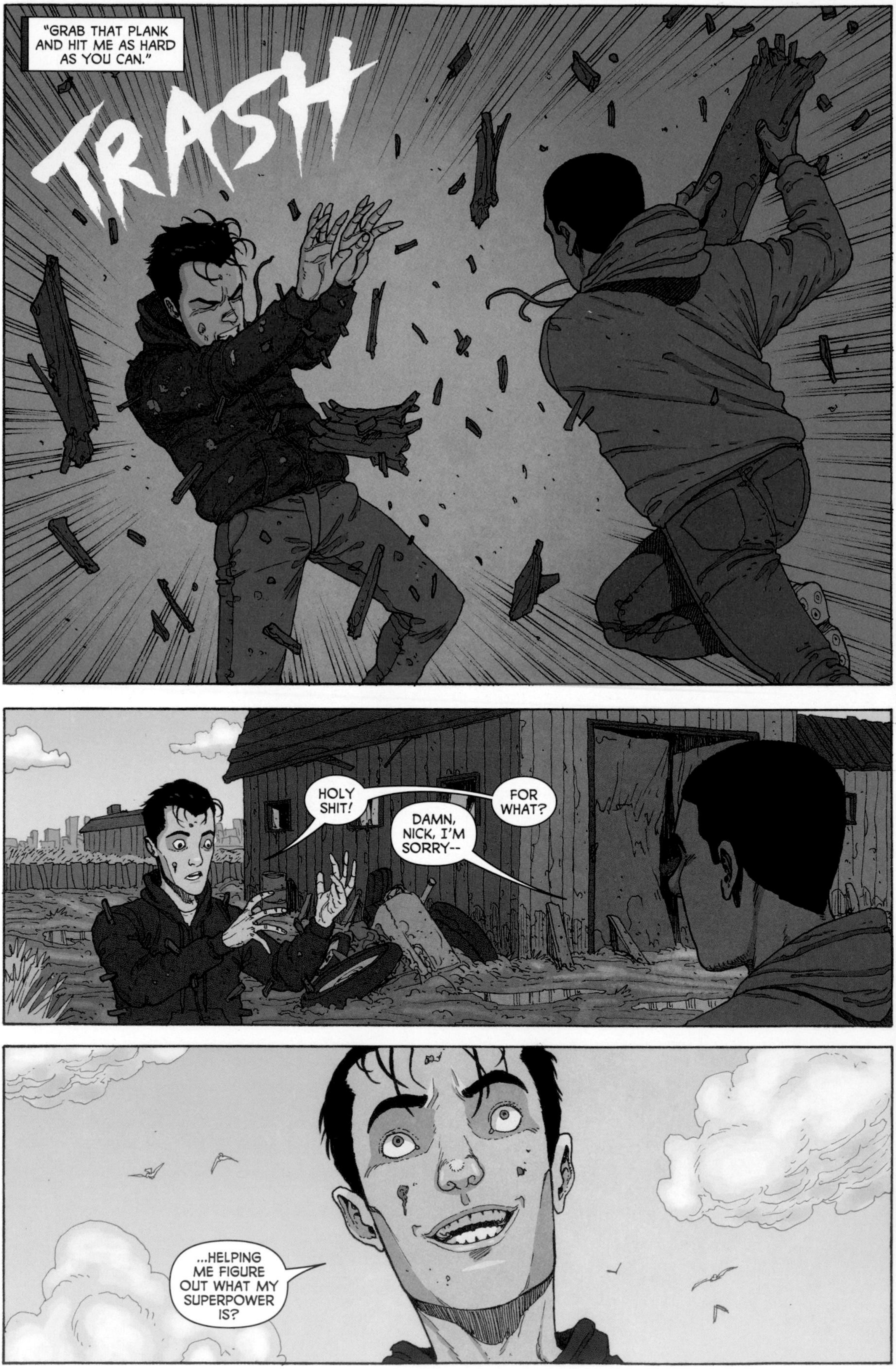
"GRAB THAT PLANK AND HIT ME AS HARD AS YOU CAN."
TRASH
HOLY SHIT!
DAMN, NICK, I'M SORRY--
FOR WHAT?
...HELPING ME FIGURE OUT WHAT MY SUPERPOWER IS?

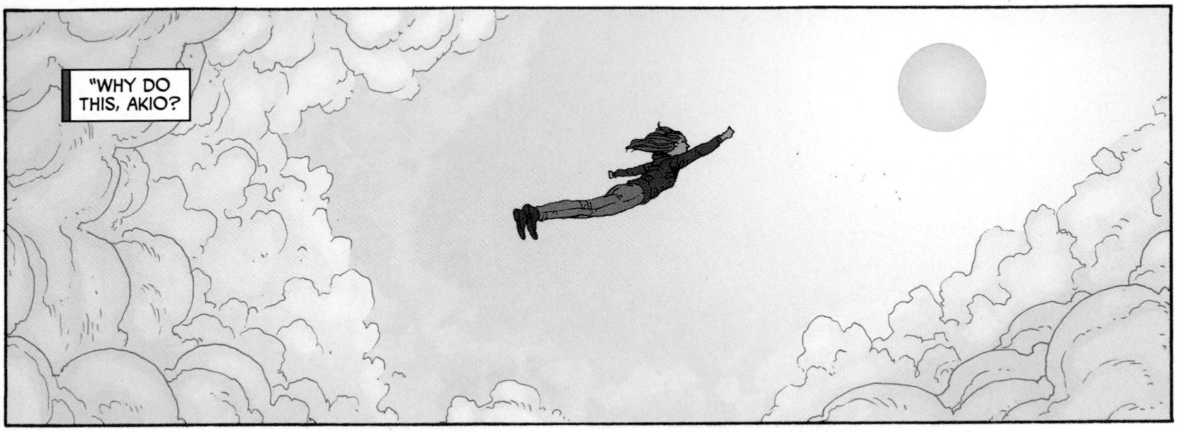
"WHY DO THIS, AKIO?

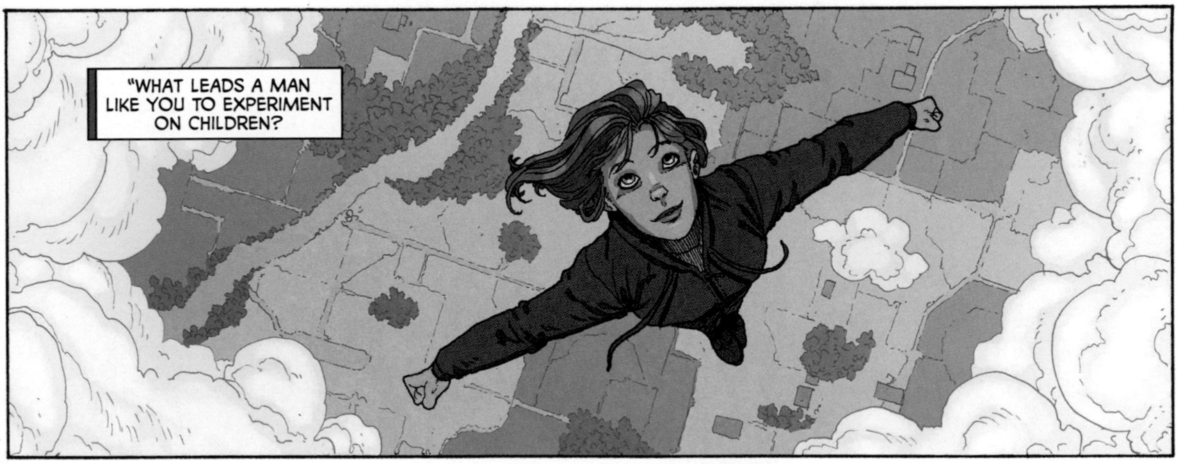
"WHAT LEADS A MAN LIKE YOU TO EXPERIMENT ON CHILDREN?

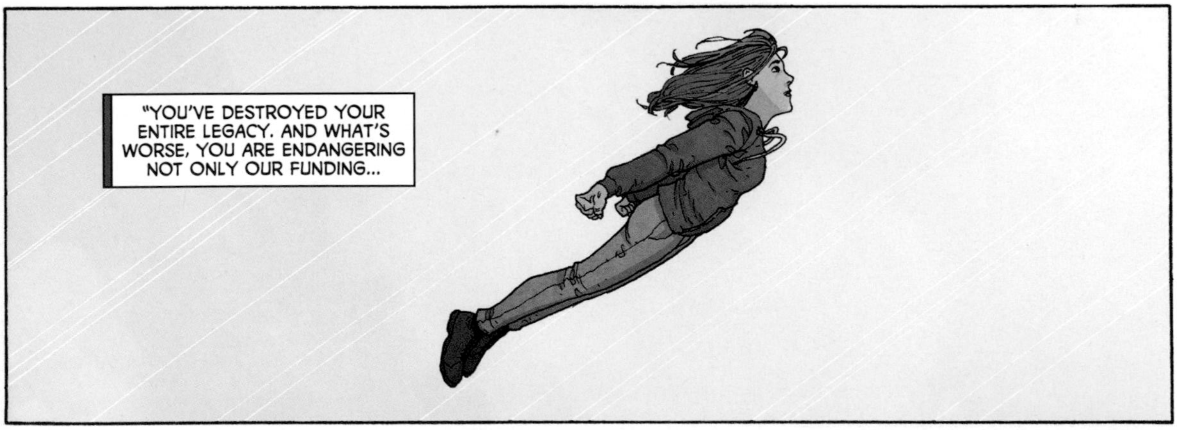
"YOU'VE DESTROYED YOUR ENTIRE LEGACY. AND WHAT'S WORSE, YOU ARE ENDANGERING NOT ONLY OUR FUNDING...

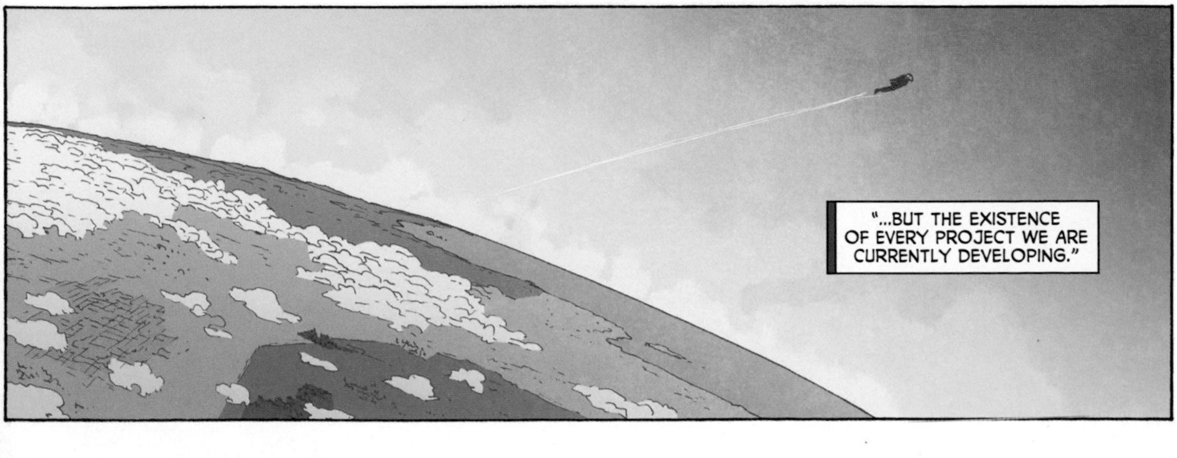
"...BUT THE EXISTENCE OF EVERY PROJECT WE ARE CURRENTLY DEVELOPING."

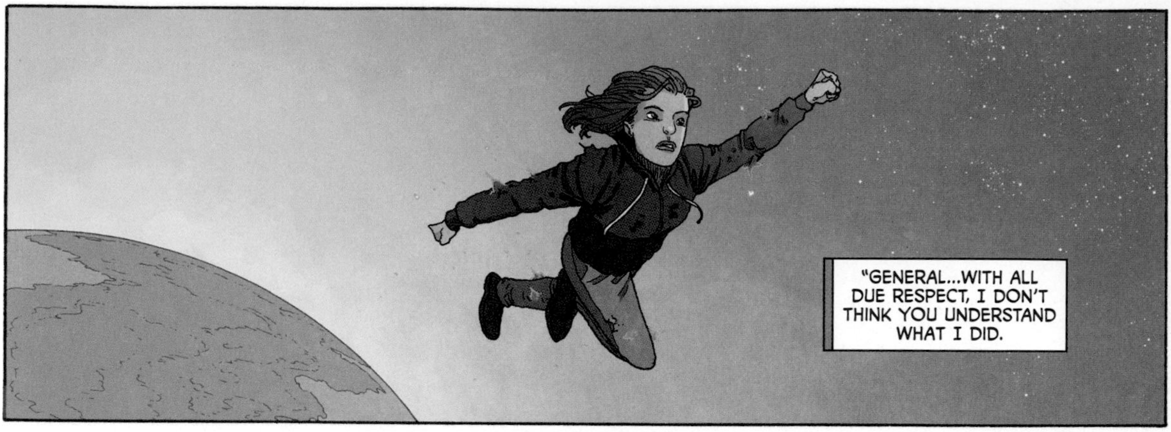
"GENERAL...WITH ALL DUE RESPECT, I DON'T THINK YOU UNDERSTAND WHAT I DID.

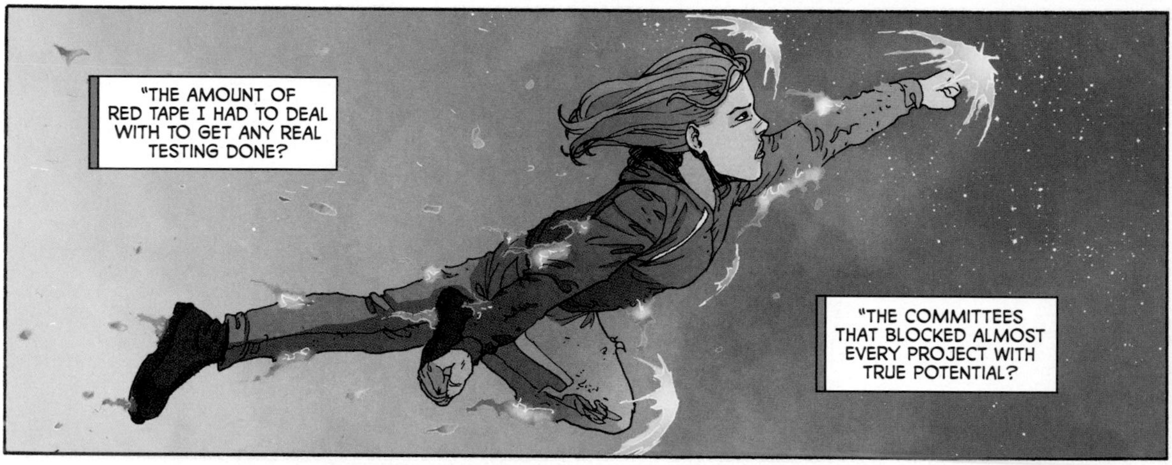
"THE AMOUNT OF RED TAPE I HAD TO DEAL WITH TO GET ANY REAL TESTING DONE?
"THE COMMITTEES THAT BLOCKED ALMOST EVERY PROJECT WITH TRUE POTENTIAL?

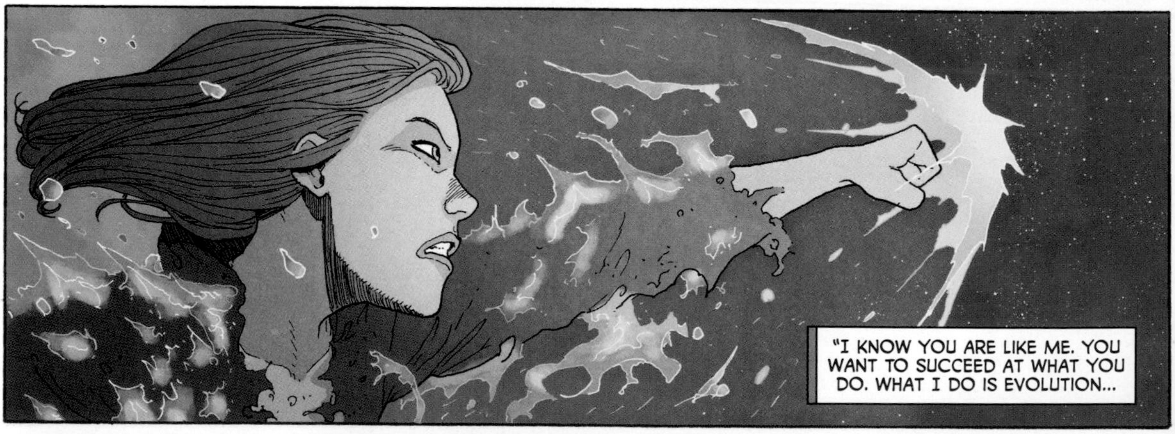
"I KNOW YOU ARE LIKE ME. YOU WANT TO SUCCEED AT WHAT YOU DO. WHAT I DO IS EVOLUTION...

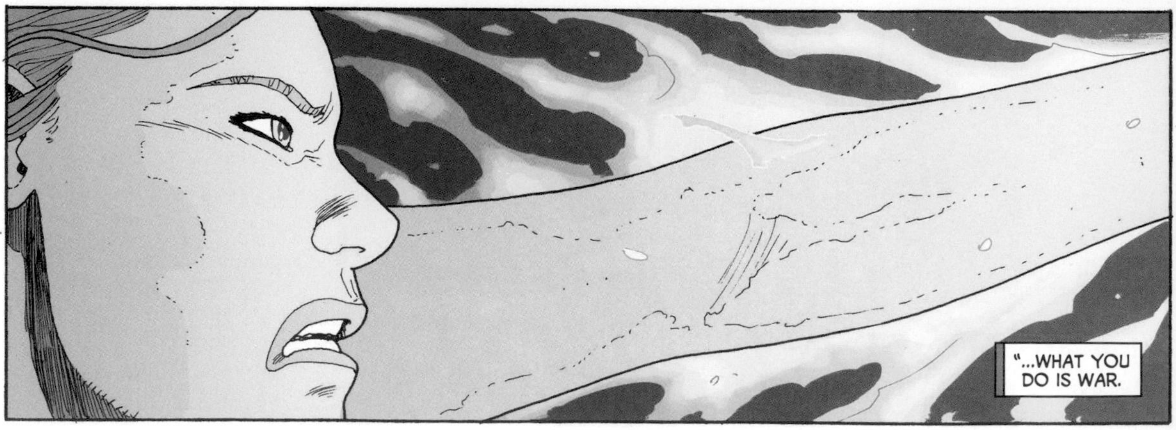
"...WHAT YOU DO IS WAR.

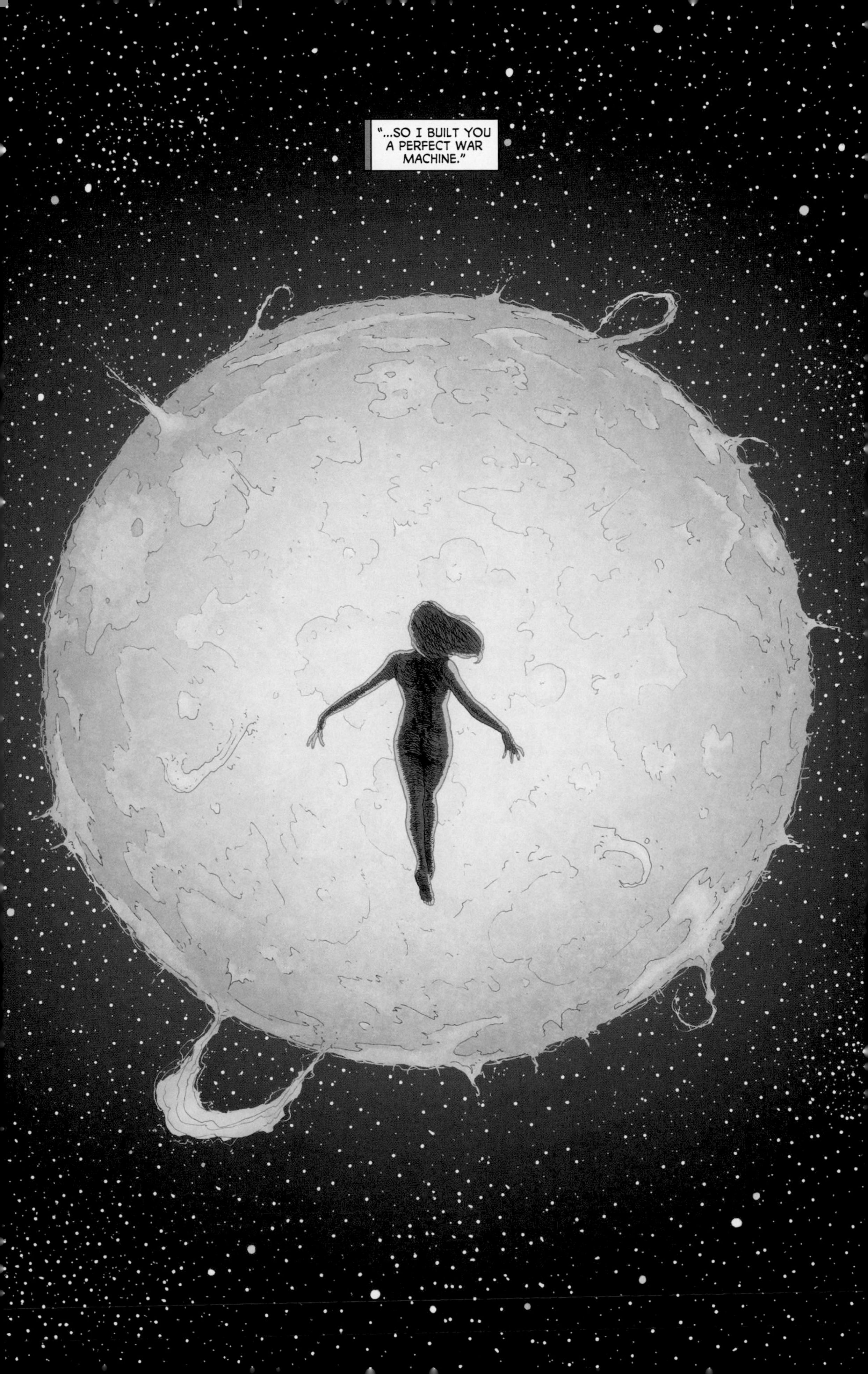
"...SO I BUILT YOU A PERFECT WAR MACHINE."

NEVERTHELESS.

PRESENTLY, THESE CHILDREN ARE STILL WEAK. THEY LACK TRAINING, AND THEIR POWERS WILL BE DEVELOPING VERY GRADUALLY.

SURE. ONE OF THEM CAN FIGHT A BIT, AND THE GIRL HAS A MENTAL ENDURANCE AND OVERALL ADAPTABILITY TO ADVERSE CONDITIONS THAT IS QUITE REMARKABLE...BUT REGARDLESS, THEY ARE JUST CHILDREN IN THEIR LATE TEENS.

THEREFORE, I STILL BELIEVE THE BEST WAY TO APPROACH THIS WOULD BE TO SIMPLY SEND ME ALONG WITH A FEW SOLDIERS AS A BACKUP.

WE KNOW WHERE THEY LIVE. WE CAN PICK THEM UP, AND I'LL MAKE SURE THEY COOPERATE.

ALL YOU HAVE TO DO...IS LET ME OUT OF THIS PLACE FOR FORTY-EIGHT HOURS AND THEY WILL BE BACK WITH YOU.

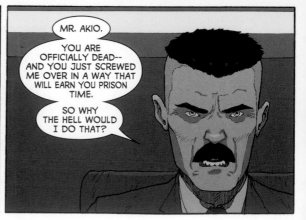

MR. AKIO.

YOU ARE OFFICIALLY DEAD-- AND YOU JUST SCREWED ME OVER IN A WAY THAT WILL EARN YOU PRISON TIME.

SO WHY THE HELL WOULD I DO THAT?

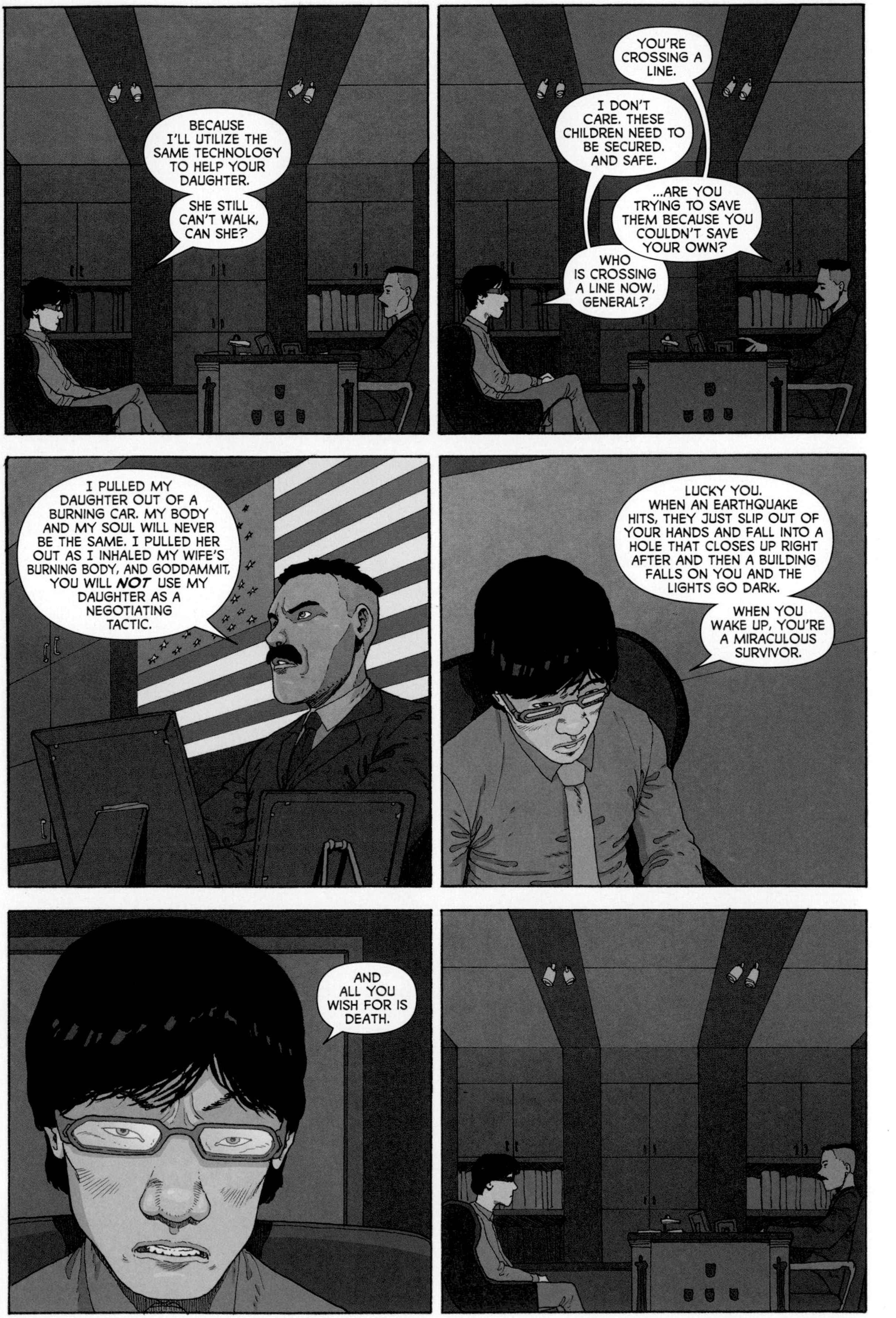
BECAUSE I'LL UTILIZE THE SAME TECHNOLOGY TO HELP YOUR DAUGHTER.
SHE STILL CAN'T WALK, CAN SHE?
YOU'RE CROSSING A LINE.
I DON'T CARE. THESE CHILDREN NEED TO BE SECURED. AND SAFE.
...ARE YOU TRYING TO SAVE THEM BECAUSE YOU COULDN'T SAVE YOUR OWN?
WHO IS CROSSING A LINE NOW, GENERAL?
I PULLED MY DAUGHTER OUT OF A BURNING CAR. MY BODY AND MY SOUL WILL NEVER BE THE SAME. I PULLED HER OUT AS I INHALED MY WIFE'S BURNING BODY, AND GODDAMMIT, YOU WILL ***NOT*** USE MY DAUGHTER AS A NEGOTIATING TACTIC.
LUCKY YOU. WHEN AN EARTHQUAKE HITS, THEY JUST SLIP OUT OF YOUR HANDS AND FALL INTO A HOLE THAT CLOSES UP RIGHT AFTER AND THEN A BUILDING FALLS ON YOU AND THE LIGHTS GO DARK.
WHEN YOU WAKE UP, YOU'RE A MIRACULOUS SURVIVOR.
AND ALL YOU WISH FOR IS DEATH.

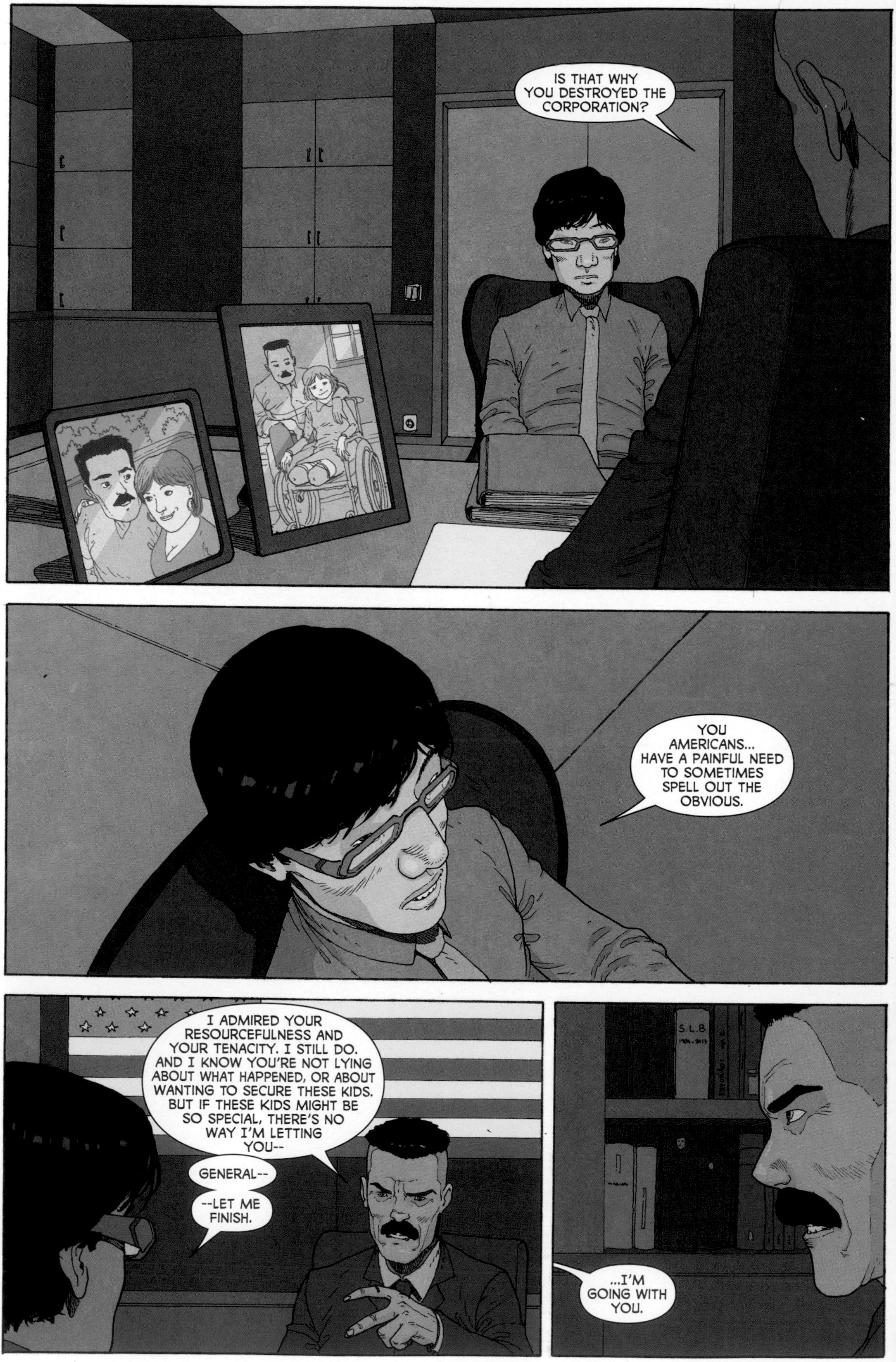
IS THAT WHY YOU DESTROYED THE CORPORATION?
YOU AMERICANS... HAVE A PAINFUL NEED TO SOMETIMES SPELL OUT THE OBVIOUS.
I ADMIRED YOUR RESOURCEFULNESS AND YOUR TENACITY. I STILL DO. AND I KNOW YOU'RE NOT LYING ABOUT WHAT HAPPENED, OR ABOUT WANTING TO SECURE THESE KIDS. BUT IF THESE KIDS MIGHT BE SO SPECIAL, THERE'S NO WAY I'M LETTING YOU--
GENERAL--
--LET ME FINISH.
...I'M GOING WITH YOU.

...AND THEN I HIT WHAT I GUESS IS MY OXYGEN LIMIT?

SO...UM... YEAH. I FLEW DOWN AND STOLE SOME CLOTHES, WHICH WAS A SORTA TRICKY THING TO DO AND I FEEL KINDA BAD ABOUT IT, BUT I WAS KINDA COLD AND PANICKED?

...RADICAL.

AND MY PHONE BURNED DOWN TOO SO I COULDN'T EVEN CALL YOU GUYS. AND NOW YOU'RE MR. INVULNERABLE AND YOU'RE...YOU FIGURE OUT WHAT YOUR *SUPERPOWER* IS, BALDWIN?

I DO ALL THE FREE EMOTIONAL LABOR FOR NICK WHILE YOU'RE GONE, GIRL. WHY THE HELL WOULD I NEED ANOTHER SUPERPOWER?

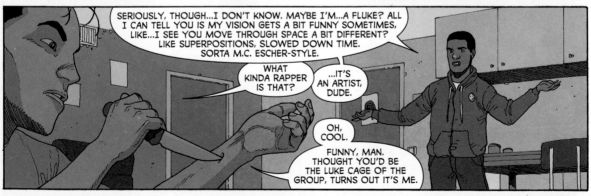

SERIOUSLY, THOUGH...I DON'T KNOW. MAYBE I'M...A FLUKE? ALL I CAN TELL YOU IS MY VISION GETS A BIT FUNNY SOMETIMES, LIKE...I SEE YOU MOVE THROUGH SPACE A BIT DIFFERENT? LIKE SUPERPOSITIONS, SLOWED DOWN TIME. SORTA M.C. ESCHER-STYLE.

WHAT KINDA RAPPER IS THAT?

...IT'S AN ARTIST, DUDE.

OH, COOL.

FUNNY, MAN. THOUGHT YOU'D BE THE LUKE CAGE OF THE GROUP, TURNS OUT IT'S ME.

...I'M NOT EVEN GONNA...

ANY NEW MESSAGES FROM OUR MYSTERY... BENEFACTOR, I GUESS?

...NOTHING.

...WHAT DO YOU THINK HAPPENED TO US, ELLIE?

...I DON'T KNOW. ALL I KNOW IS WE SOMEHOW...

"...I DON'T KNOW, BALDWIN."

"I'M GLAD WE SURVIVED?"

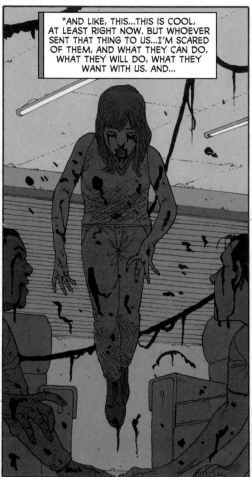

"AND LIKE, THIS...THIS IS COOL, AT LEAST RIGHT NOW. BUT WHOEVER SENT THAT THING TO US...I'M SCARED OF THEM, AND WHAT THEY CAN DO, WHAT THEY WILL DO, WHAT THEY WANT WITH US. AND..."

"...WE DON'T HAVE THE CASH. I NEED THE CASH."

...AND I GOTTA TAKE A LEAK BEFORE WE FIGURE OUT HOW TO GET IT. TO BE CONTINUED IN TWO MINUTES? MY LIVER'S BEEN KILLING ME. MAYBE I'M GROWING NEW ORGANS?

AWESOME.

EW!

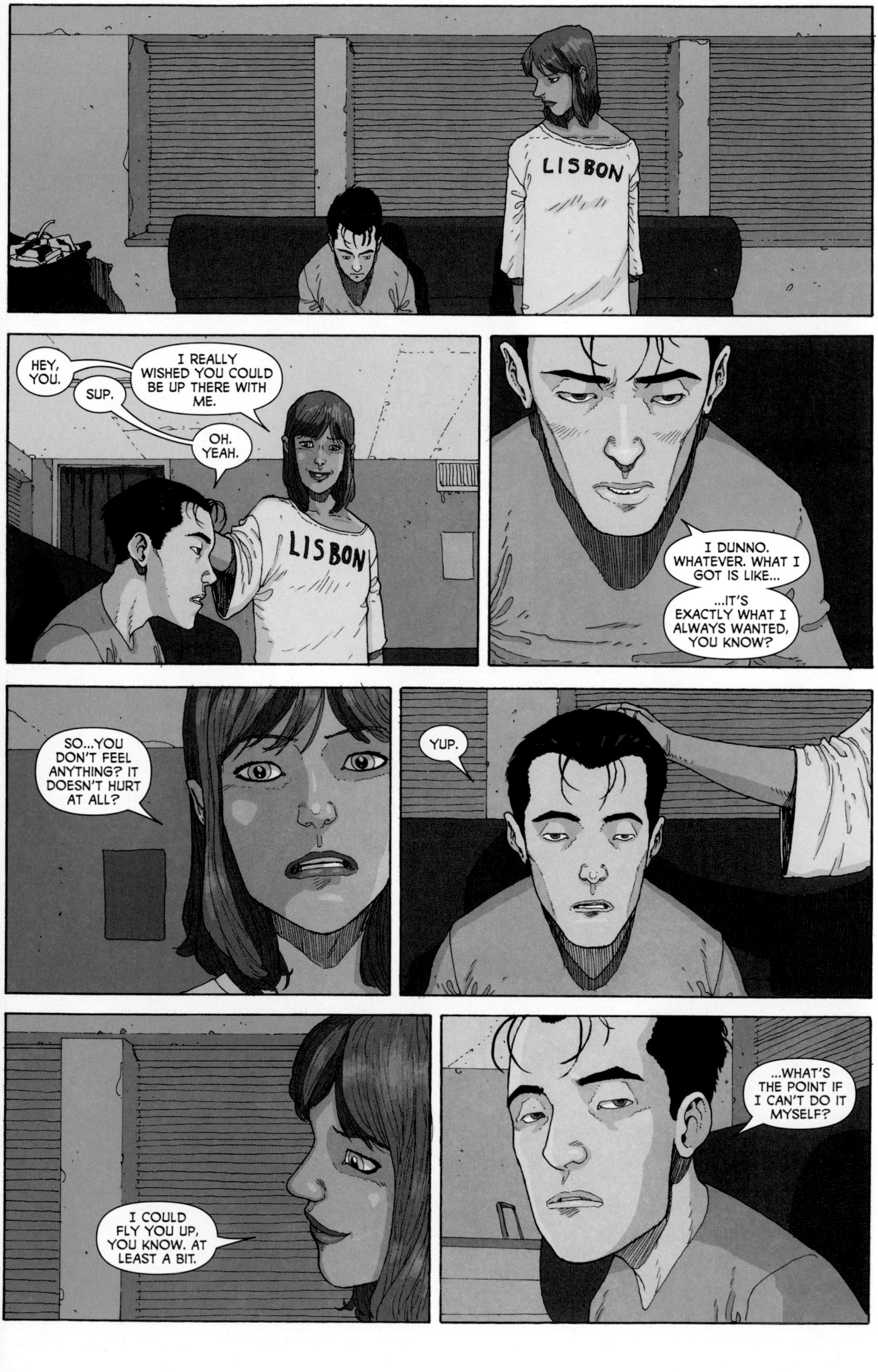
LISBON
HEY, YOU.
I REALLY WISHED YOU COULD BE UP THERE WITH ME.
SUP.
OH. YEAH.
LISBON
I DUNNO. WHATEVER. WHAT I GOT IS LIKE...
...IT'S EXACTLY WHAT I ALWAYS WANTED, YOU KNOW?
SO...YOU DON'T FEEL ANYTHING? IT DOESN'T HURT AT ALL?
YUP.
I COULD FLY YOU UP, YOU KNOW. AT LEAST A BIT.
...WHAT'S THE POINT IF I CAN'T DO IT MYSELF?

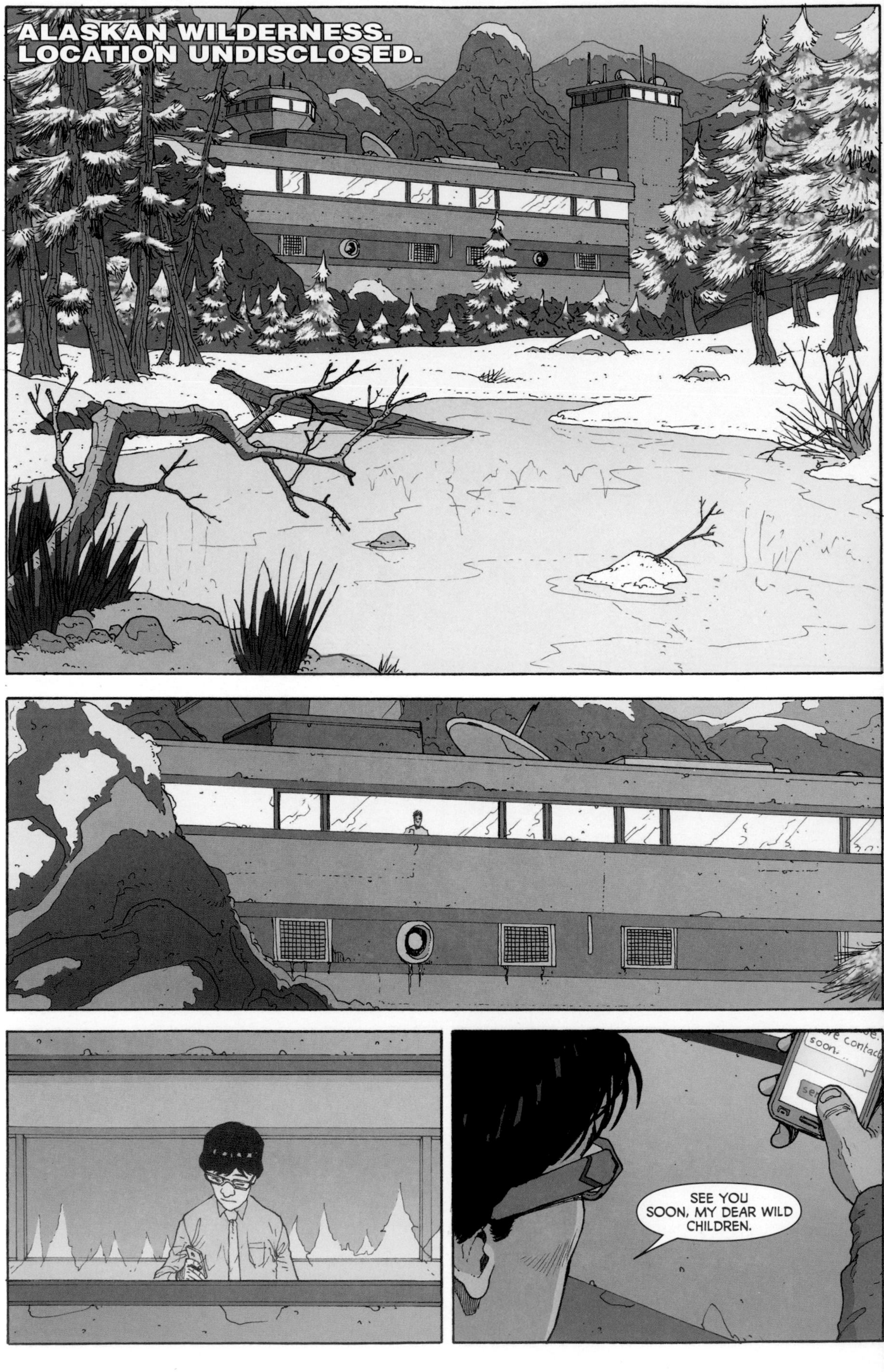
ALASKAN WILDERNESS.
LOCATION UNDISCLOSED.
SEE YOU SOON, MY DEAR WILD CHILDREN.

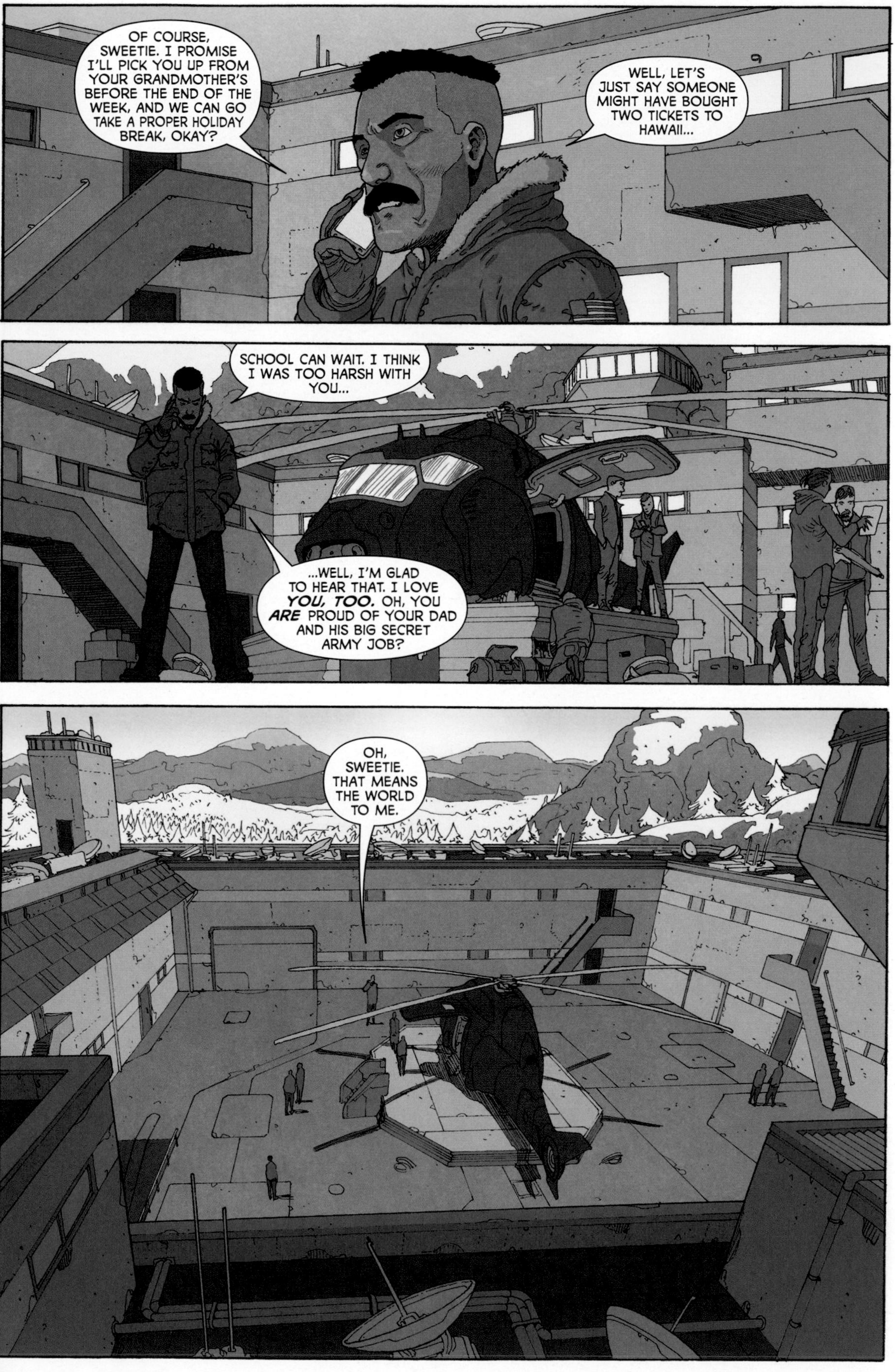
OF COURSE, SWEETIE. I PROMISE I'LL PICK YOU UP FROM YOUR GRANDMOTHER'S BEFORE THE END OF THE WEEK, AND WE CAN GO TAKE A PROPER HOLIDAY BREAK, OKAY?
WELL, LET'S JUST SAY SOMEONE MIGHT HAVE BOUGHT TWO TICKETS TO HAWAII...
SCHOOL CAN WAIT. I THINK I WAS TOO HARSH WITH YOU...
...WELL, I'M GLAD TO HEAR THAT. I LOVE ***YOU, TOO.*** OH, YOU ***ARE*** PROUD OF YOUR DAD AND HIS BIG SECRET ARMY JOB?
OH, SWEETIE. THAT MEANS THE WORLD TO ME.

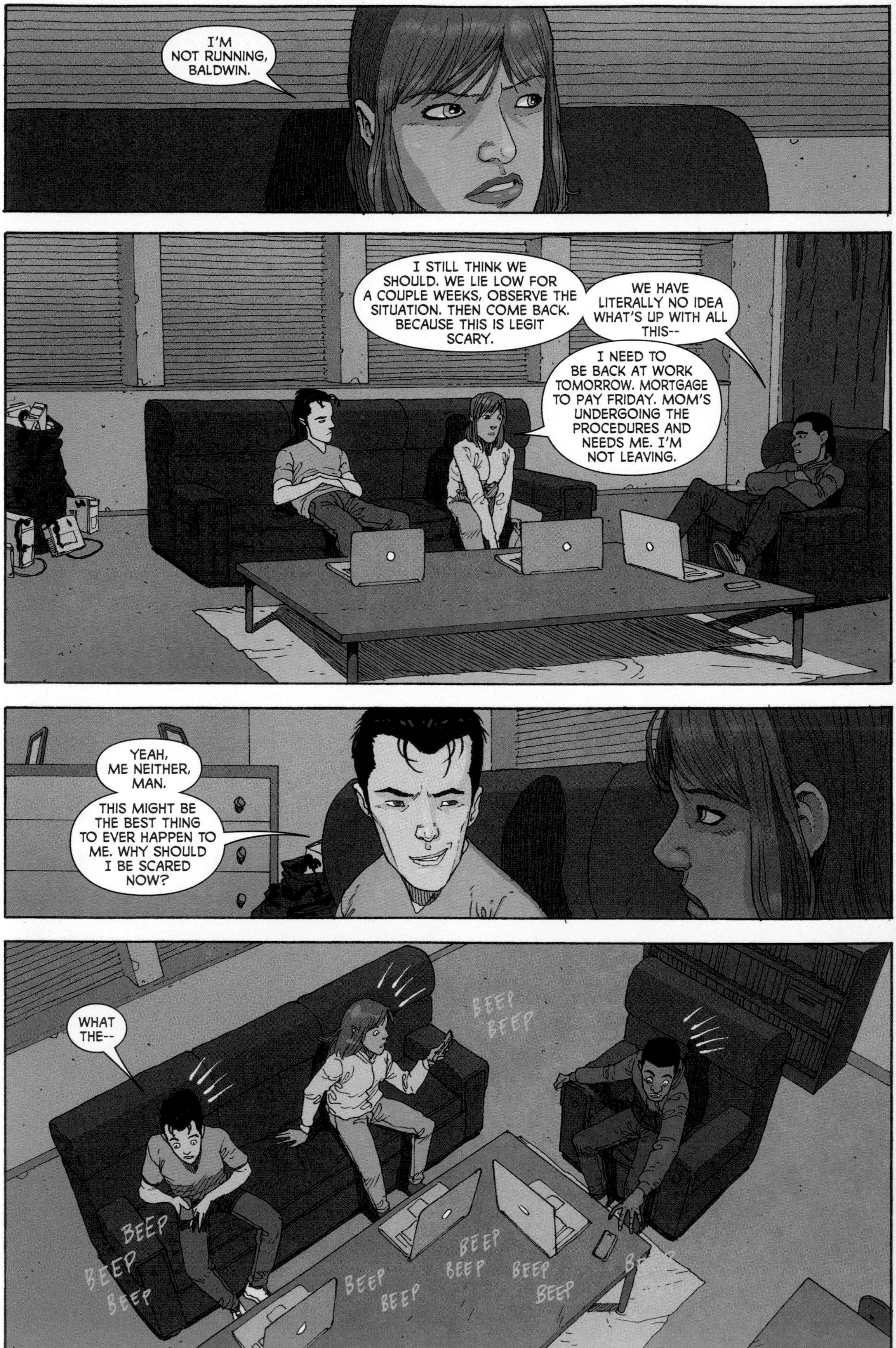
I'M NOT RUNNING, BALDWIN.
I STILL THINK WE SHOULD. WE LIE LOW FOR A COUPLE WEEKS, OBSERVE THE SITUATION. THEN COME BACK. BECAUSE THIS IS LEGIT SCARY.
WE HAVE LITERALLY NO IDEA WHAT'S UP WITH ALL THIS--
I NEED TO BE BACK AT WORK TOMORROW. MORTGAGE TO PAY FRIDAY. MOM'S UNDERGOING THE PROCEDURES AND NEEDS ME. I'M NOT LEAVING.
YEAH, ME NEITHER, MAN.
THIS MIGHT BE THE BEST THING TO EVER HAPPEN TO ME. WHY SHOULD I BE SCARED NOW?
WHAT THE--
BEEP BEEP
BEEP BEEP BEEP
BEEP BEEP
BEEP BEEP
BEEP BEEP

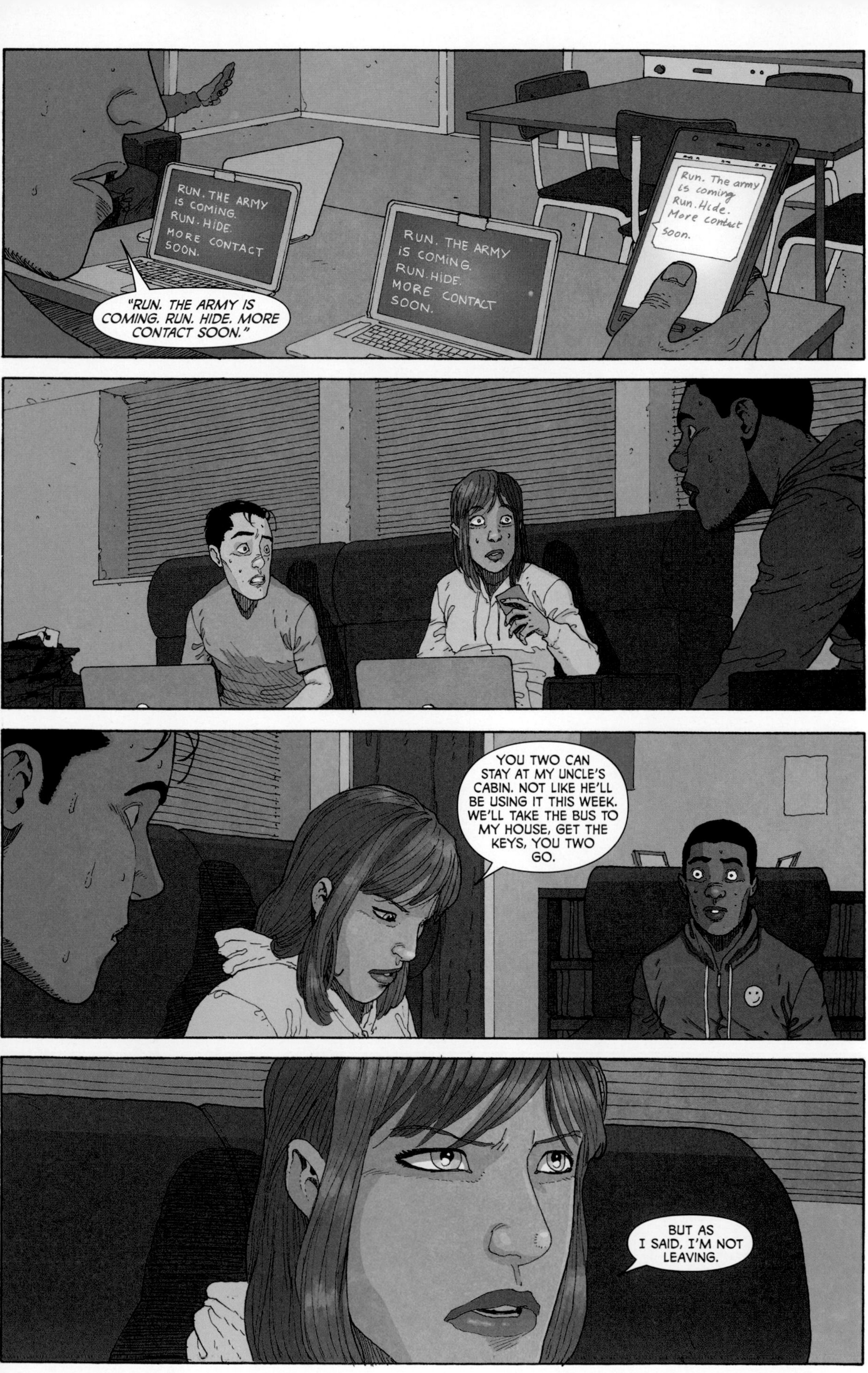

RUN. THE ARMY IS COMING. RUN. HIDE. MORE CONTACT SOON.
RUN. THE ARMY IS COMING. RUN. HIDE. MORE CONTACT SOON.
Run. The army is coming Run. Hide. More contact soon.
"RUN. THE ARMY IS COMING. RUN. HIDE. MORE CONTACT SOON."
YOU TWO CAN STAY AT MY UNCLE'S CABIN. NOT LIKE HE'LL BE USING IT THIS WEEK. WE'LL TAKE THE BUS TO MY HOUSE, GET THE KEYS, YOU TWO GO.
BUT AS I SAID, I'M NOT LEAVING.

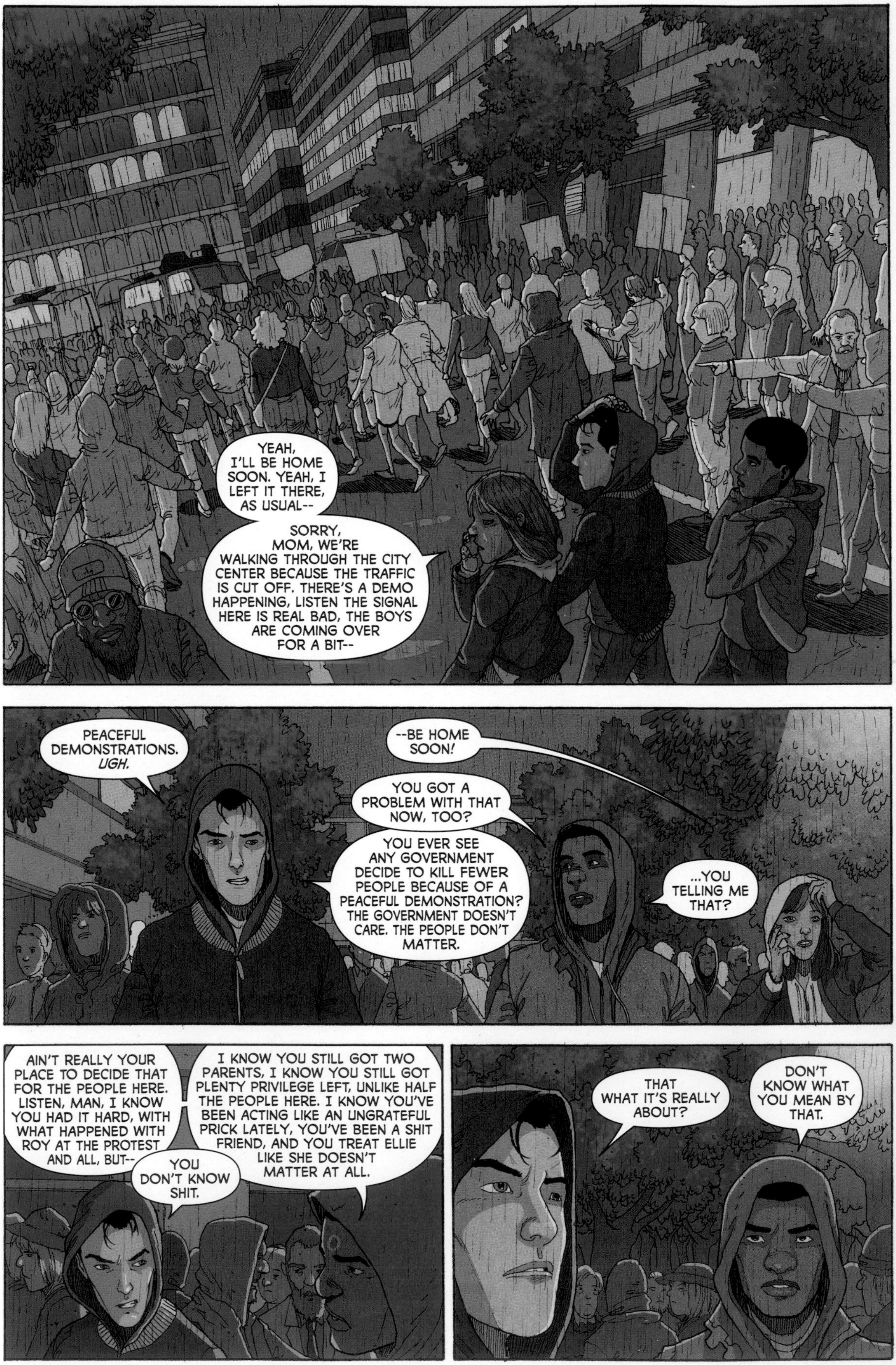
YEAH, I'LL BE HOME SOON. YEAH, I LEFT IT THERE, AS USUAL--
SORRY, MOM, WE'RE WALKING THROUGH THE CITY CENTER BECAUSE THE TRAFFIC IS CUT OFF. THERE'S A DEMO HAPPENING, LISTEN THE SIGNAL HERE IS REAL BAD, THE BOYS ARE COMING OVER FOR A BIT--
PEACEFUL DEMONSTRATIONS. *UGH.*
--BE HOME SOON!
YOU GOT A PROBLEM WITH THAT NOW, TOO?
YOU EVER SEE ANY GOVERNMENT DECIDE TO KILL FEWER PEOPLE BECAUSE OF A PEACEFUL DEMONSTRATION? THE GOVERNMENT DOESN'T CARE. THE PEOPLE DON'T MATTER.
...YOU TELLING ME THAT?
AIN'T REALLY YOUR PLACE TO DECIDE THAT FOR THE PEOPLE HERE. LISTEN, MAN, I KNOW YOU HAD IT HARD, WITH WHAT HAPPENED WITH ROY AT THE PROTEST AND ALL, BUT--
YOU DON'T KNOW SHIT.
I KNOW YOU STILL GOT TWO PARENTS, I KNOW YOU STILL GOT PLENTY PRIVILEGE LEFT, UNLIKE HALF THE PEOPLE HERE. I KNOW YOU'VE BEEN ACTING LIKE AN UNGRATEFUL PRICK LATELY, YOU'VE BEEN A SHIT FRIEND, AND YOU TREAT ELLIE LIKE SHE DOESN'T MATTER AT ALL.
THAT WHAT IT'S REALLY ABOUT?
DON'T KNOW WHAT YOU MEAN BY THAT.

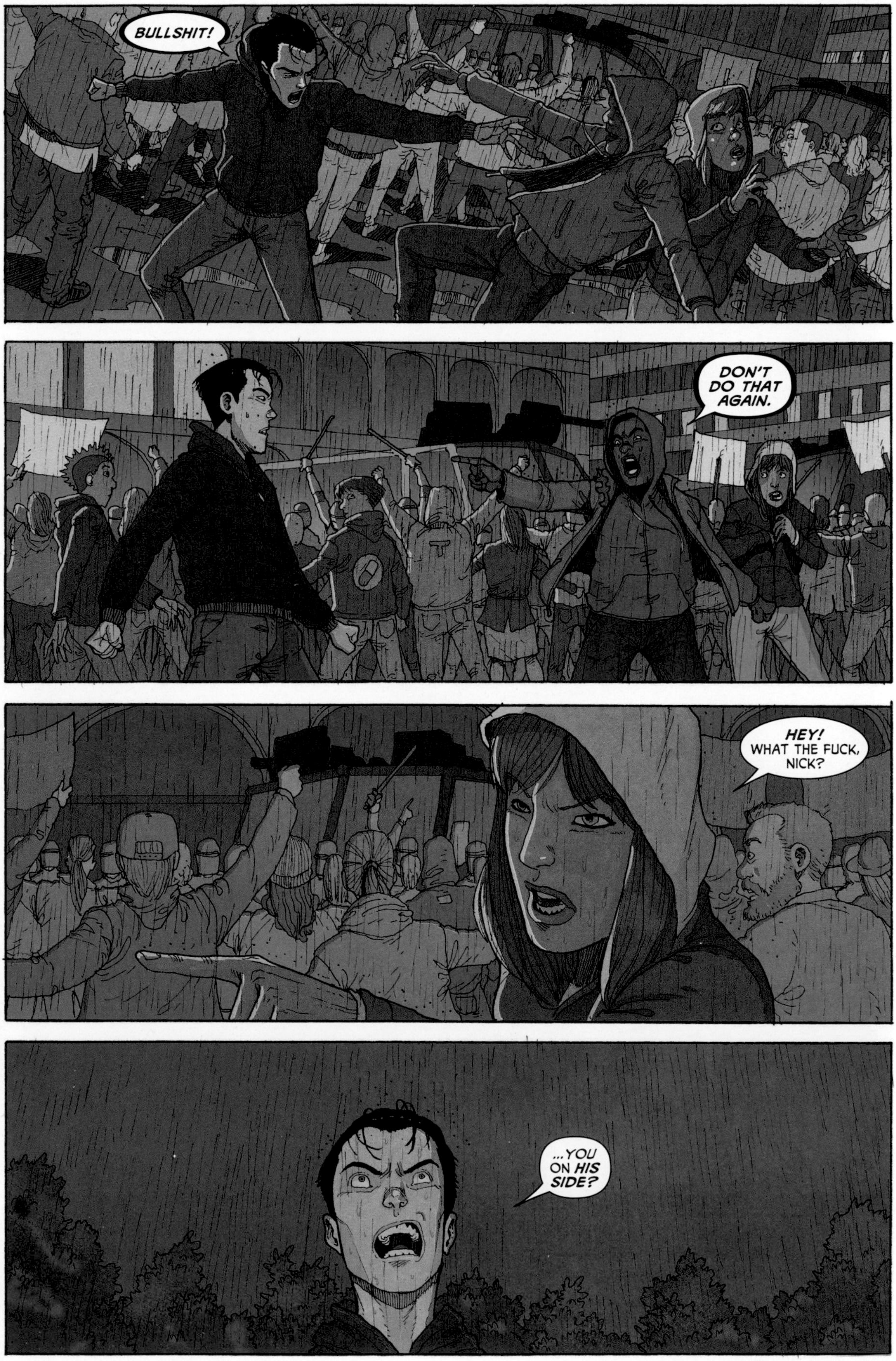
BULLSHIT!
DON'T DO THAT AGAIN.
HEY! WHAT THE FUCK, NICK?
...YOU ON HIS SIDE?

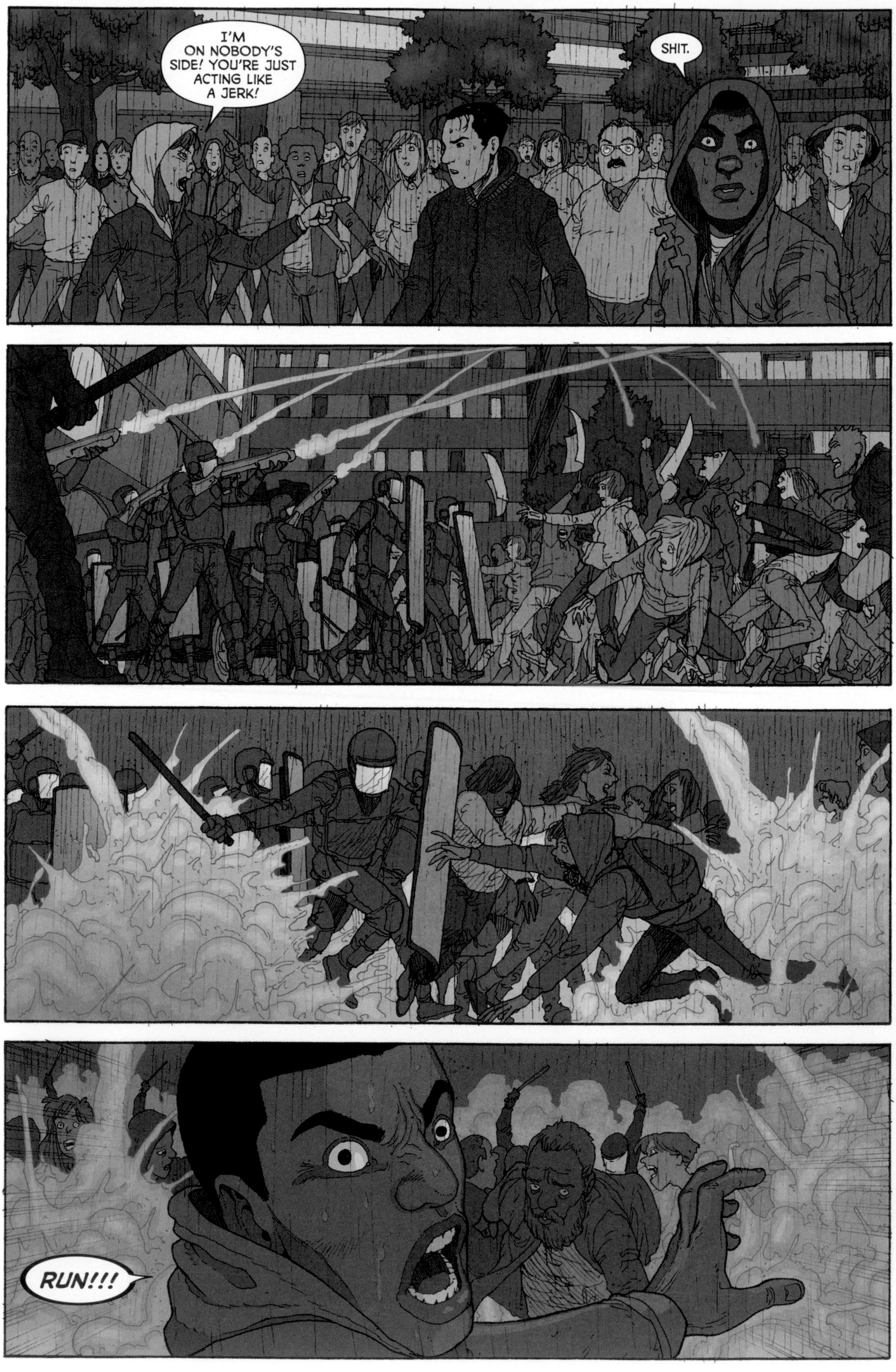
I'M ON NOBODY'S SIDE! YOU'RE JUST ACTING LIKE A JERK!
SHIT.
RUN!!!

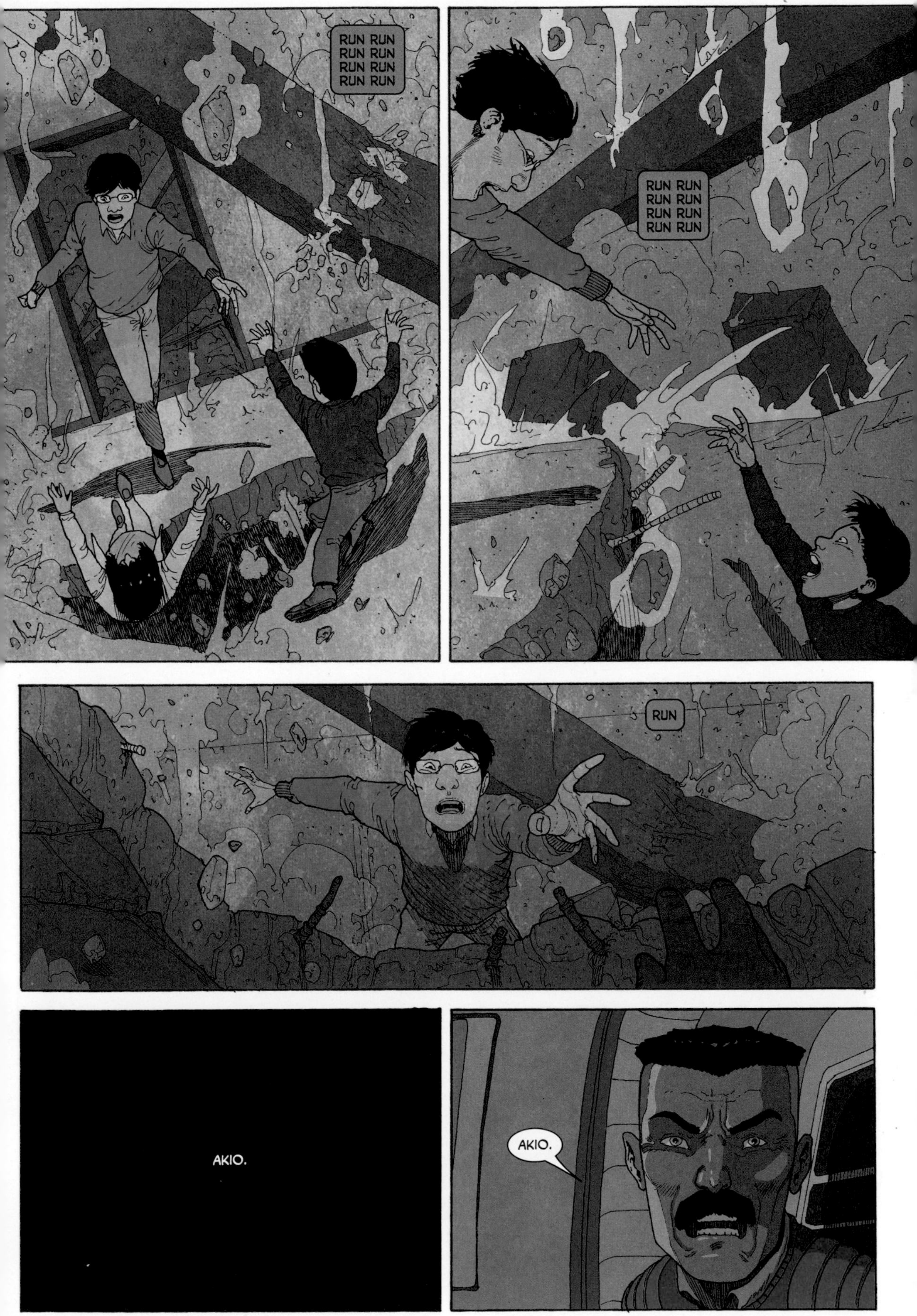
RUN RUN
RUN RUN
RUN RUN
RUN RUN
RUN RUN
RUN RUN
RUN RUN
RUN RUN
RUN
AKIO.
AKIO.

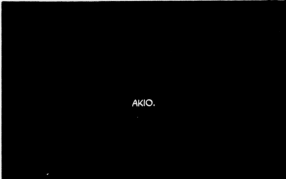

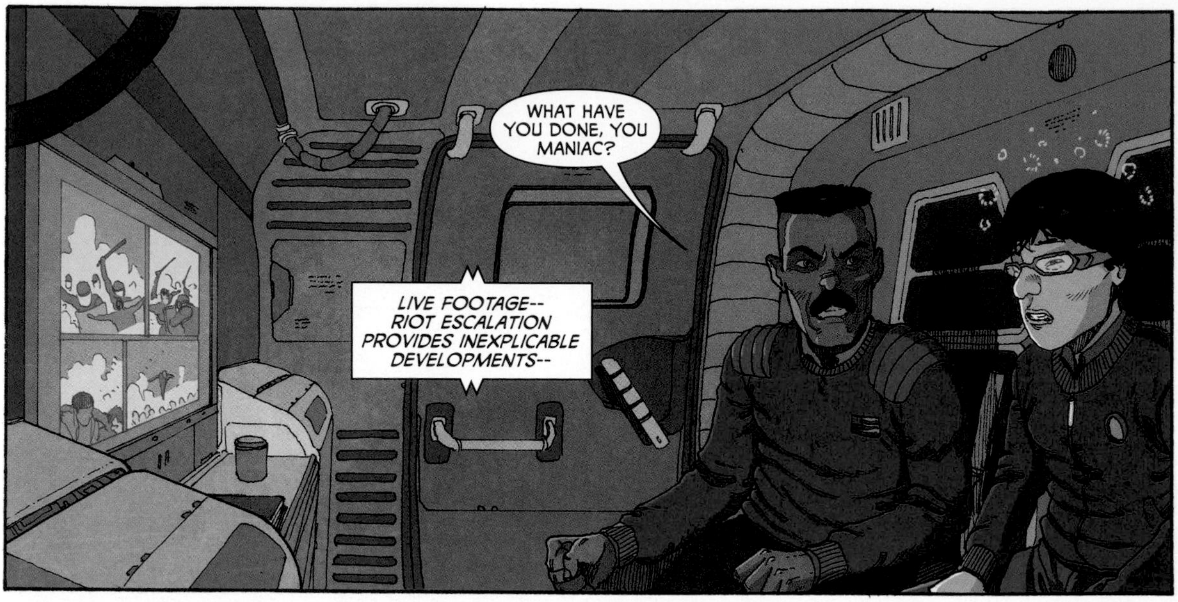
WHAT HAVE YOU DONE, YOU MANIAC?
LIVE FOOTAGE-- RIOT ESCALATION PROVIDES INEXPLICABLE DEVELOPMENTS--

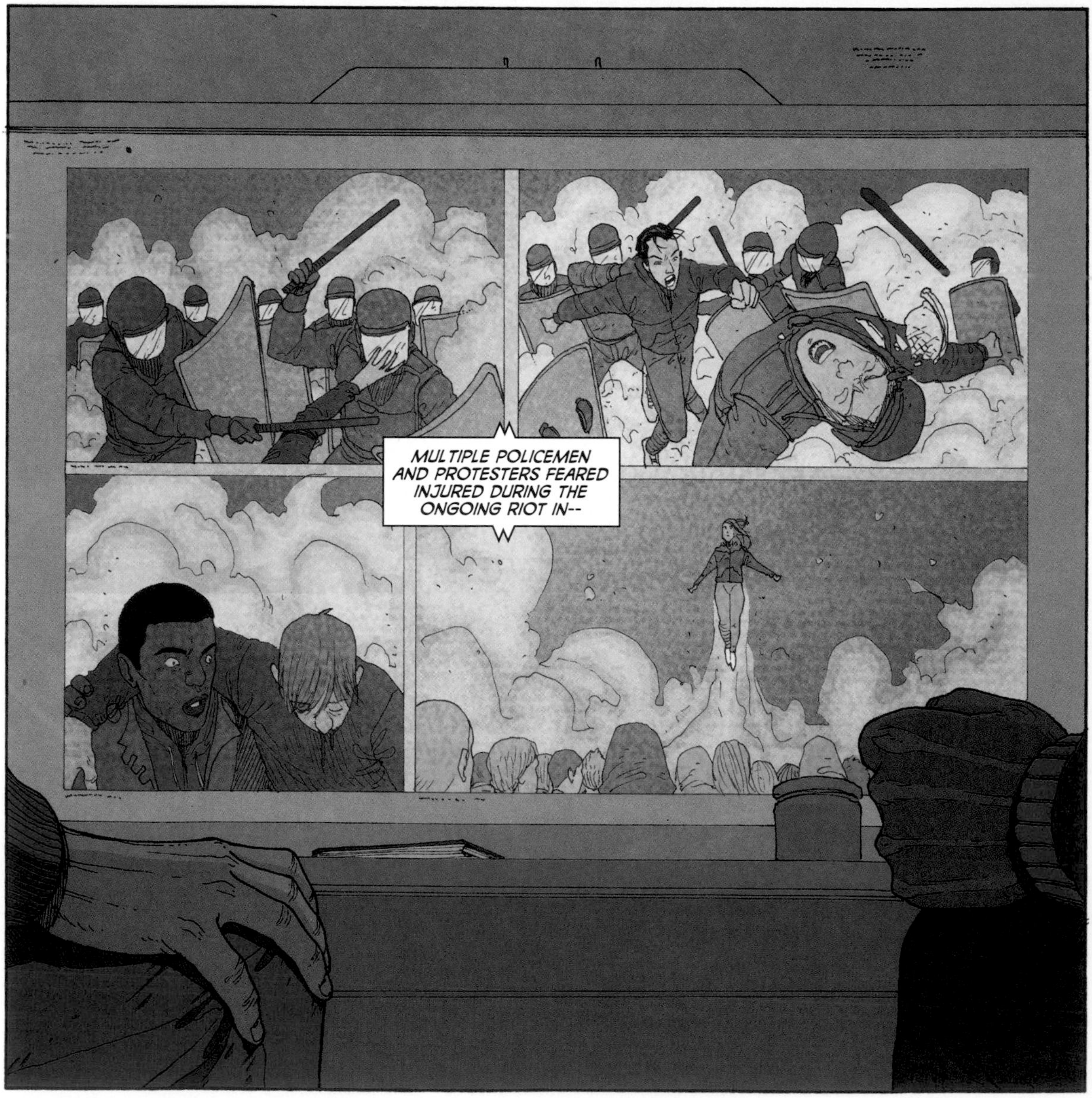
MULTIPLE POLICEMEN AND PROTESTERS FEARED INJURED DURING THE ONGOING RIOT IN--

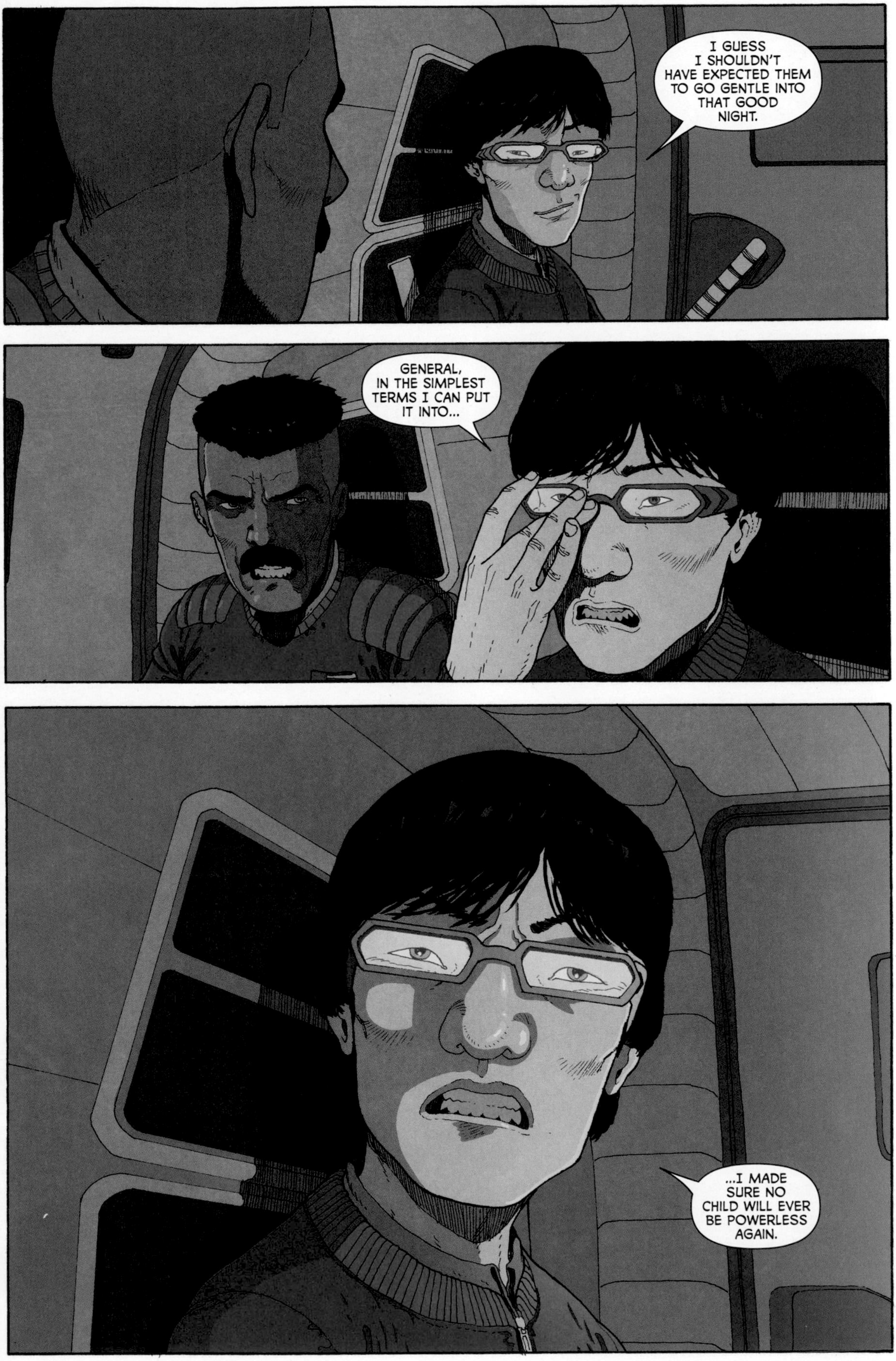
I GUESS I SHOULDN'T HAVE EXPECTED THEM TO GO GENTLE INTO THAT GOOD NIGHT.
GENERAL, IN THE SIMPLEST TERMS I CAN PUT IT INTO...
...I MADE SURE NO CHILD WILL EVER BE POWERLESS AGAIN.

REFUSE DREAM R

CHAPTER THREE

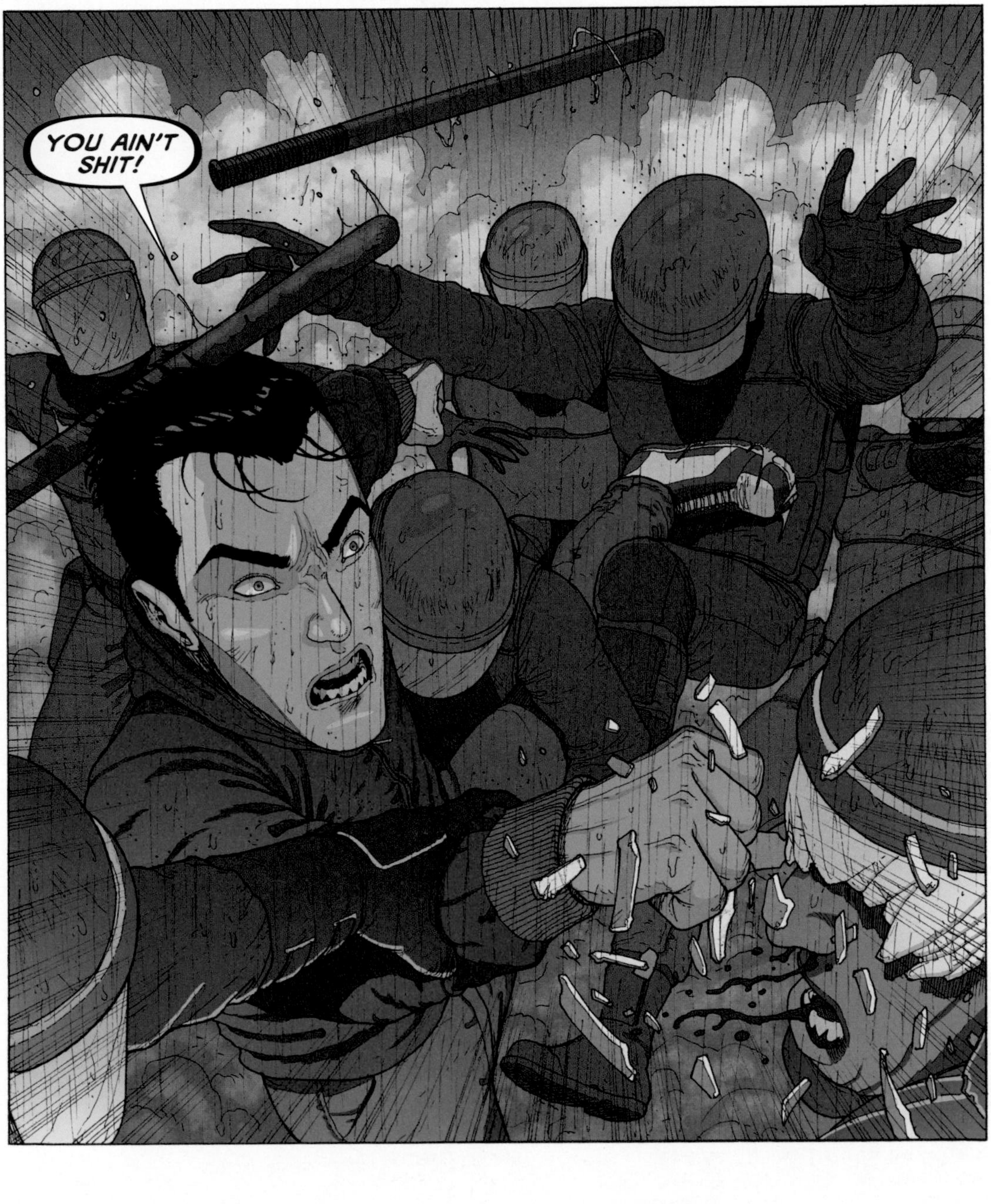
YOU AIN'T SHIT!

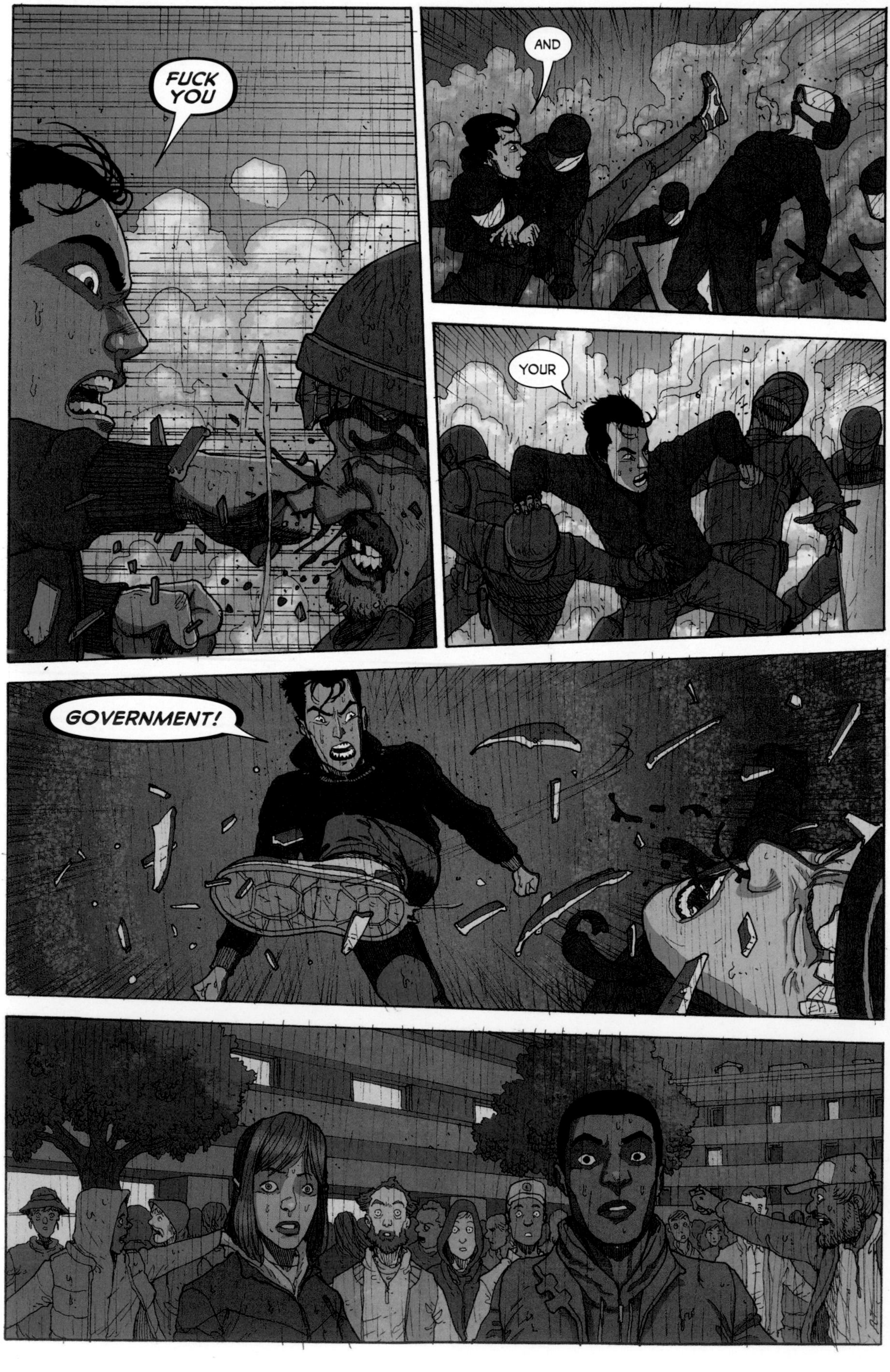
FUCK YOU
AND
YOUR
GOVERNMENT!

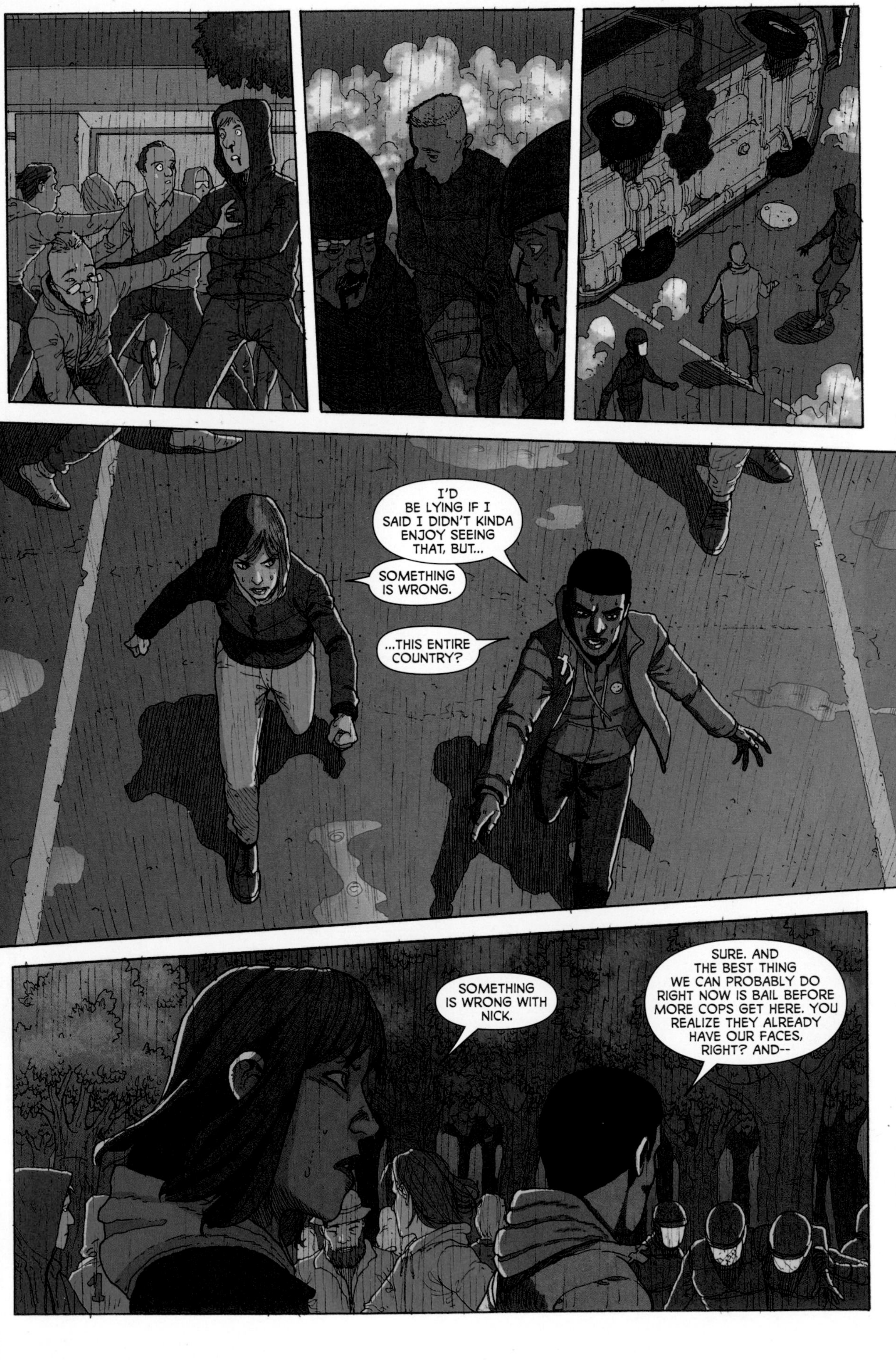
I'D BE LYING IF I SAID I DIDN'T KINDA ENJOY SEEING THAT, BUT...
SOMETHING IS WRONG.
...THIS ENTIRE COUNTRY?
SOMETHING IS WRONG WITH NICK.
SURE. AND THE BEST THING WE CAN PROBABLY DO RIGHT NOW IS BAIL BEFORE MORE COPS GET HERE. YOU REALIZE THEY ALREADY HAVE OUR FACES, RIGHT? AND--

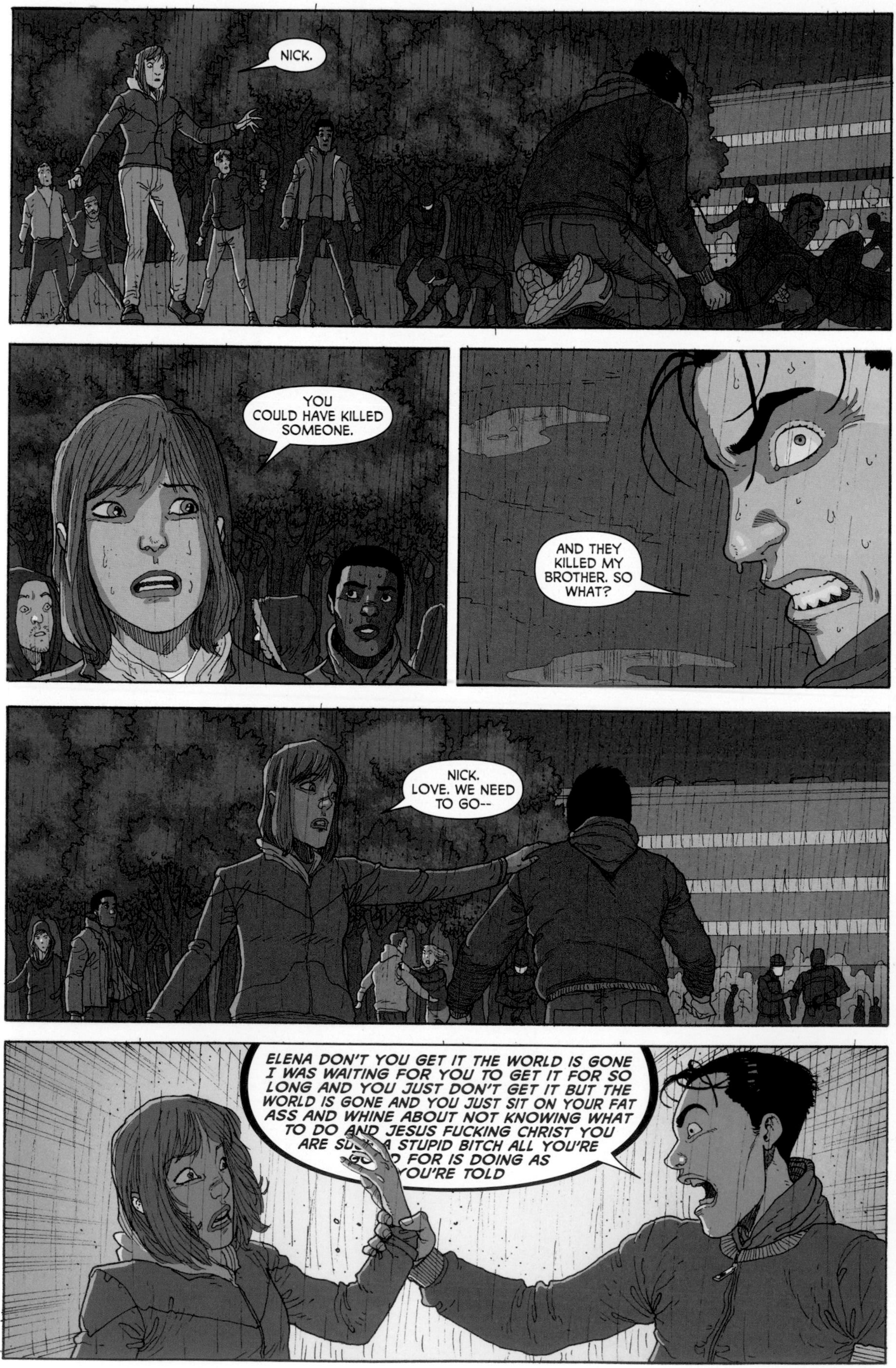
NICK.
YOU COULD HAVE KILLED SOMEONE.
AND THEY KILLED MY BROTHER. SO WHAT?
NICK. LOVE. WE NEED TO GO--
ELENA DON'T YOU GET IT THE WORLD IS GONE I WAS WAITING FOR YOU TO GET IT FOR SO LONG AND YOU JUST DON'T GET IT BUT THE WORLD IS GONE AND YOU JUST SIT ON YOUR FAT ASS AND WHINE ABOUT NOT KNOWING WHAT TO DO AND JESUS FUCKING CHRIST YOU ARE SU A STUPID BITCH ALL YOU'RE D FOR IS DOING AS YOU'RE TOLD

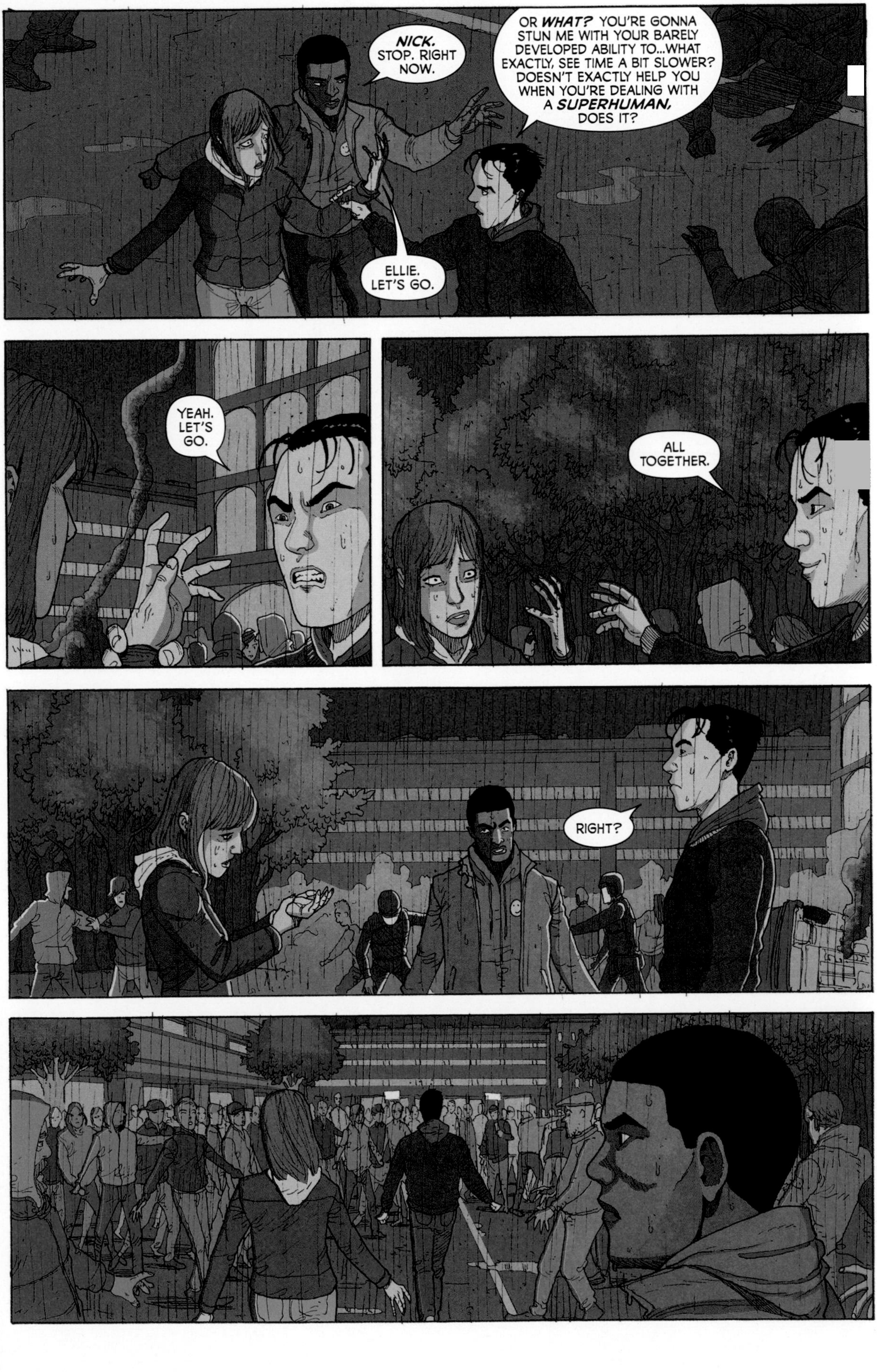
NICK. STOP. RIGHT NOW.
OR WHAT? YOU'RE GONNA STUN ME WITH YOUR BARELY DEVELOPED ABILITY TO...WHAT EXACTLY, SEE TIME A BIT SLOWER? DOESN'T EXACTLY HELP YOU WHEN YOU'RE DEALING WITH A SUPERHUMAN, DOES IT?
ELLIE. LET'S GO.
YEAH. LET'S GO.
ALL TOGETHER.
RIGHT?

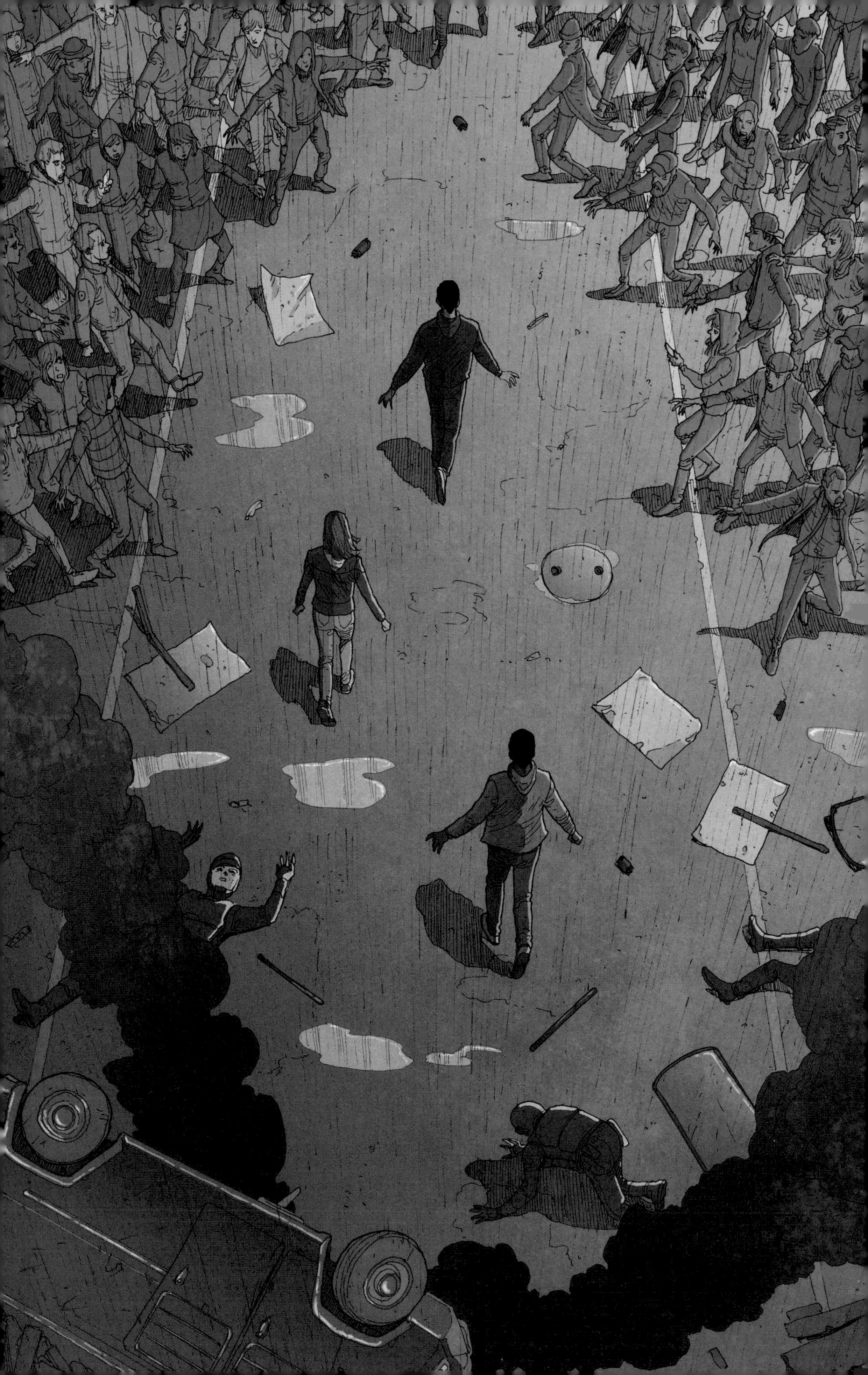

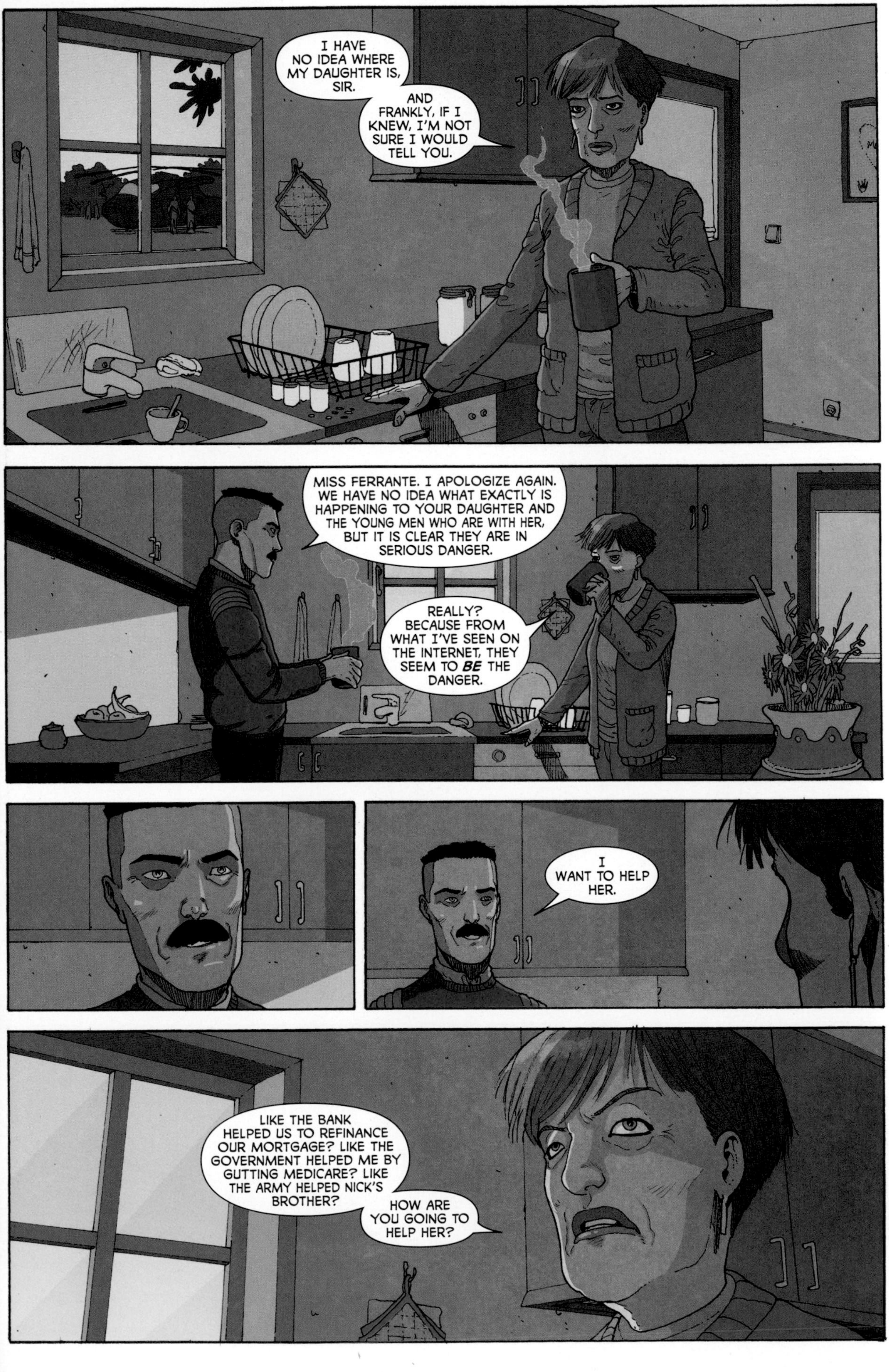
I HAVE NO IDEA WHERE MY DAUGHTER IS, SIR.
AND FRANKLY, IF I KNEW, I'M NOT SURE I WOULD TELL YOU.
MISS FERRANTE. I APOLOGIZE AGAIN. WE HAVE NO IDEA WHAT EXACTLY IS HAPPENING TO YOUR DAUGHTER AND THE YOUNG MEN WHO ARE WITH HER, BUT IT IS CLEAR THEY ARE IN SERIOUS DANGER.
REALLY? BECAUSE FROM WHAT I'VE SEEN ON THE INTERNET, THEY SEEM TO ***BE*** THE DANGER.
I WANT TO HELP HER.
LIKE THE BANK HELPED US TO REFINANCE OUR MORTGAGE? LIKE THE GOVERNMENT HELPED ME BY GUTTING MEDICARE? LIKE THE ARMY HELPED NICK'S BROTHER?
HOW ARE YOU GOING TO HELP HER?

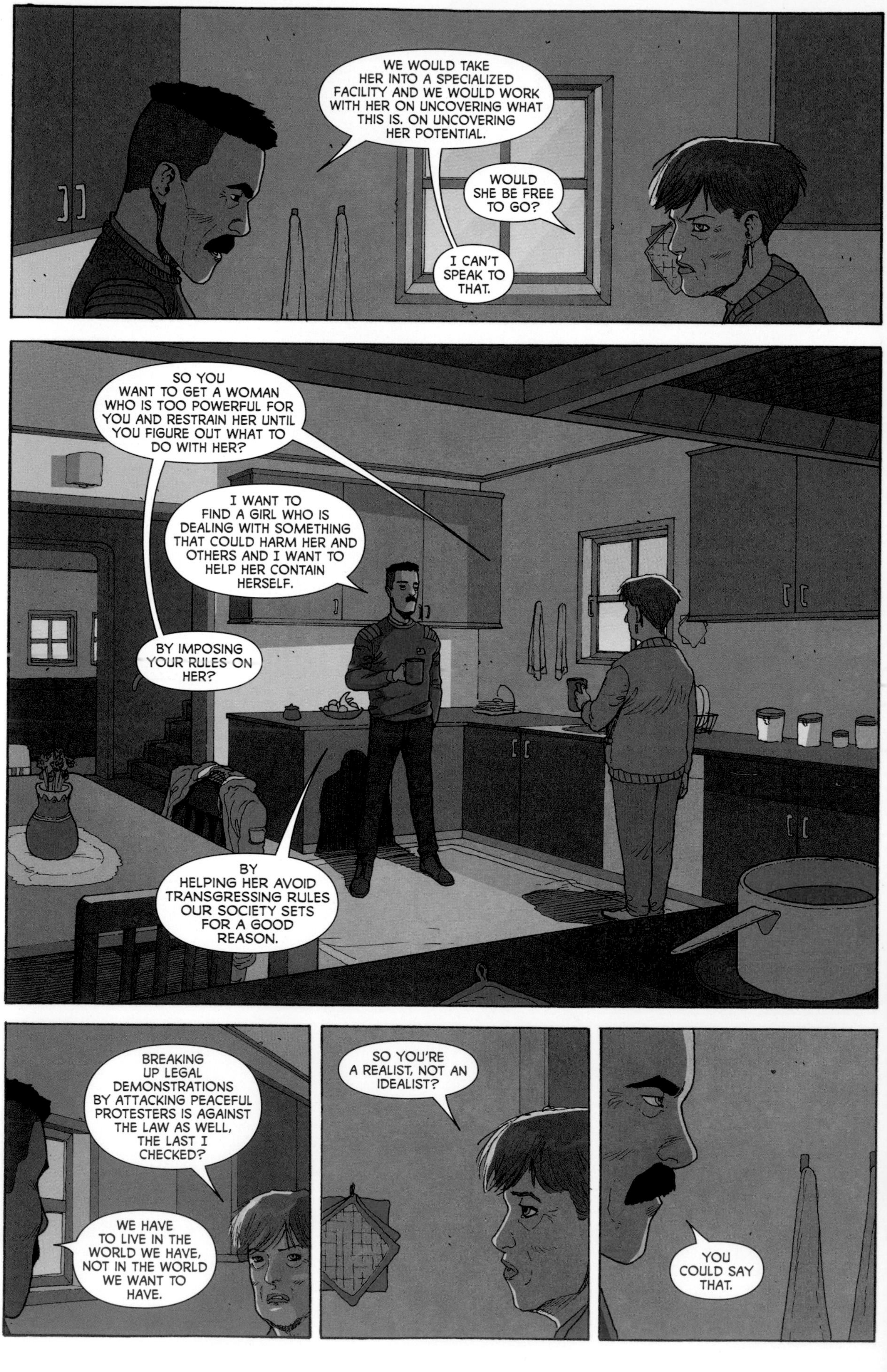
WE WOULD TAKE HER INTO A SPECIALIZED FACILITY AND WE WOULD WORK WITH HER ON UNCOVERING WHAT THIS IS. ON UNCOVERING HER POTENTIAL.
WOULD SHE BE FREE TO GO?
I CAN'T SPEAK TO THAT.
SO YOU WANT TO GET A WOMAN WHO IS TOO POWERFUL FOR YOU AND RESTRAIN HER UNTIL YOU FIGURE OUT WHAT TO DO WITH HER?
I WANT TO FIND A GIRL WHO IS DEALING WITH SOMETHING THAT COULD HARM HER AND OTHERS AND I WANT TO HELP HER CONTAIN HERSELF.
BY IMPOSING YOUR RULES ON HER?
BY HELPING HER AVOID TRANSGRESSING RULES OUR SOCIETY SETS FOR A GOOD REASON.
BREAKING UP LEGAL DEMONSTRATIONS BY ATTACKING PEACEFUL PROTESTERS IS AGAINST THE LAW AS WELL, THE LAST I CHECKED?
WE HAVE TO LIVE IN THE WORLD WE HAVE, NOT IN THE WORLD WE WANT TO HAVE.
SO YOU'RE A REALIST, NOT AN IDEALIST?
YOU COULD SAY THAT.

I HAVE CANCER. IT'S LIKELY TO KILL ME WITHIN THE NEXT SIX MONTHS. MY DAUGHTER WILL NOT ACCEPT THIS UNTIL LONG AFTER I'M BURIED IN THE GROUND.

I'D LIKE TO THINK ONE OF THE REASONS SHE WON'T ACCEPT THIS IS BECAUSE I RAISED HER THAT WAY. WHEN SHE WAS YOUNG, I TOLD HER--"WORK TO BE ANYTHING YOU WANT TO BE, AS LONG AS IT ISN'T HARMING OTHERS. BECAUSE YOU CAN VERY LIKELY ACHIEVE IT."

YOU COULD SAY I WAS NAIVE. YOU COULD SAY I WAS "AN IDEALIST."

NOW I GIVE UP NEARLY EVERY DAY.

AND SHE DOESN'T.

SHE HOLDS DOWN TWO JOBS TO KEEP THIS HOME OVER OUR HEADS. SHE PAYS FOR MY BILLS, AND SHE'S AN IDEALIST, AND YOU KNOW WHAT? THAT MEANS SHE'S A REALIST, DAMMIT. BECAUSE SHE STILL BELIEVES, DESPITE THE STATE OF THIS COUNTRY AND THIS HUMANITY, DEEP DOWN SHE STILL BELIEVES HER DREAMS AND A BETTER WORLD ARE TRULY POSSIBLE.

THAT'S WHAT KEEPS ME ALIVE WHEN I STRUGGLE TO SEE THE POINT.

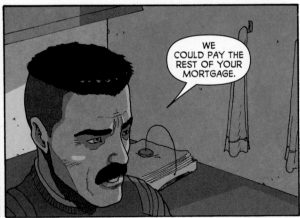

WE COULD PAY THE REST OF YOUR MORTGAGE.

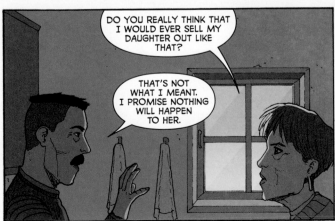

DO YOU REALLY THINK THAT I WOULD EVER SELL MY DAUGHTER OUT LIKE THAT?

THAT'S NOT WHAT I MEANT. I PROMISE NOTHING WILL HAPPEN TO HER.

GENERAL... HAS LIFE NOT TAUGHT YOU THAT THERE ARE SOME PROMISES YOU CAN'T KEEP?

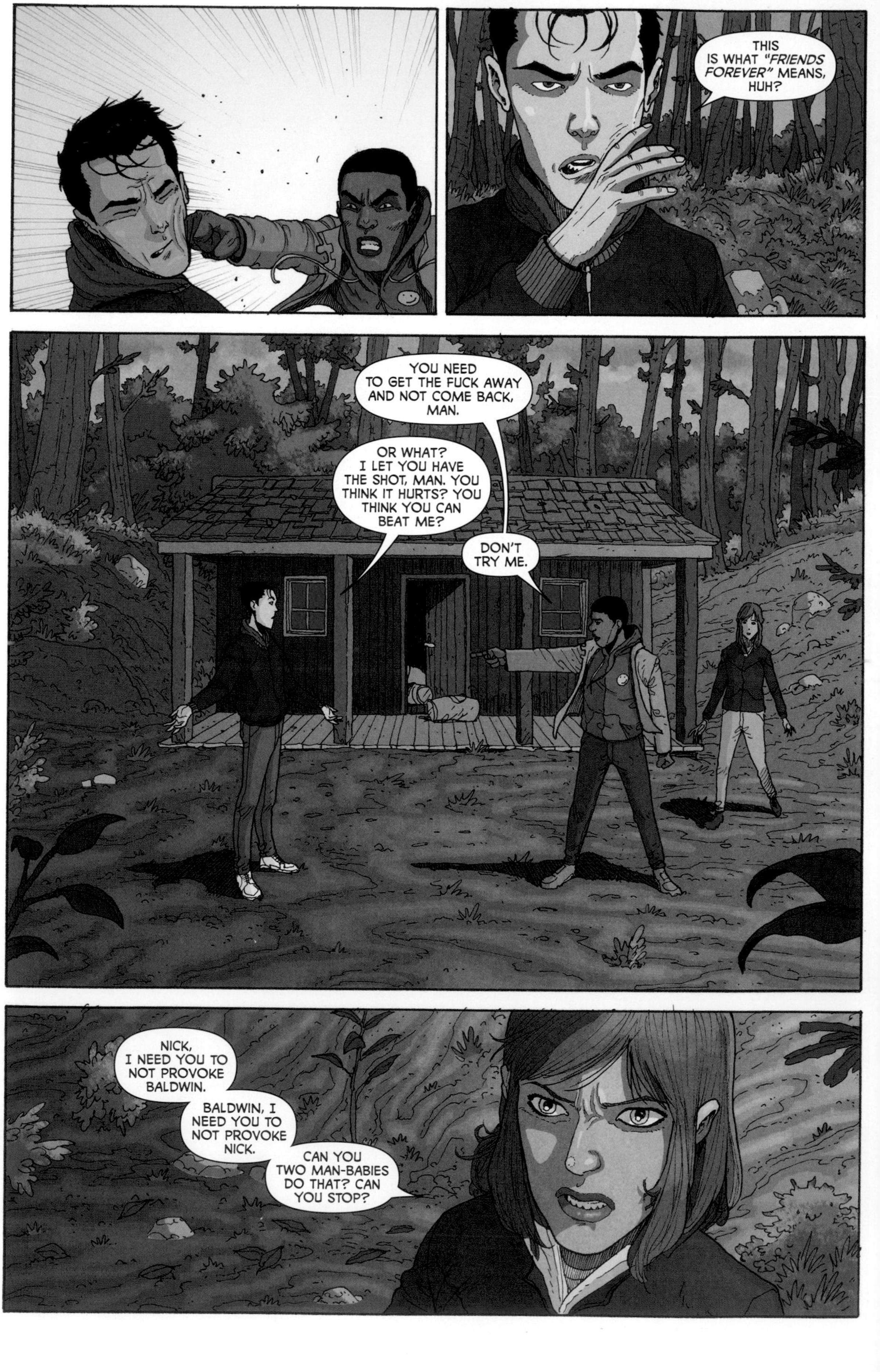
THIS IS WHAT "FRIENDS FOREVER" MEANS, HUH?
YOU NEED TO GET THE FUCK AWAY AND NOT COME BACK, MAN.
OR WHAT? I LET YOU HAVE THE SHOT, MAN. YOU THINK IT HURTS? YOU THINK YOU CAN BEAT ME?
DON'T TRY ME.
NICK, I NEED YOU TO NOT PROVOKE BALDWIN.
BALDWIN, I NEED YOU TO NOT PROVOKE NICK.
CAN YOU TWO MAN-BABIES DO THAT? CAN YOU STOP?

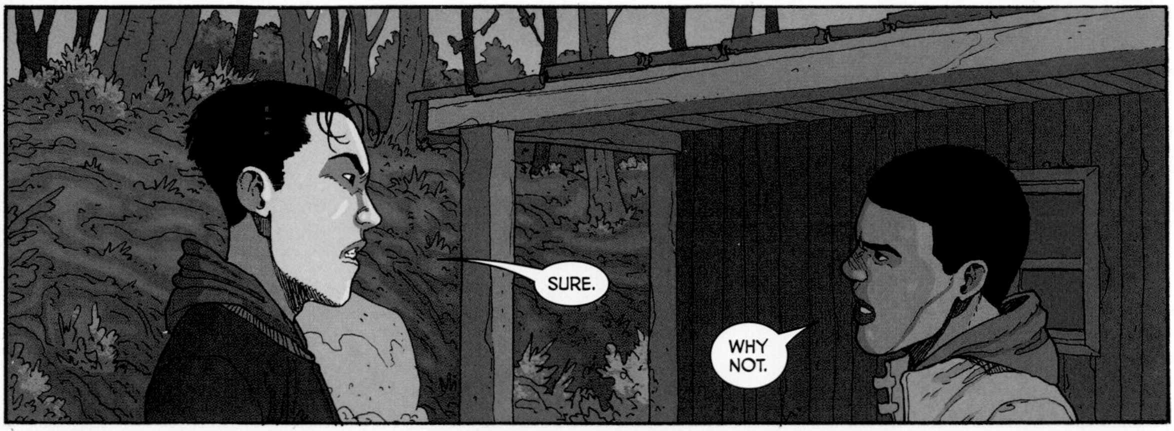
SURE.
WHY NOT.
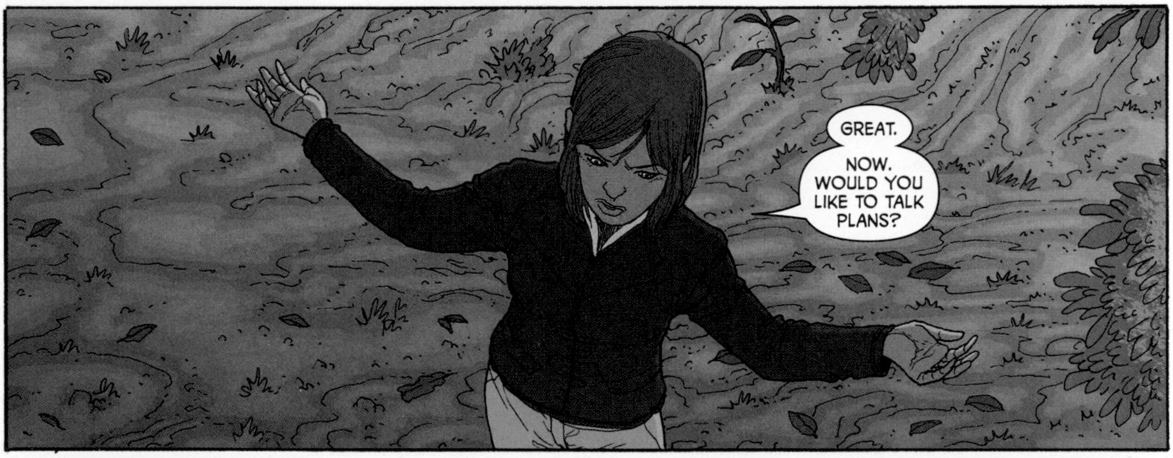
GREAT.
NOW. WOULD YOU LIKE TO TALK PLANS?
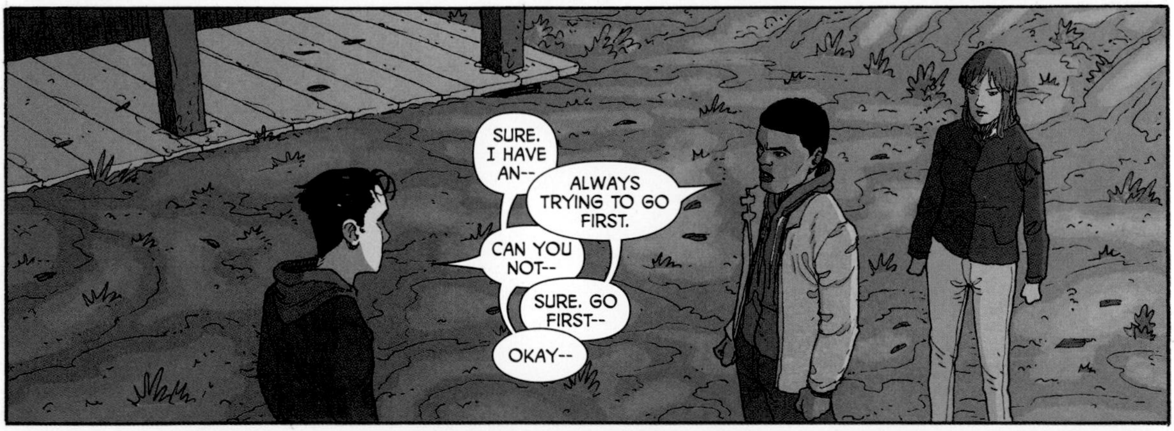
SURE. I HAVE AN--
ALWAYS TRYING TO GO FIRST.
CAN YOU NOT--
SURE. GO FIRST--
OKAY--
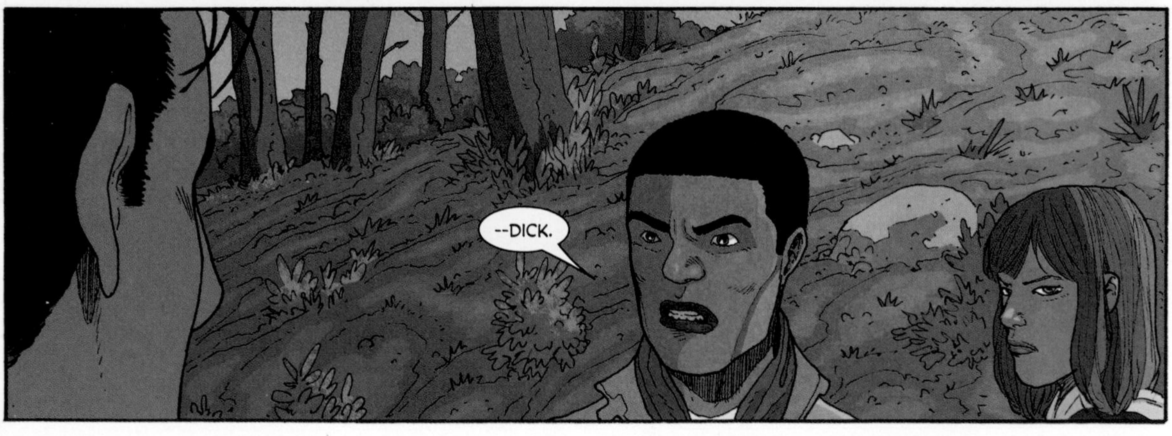
--DICK.

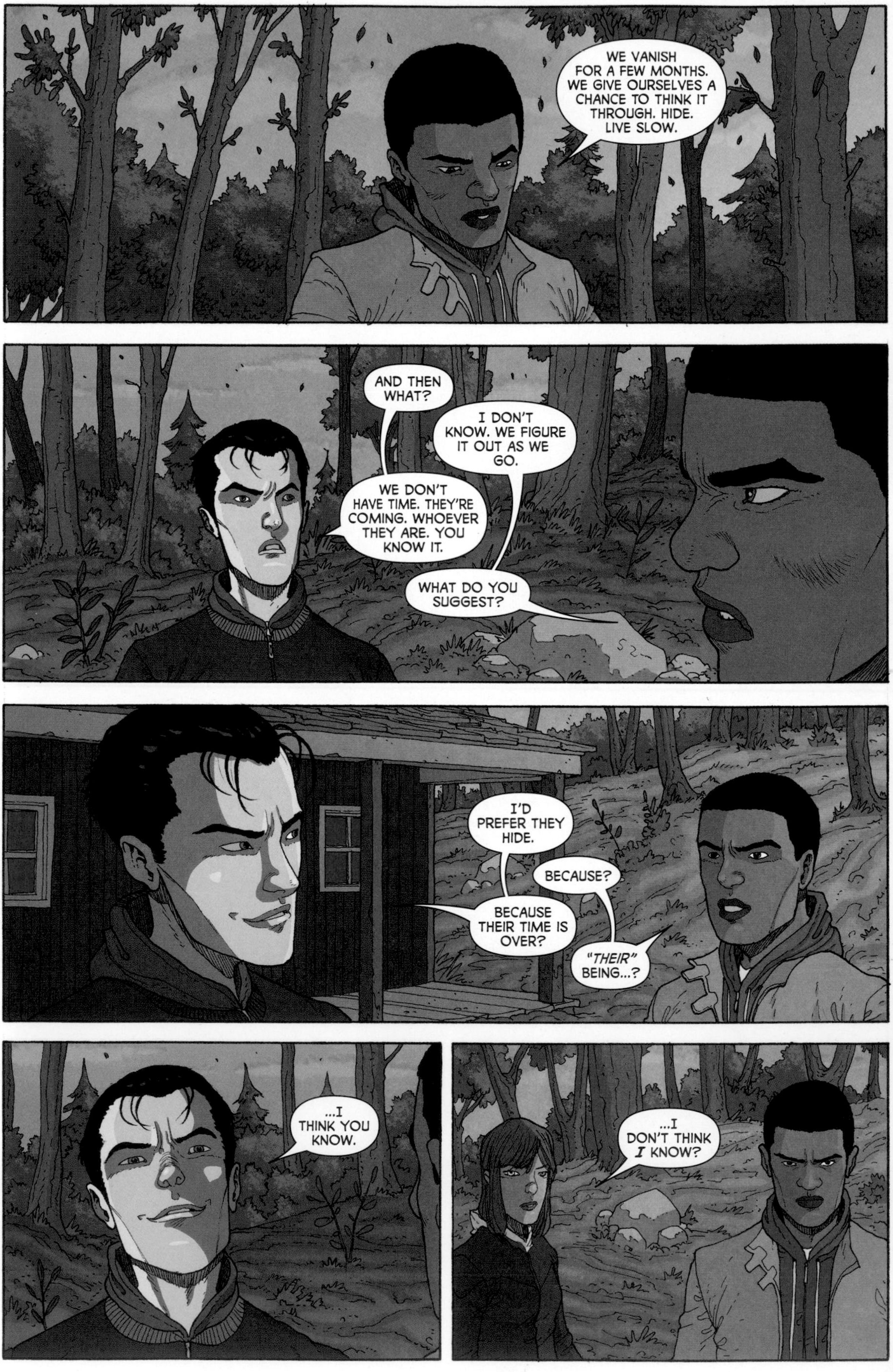
WE VANISH FOR A FEW MONTHS. WE GIVE OURSELVES A CHANCE TO THINK IT THROUGH. HIDE. LIVE SLOW.
AND THEN WHAT?
I DON'T KNOW. WE FIGURE IT OUT AS WE GO.
WE DON'T HAVE TIME. THEY'RE COMING. WHOEVER THEY ARE. YOU KNOW IT.
WHAT DO YOU SUGGEST?
I'D PREFER THEY HIDE.
BECAUSE?
BECAUSE THEIR TIME IS OVER?
"THEIR" BEING...?
...I THINK YOU KNOW.
...I DON'T THINK I KNOW?

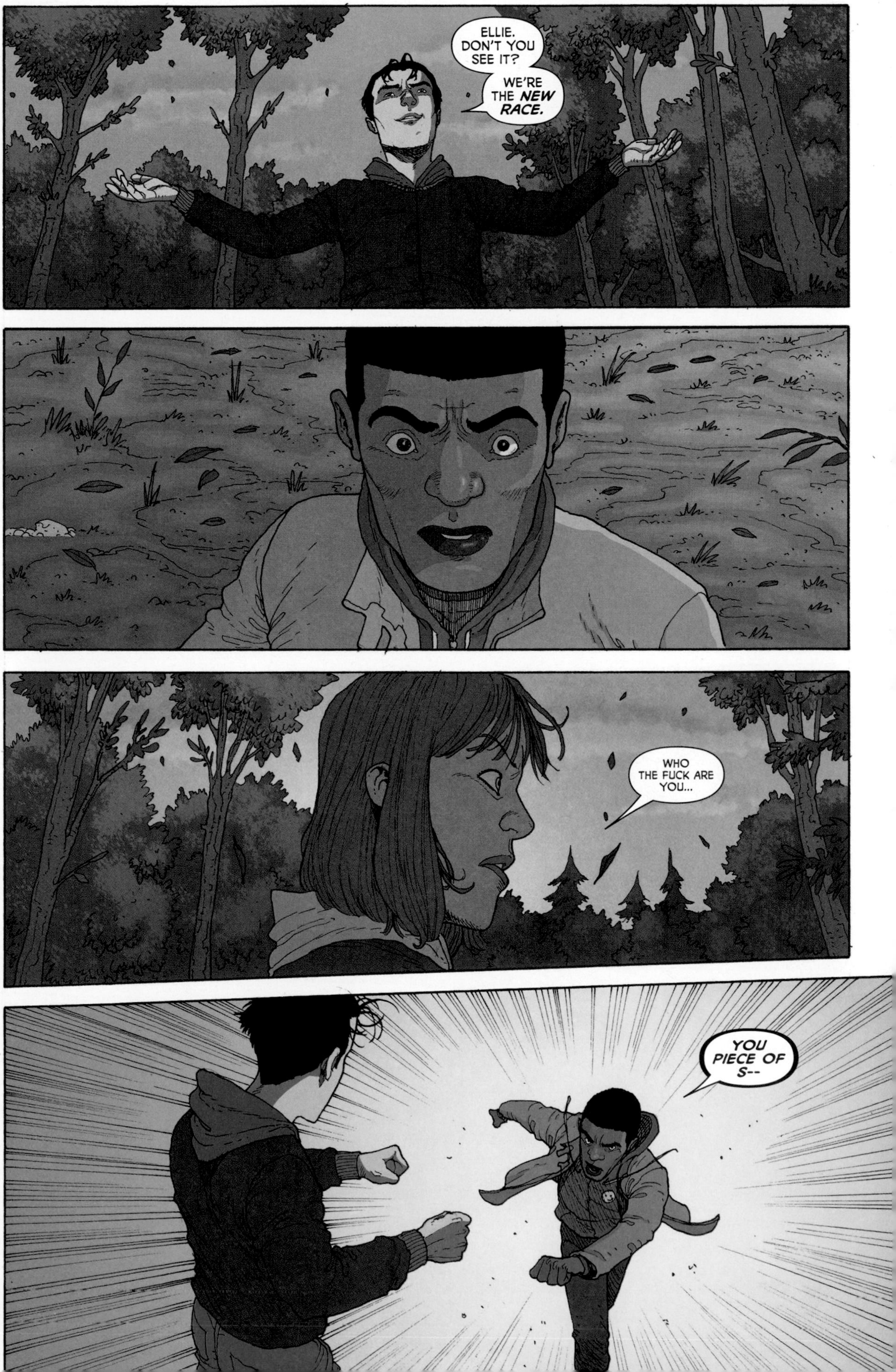
ELLIE. DON'T YOU SEE IT?
WE'RE THE *NEW RACE.*
WHO THE FUCK ARE YOU...
YOU PIECE OF S--

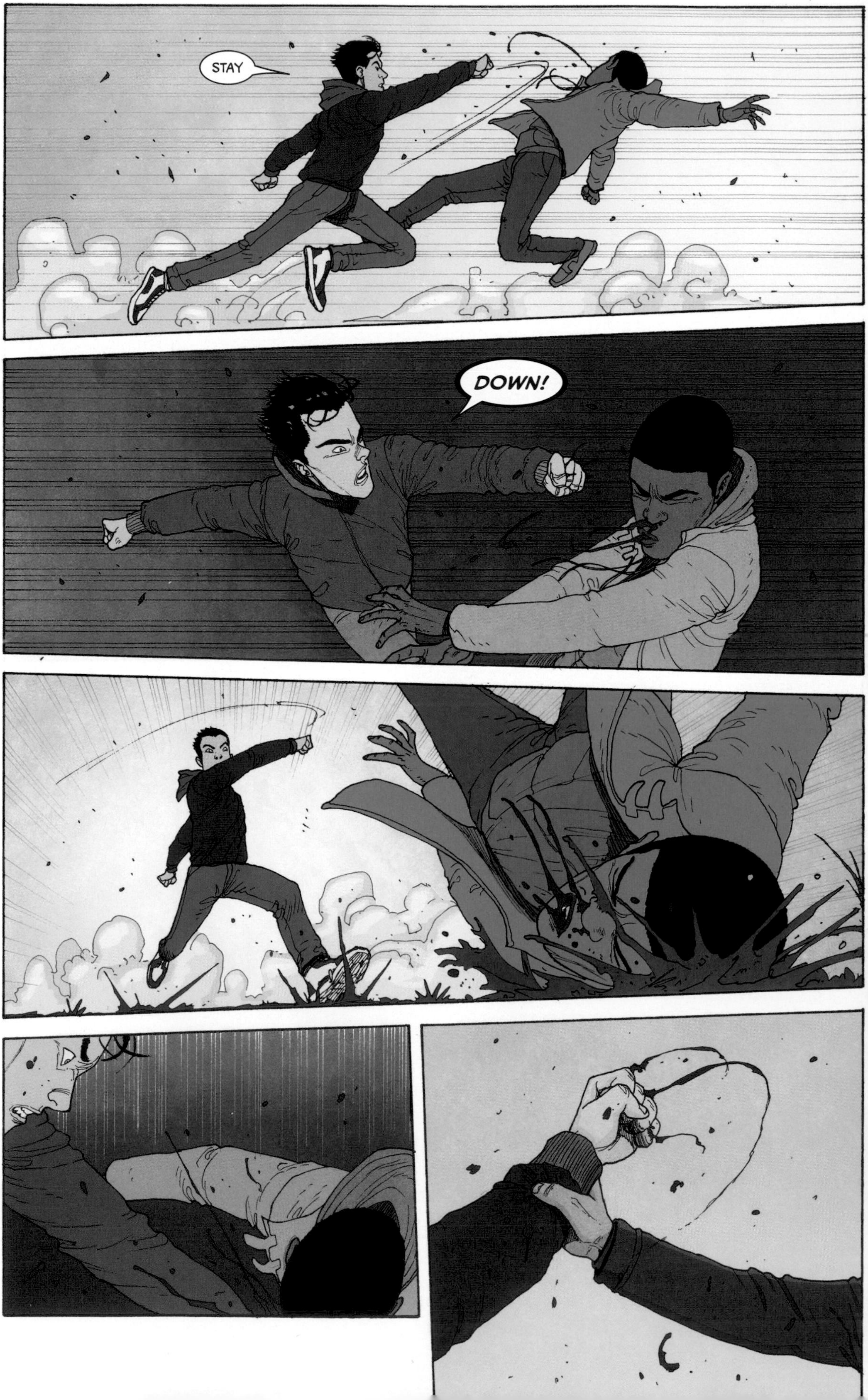
STAY
DOWN!

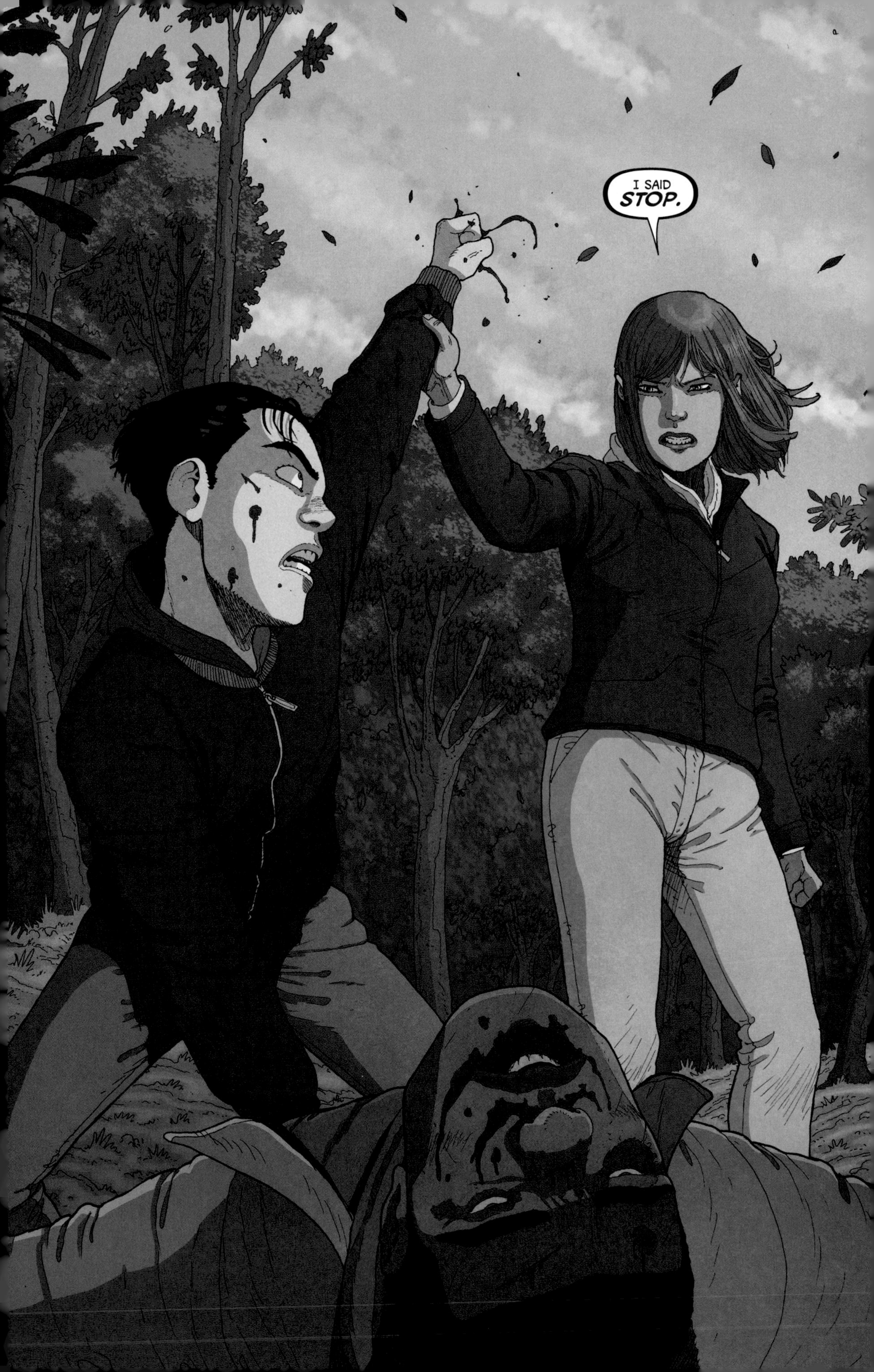
I SAID STOP.

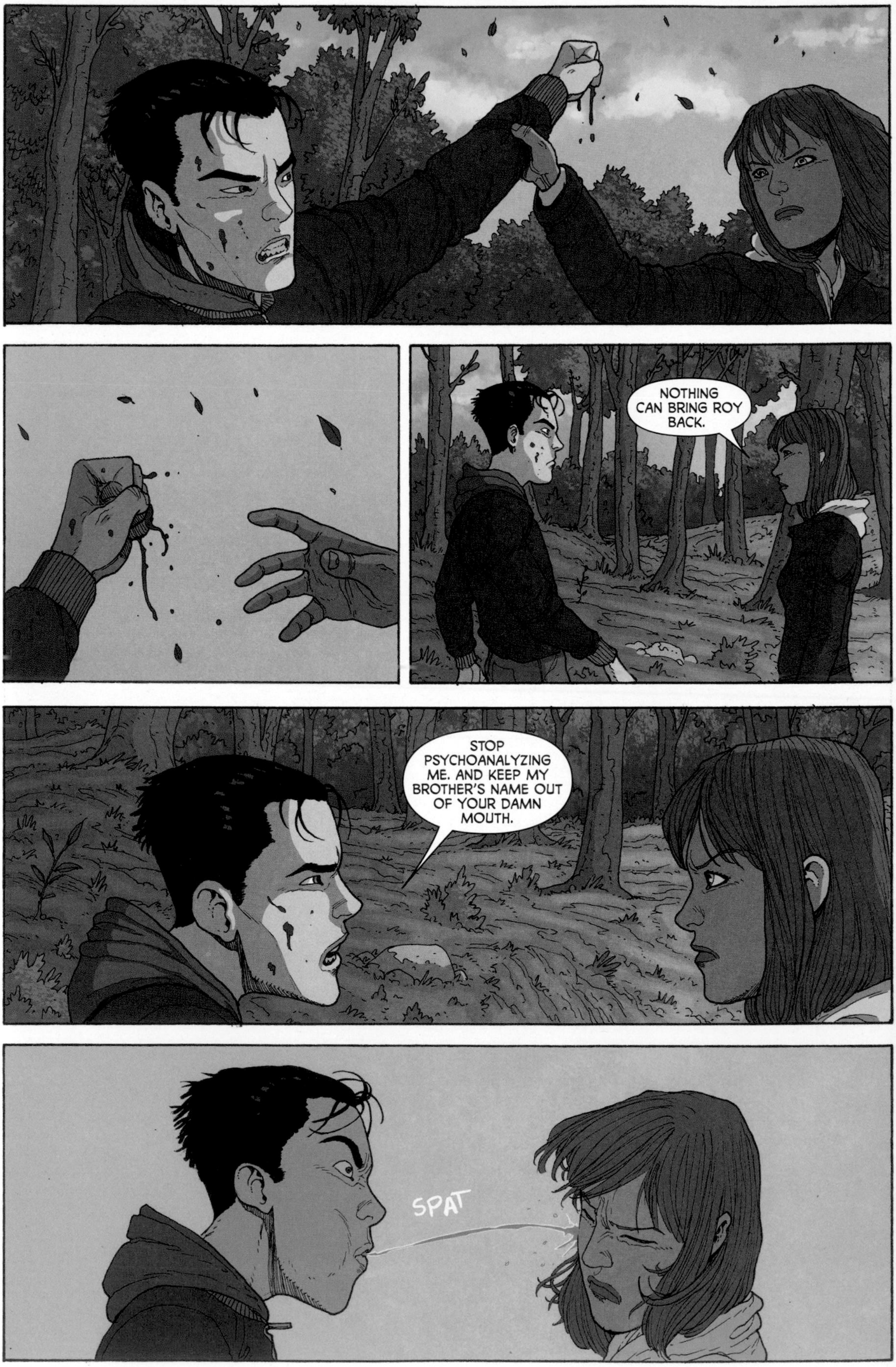
NOTHING CAN BRING ROY BACK.
STOP PSYCHOANALYZING ME. AND KEEP MY BROTHER'S NAME OUT OF YOUR DAMN MOUTH.
SPAT

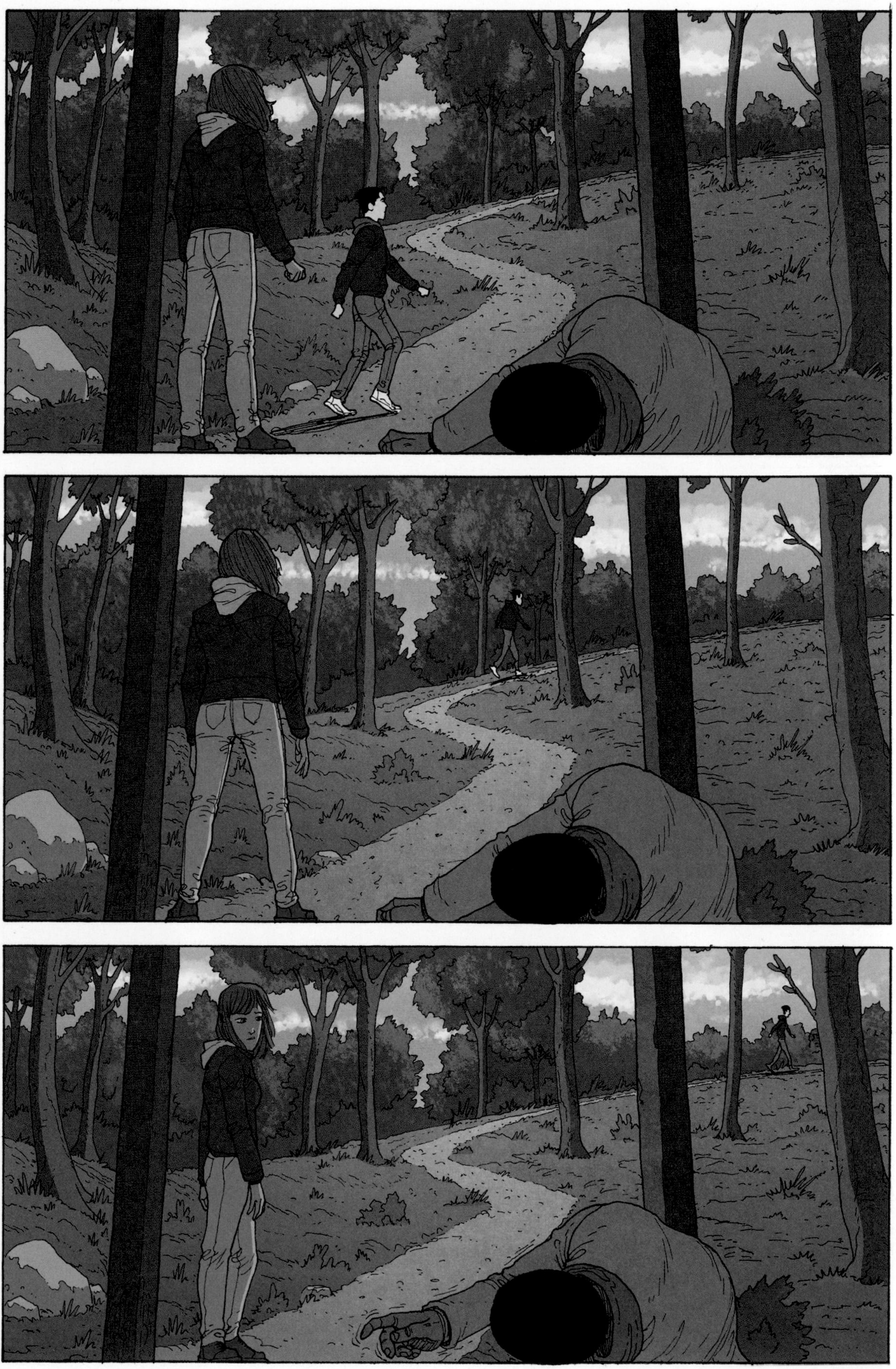

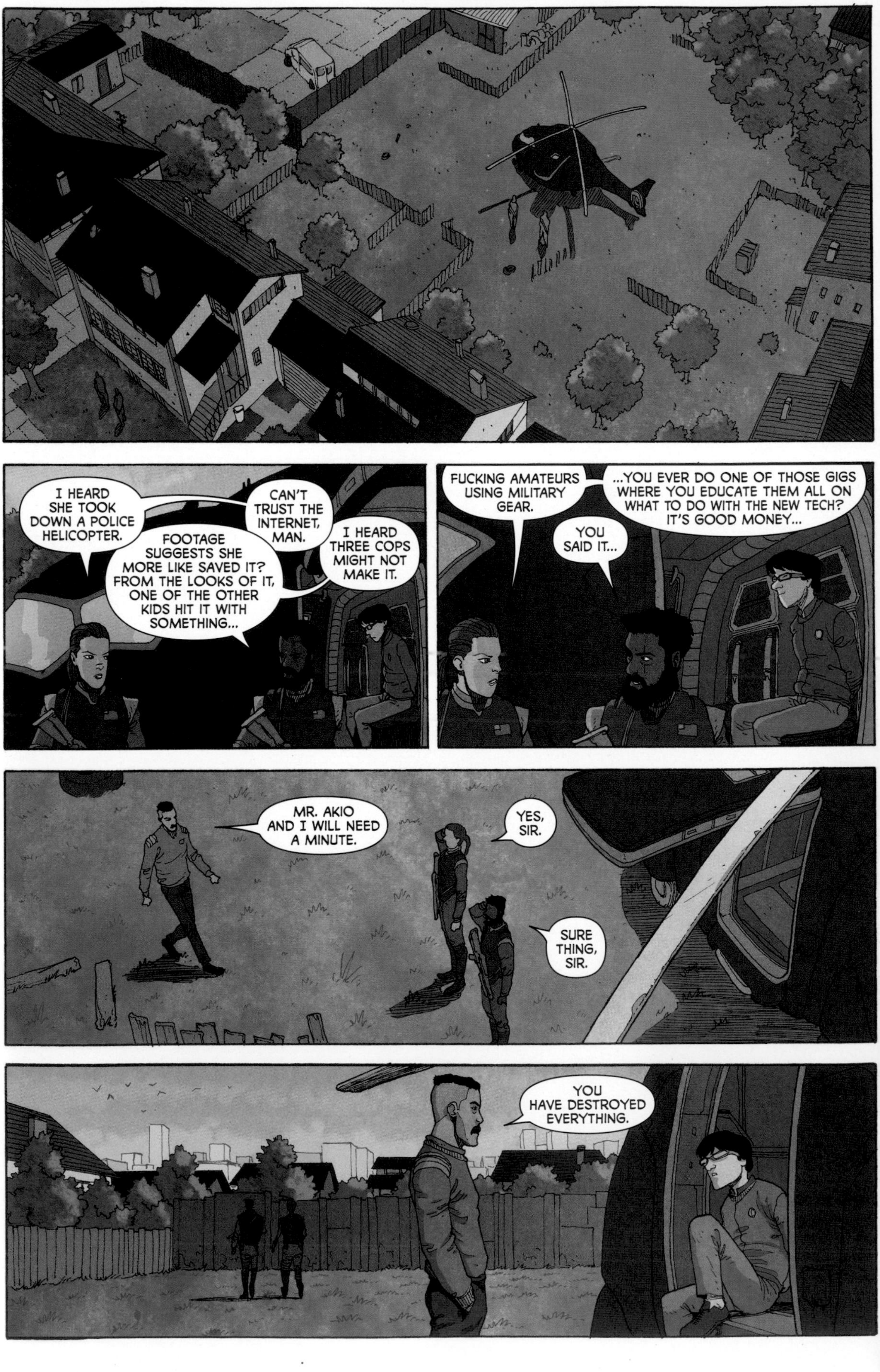
I HEARD SHE TOOK DOWN A POLICE HELICOPTER.
CAN'T TRUST THE INTERNET, MAN.
FOOTAGE SUGGESTS SHE MORE LIKE SAVED IT? FROM THE LOOKS OF IT, ONE OF THE OTHER KIDS HIT IT WITH SOMETHING...
I HEARD THREE COPS MIGHT NOT MAKE IT.
FUCKING AMATEURS USING MILITARY GEAR.
...YOU EVER DO ONE OF THOSE GIGS WHERE YOU EDUCATE THEM ALL ON WHAT TO DO WITH THE NEW TECH? IT'S GOOD MONEY...
YOU SAID IT...
MR. AKIO AND I WILL NEED A MINUTE.
YES, SIR.
SURE THING, SIR.
YOU HAVE DESTROYED EVERYTHING.

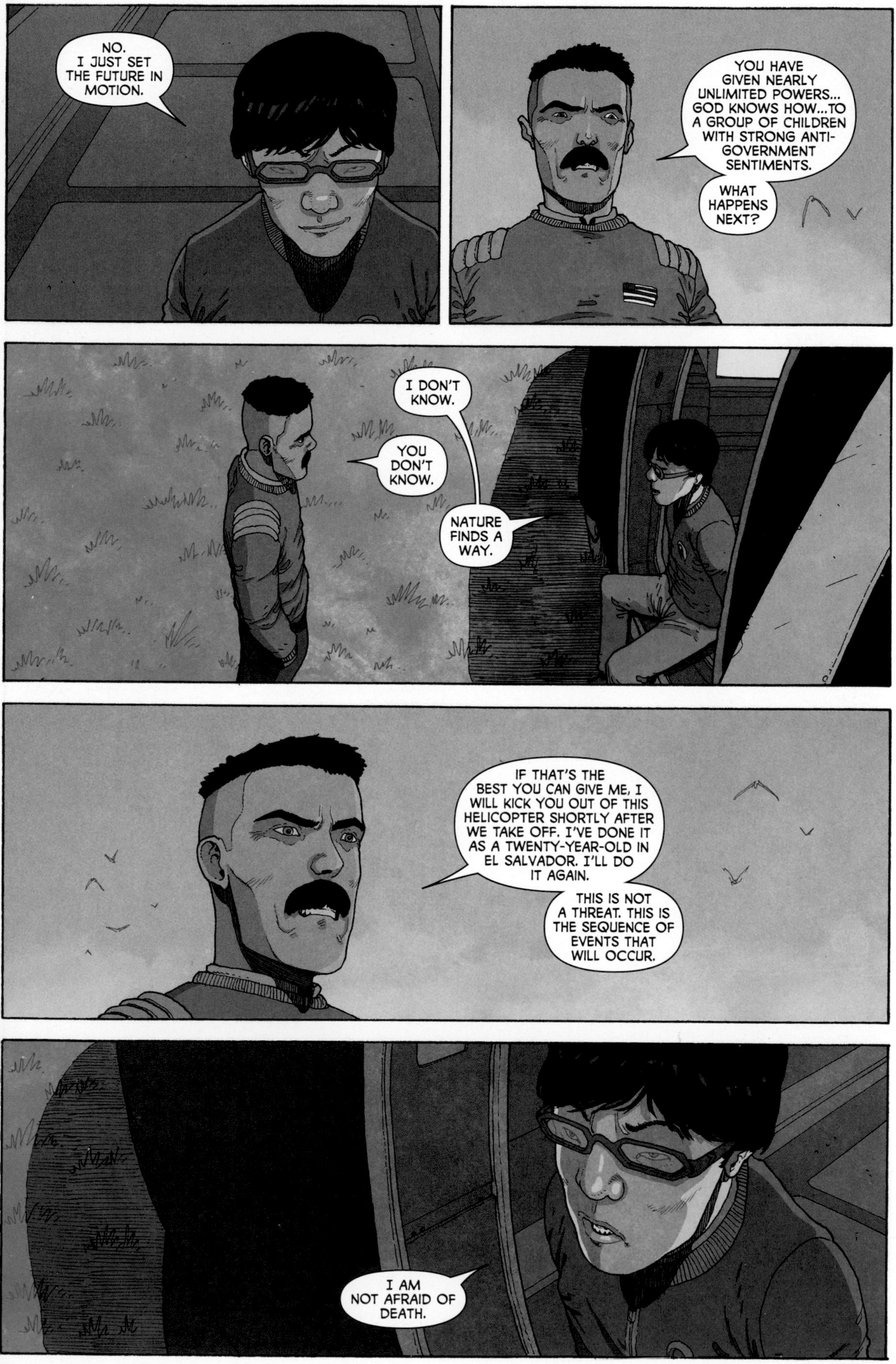
NO. I JUST SET THE FUTURE IN MOTION.
YOU HAVE GIVEN NEARLY UNLIMITED POWERS... GOD KNOWS HOW...TO A GROUP OF CHILDREN WITH STRONG ANTI-GOVERNMENT SENTIMENTS.
WHAT HAPPENS NEXT?
I DON'T KNOW.
YOU DON'T KNOW.
NATURE FINDS A WAY.
IF THAT'S THE BEST YOU CAN GIVE ME, I WILL KICK YOU OUT OF THIS HELICOPTER SHORTLY AFTER WE TAKE OFF. I'VE DONE IT AS A TWENTY-YEAR-OLD IN EL SALVADOR. I'LL DO IT AGAIN.
THIS IS NOT A THREAT. THIS IS THE SEQUENCE OF EVENTS THAT WILL OCCUR.
I AM NOT AFRAID OF DEATH.

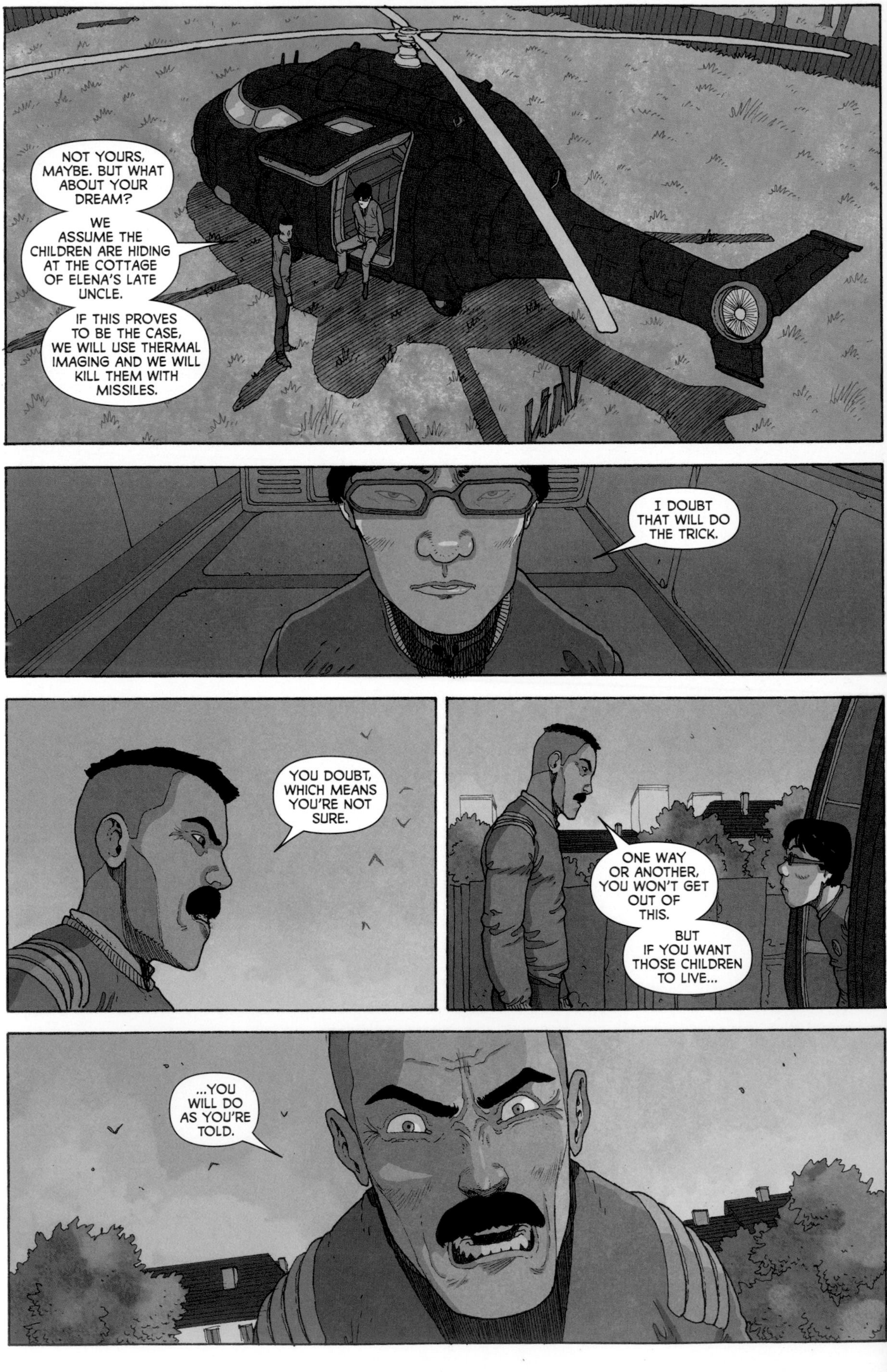
NOT YOURS, MAYBE. BUT WHAT ABOUT YOUR DREAM?
WE ASSUME THE CHILDREN ARE HIDING AT THE COTTAGE OF ELENA'S LATE UNCLE.
IF THIS PROVES TO BE THE CASE, WE WILL USE THERMAL IMAGING AND WE WILL KILL THEM WITH MISSILES.
I DOUBT THAT WILL DO THE TRICK.
YOU DOUBT, WHICH MEANS YOU'RE NOT SURE.
ONE WAY OR ANOTHER, YOU WON'T GET OUT OF THIS.
BUT IF YOU WANT THOSE CHILDREN TO LIVE...
...YOU WILL DO AS YOU'RE TOLD.

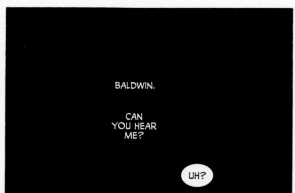

BALDWIN.

CAN YOU HEAR ME?

UH?

YOU'RE HEALING.

HUH.

I GUESS THE POWERS ARE DIFFERENT FOR EACH ONE OF US?

YEAH... I GUESS I GOT SOME OF THE HEALING FACTOR AFTER ALL... HE CAN'T FLY, CAN HE...?

NO, I DON'T THINK HE CAN.

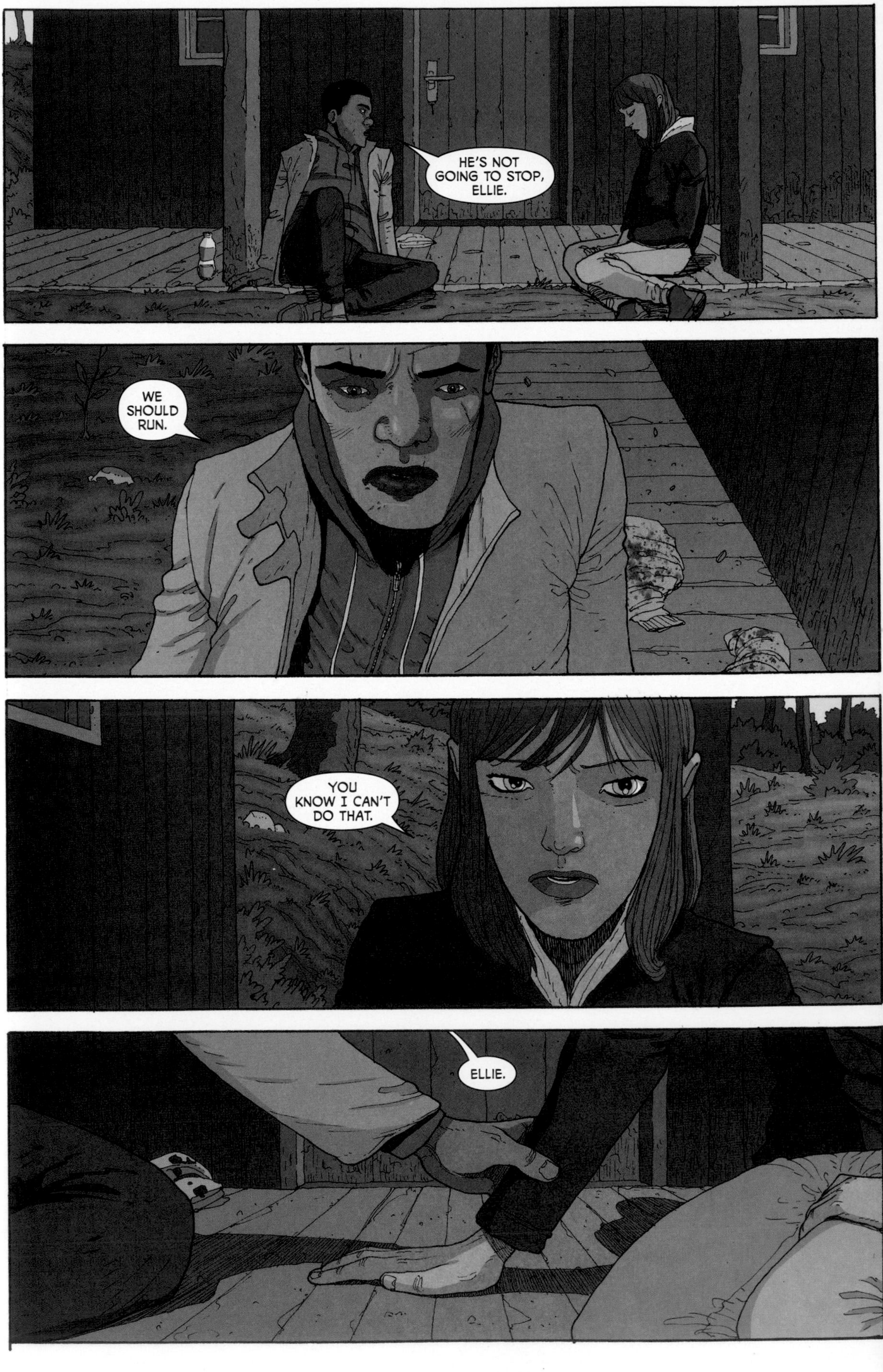
HE'S NOT GOING TO STOP, ELLIE.
WE SHOULD RUN.
YOU KNOW I CAN'T DO THAT.
ELLIE.

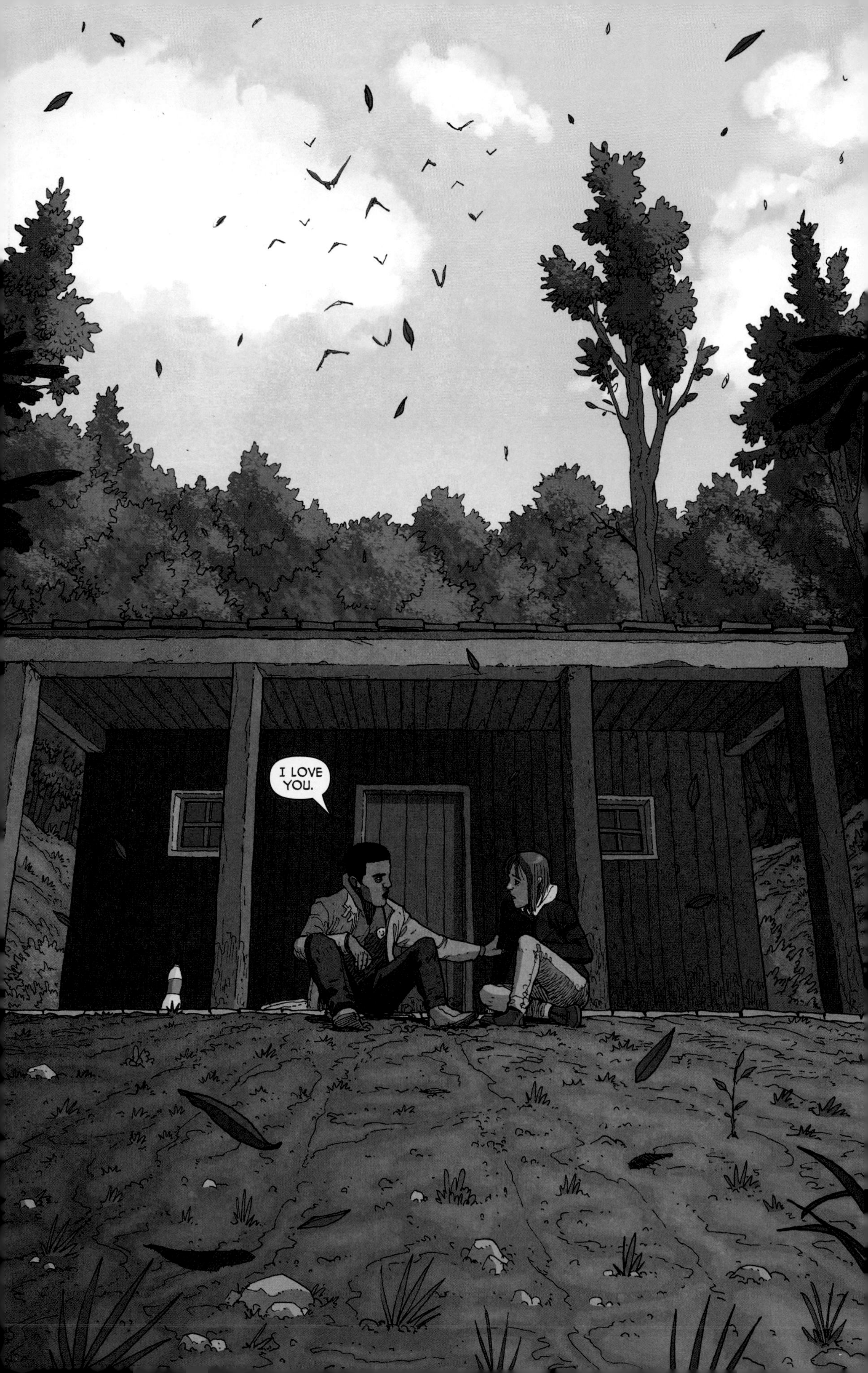
I LOVE YOU.

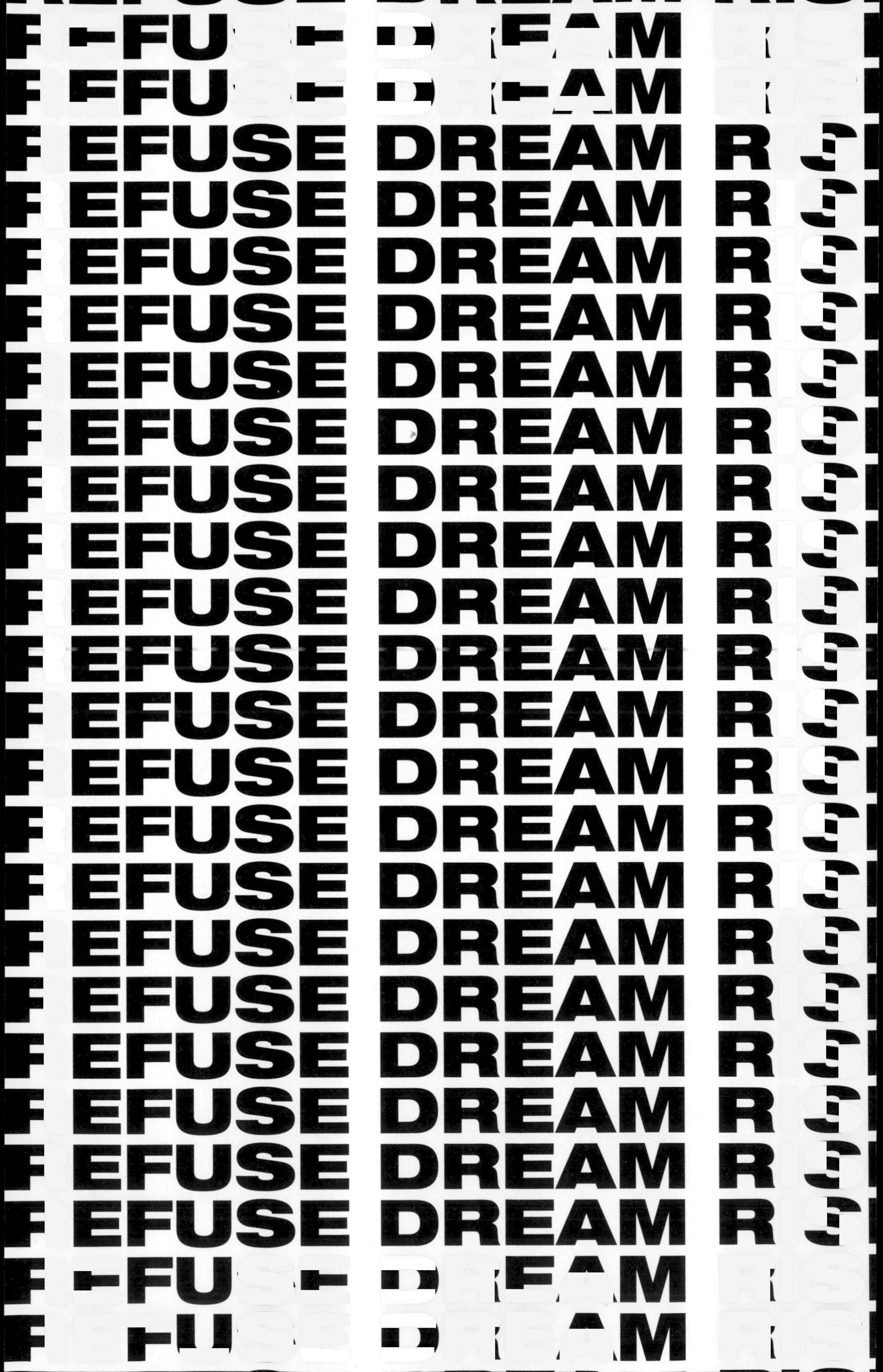
REFUSE DREAM RISE
REFUSE DREAM RISE
REFUSE DREAM RISE
REFUSE DREAM RISE
REFUSE DREAM RISE
REFUSE DREAM RISE
REFUSE DREAM RISE
REFUSE DREAM RISE
REFUSE DREAM RISE
REFUSE DREAM RISE
REFUSE DREAM RISE
REFUSE DREAM RISE
REFUSE DREAM RISE
REFUSE DREAM RISE
REFUSE DREAM RISE
REFUSE DREAM RISE
REFUSE DREAM RISE
REFUSE DREAM RISE
REFUSE DREAM RISE

CHAPTER FOUR

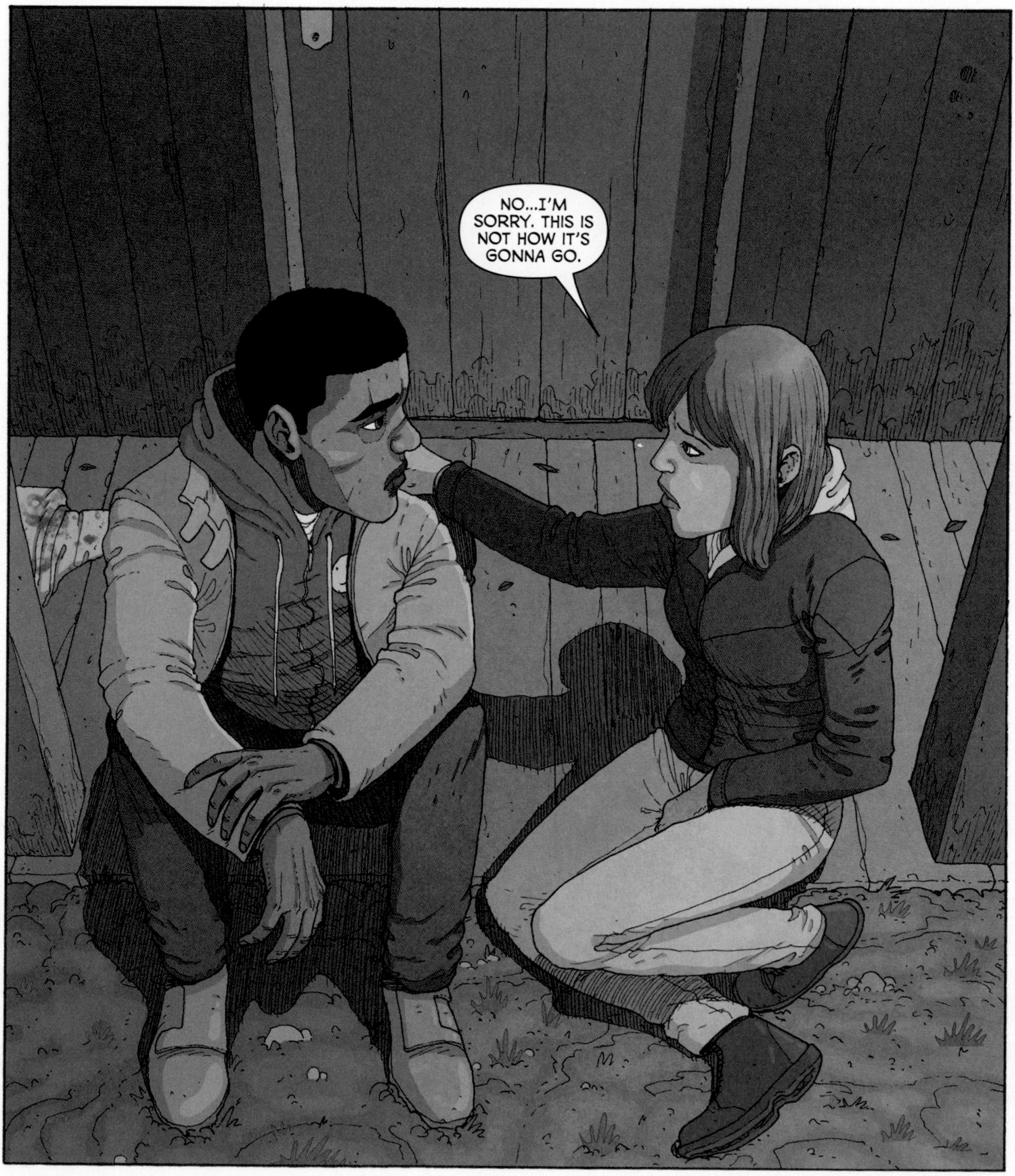
NO...I'M SORRY. THIS IS NOT HOW IT'S GONNA GO.

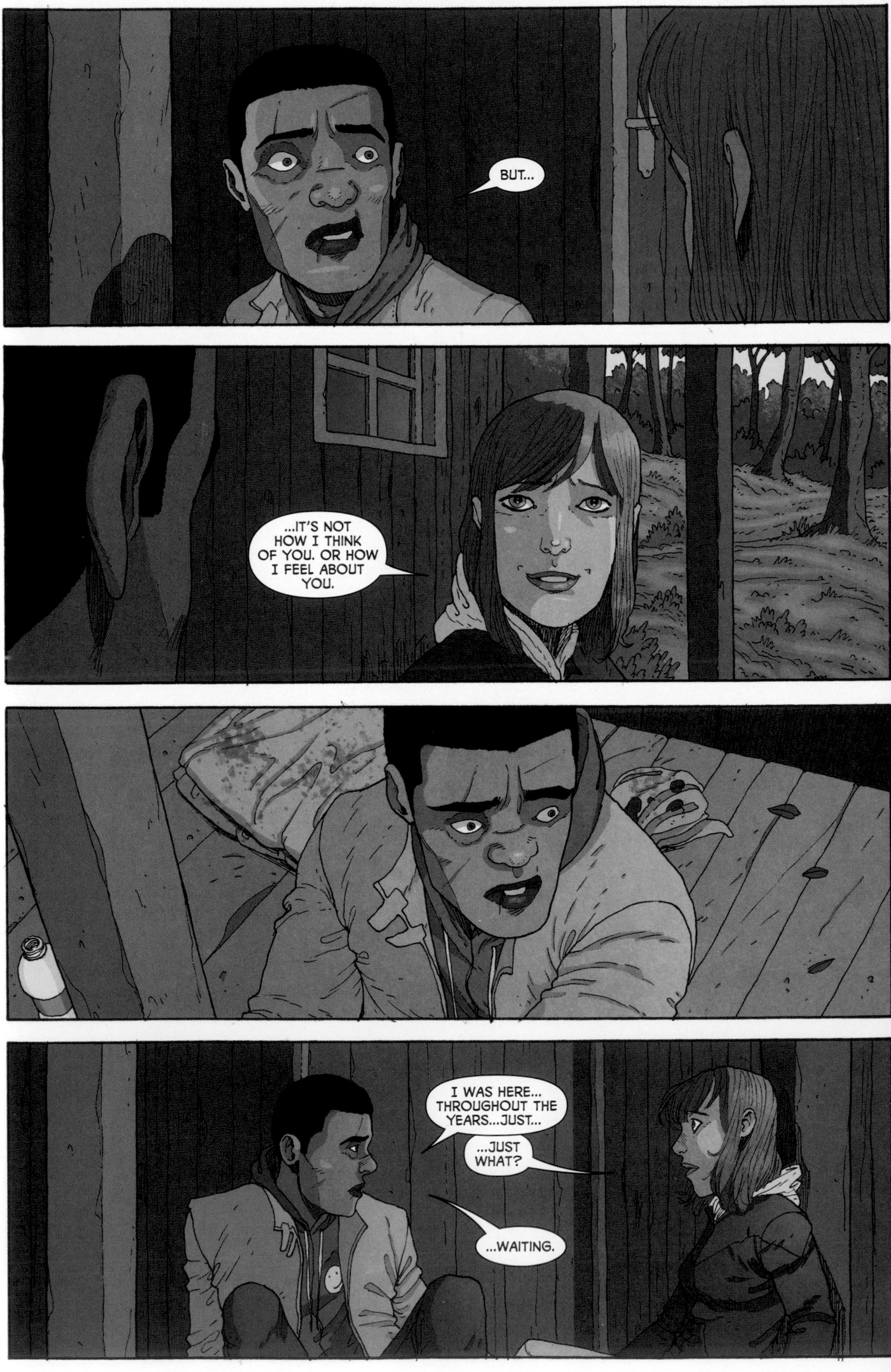
BUT...
...IT'S NOT HOW I THINK OF YOU. OR HOW I FEEL ABOUT YOU.
I WAS HERE... THROUGHOUT THE YEARS...JUST...
...JUST WHAT?
...WAITING.

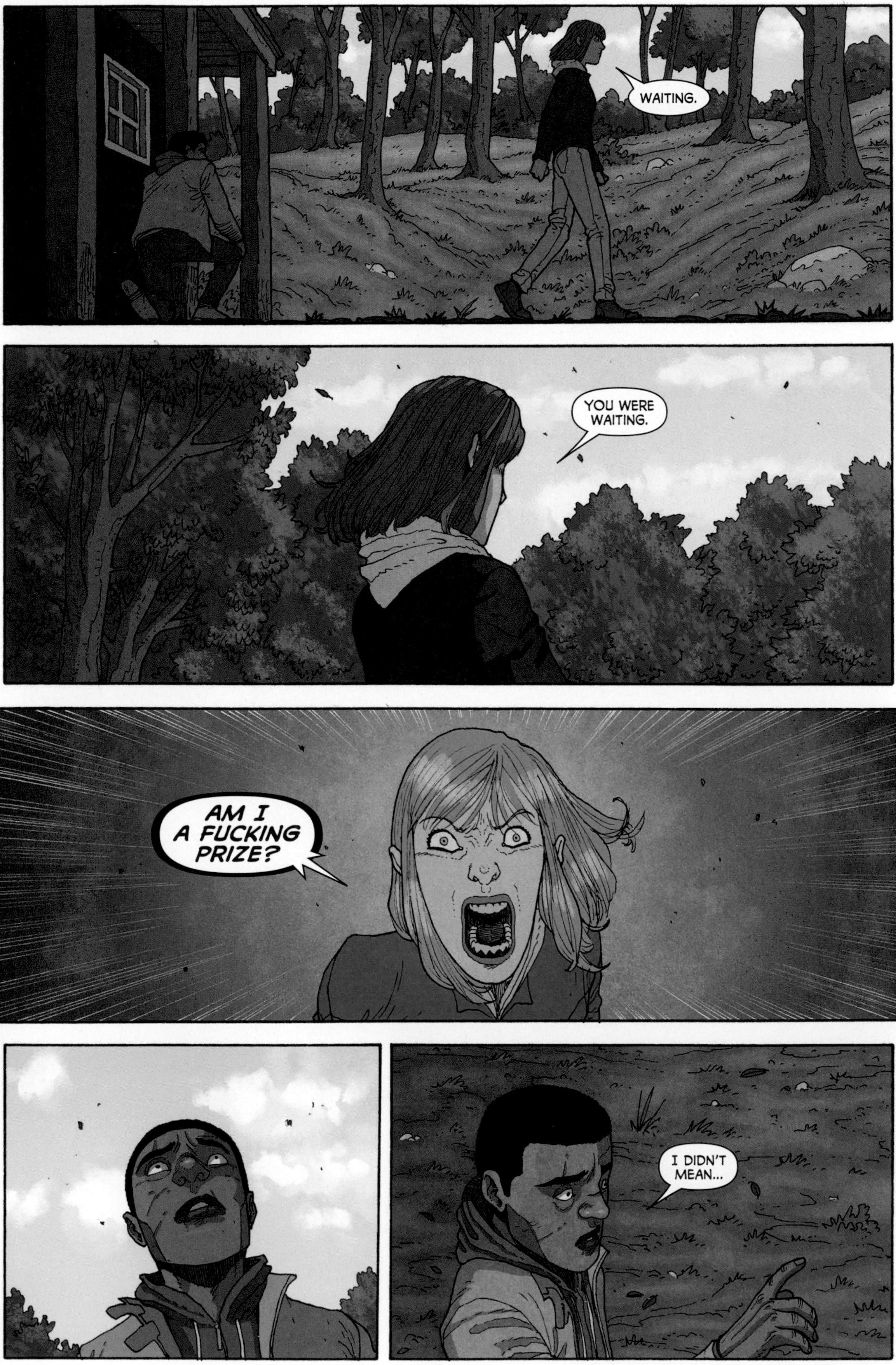
WAITING.
YOU WERE WAITING.
AM I A FUCKING PRIZE?
I DIDN'T MEAN...

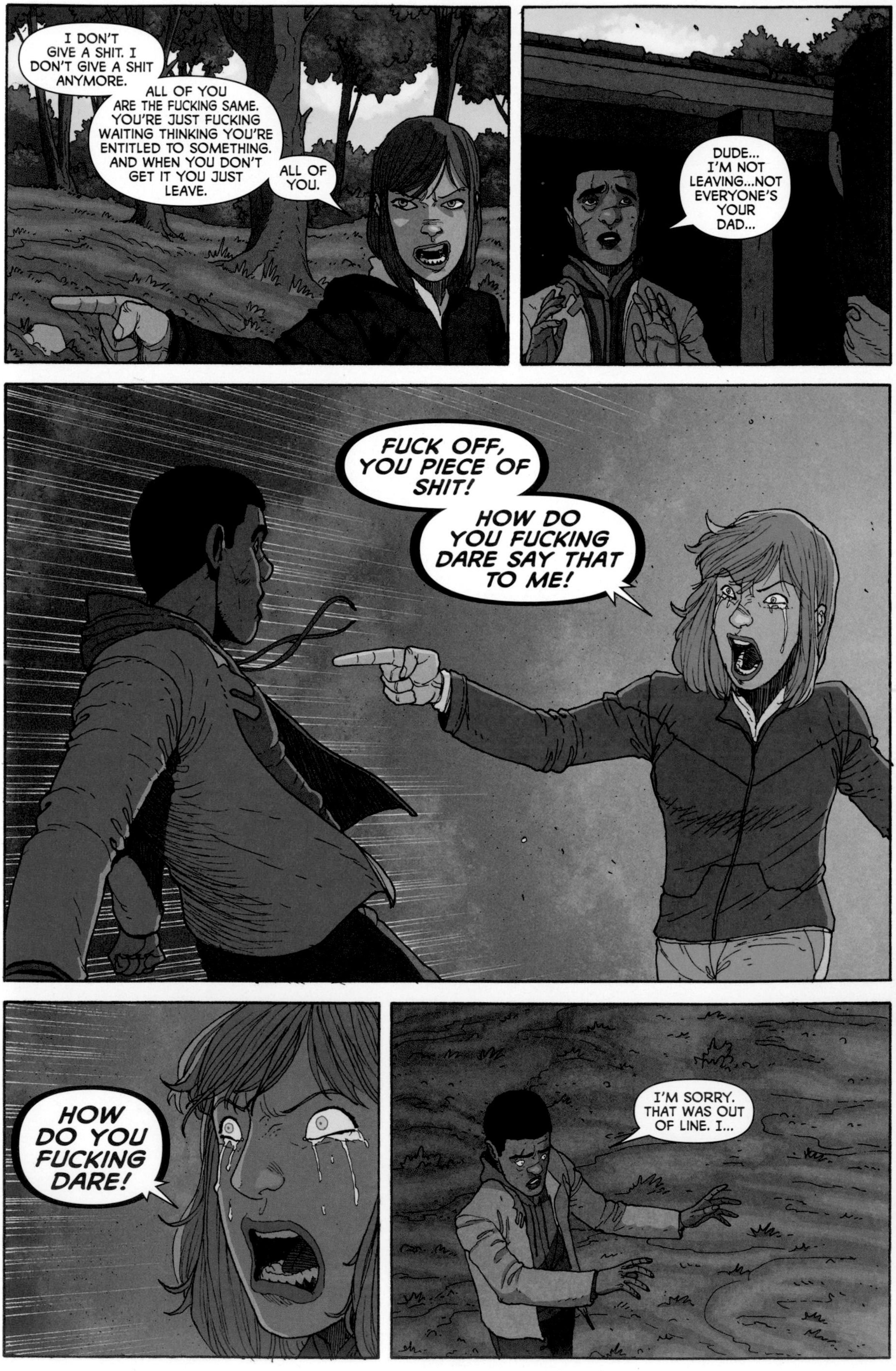
I DON'T GIVE A SHIT. I DON'T GIVE A SHIT ANYMORE.
ALL OF YOU ARE THE FUCKING SAME. YOU'RE JUST FUCKING WAITING THINKING YOU'RE ENTITLED TO SOMETHING. AND WHEN YOU DON'T GET IT YOU JUST LEAVE.
ALL OF YOU.
DUDE... I'M NOT LEAVING...NOT EVERYONE'S YOUR DAD...
FUCK OFF, YOU PIECE OF SHIT!
HOW DO YOU FUCKING DARE SAY THAT TO ME!
HOW DO YOU FUCKING DARE!
I'M SORRY. THAT WAS OUT OF LINE. I...

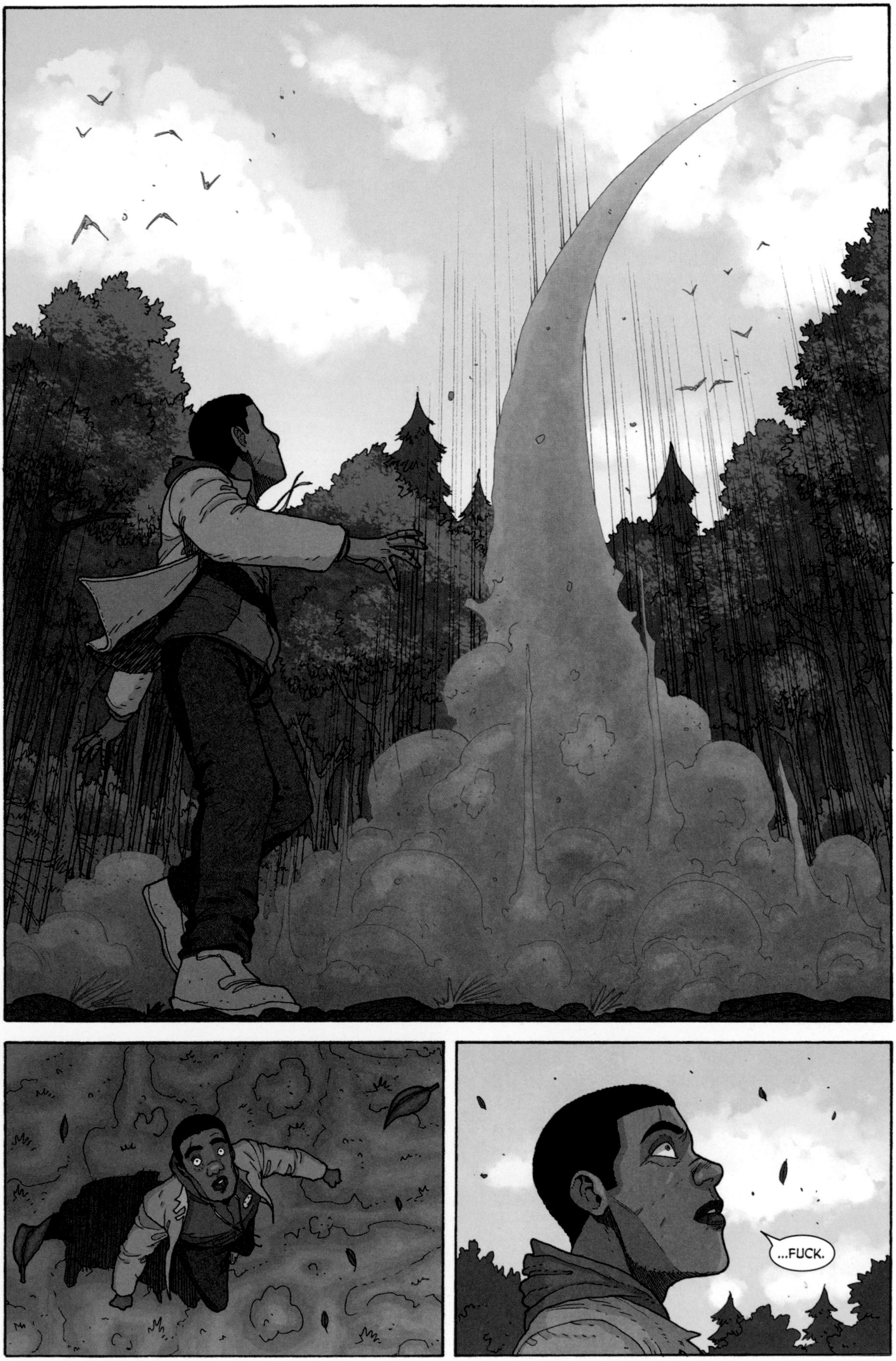
...FUCK.

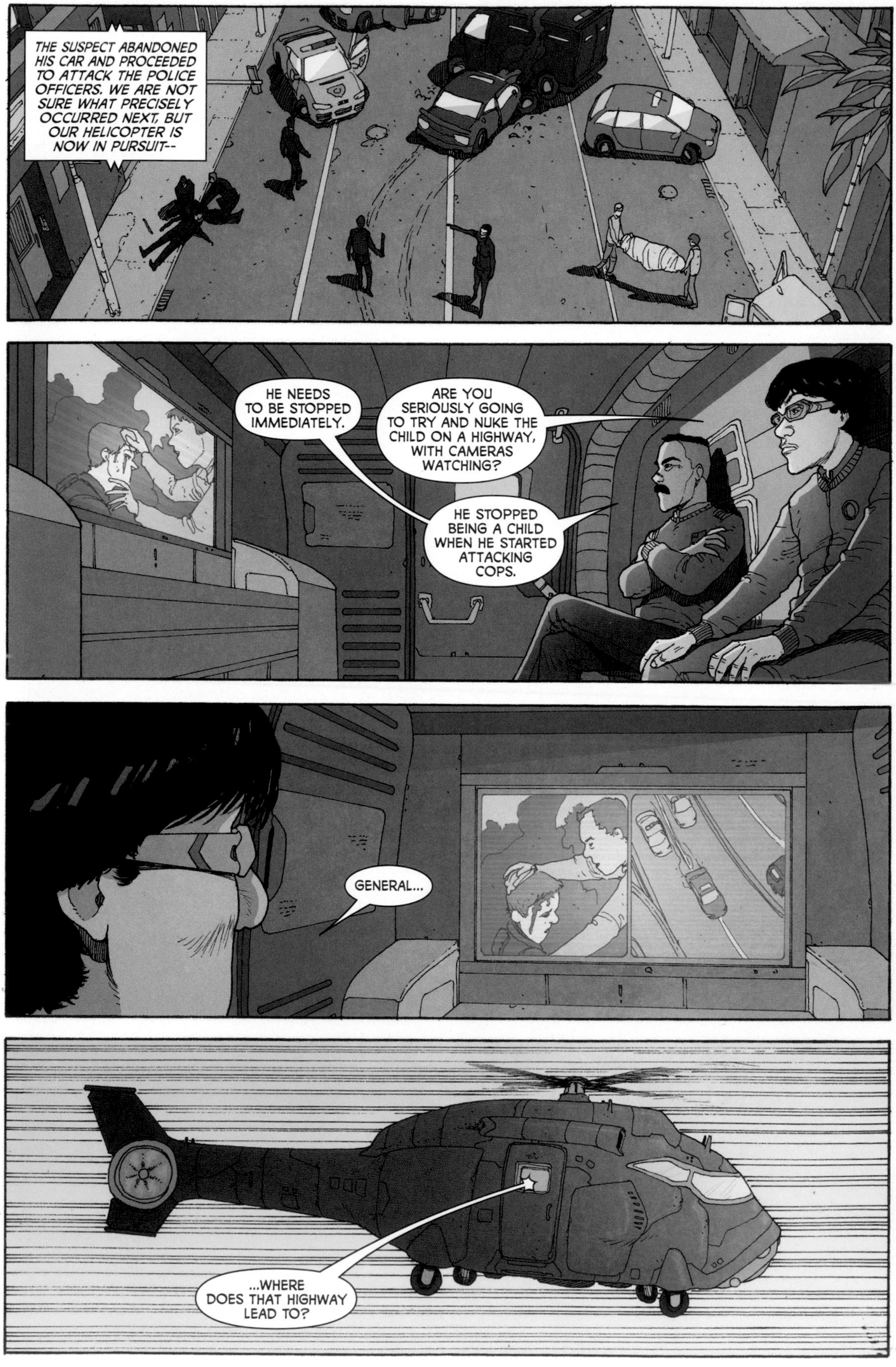
THE SUSPECT ABANDONED HIS CAR AND PROCEEDED TO ATTACK THE POLICE OFFICERS. WE ARE NOT SURE WHAT PRECISELY OCCURRED NEXT, BUT OUR HELICOPTER IS NOW IN PURSUIT--
ARE YOU SERIOUSLY GOING TO TRY AND NUKE THE CHILD ON A HIGHWAY, WITH CAMERAS WATCHING?
HE NEEDS TO BE STOPPED IMMEDIATELY.
HE STOPPED BEING A CHILD WHEN HE STARTED ATTACKING COPS.
GENERAL...
...WHERE DOES THAT HIGHWAY LEAD TO?

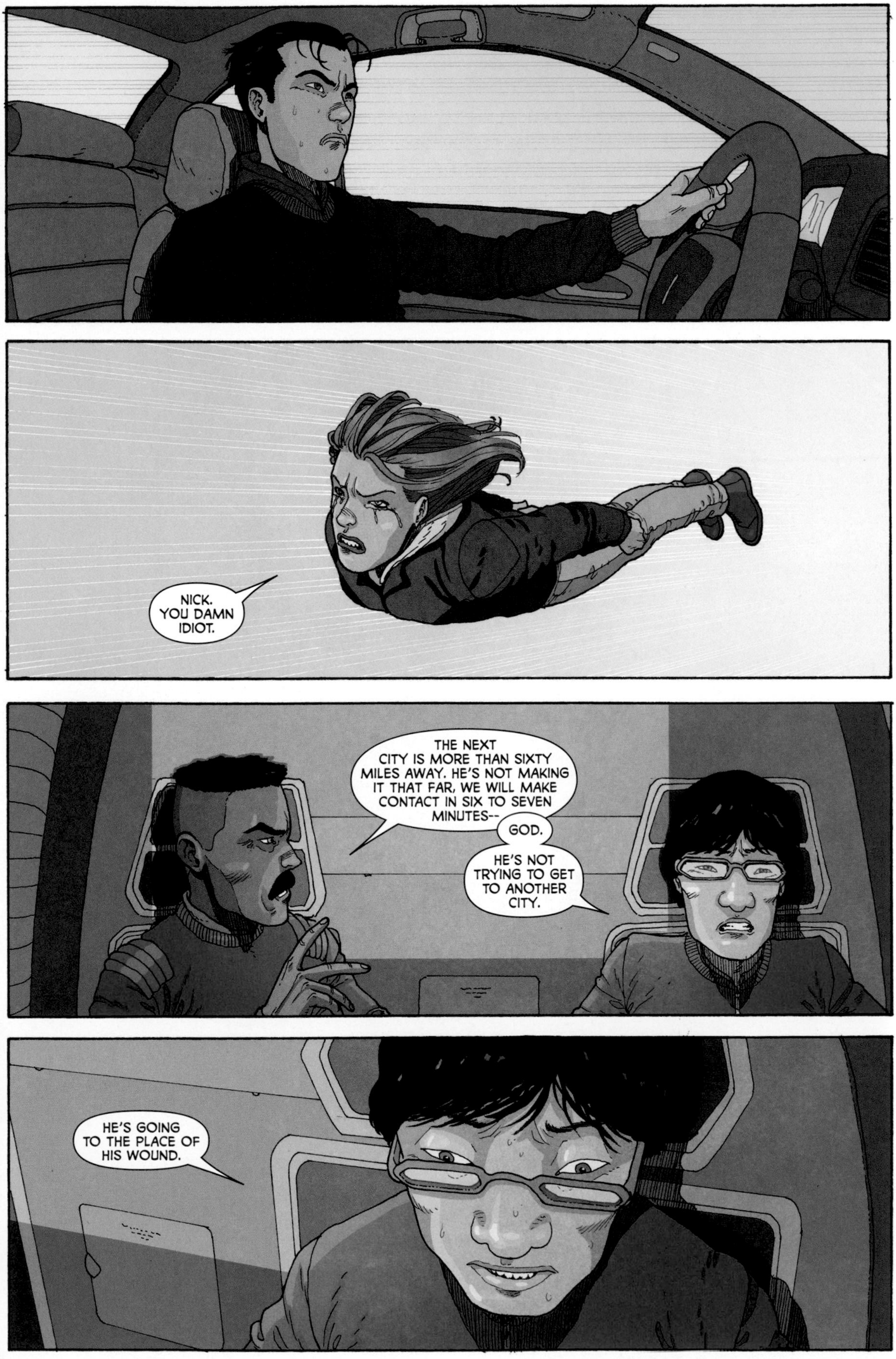
NICK. YOU DAMN IDIOT.
THE NEXT CITY IS MORE THAN SIXTY MILES AWAY. HE'S NOT MAKING IT THAT FAR, WE WILL MAKE CONTACT IN SIX TO SEVEN MINUTES--
GOD.
HE'S NOT TRYING TO GET TO ANOTHER CITY.
HE'S GOING TO THE PLACE OF HIS WOUND.

I REALLY HOPE YOU WON'T TRY ANYTHING THAT STUPID. I REALLY DO. YOU FUCKING IDIOT. HOW COULD YOU. I LOVED YOU.
I LOVED YOU.
KNEW I SHOULD HAVE NEVER TRUSTED YOUR CRAZY WHITE ASS, NICK--
NO. NOT EVEN *YOU* CAN BE THAT FUCKED UP--

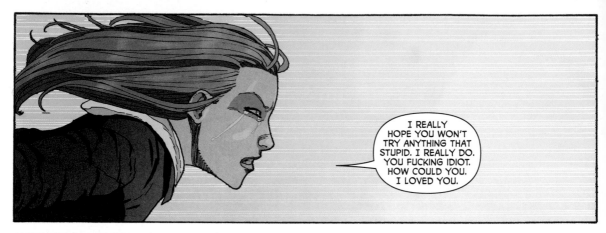

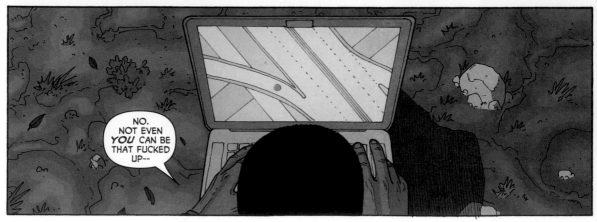

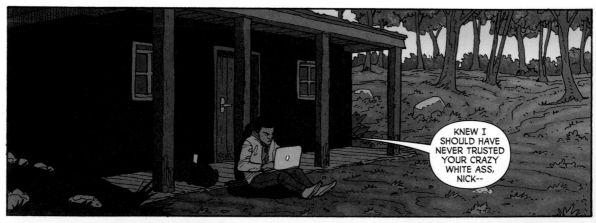

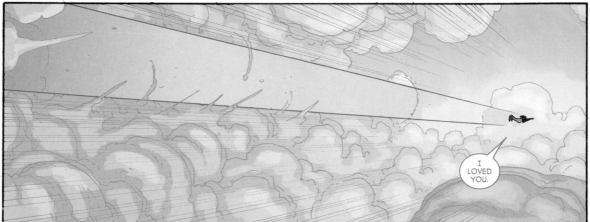

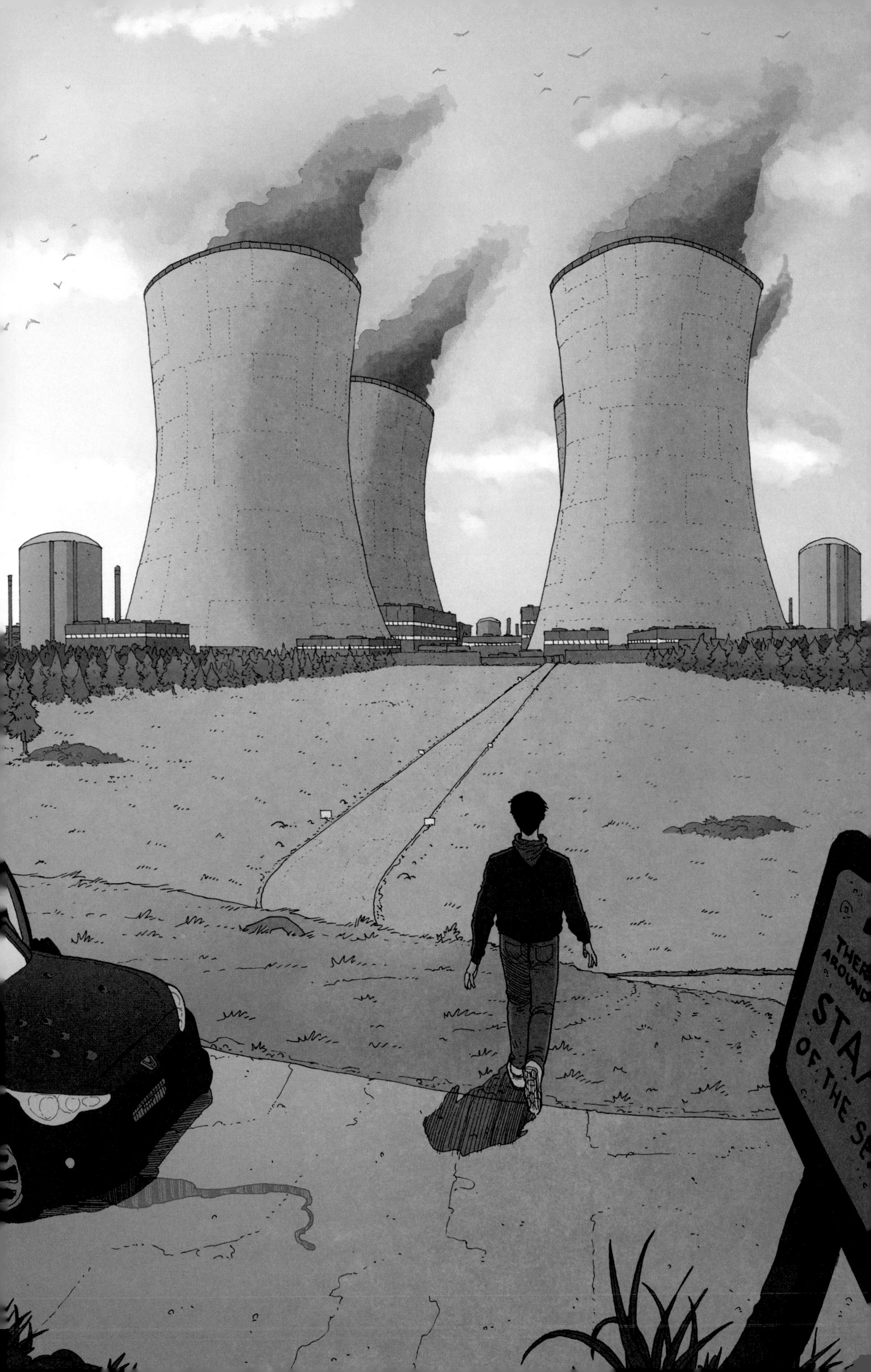

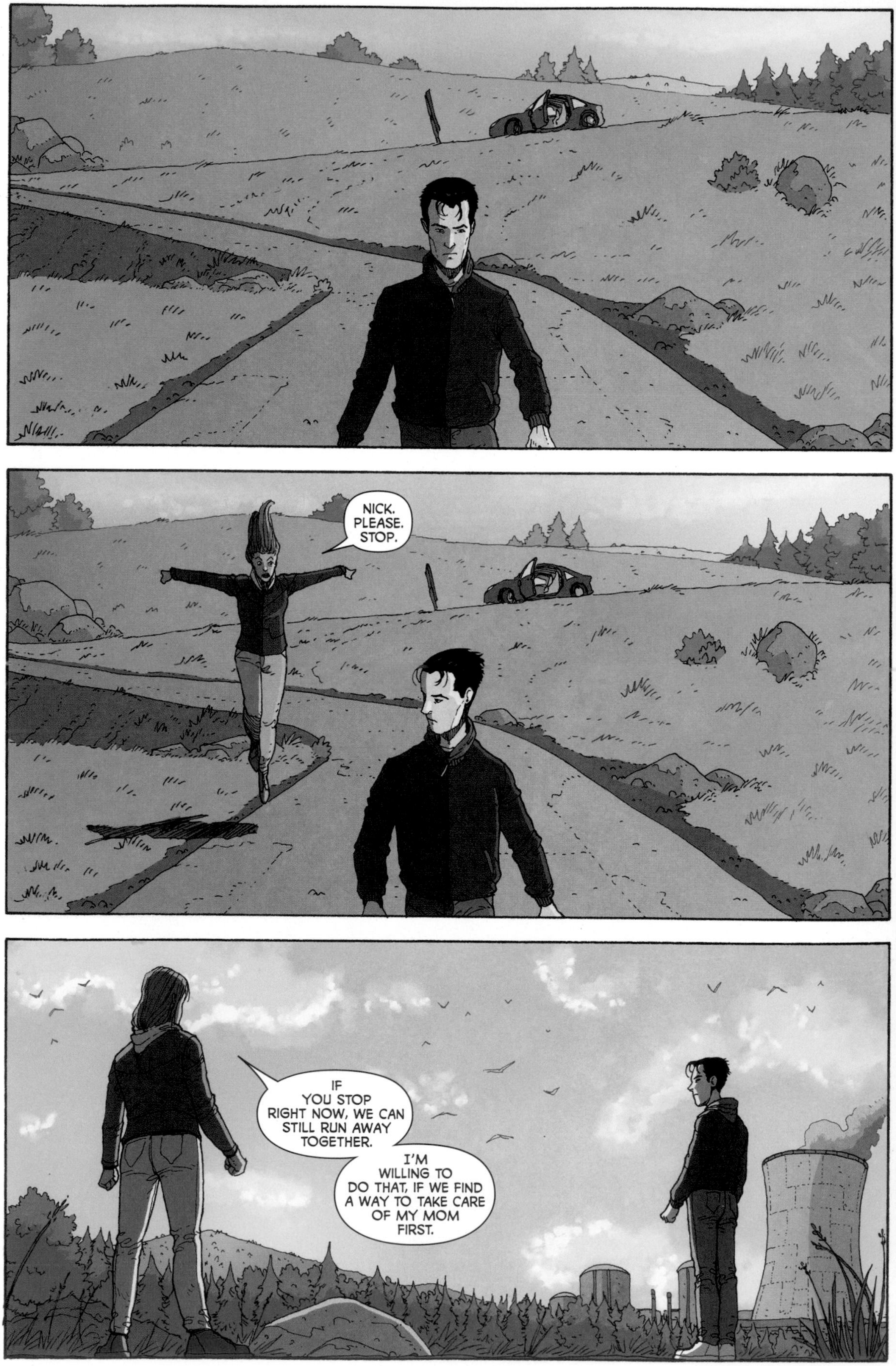
NICK. PLEASE. STOP.
IF YOU STOP RIGHT NOW, WE CAN STILL RUN AWAY TOGETHER.
I'M WILLING TO DO THAT, IF WE FIND A WAY TO TAKE CARE OF MY MOM FIRST.

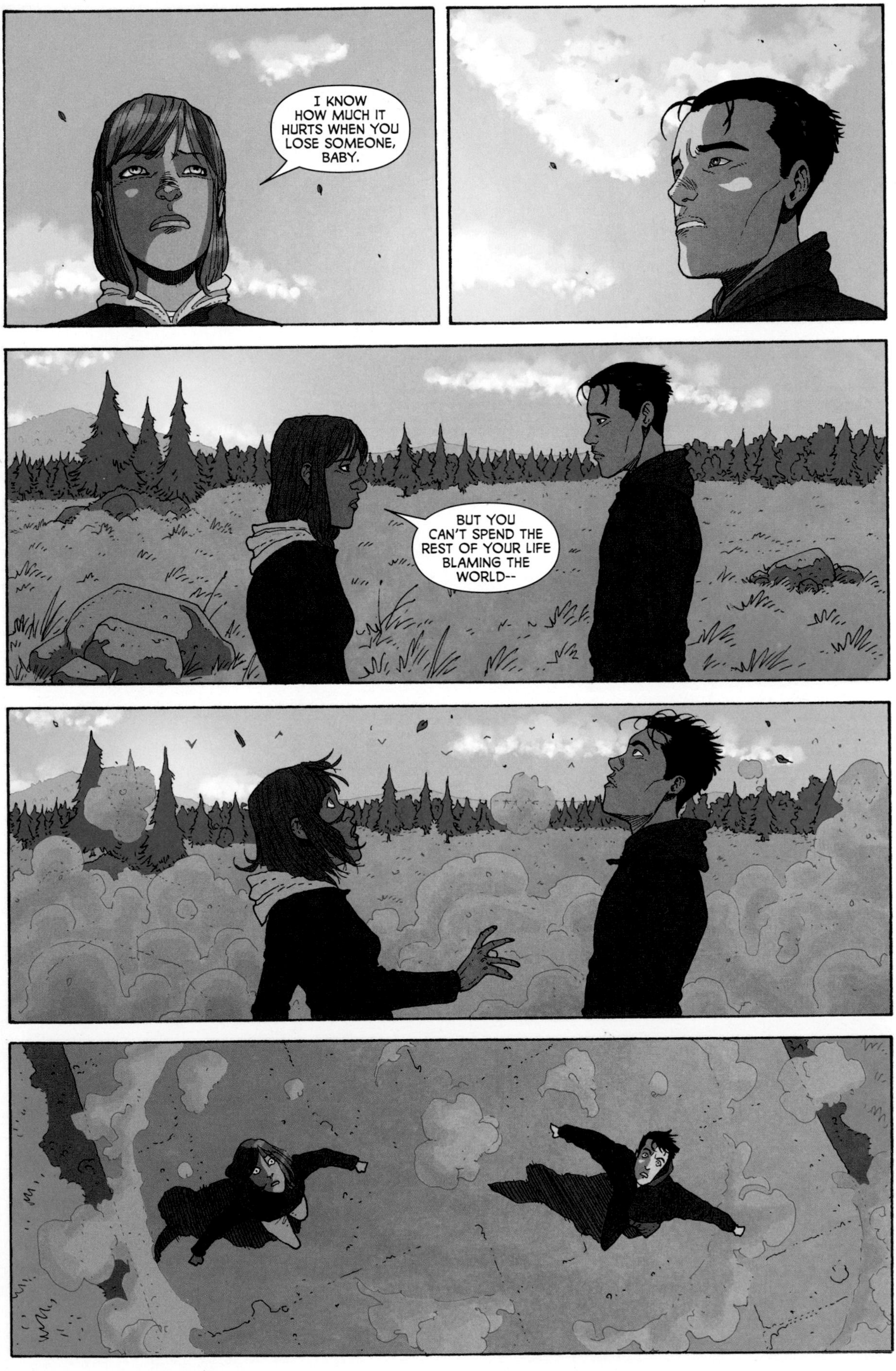
I KNOW HOW MUCH IT HURTS WHEN YOU LOSE SOMEONE, BABY.
BUT YOU CAN'T SPEND THE REST OF YOUR LIFE BLAMING THE WORLD--

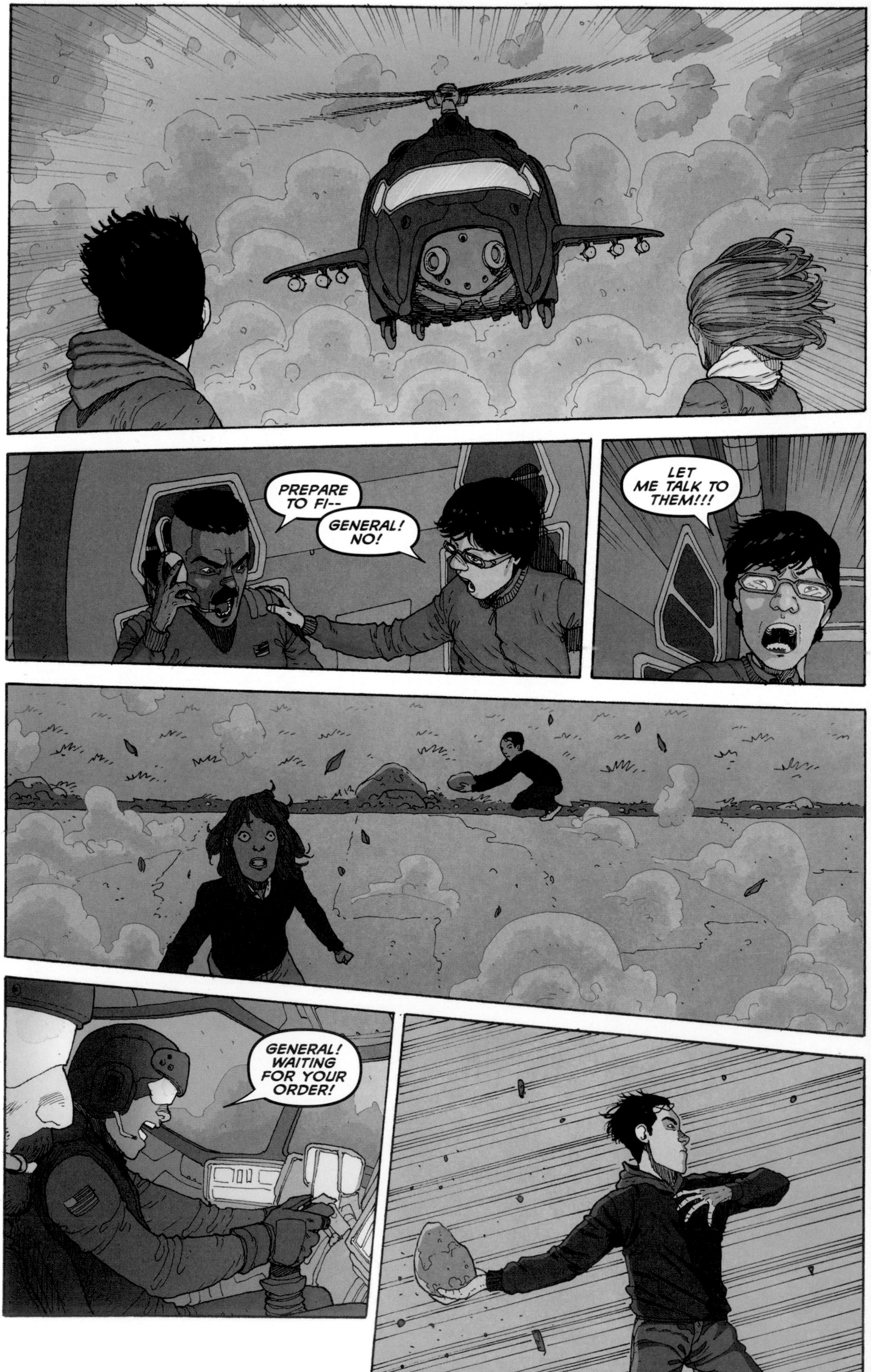
PREPARE TO FI--
GENERAL! NO!
LET ME TALK TO THEM!!!
GENERAL! WAITING FOR YOUR ORDER!

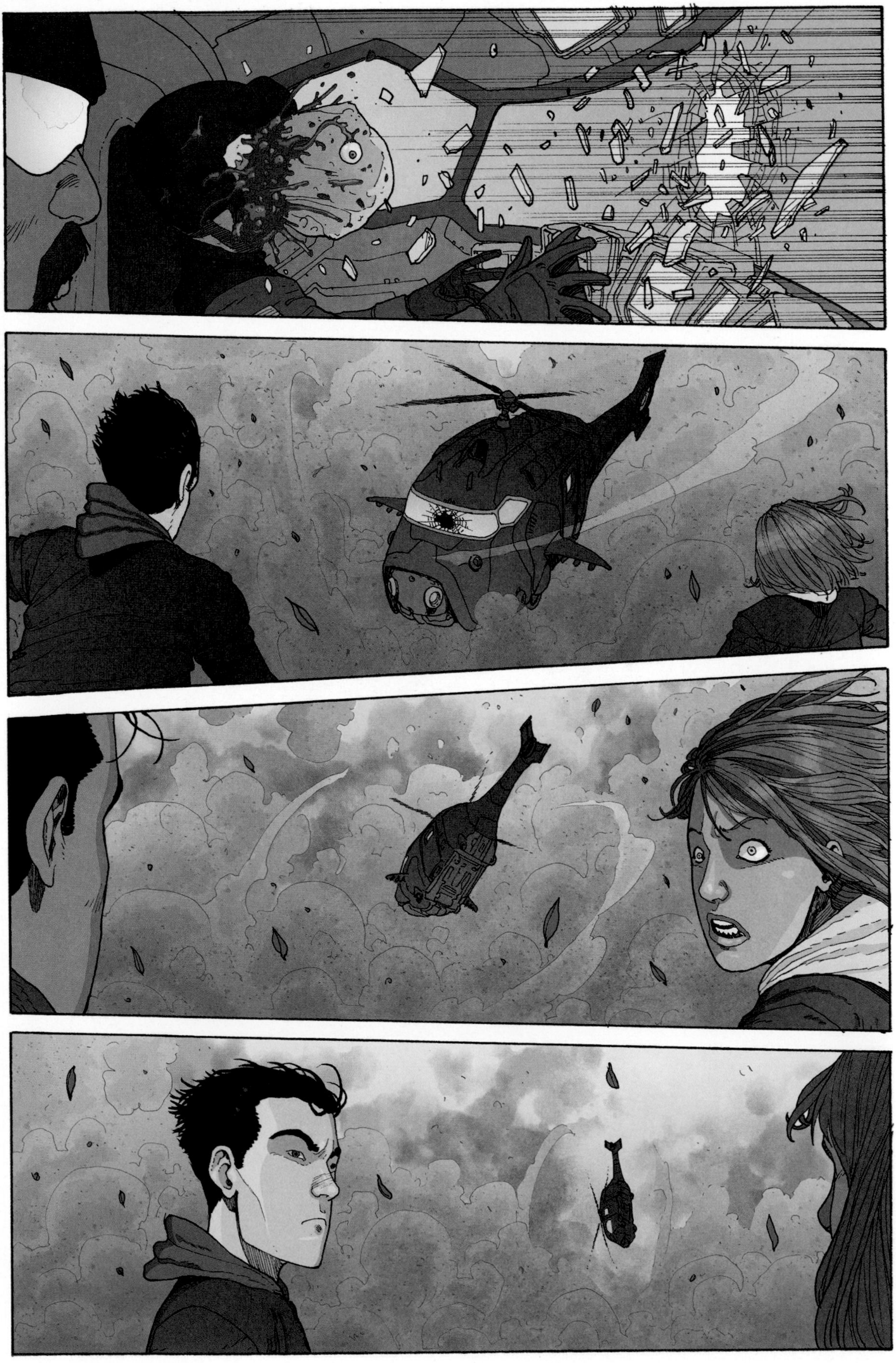

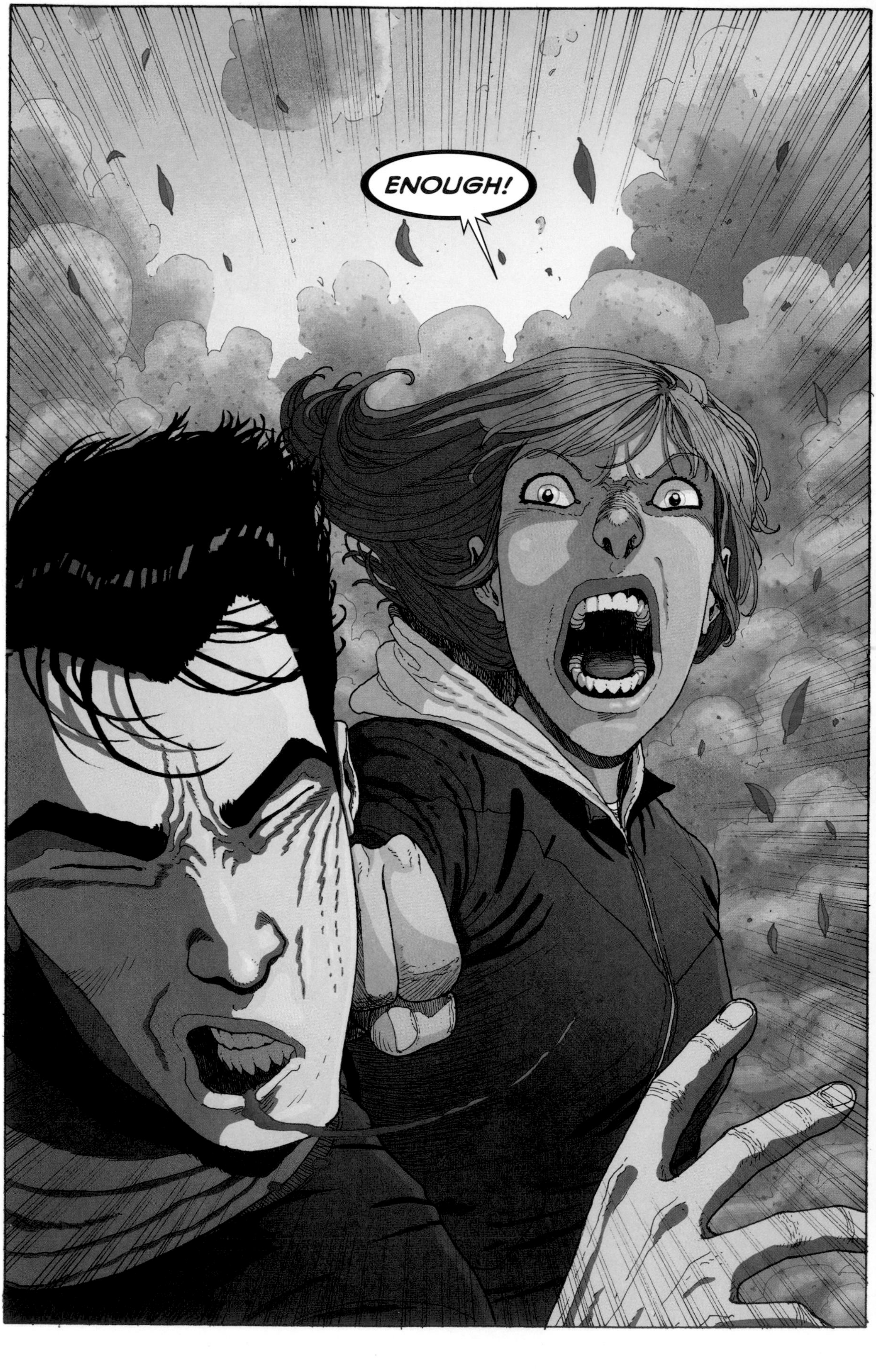
ENOUGH!

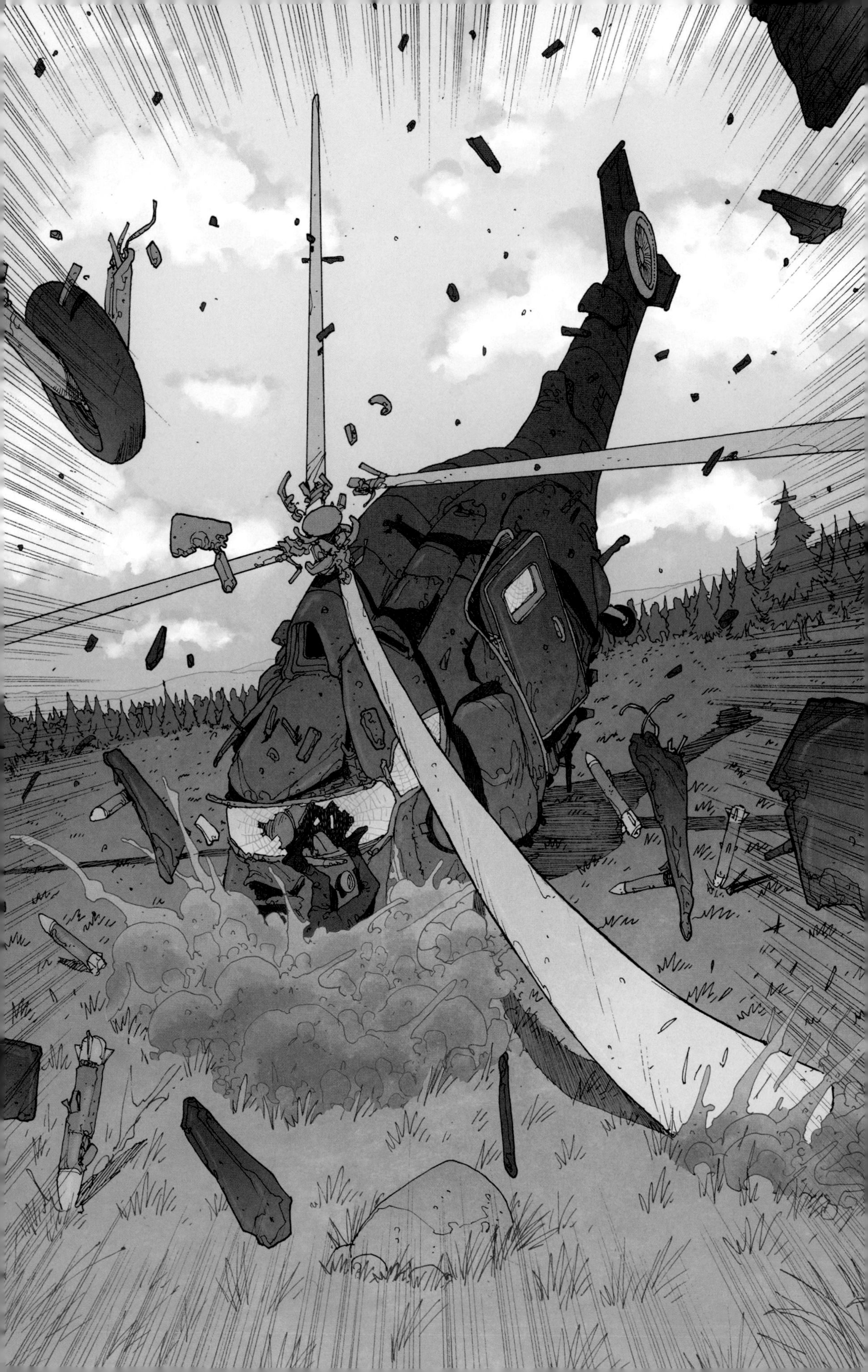

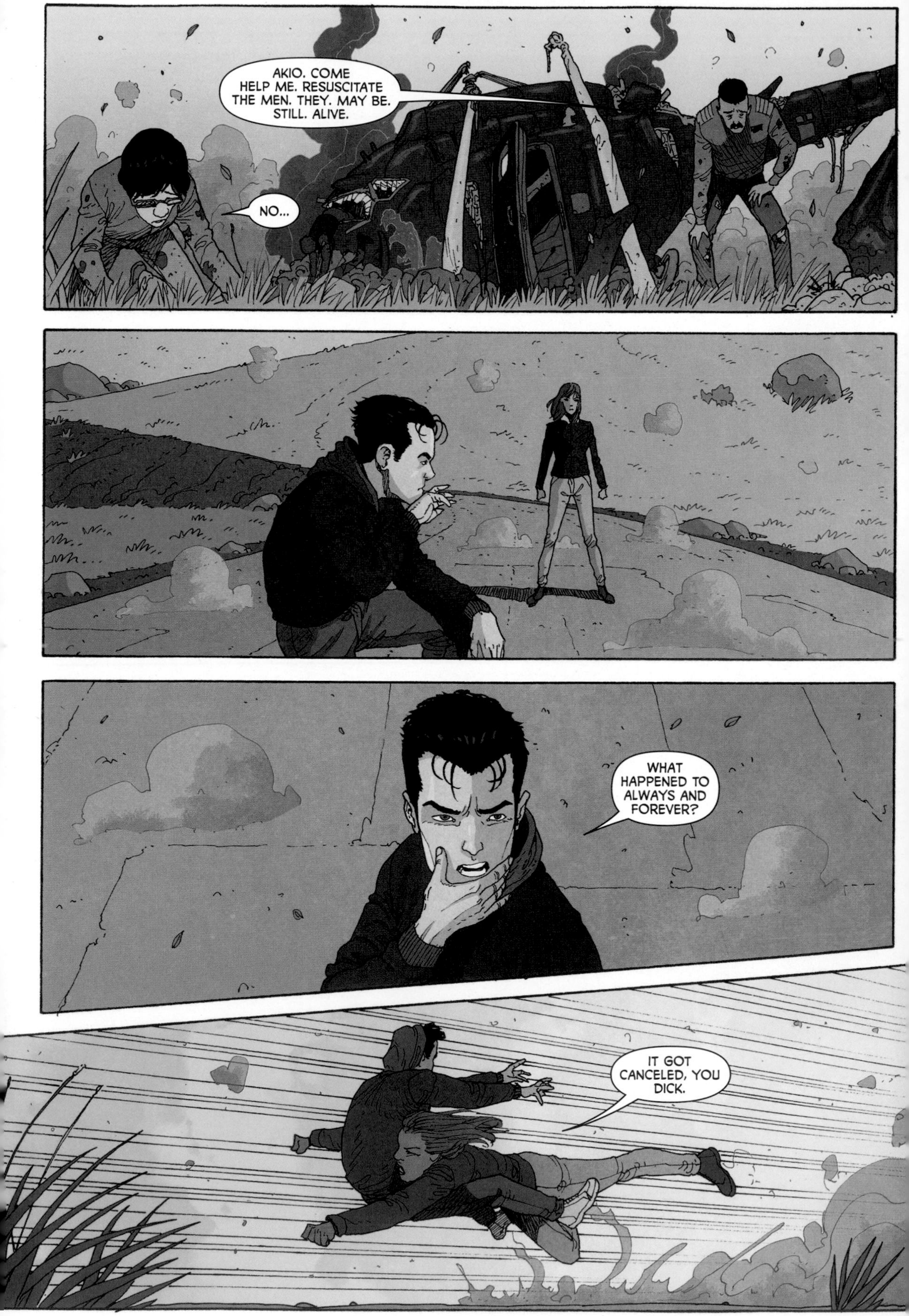
AKIO. COME HELP ME. RESUSCITATE THE MEN. THEY. MAY BE. STILL. ALIVE.
NO...
WHAT HAPPENED TO ALWAYS AND FOREVER?
IT GOT CANCELED, YOU DICK.

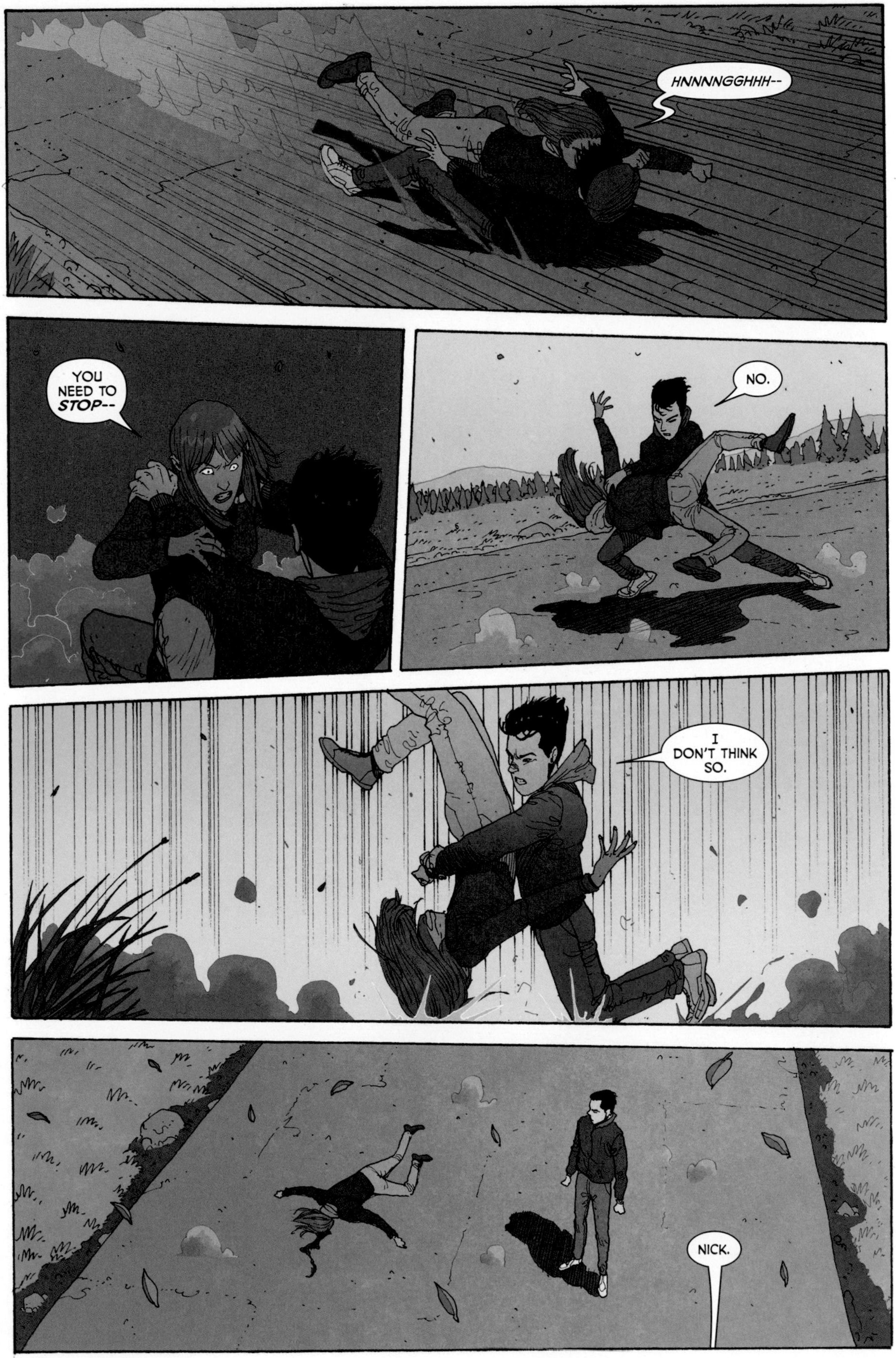
HNNNNGGHHH--
YOU NEED TO STOP--
NO.
I DON'T THINK SO.
NICK.

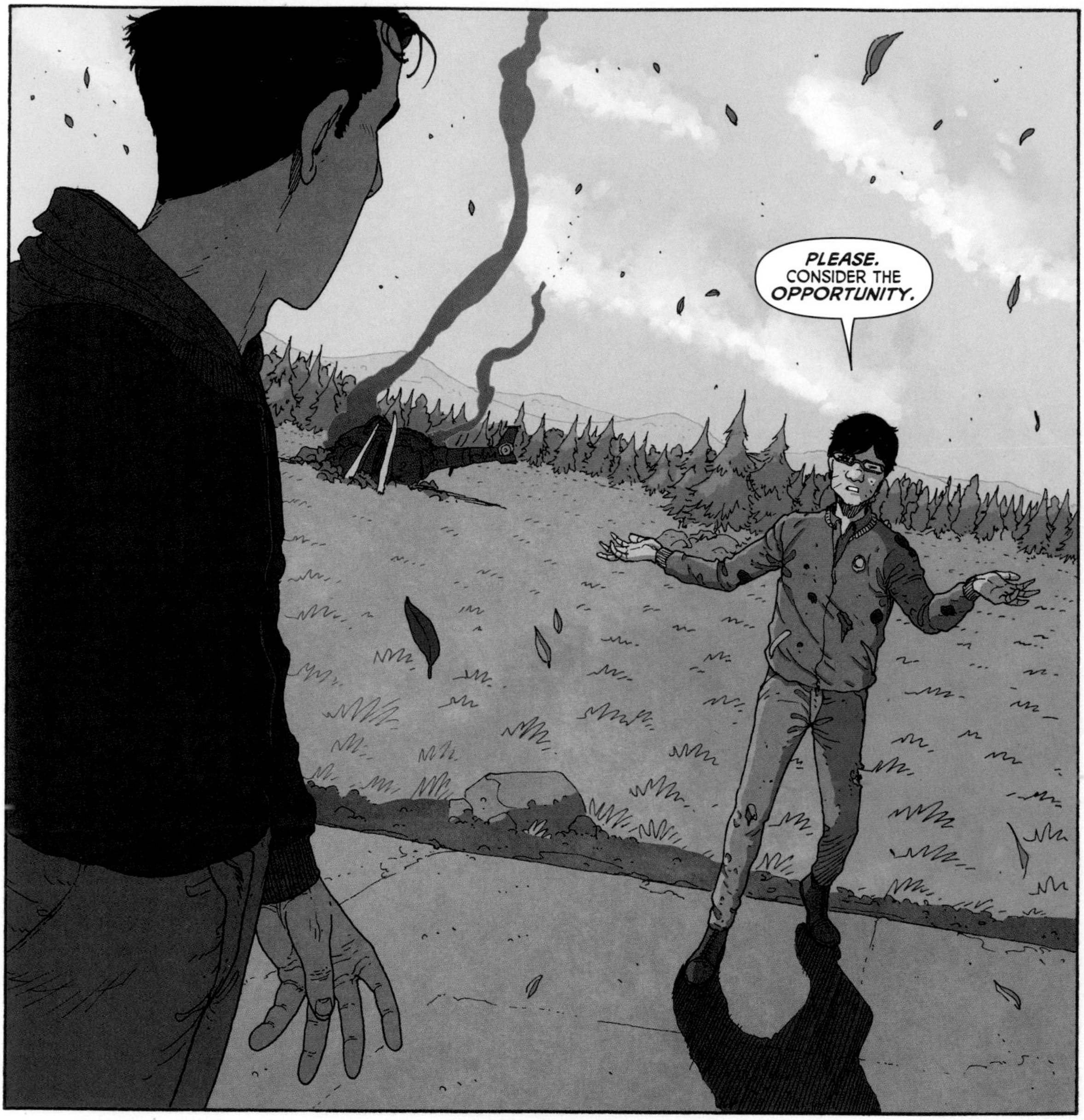
PLEASE. CONSIDER THE OPPORTUNITY.

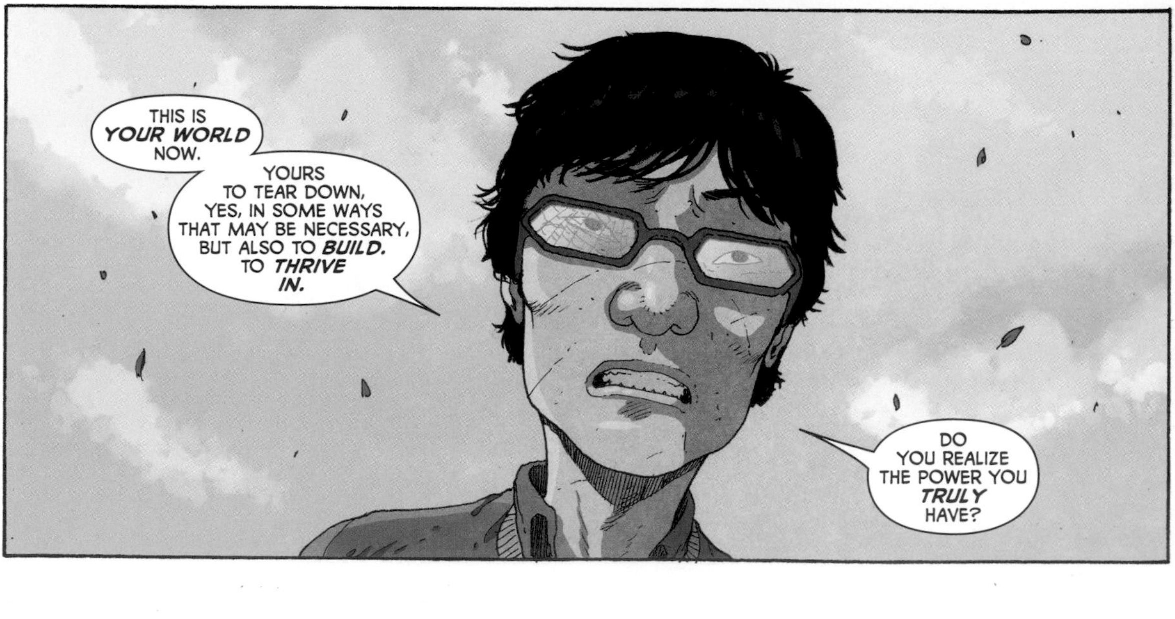
THIS IS YOUR WORLD NOW.
YOURS TO TEAR DOWN, YES, IN SOME WAYS THAT MAY BE NECESSARY, BUT ALSO TO BUILD. TO THRIVE IN.
DO YOU REALIZE THE POWER YOU TRULY HAVE?

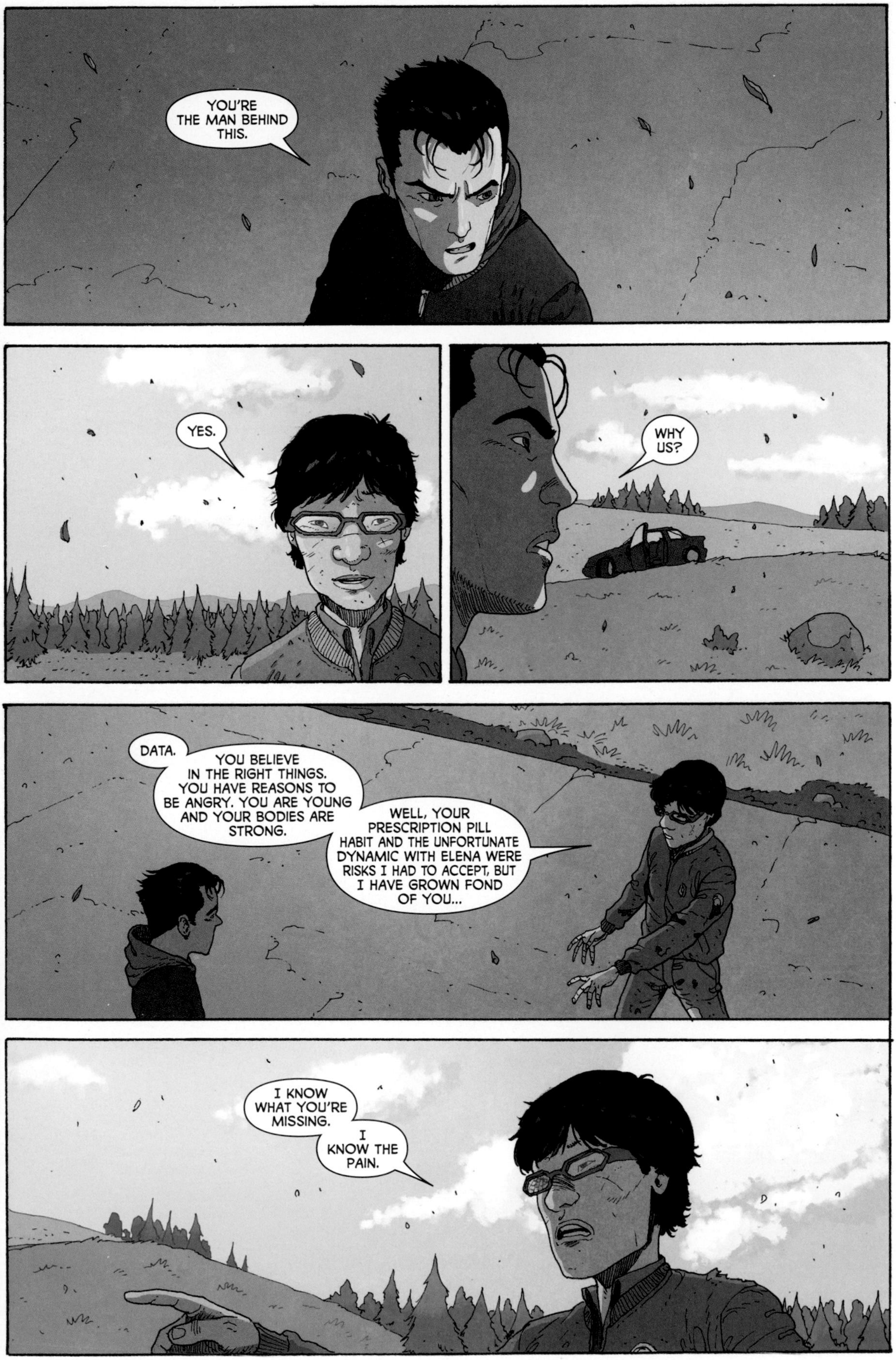
YOU'RE THE MAN BEHIND THIS.
YES.
WHY US?
DATA.
YOU BELIEVE IN THE RIGHT THINGS. YOU HAVE REASONS TO BE ANGRY. YOU ARE YOUNG AND YOUR BODIES ARE STRONG.
WELL, YOUR PRESCRIPTION PILL HABIT AND THE UNFORTUNATE DYNAMIC WITH ELENA WERE RISKS I HAD TO ACCEPT, BUT I HAVE GROWN FOND OF YOU...
I KNOW WHAT YOU'RE MISSING.
I KNOW THE PAIN.

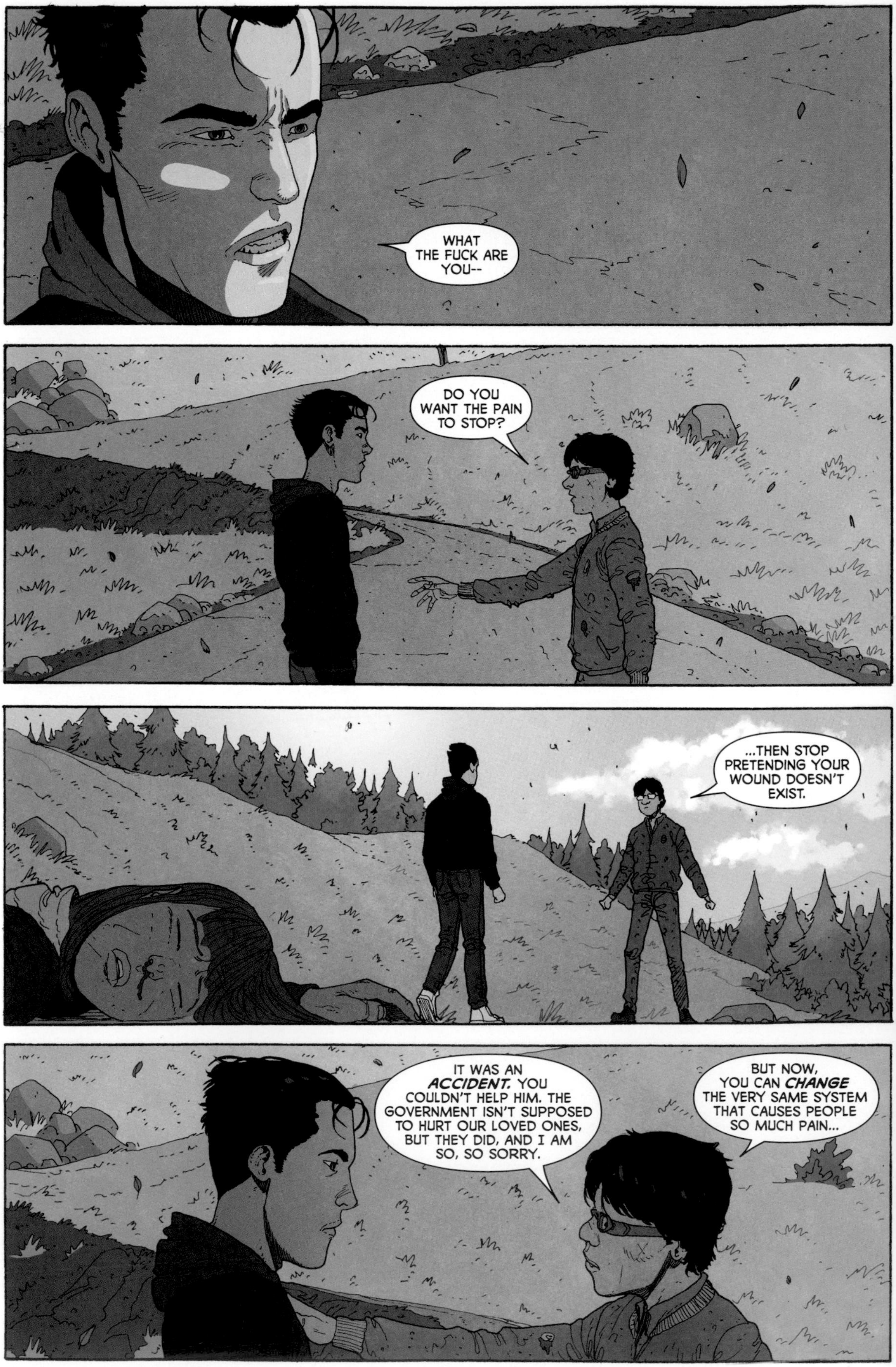
WHAT THE FUCK ARE YOU--
DO YOU WANT THE PAIN TO STOP?
...THEN STOP PRETENDING YOUR WOUND DOESN'T EXIST.
IT WAS AN ACCIDENT. YOU COULDN'T HELP HIM. THE GOVERNMENT ISN'T SUPPOSED TO HURT OUR LOVED ONES, BUT THEY DID, AND I AM SO, SO SORRY.
BUT NOW, YOU CAN CHANGE THE VERY SAME SYSTEM THAT CAUSES PEOPLE SO MUCH PAIN...

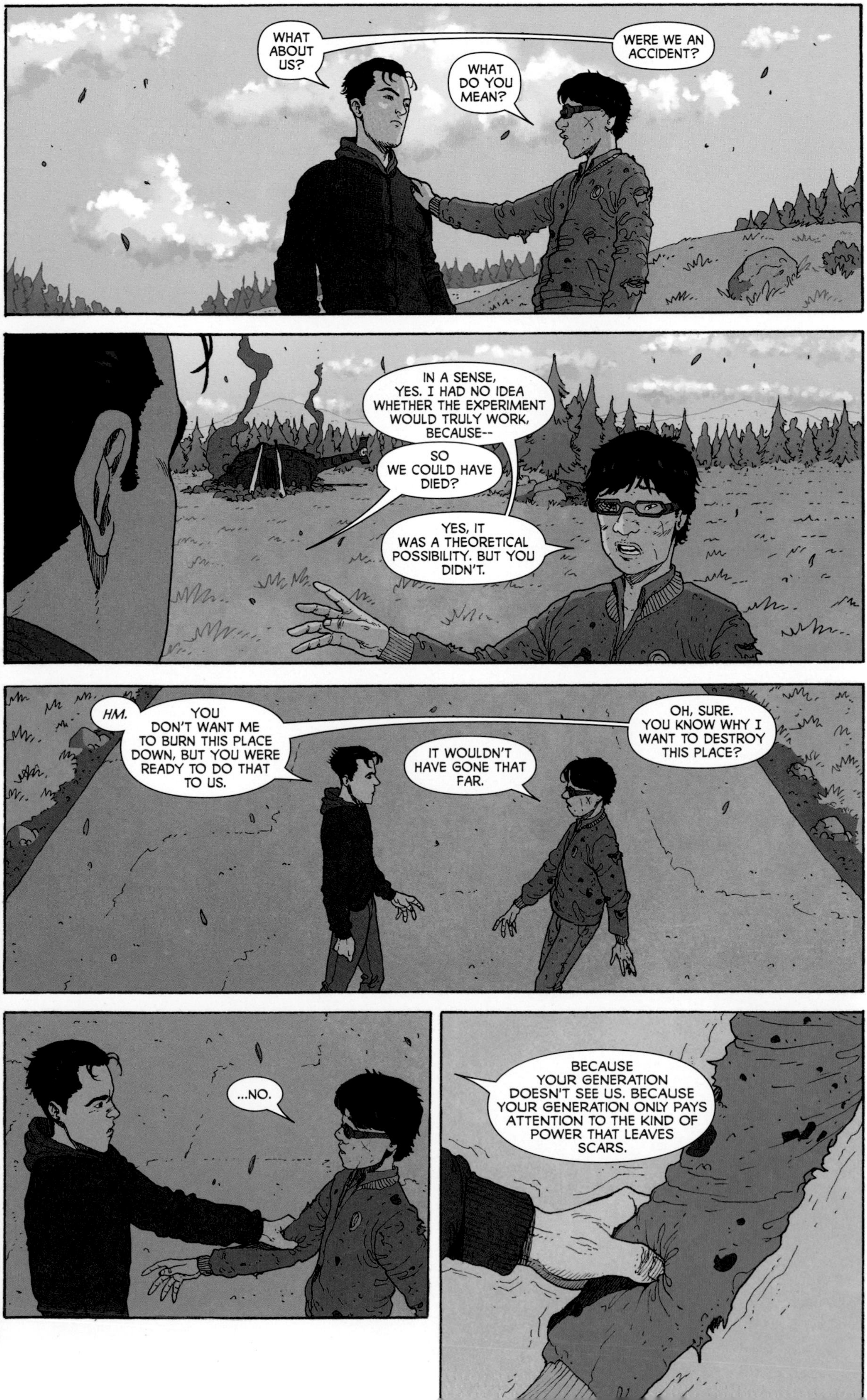
WHAT ABOUT US?
WHAT DO YOU MEAN?
WERE WE AN ACCIDENT?
IN A SENSE, YES. I HAD NO IDEA WHETHER THE EXPERIMENT WOULD TRULY WORK, BECAUSE--
SO WE COULD HAVE DIED?
YES, IT WAS A THEORETICAL POSSIBILITY. BUT YOU DIDN'T.
HM.
YOU DON'T WANT ME TO BURN THIS PLACE DOWN, BUT YOU WERE READY TO DO THAT TO US.
IT WOULDN'T HAVE GONE THAT FAR.
OH, SURE. YOU KNOW WHY I WANT TO DESTROY THIS PLACE?
...NO.
BECAUSE YOUR GENERATION DOESN'T SEE US. BECAUSE YOUR GENERATION ONLY PAYS ATTENTION TO THE KIND OF POWER THAT LEAVES SCARS.

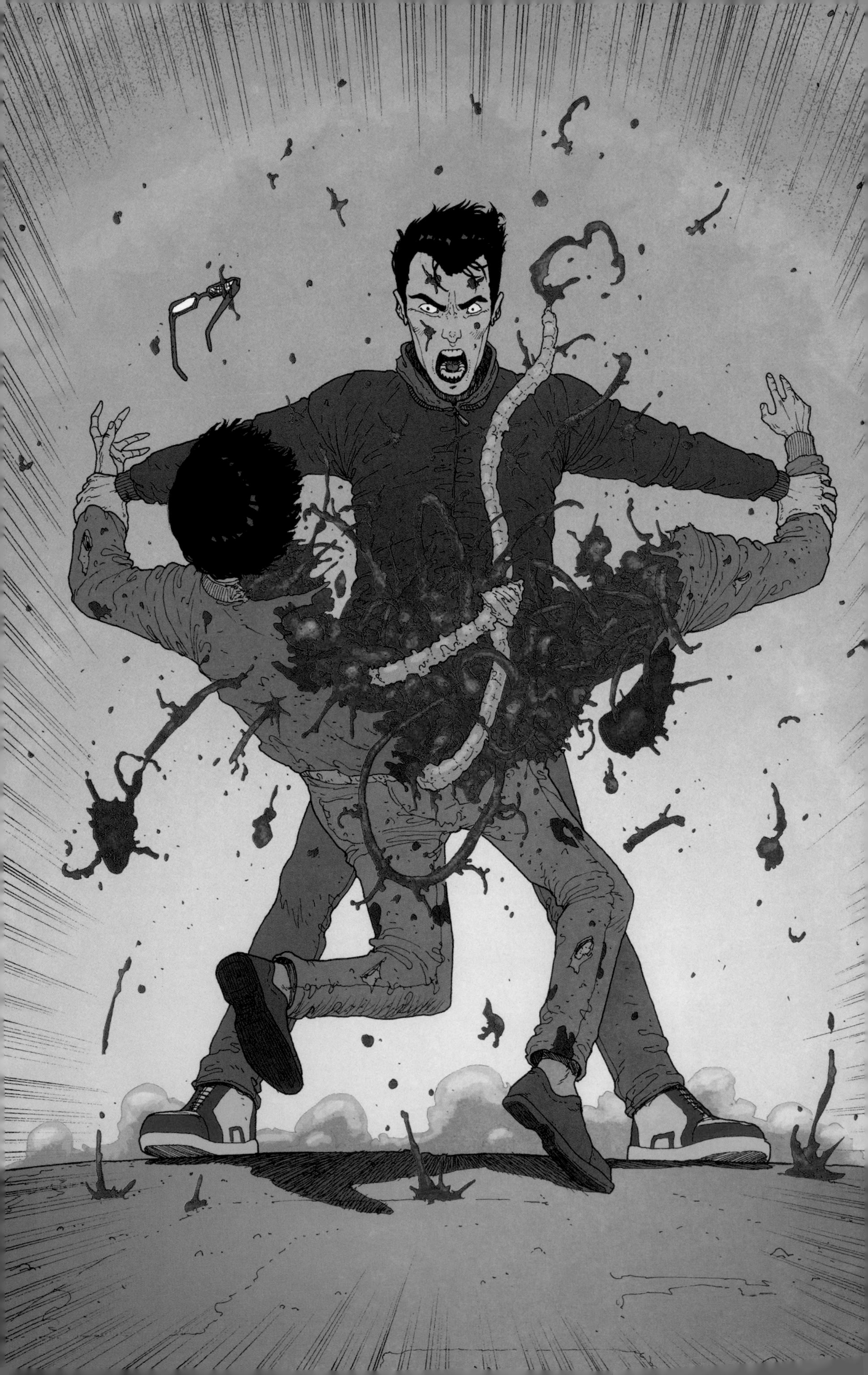

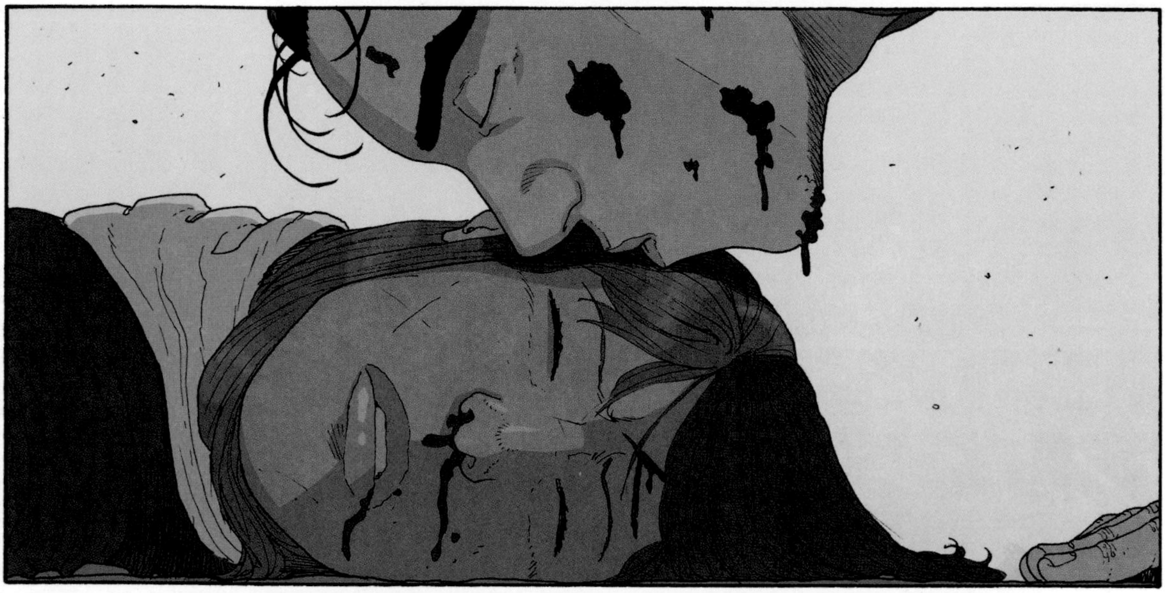

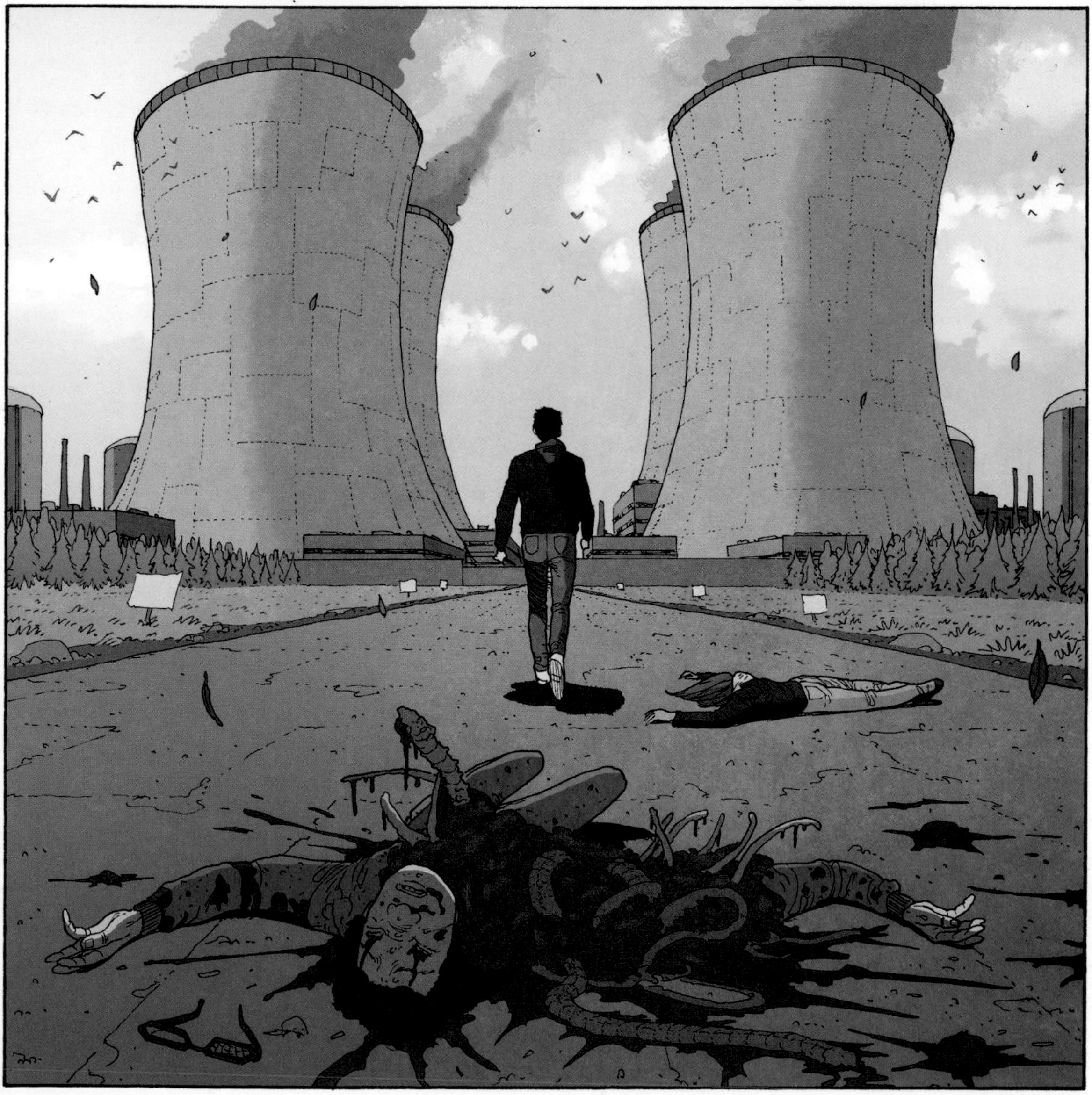

REFUSE DREAM RISE

REFUSE DREAM RISE

REFUSE DREAM RISE

REFUSE DREAM RISE

REFUSE DREAM RISE

REFUSE DREAM RISE

REFUSE DREAM RISE

REFUSE DREAM RISE

REFUSE DREAM RISE

REFUSE DREAM RISE

REFUSE DREAM RISE

REFUSE DREAM RISE

REFUSE DREAM RISE

REFUSE DREAM RISE

REFUSE DREAM RISE

REFUSE DREAM RISE

REFUSE DREAM RISE

REFUSE DREAM RISE

REFUSE DREAM RISE

REFUSE DREAM RISE

REFUSE DREAM RISE

CHAPTER FIVE

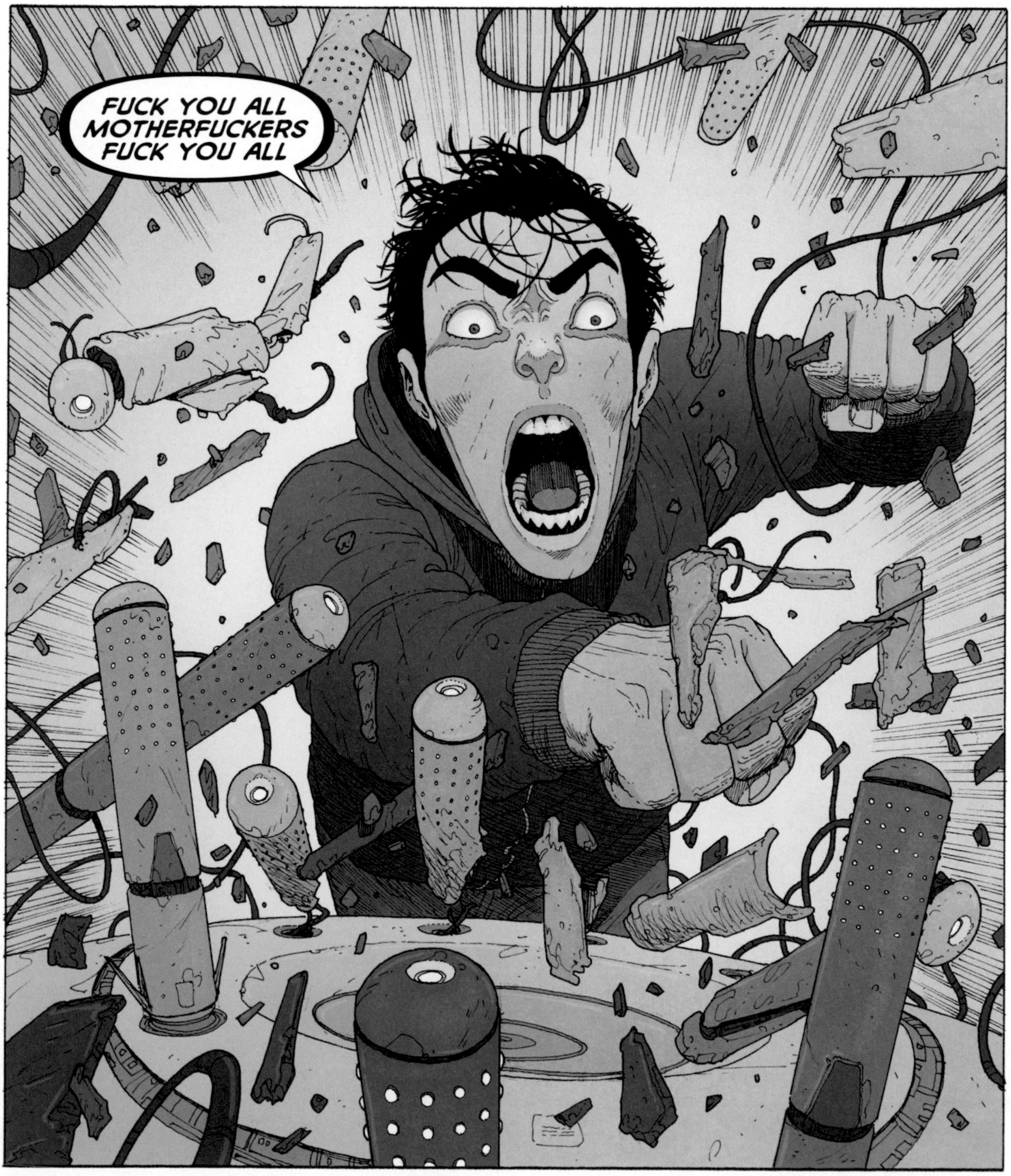
FUCK YOU ALL
MOTHERFUCKERS
FUCK YOU ALL

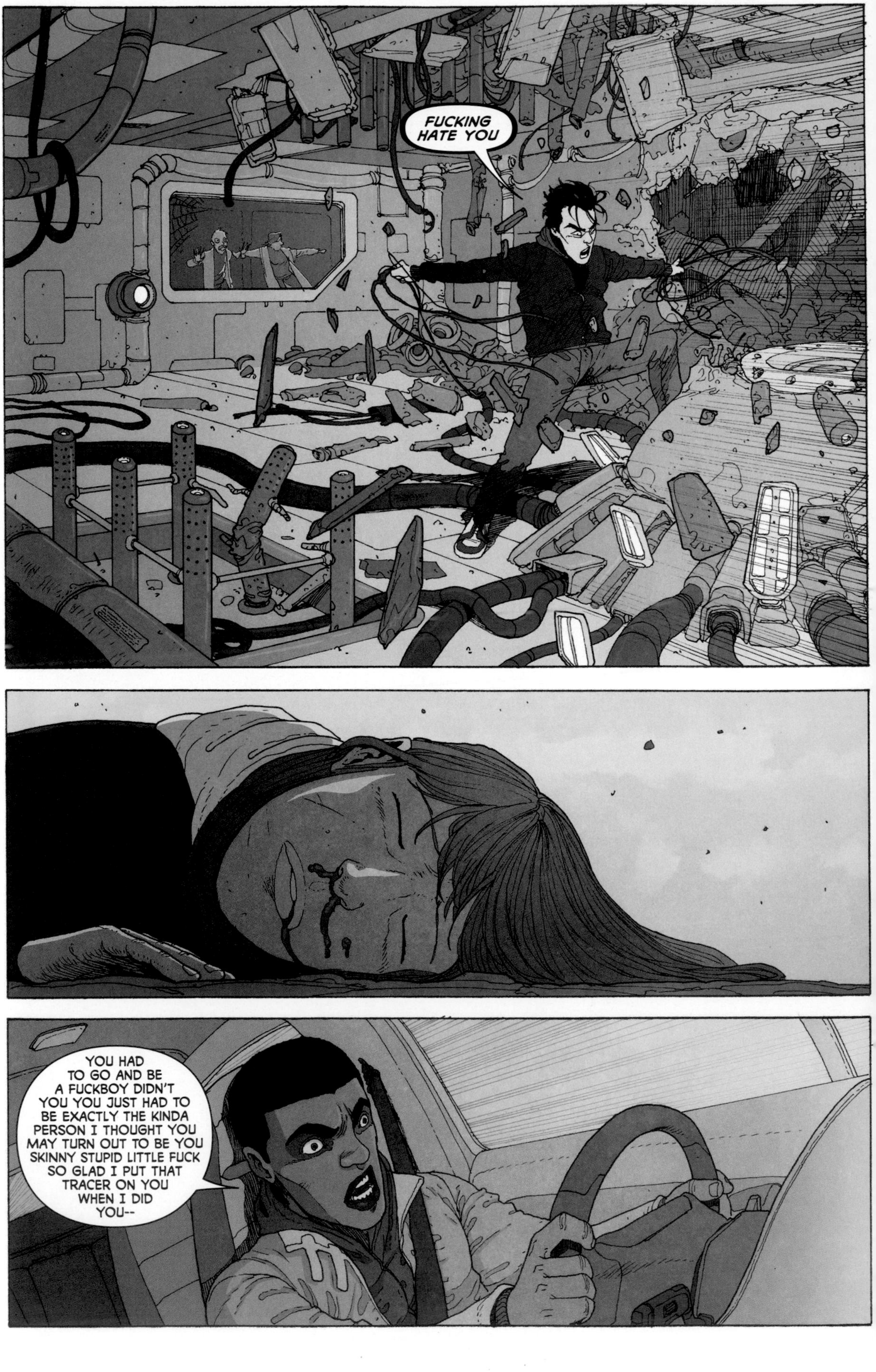
FUCKING HATE YOU
YOU HAD TO GO AND BE A FUCKBOY DIDN'T YOU YOU JUST HAD TO BE EXACTLY THE KINDA PERSON I THOUGHT YOU MAY TURN OUT TO BE YOU SKINNY STUPID LITTLE FUCK SO GLAD I PUT THAT TRACER ON YOU WHEN I DID YOU--

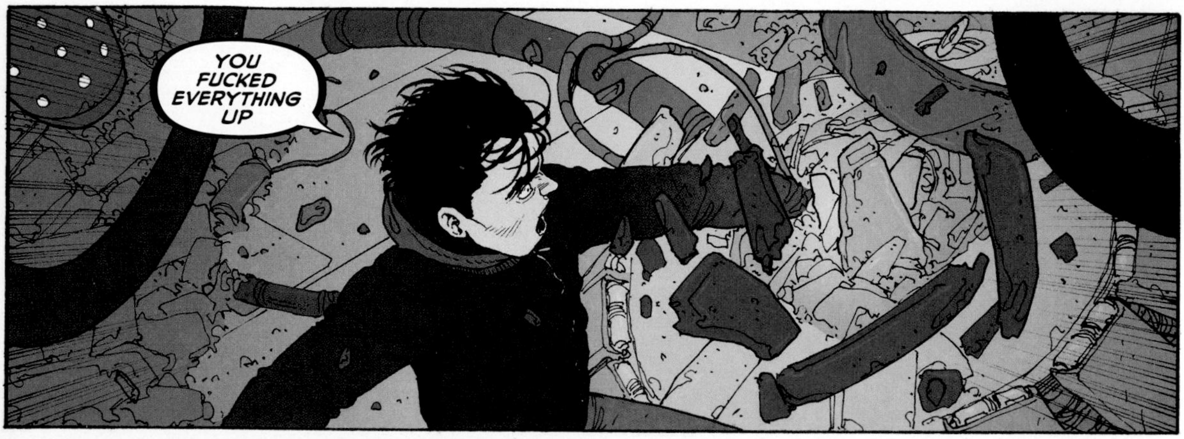
YOU FUCKED EVERYTHING UP
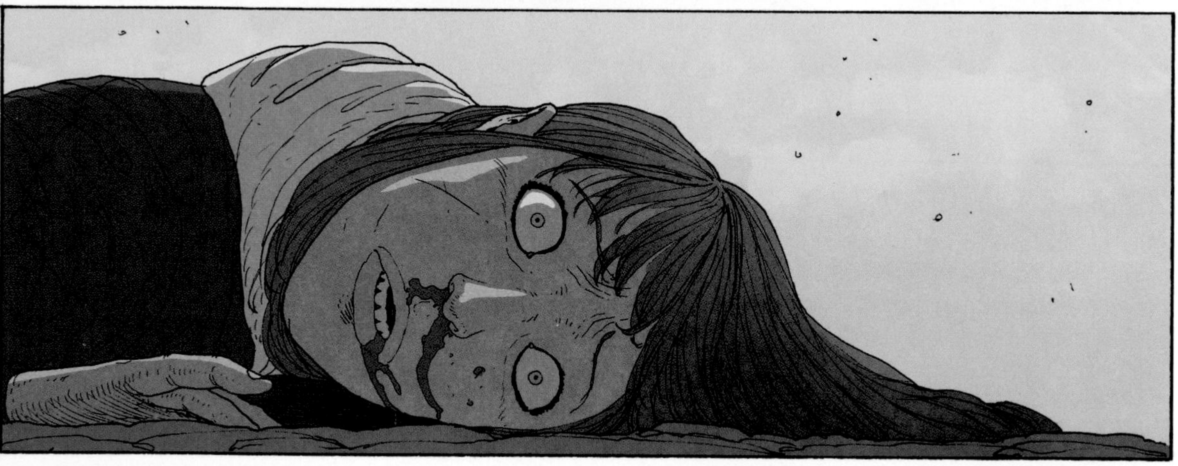
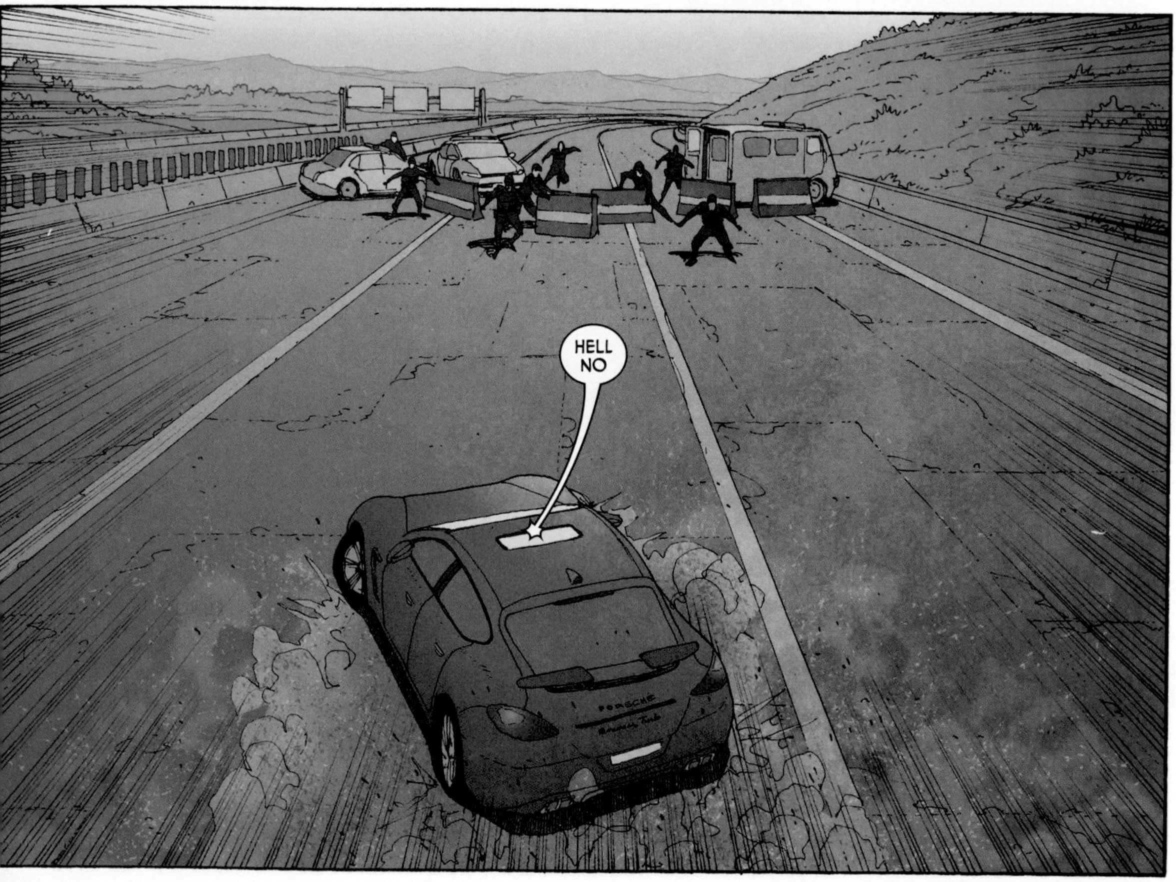
HELL NO

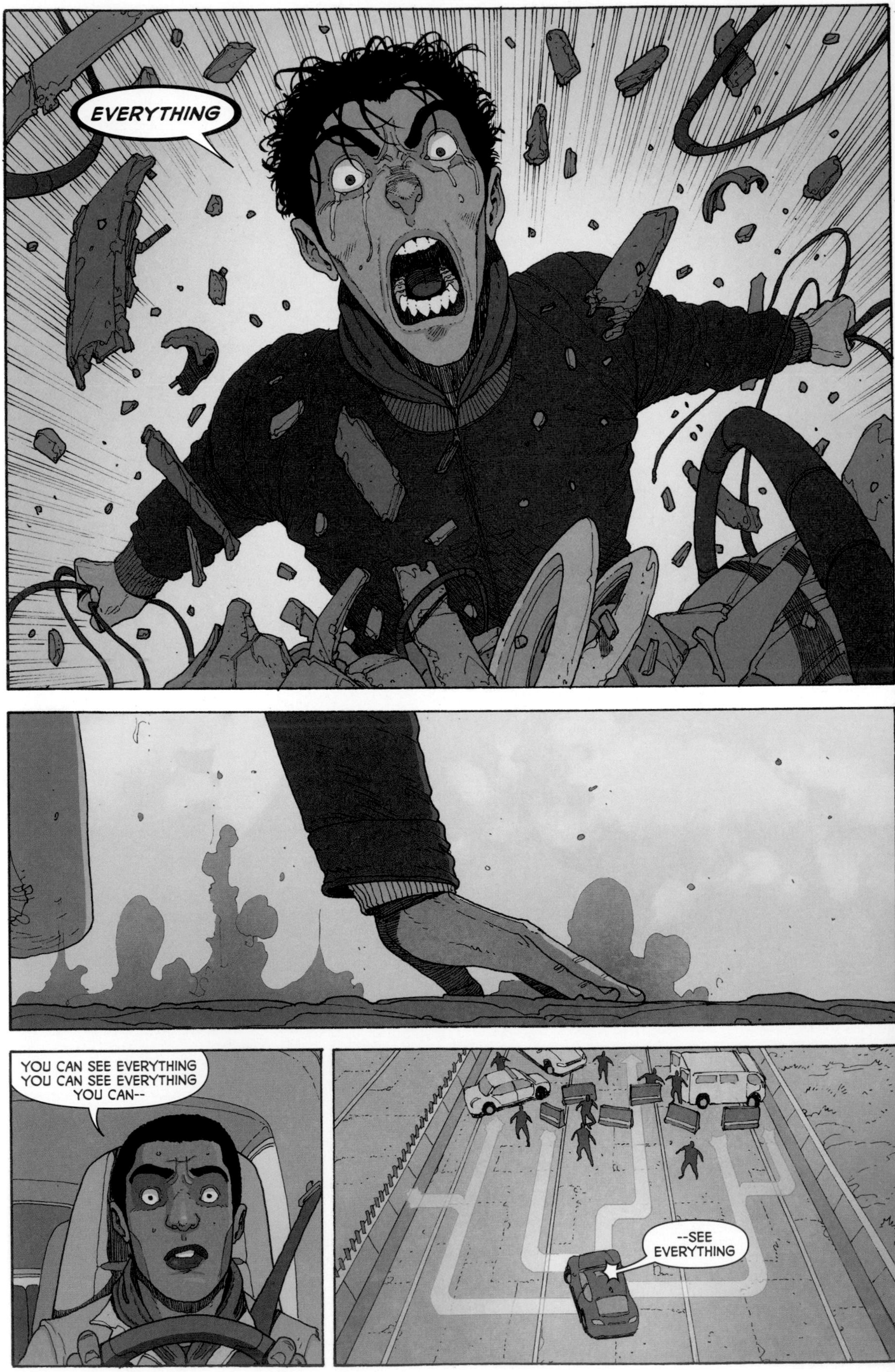
EVERYTHING
YOU CAN SEE EVERYTHING YOU CAN SEE EVERYTHING YOU CAN--
--SEE EVERYTHING

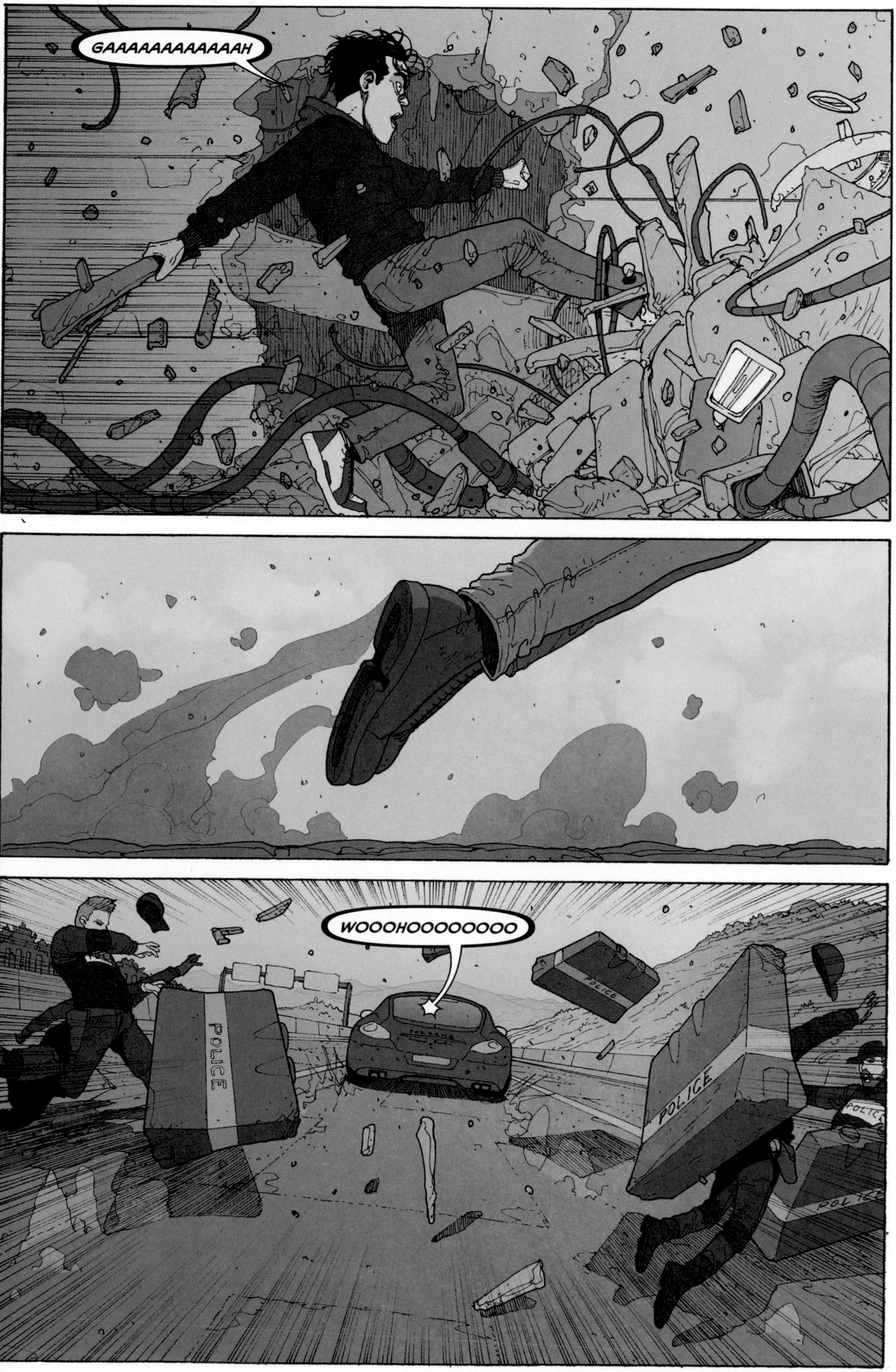
GAAAAAAAAAAAAH
WOOOHOOOOOOOO
POLICE
POLICE
POLICE

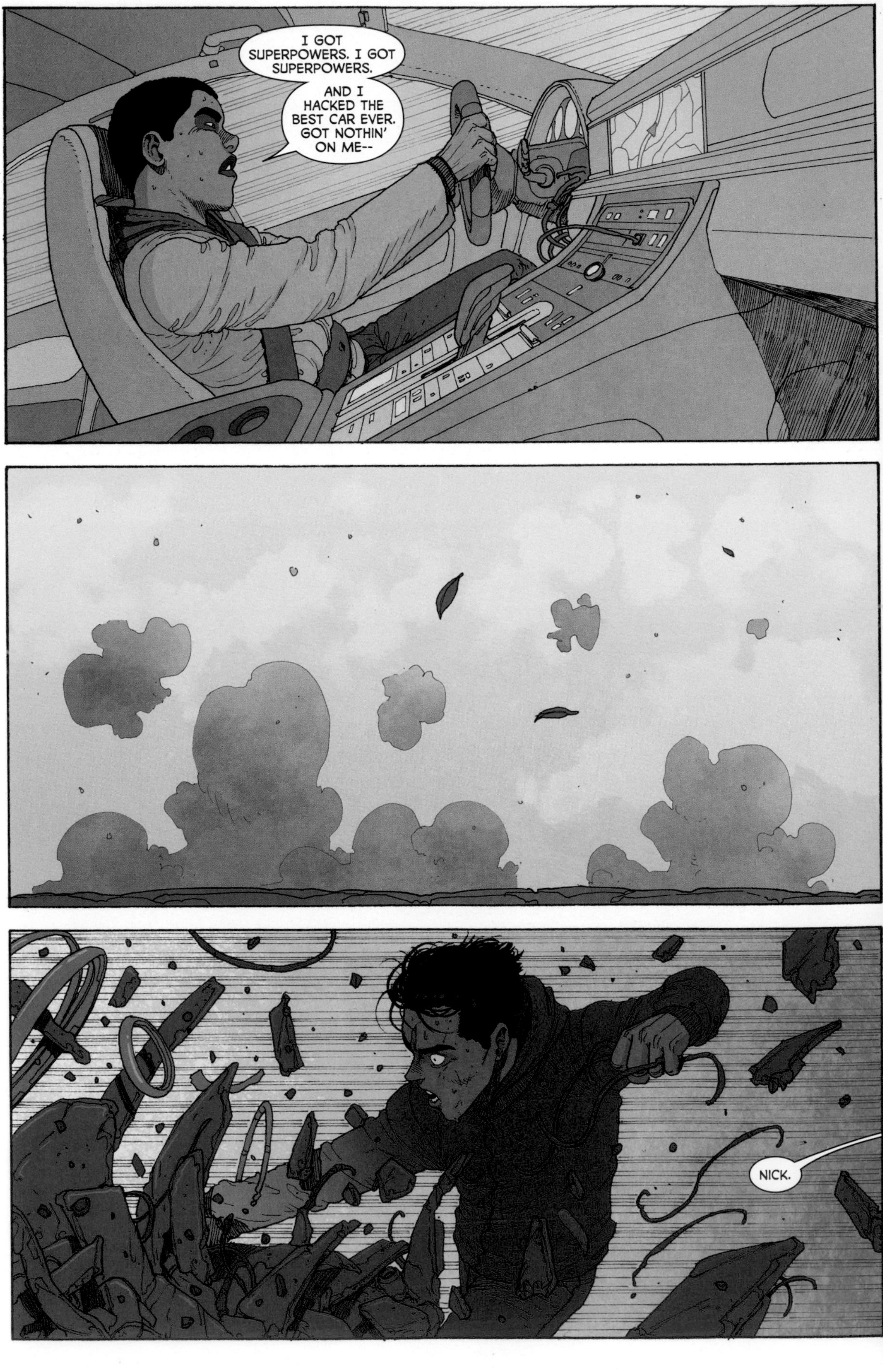
I GOT SUPERPOWERS. I GOT SUPERPOWERS.
AND I HACKED THE BEST CAR EVER. GOT NOTHIN' ON ME--
NICK.

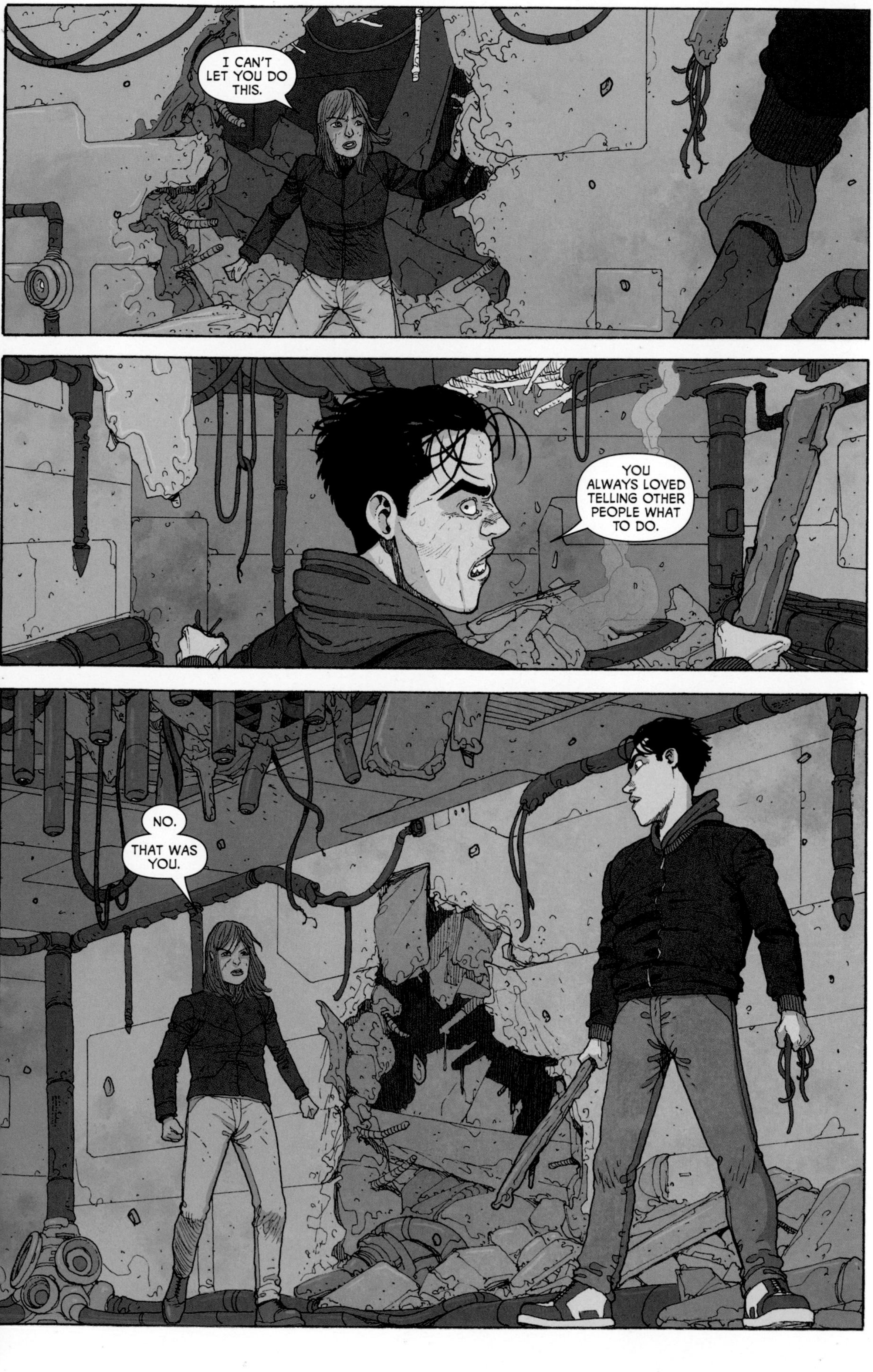
I CAN'T LET YOU DO THIS.
YOU ALWAYS LOVED TELLING OTHER PEOPLE WHAT TO DO.
NO.
THAT WAS YOU.

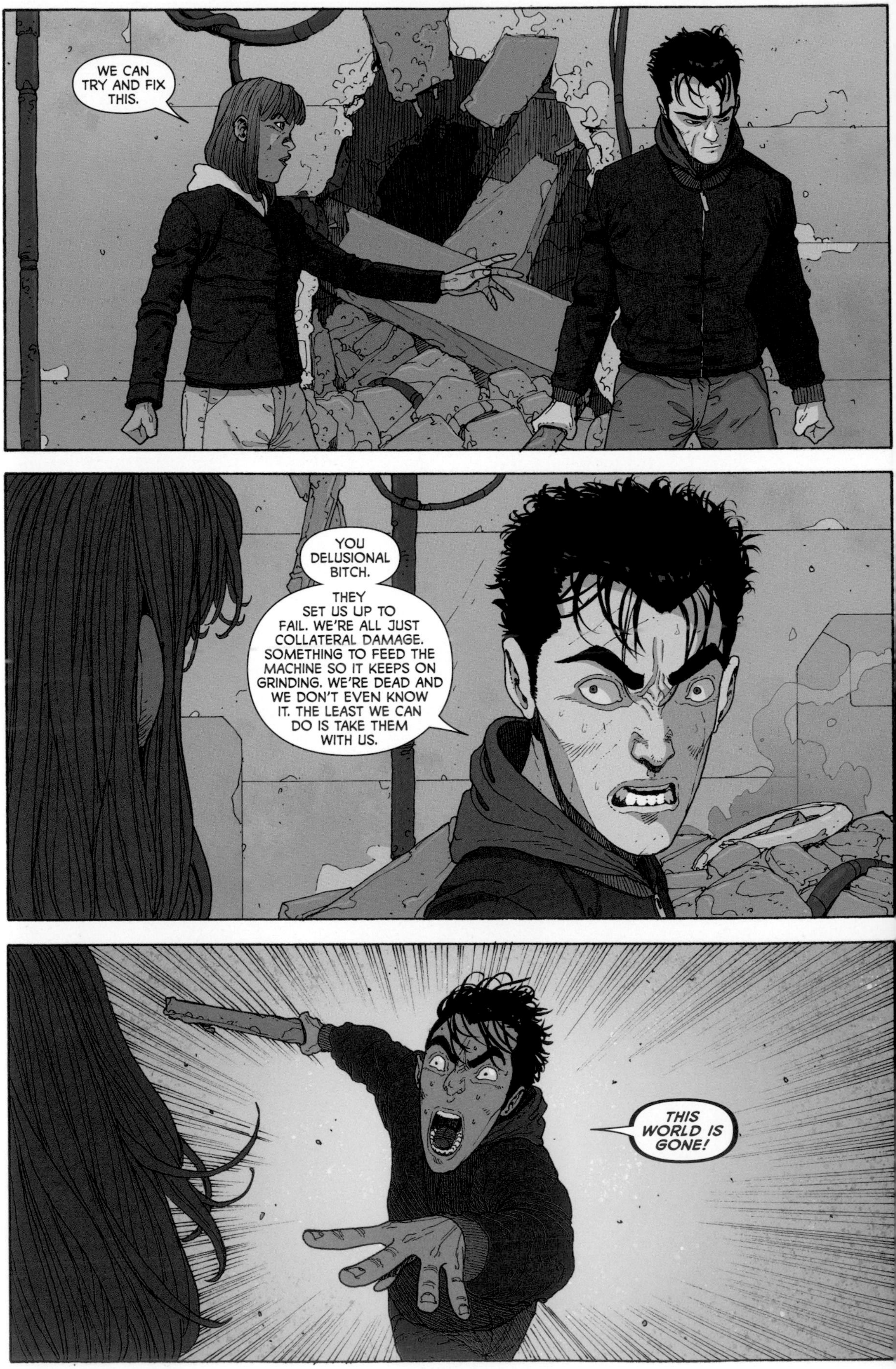
WE CAN TRY AND FIX THIS.
YOU DELUSIONAL BITCH.
THEY SET US UP TO FAIL. WE'RE ALL JUST COLLATERAL DAMAGE. SOMETHING TO FEED THE MACHINE SO IT KEEPS ON GRINDING. WE'RE DEAD AND WE DON'T EVEN KNOW IT. THE LEAST WE CAN DO IS TAKE THEM WITH US.
THIS WORLD IS GONE!

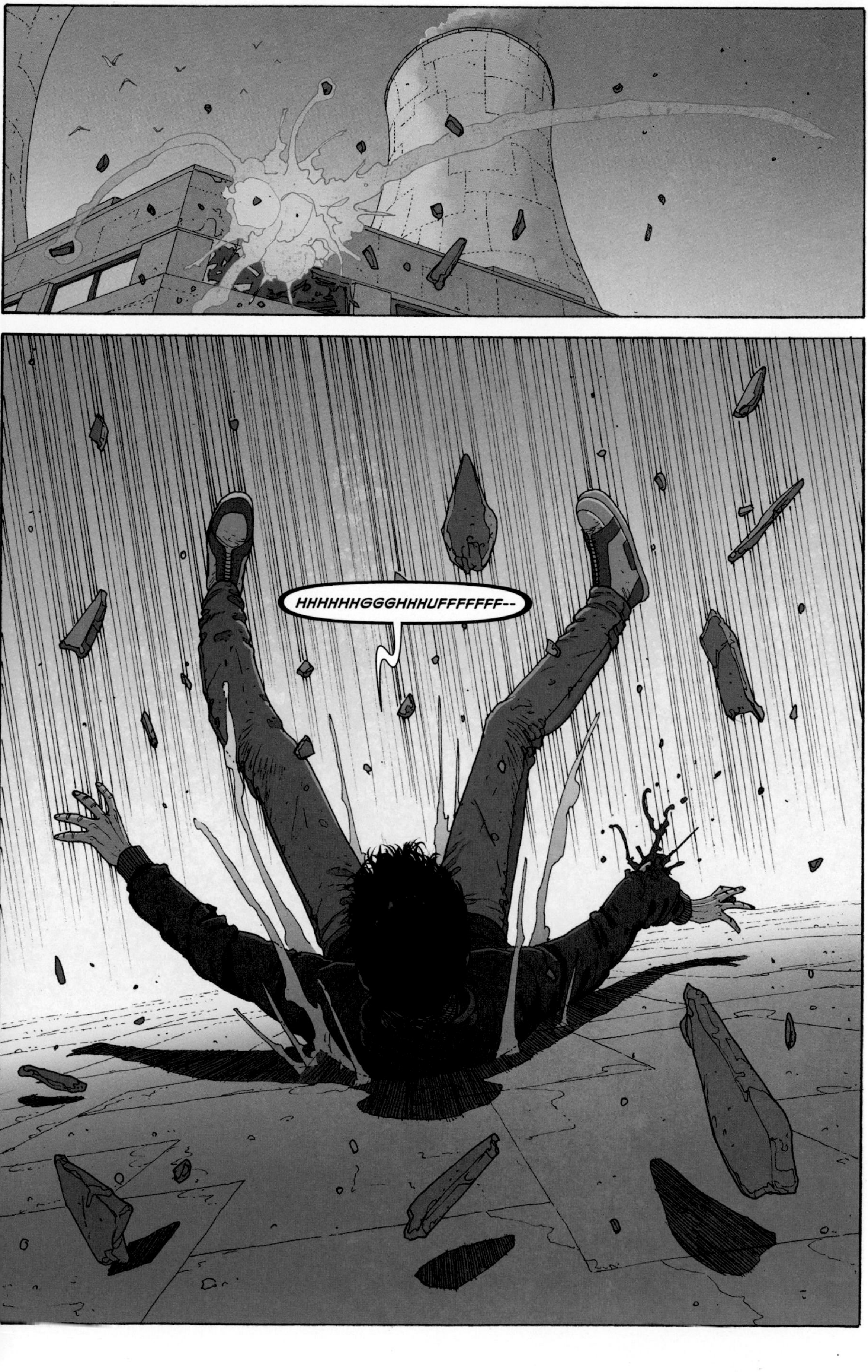
HHHHHHGGGHHHUFFFFFFF--

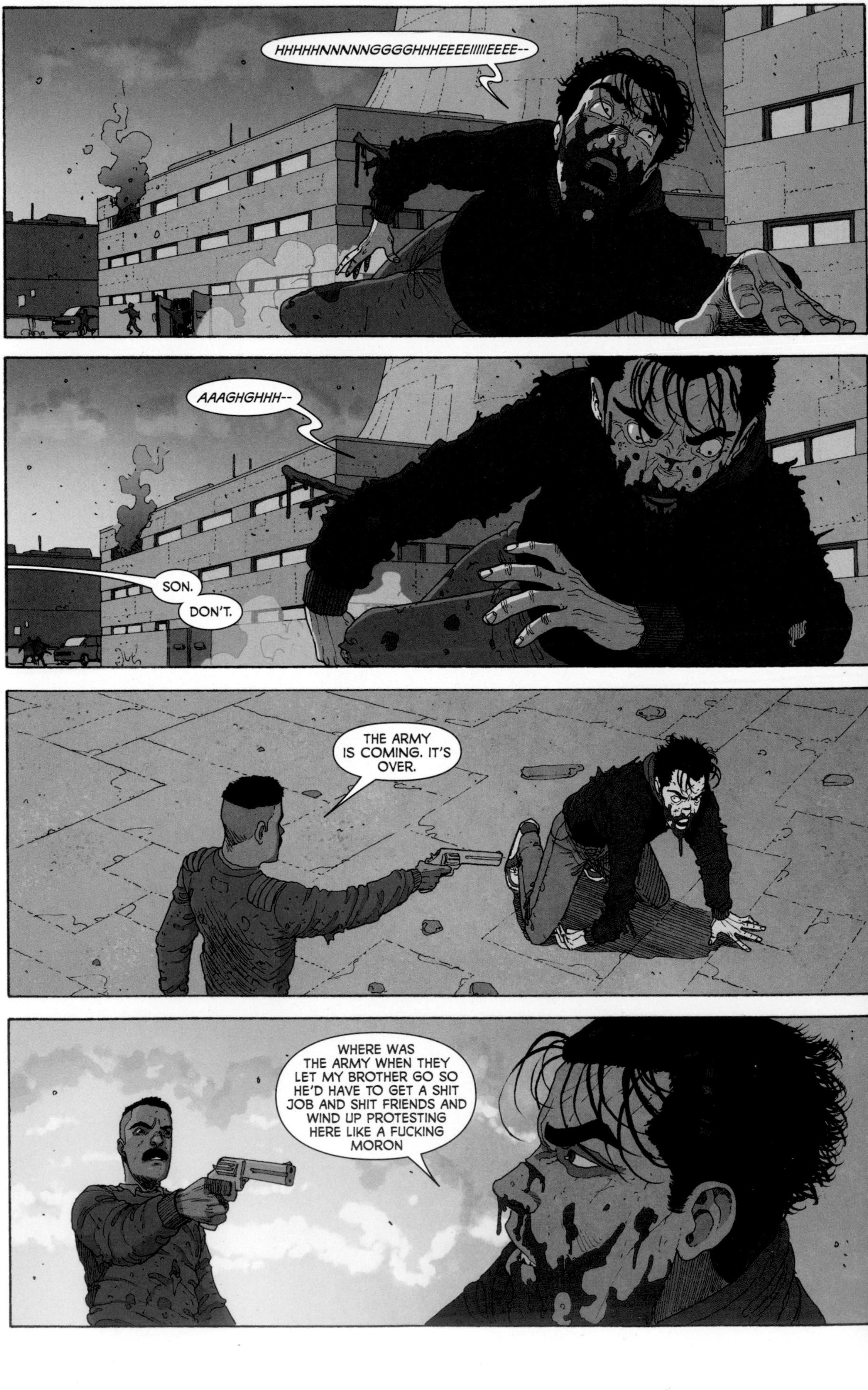
HHHHHNNNNNGGGGHHHEEEEIIIIIIEEEE--
AAAGHGHHH--
SON.
DON'T.
THE ARMY IS COMING. IT'S OVER.
WHERE WAS THE ARMY WHEN THEY LET MY BROTHER GO SO HE'D HAVE TO GET A SHIT JOB AND SHIT FRIENDS AND WIND UP PROTESTING HERE LIKE A FUCKING MORON

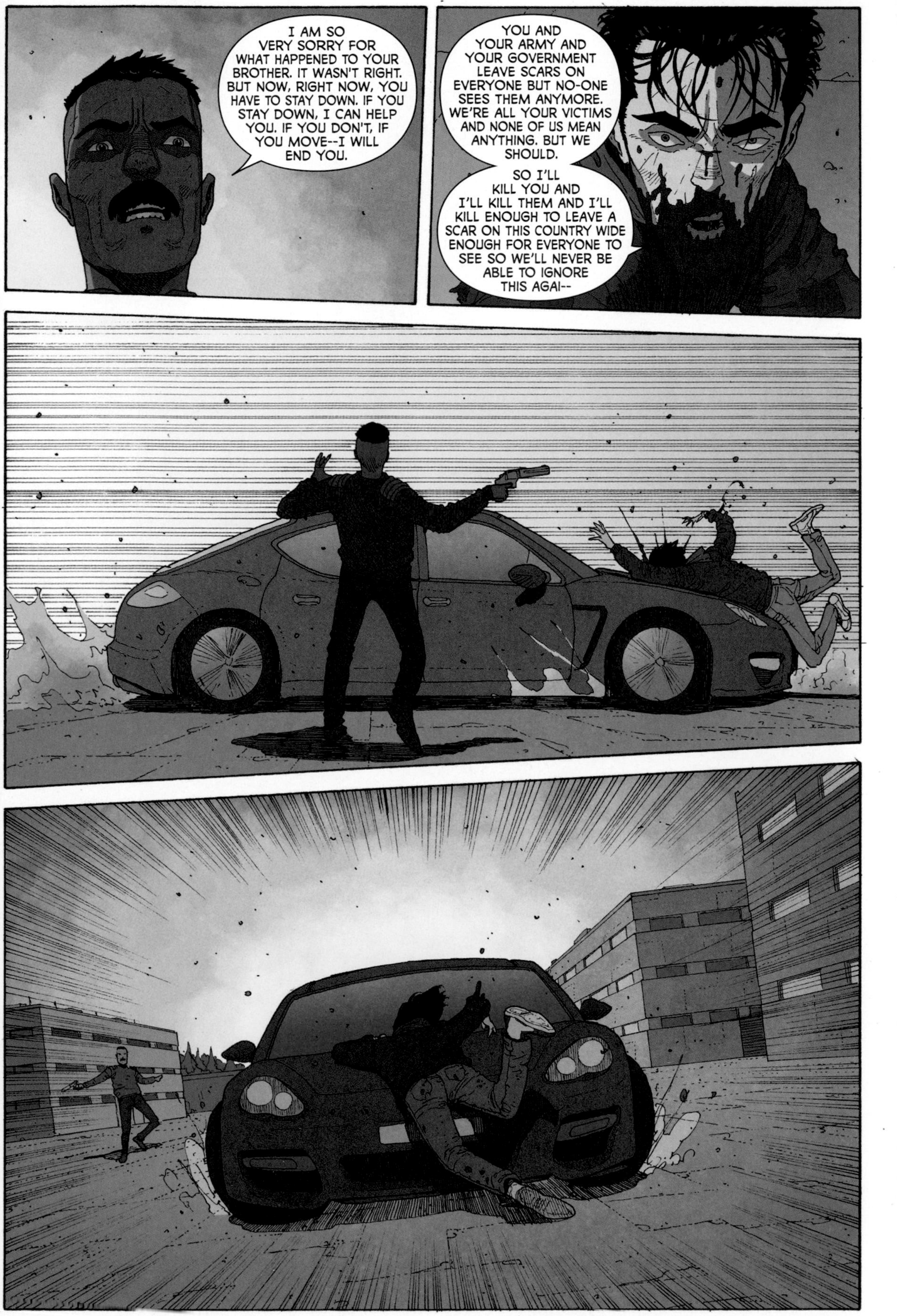
I AM SO VERY SORRY FOR WHAT HAPPENED TO YOUR BROTHER. IT WASN'T RIGHT. BUT NOW, RIGHT NOW, YOU HAVE TO STAY DOWN. IF YOU STAY DOWN, I CAN HELP YOU. IF YOU DON'T, IF YOU MOVE--I WILL END YOU.
YOU AND YOUR ARMY AND YOUR GOVERNMENT LEAVE SCARS ON EVERYONE BUT NO-ONE SEES THEM ANYMORE. WE'RE ALL YOUR VICTIMS AND NONE OF US MEAN ANYTHING. BUT WE SHOULD.
SO I'LL KILL YOU AND I'LL KILL THEM AND I'LL KILL ENOUGH TO LEAVE A SCAR ON THIS COUNTRY WIDE ENOUGH FOR EVERYONE TO SEE SO WE'LL NEVER BE ABLE TO IGNORE THIS AGAI--

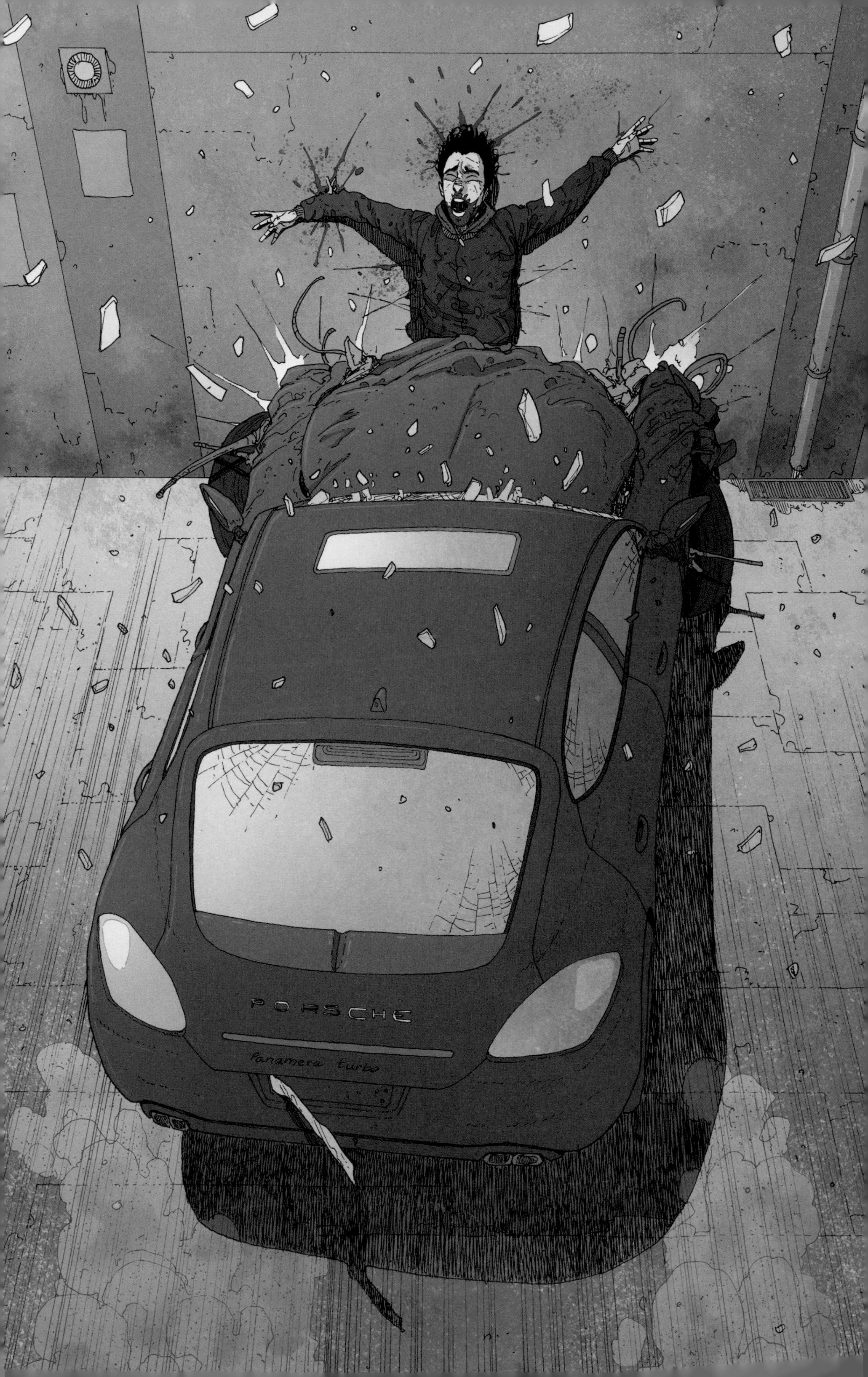
PORSCHE
Panamera turbo

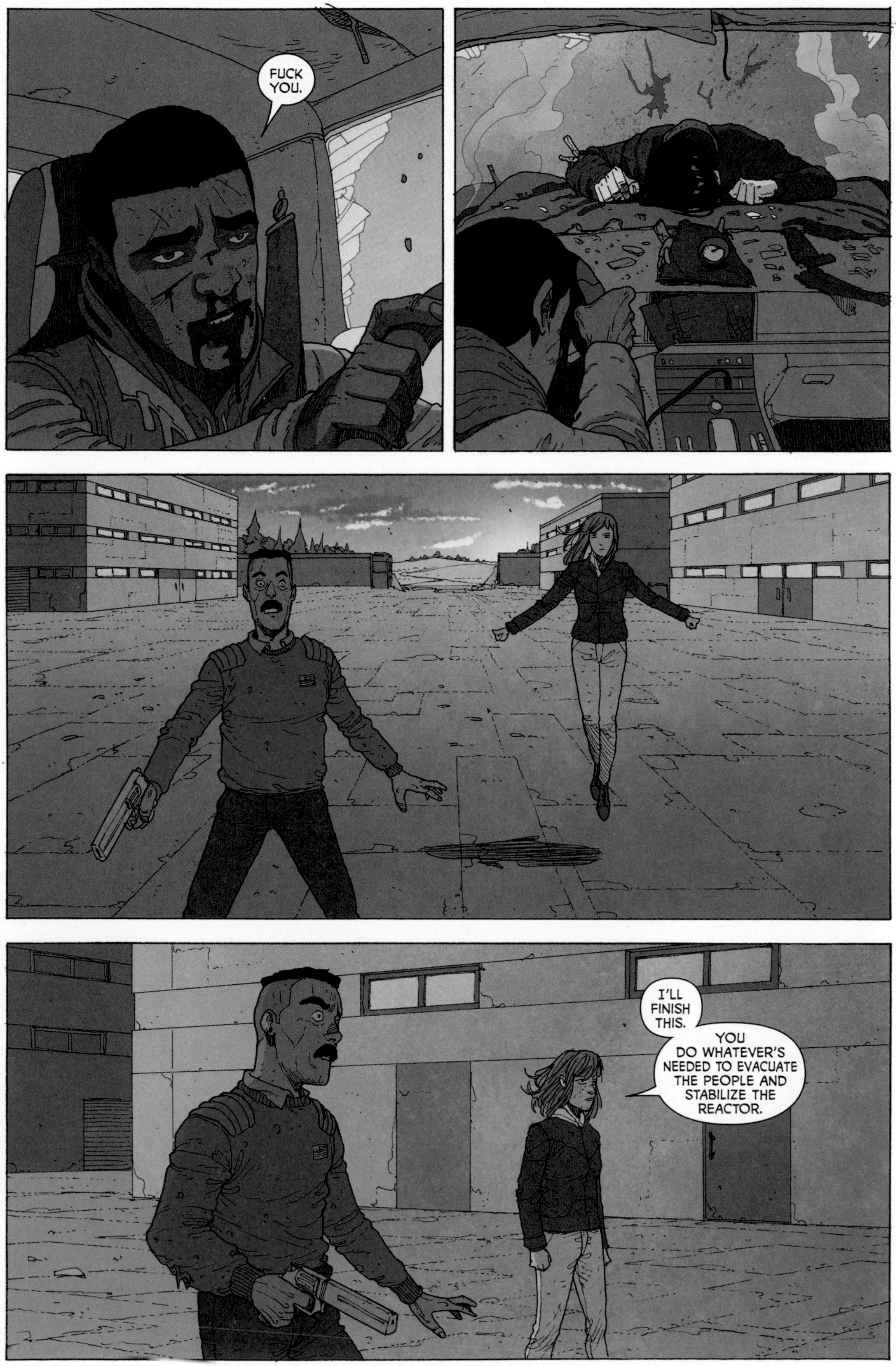
FUCK YOU.
I'LL FINISH THIS.
YOU DO WHATEVER'S NEEDED TO EVACUATE THE PEOPLE AND STABILIZE THE REACTOR.

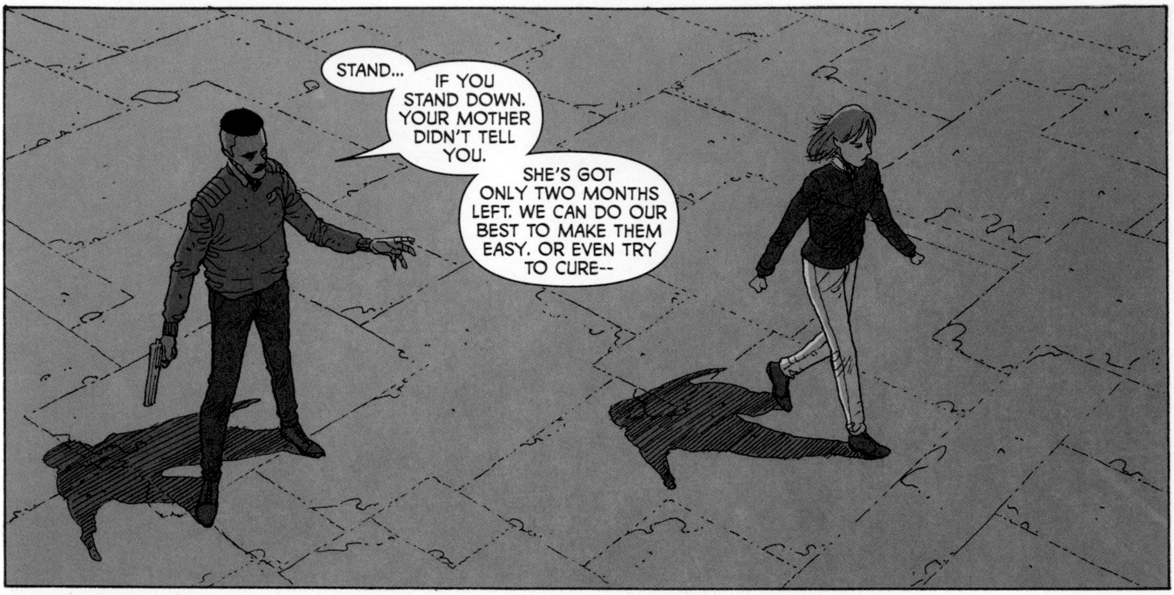
STAND...
IF YOU STAND DOWN. YOUR MOTHER DIDN'T TELL YOU.
SHE'S GOT ONLY TWO MONTHS LEFT. WE CAN DO OUR BEST TO MAKE THEM EASY. OR EVEN TRY TO CURE--

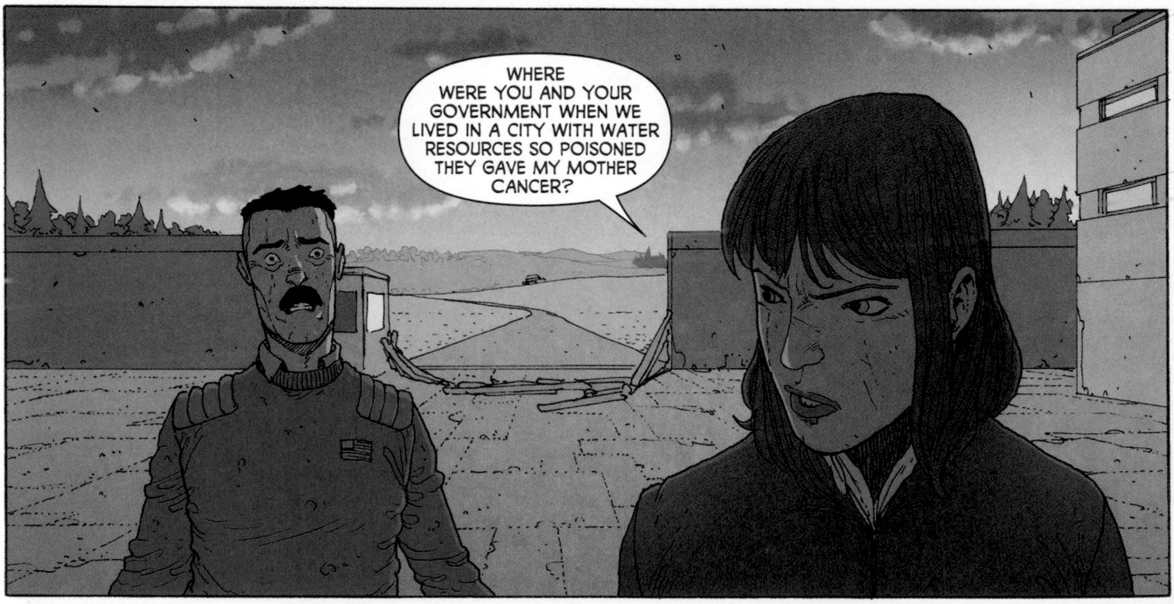
WHERE WERE YOU AND YOUR GOVERNMENT WHEN WE LIVED IN A CITY WITH WATER RESOURCES SO POISONED THEY GAVE MY MOTHER CANCER?

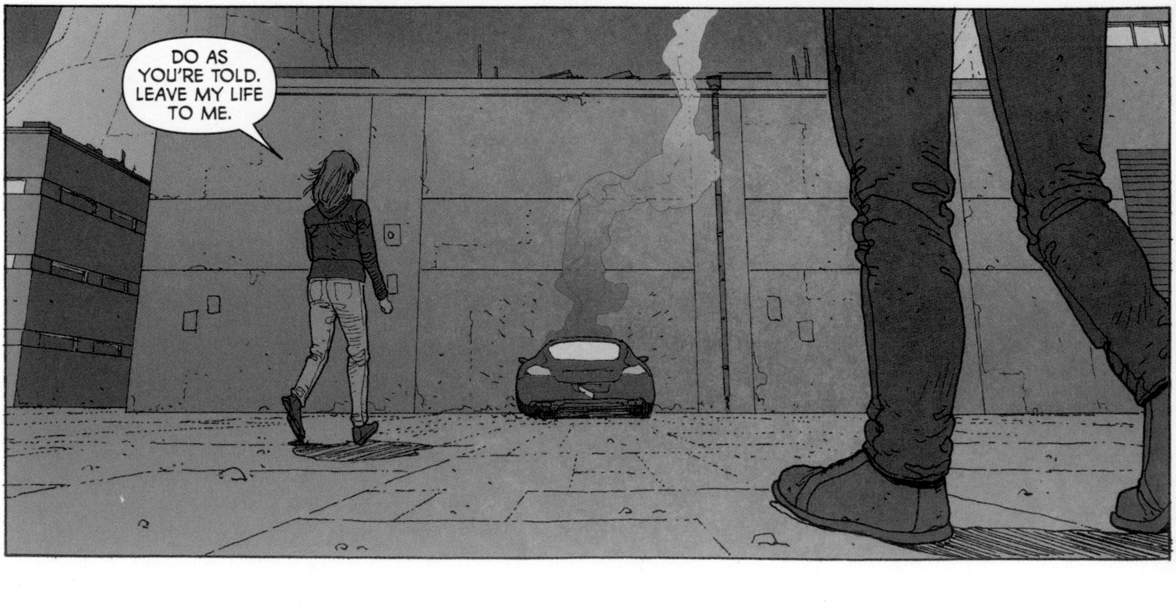
DO AS YOU'RE TOLD. LEAVE MY LIFE TO ME.

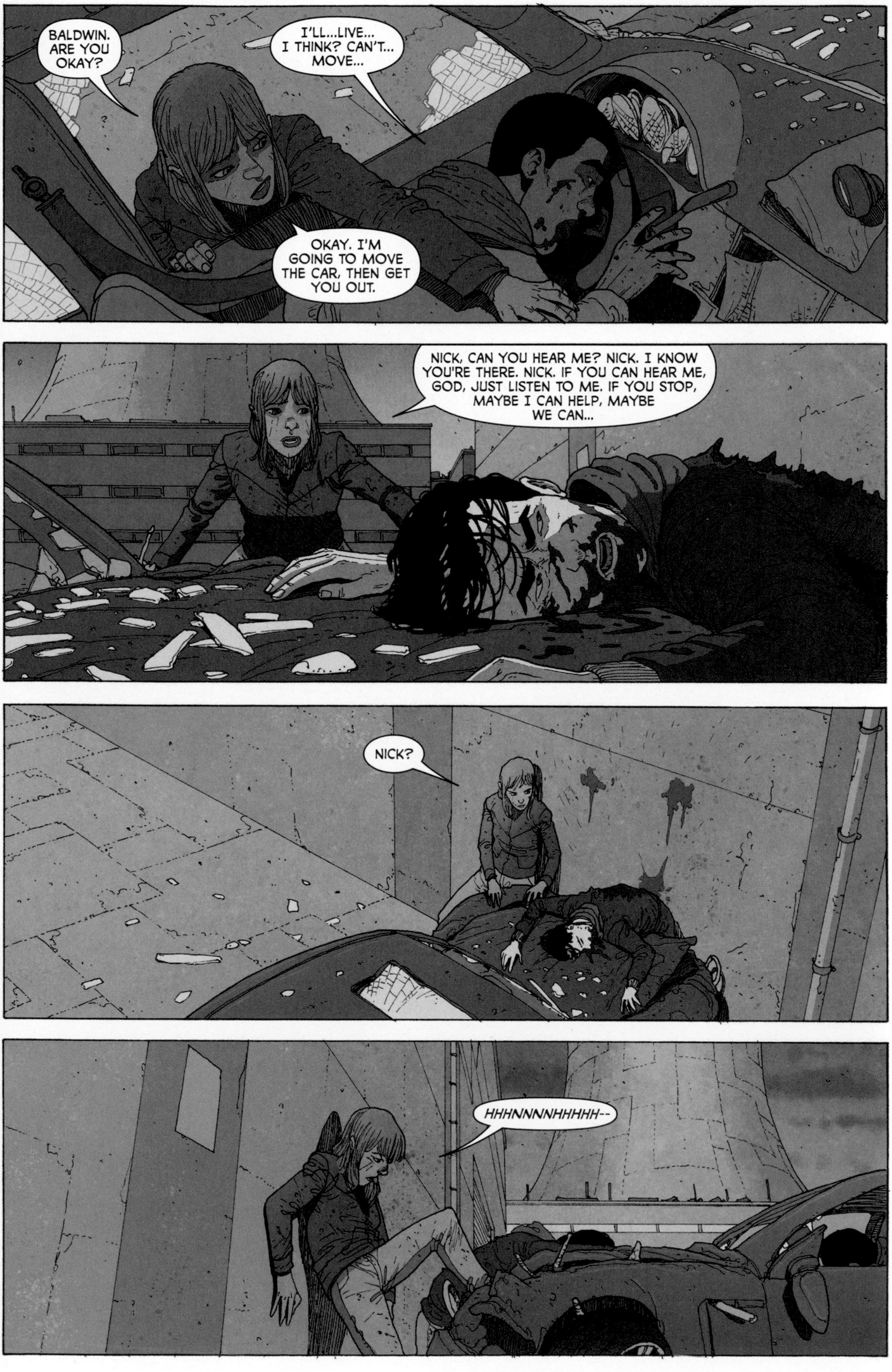
BALDWIN. ARE YOU OKAY?
I'LL...LIVE... I THINK? CAN'T... MOVE...
OKAY. I'M GOING TO MOVE THE CAR, THEN GET YOU OUT.
NICK, CAN YOU HEAR ME? NICK. I KNOW YOU'RE THERE. NICK. IF YOU CAN HEAR ME, GOD, JUST LISTEN TO ME. IF YOU STOP, MAYBE I CAN HELP, MAYBE WE CAN...
NICK?
HHHNNNNHHHHH--

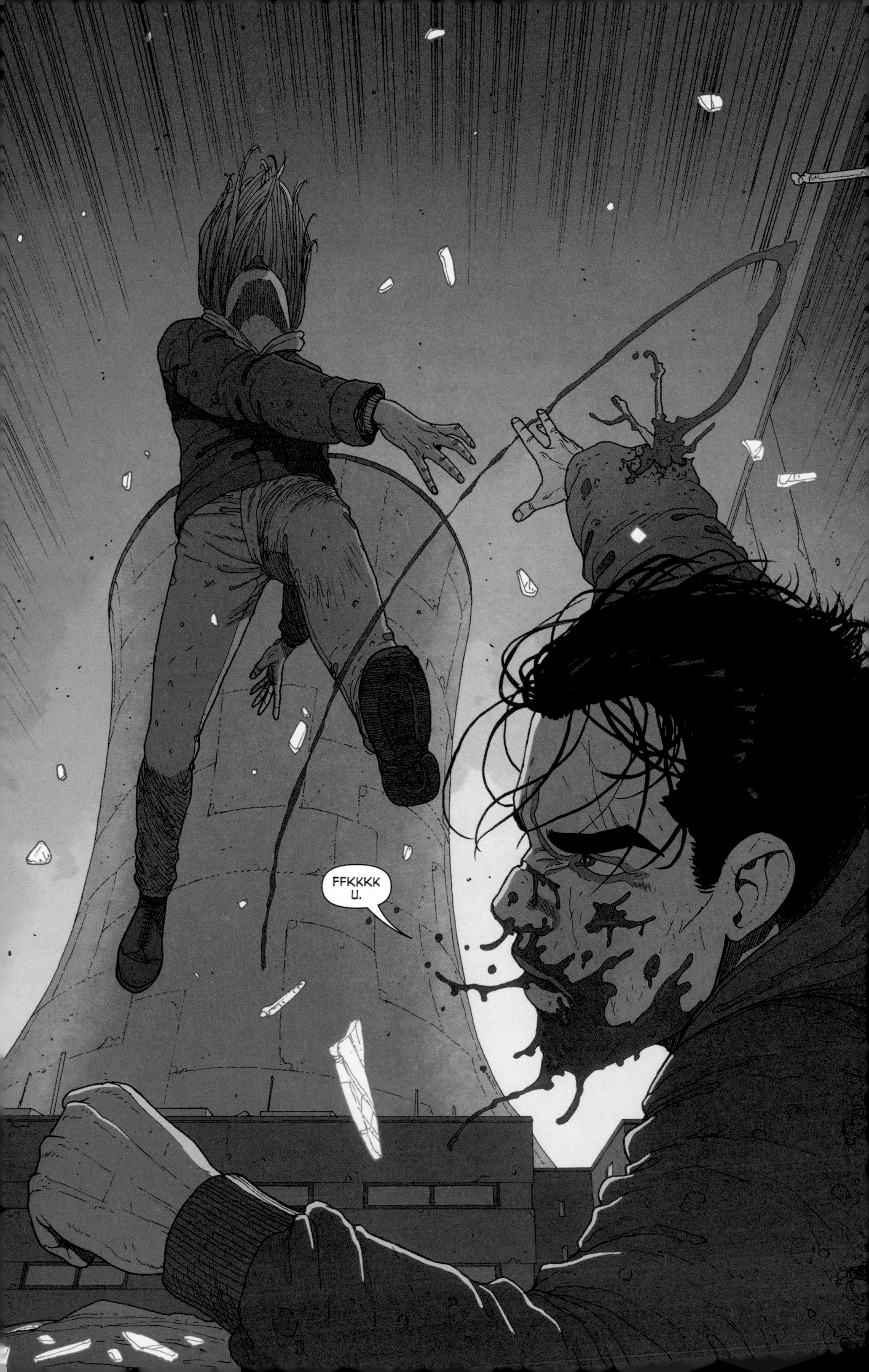
FFKKKK
U.

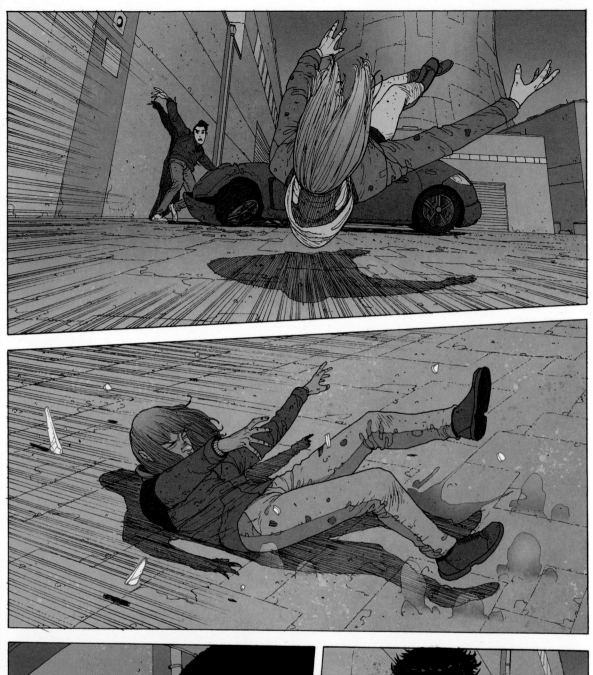

ELLIE--

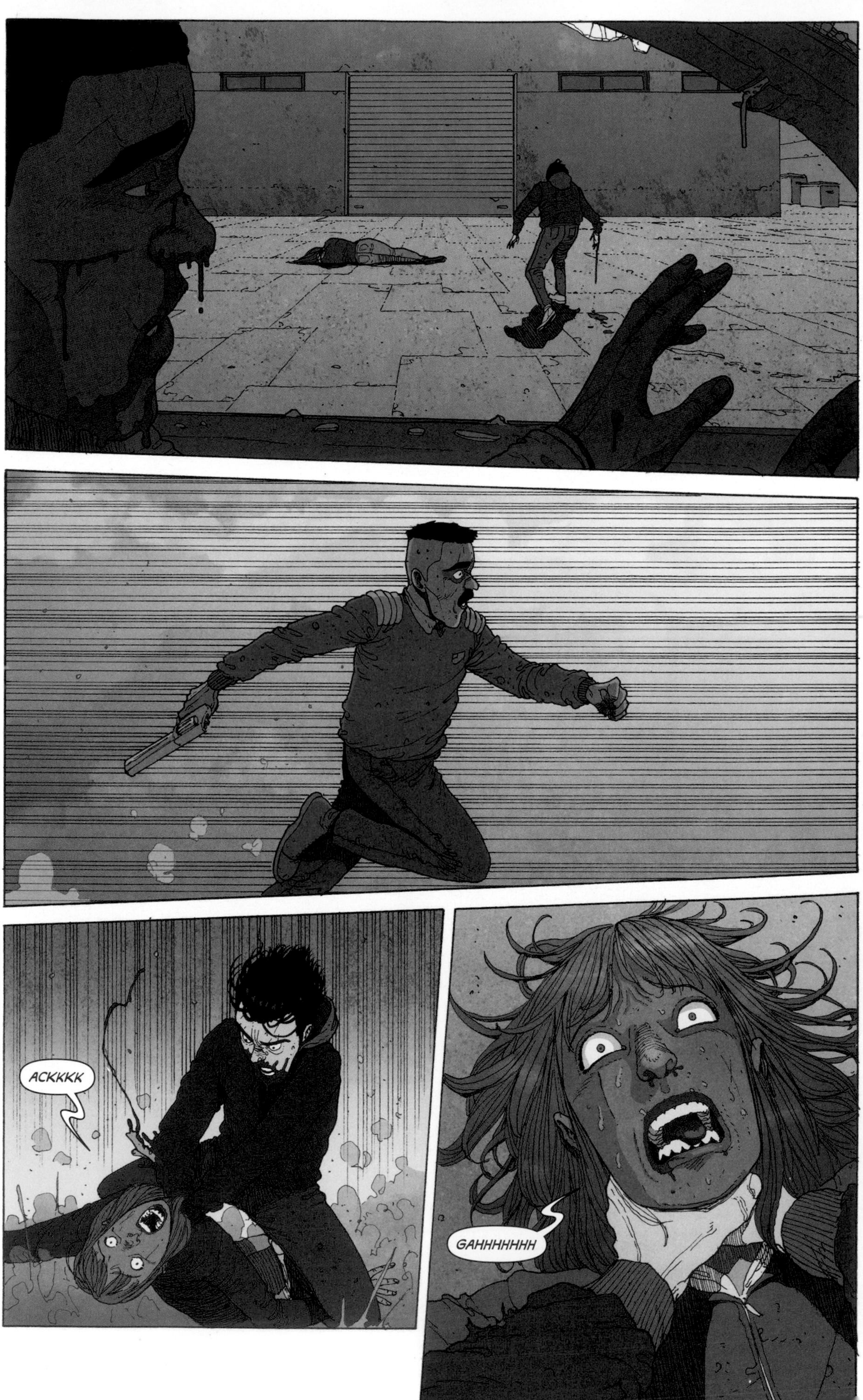
ACKKKK
GAHHHHHHH

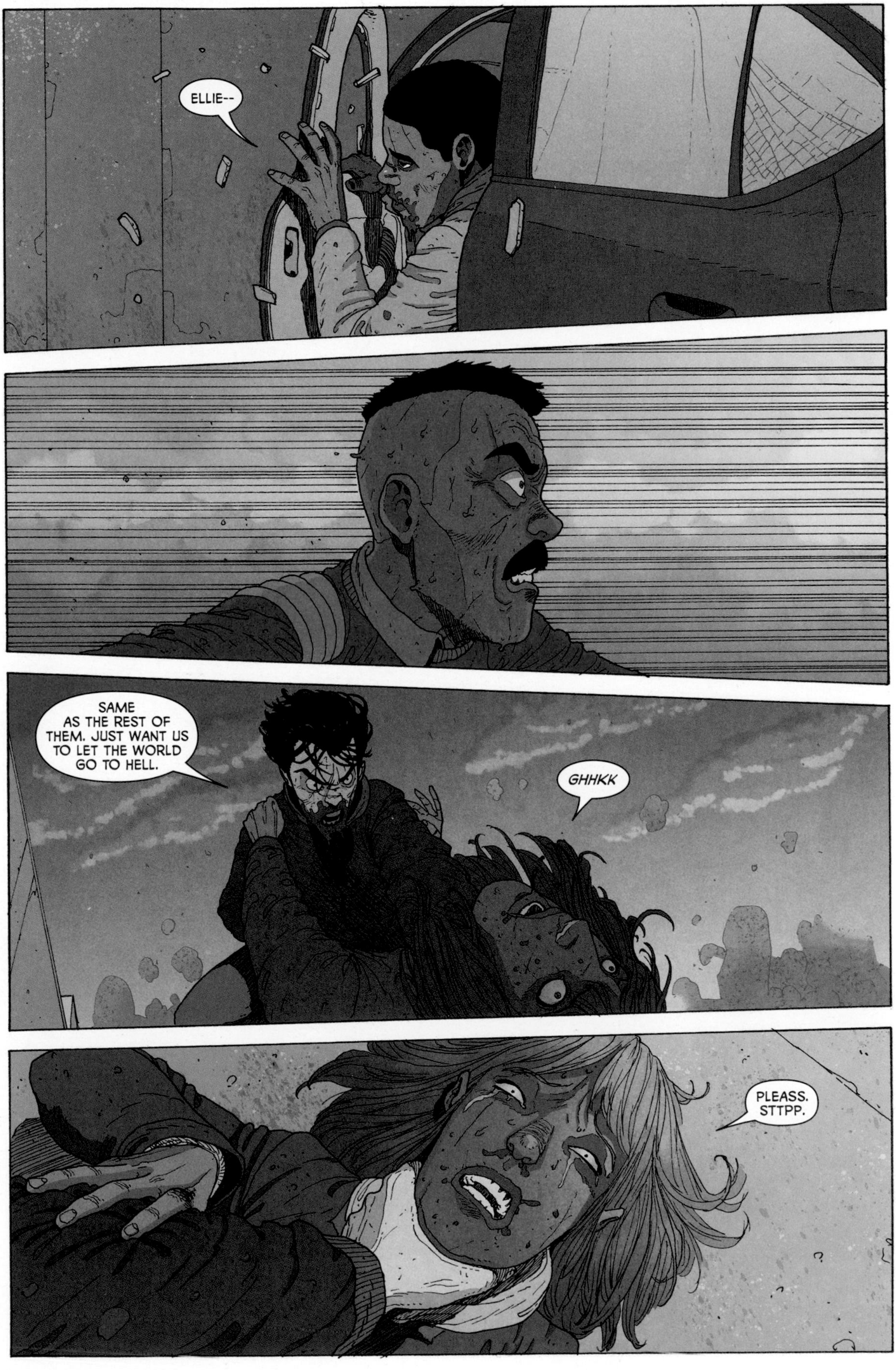
ELLIE--
SAME AS THE REST OF THEM. JUST WANT US TO LET THE WORLD GO TO HELL.
GHHKK
PLEASS. STTPP.

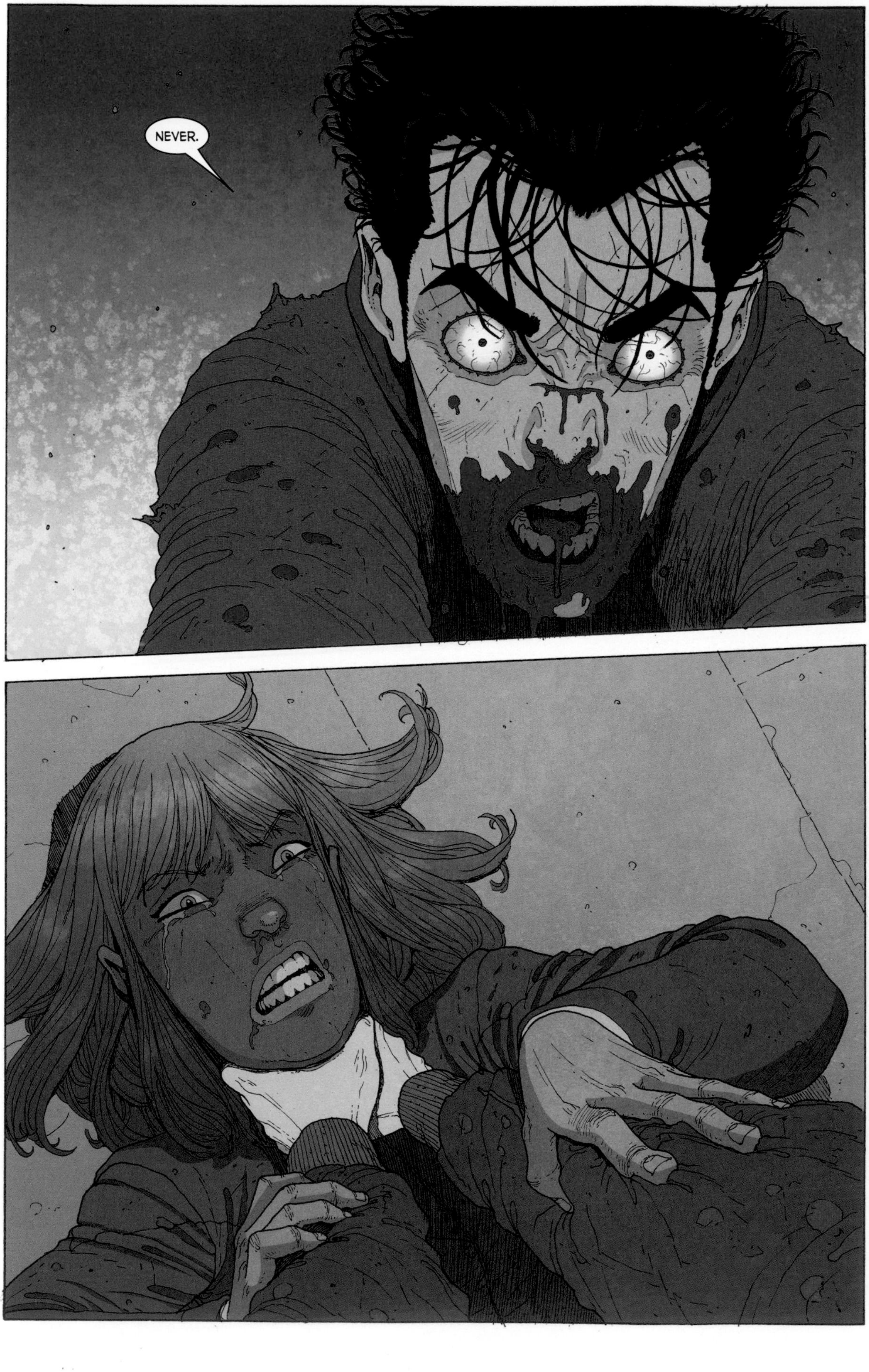
NEVER.

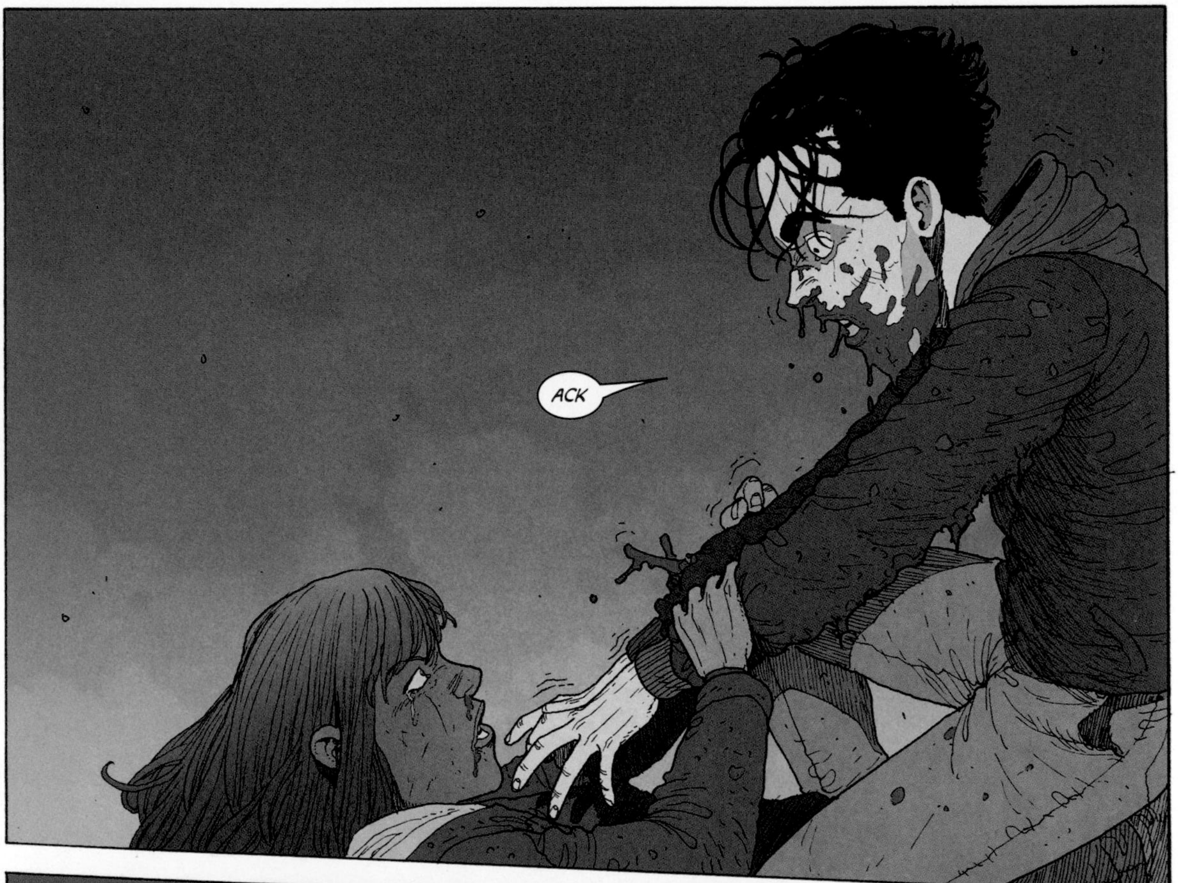
ACK

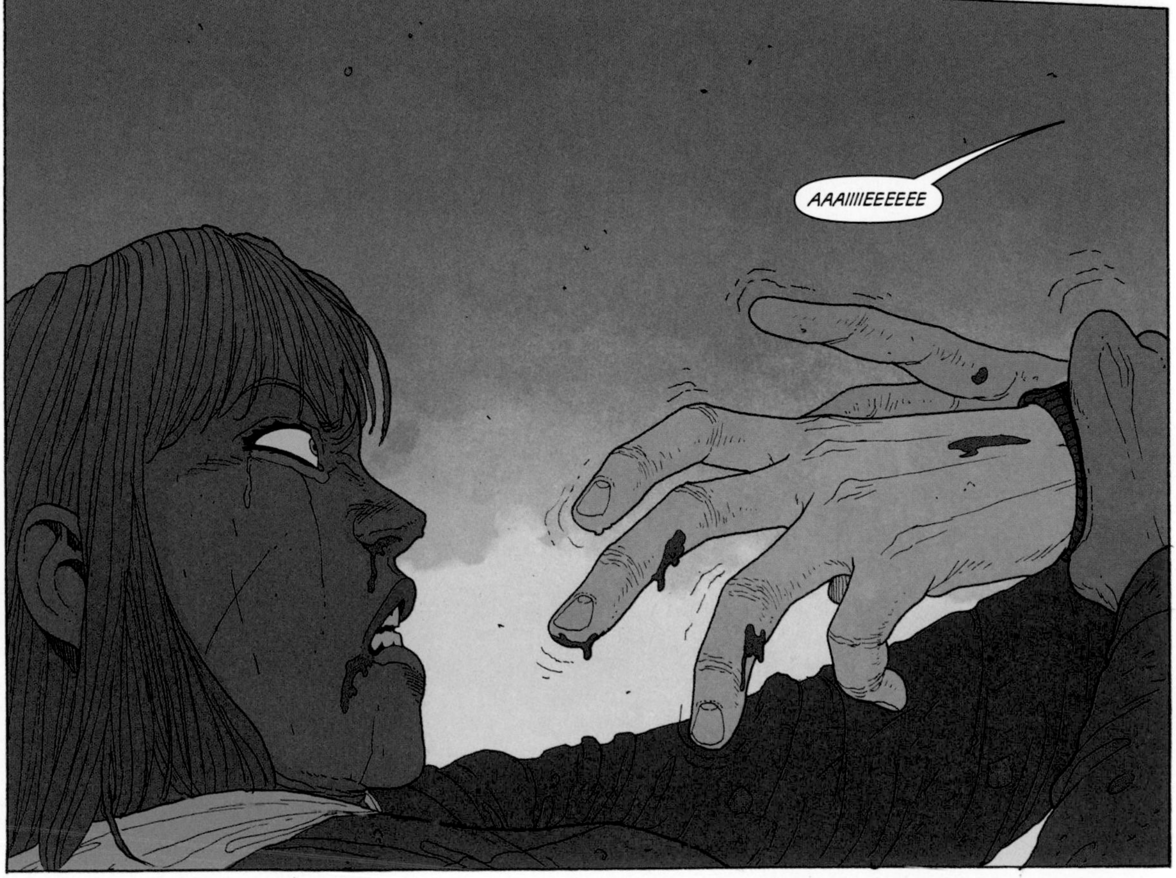
AAAIIIIIEEEEEE

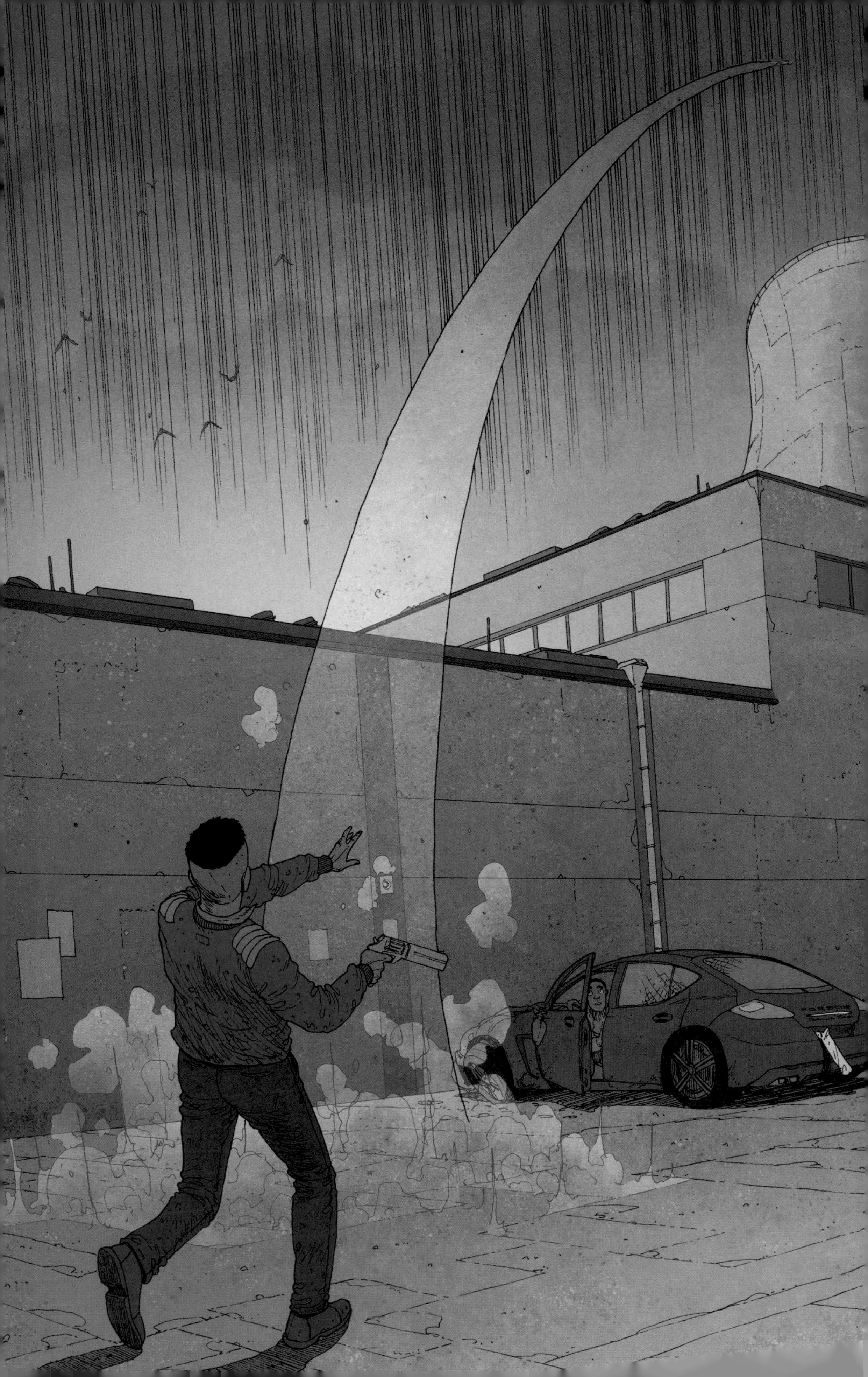

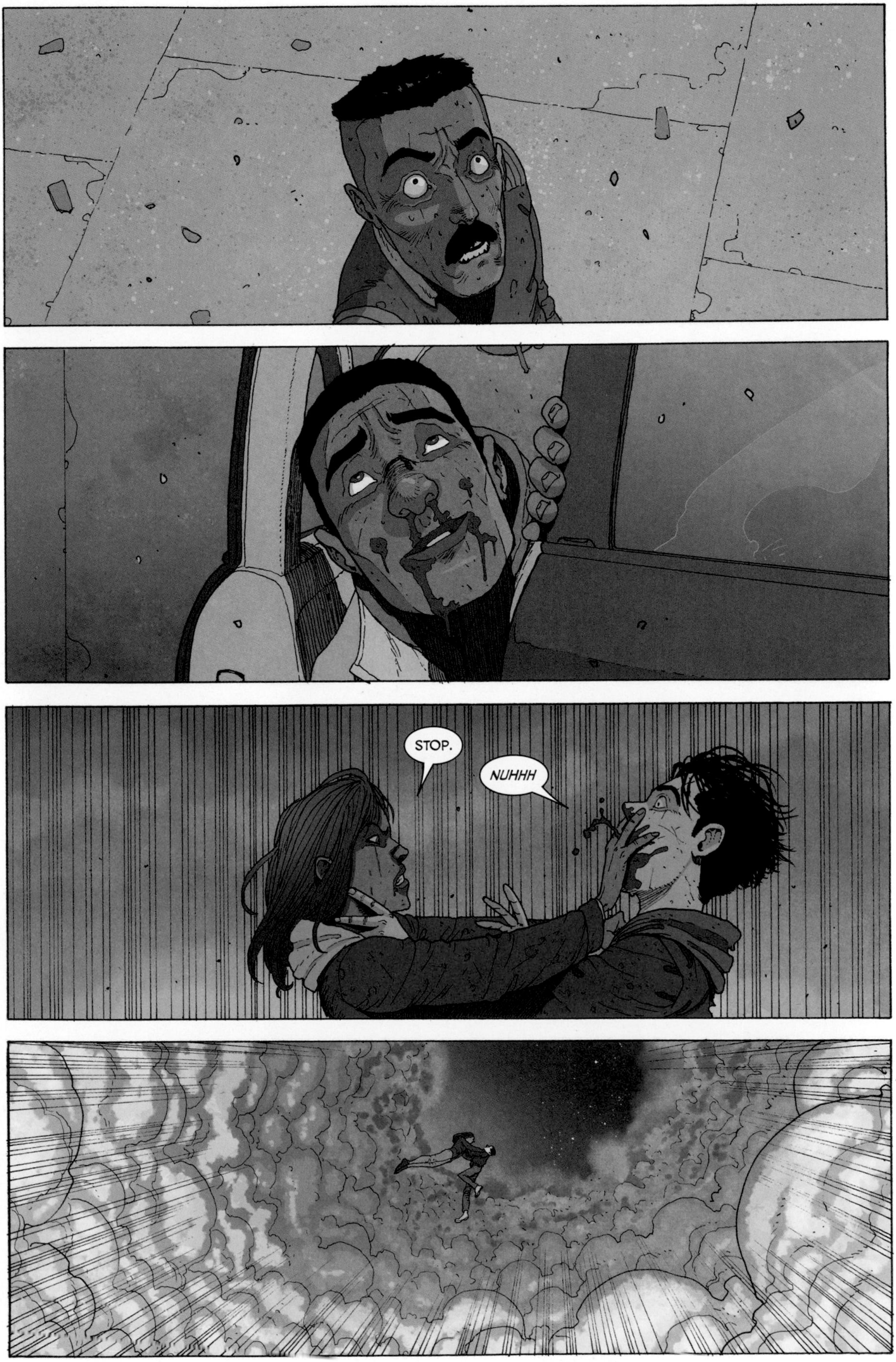
STOP.
NUHHH

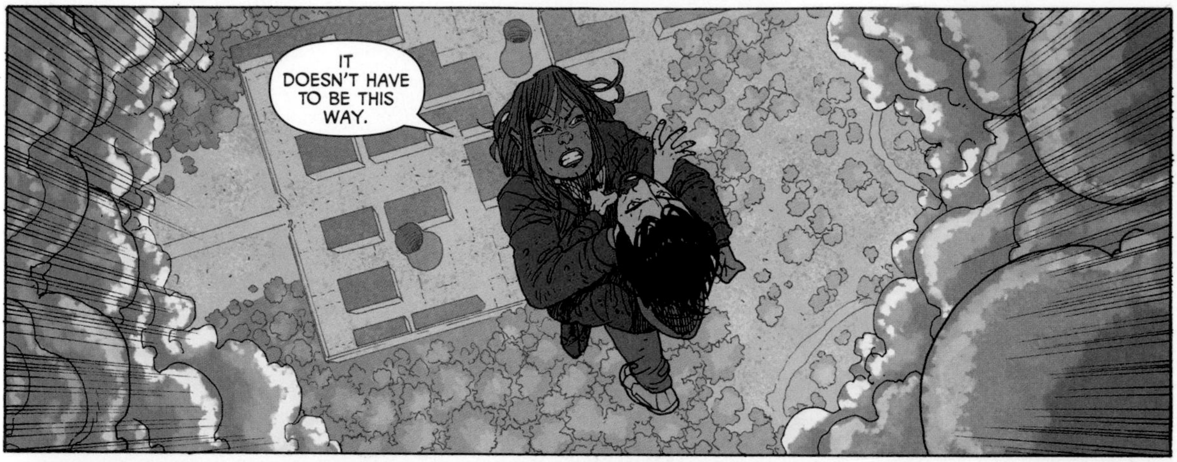
IT DOESN'T HAVE TO BE THIS WAY.
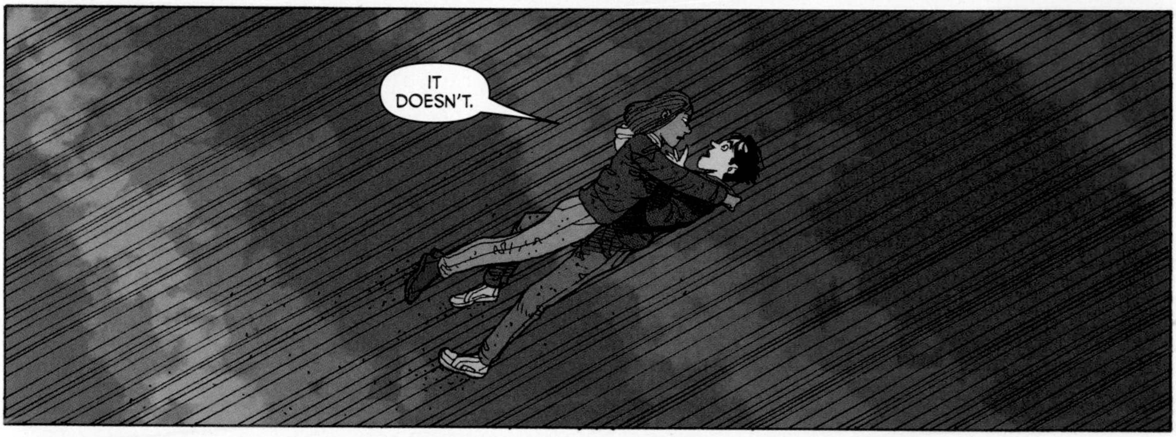
IT DOESN'T.
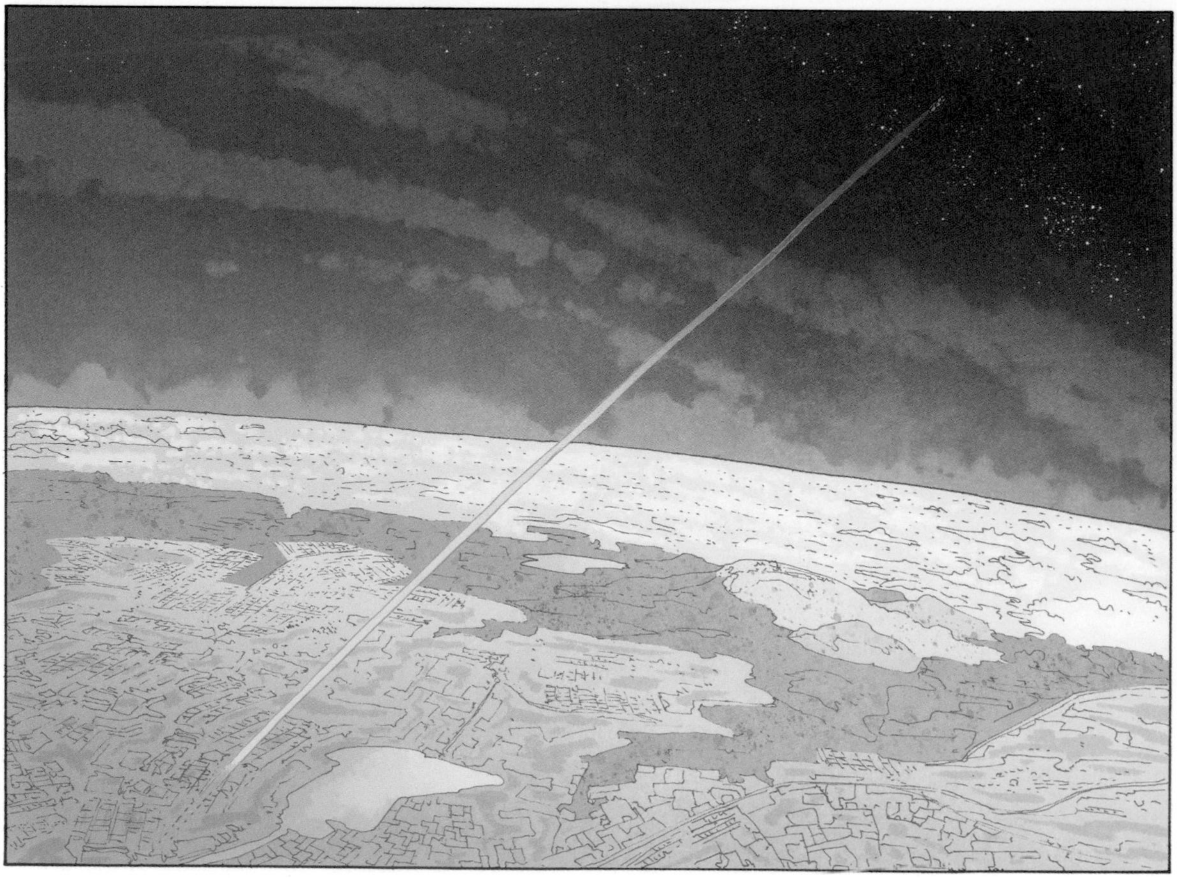

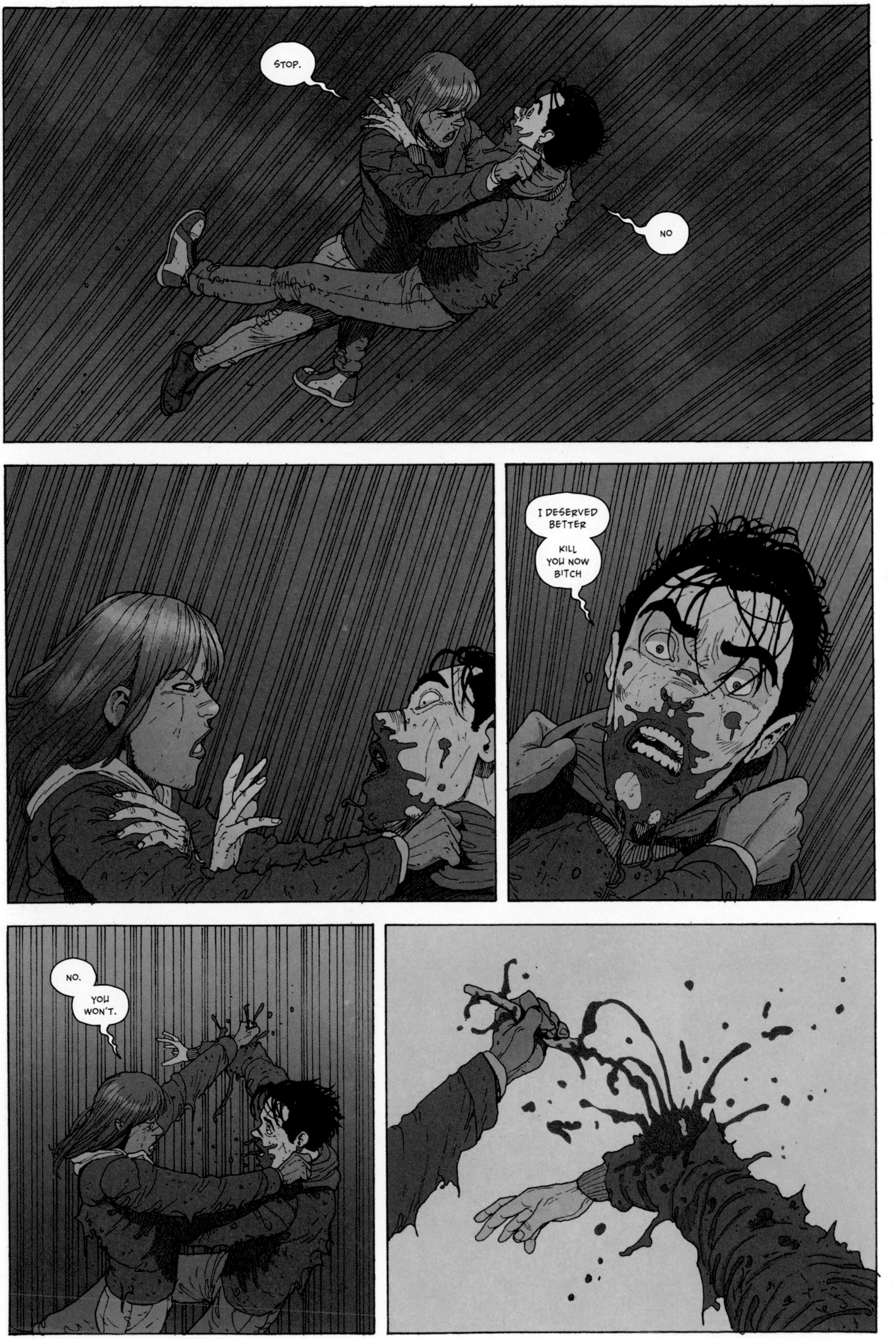
STOP.
NO
I DESERVED BETTER
KILL YOU NOW BITCH
NO.
YOU WON'T.

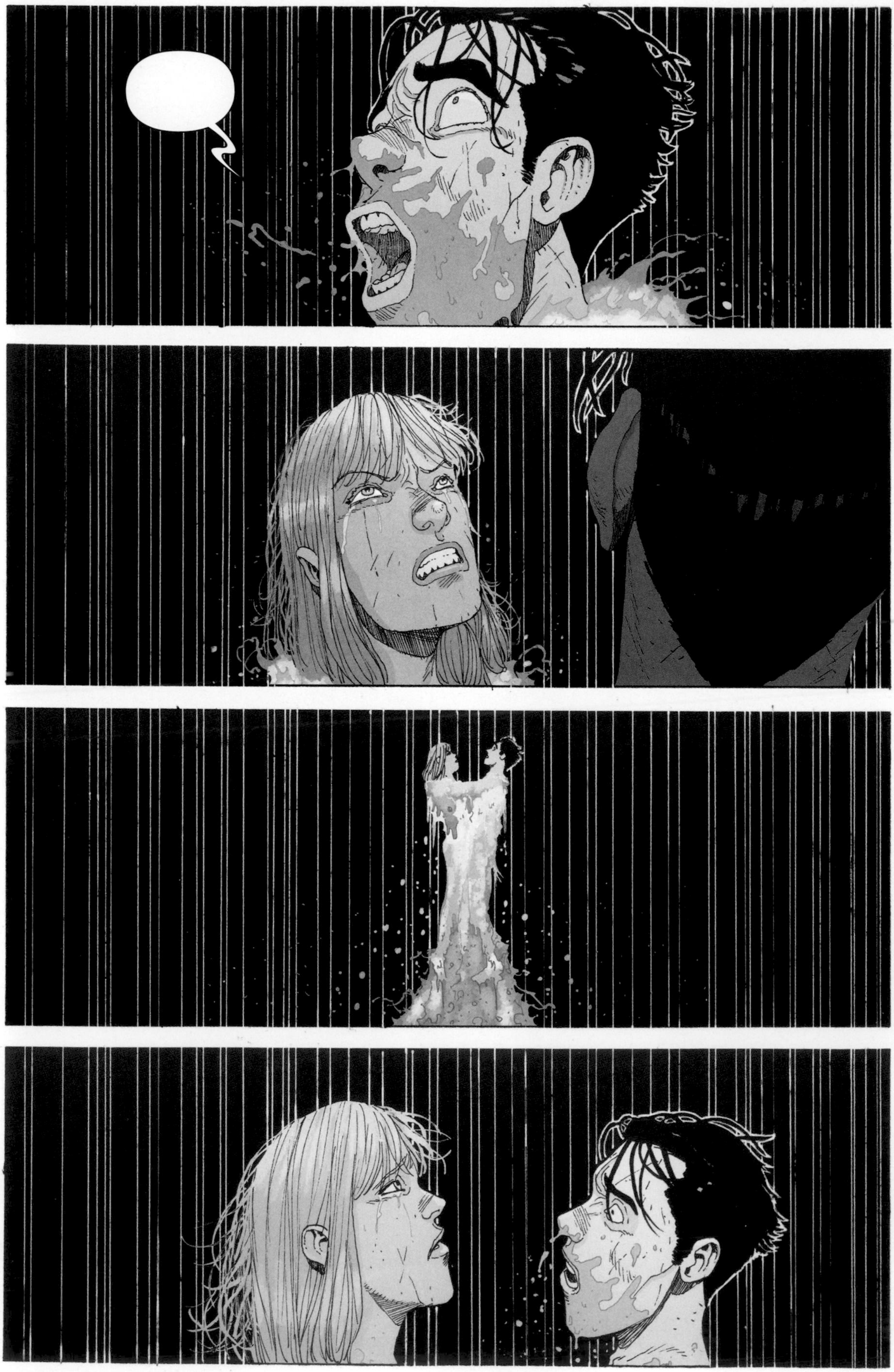

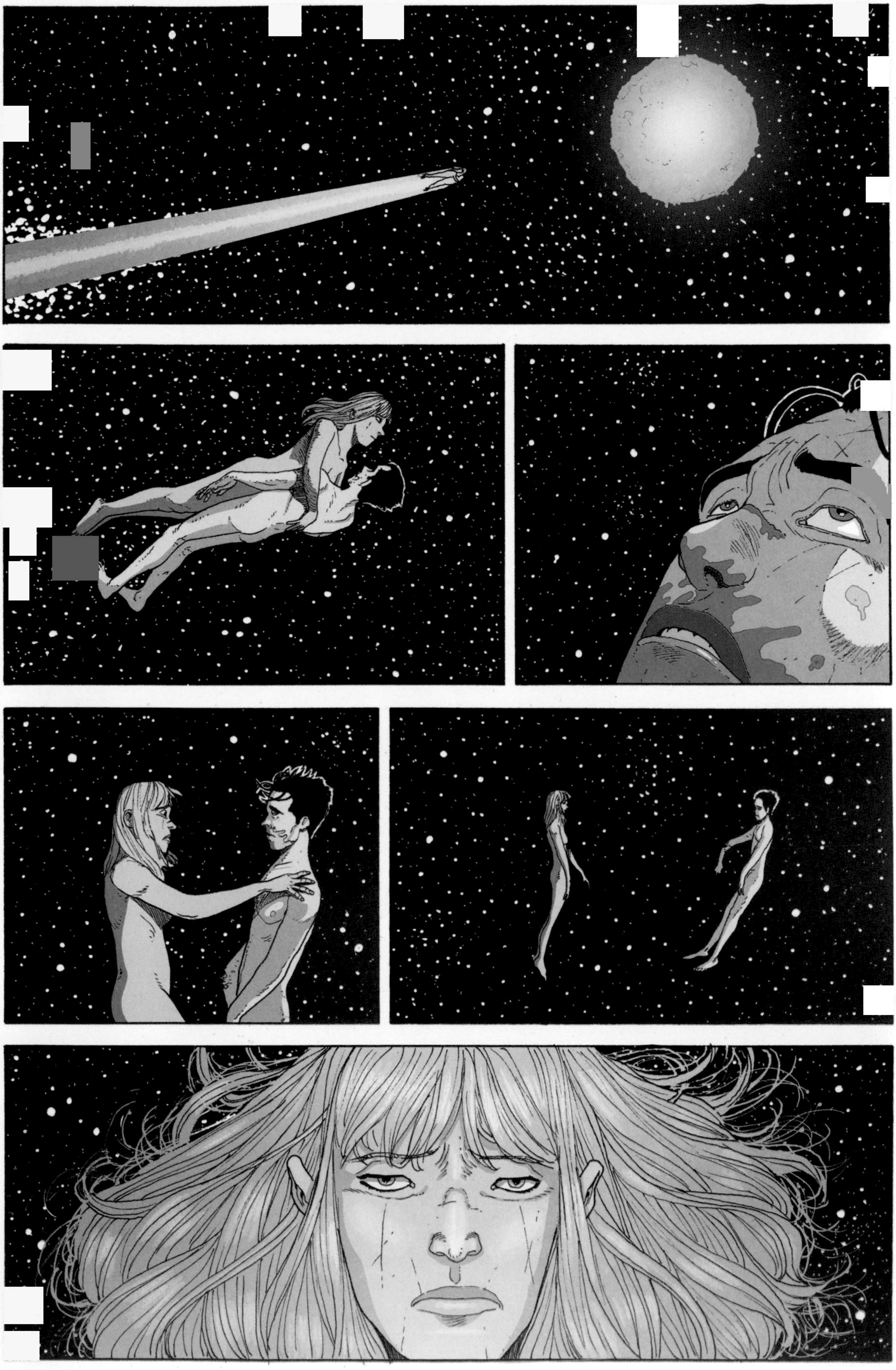

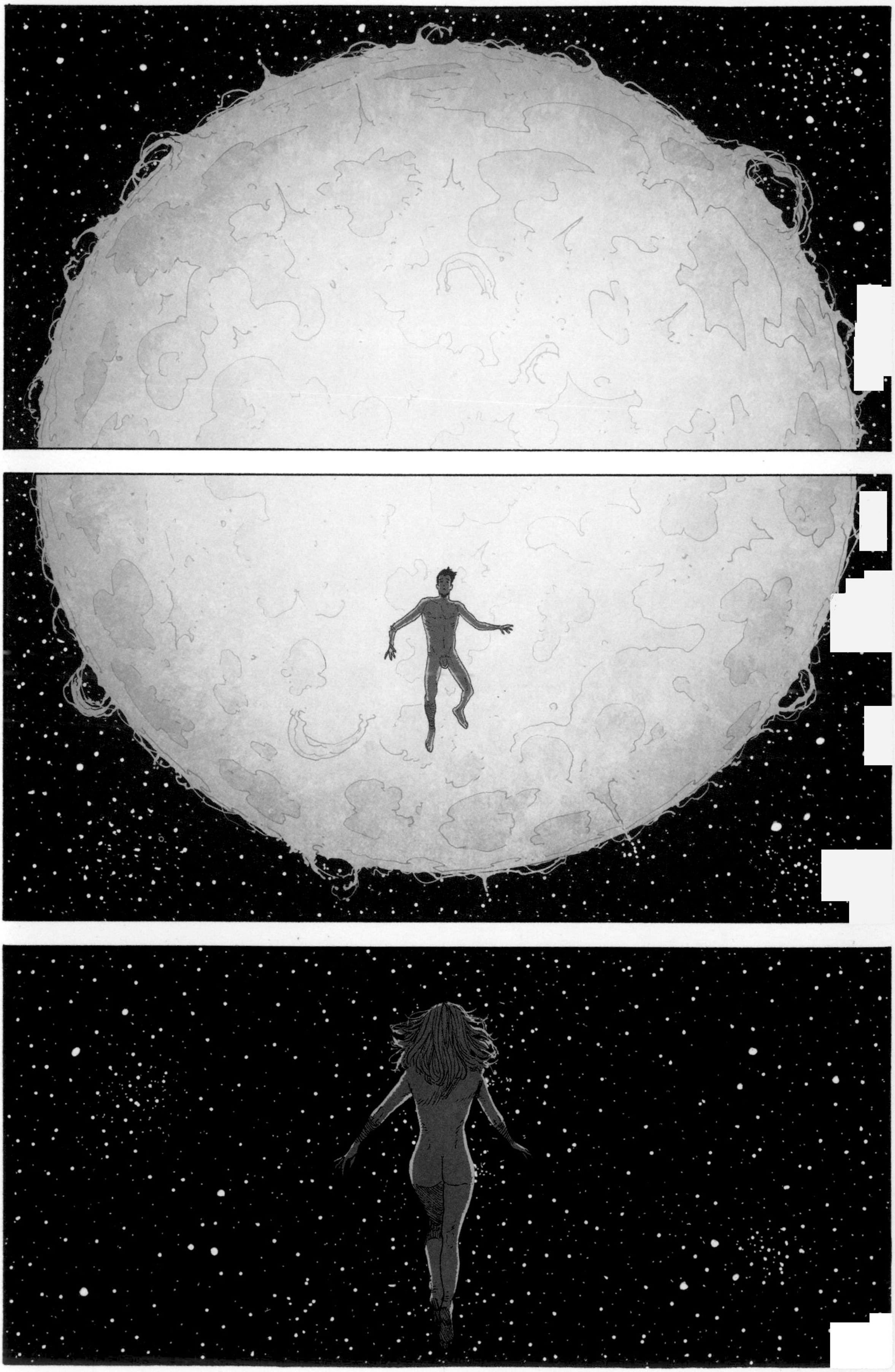

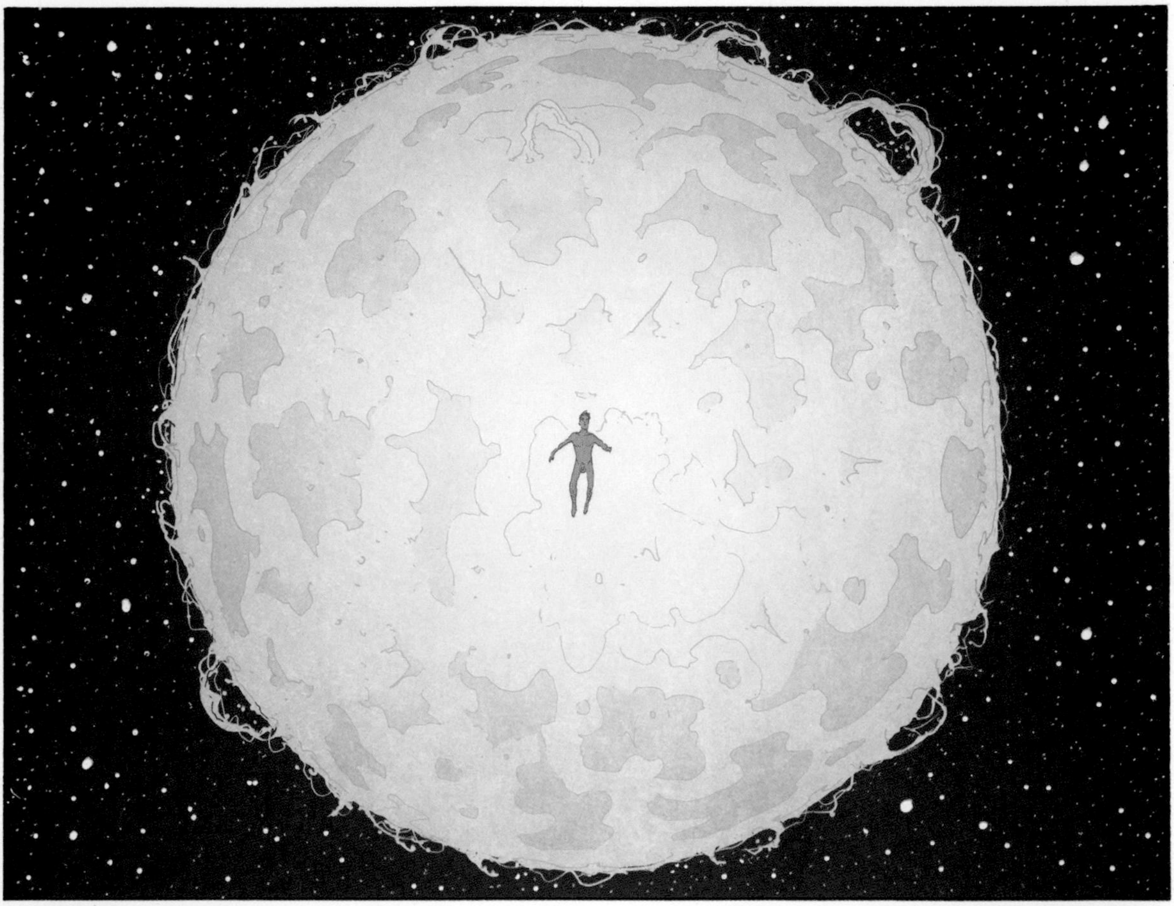
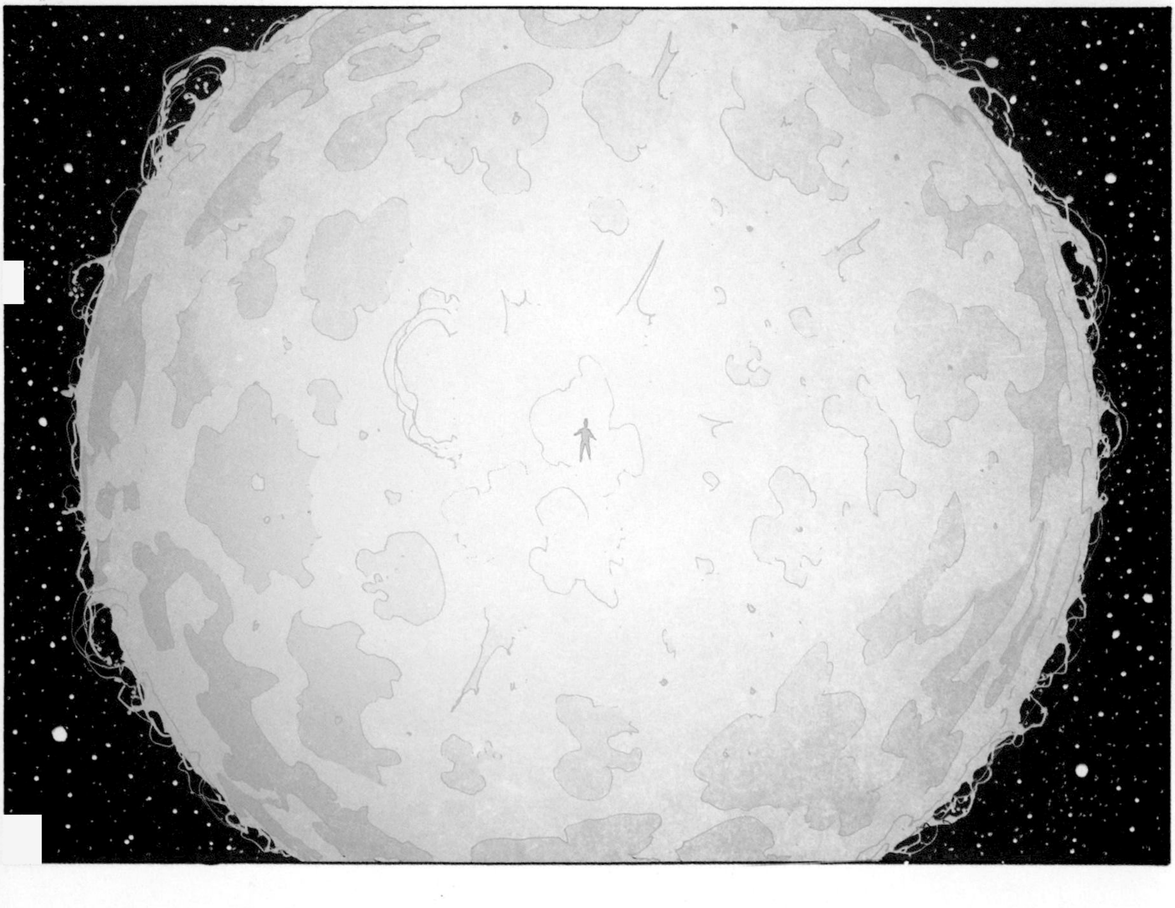

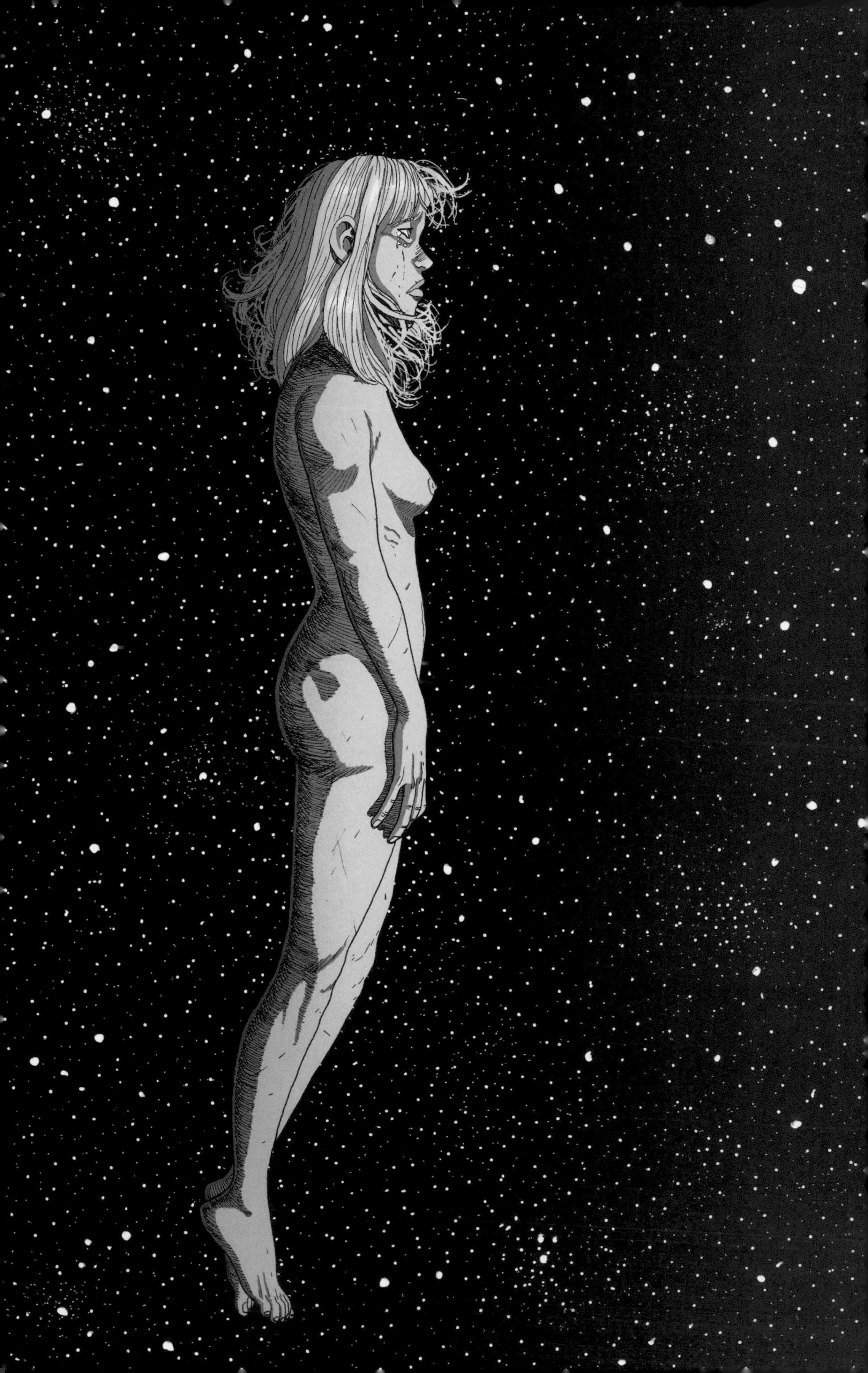

TWO MONTHS LATER.

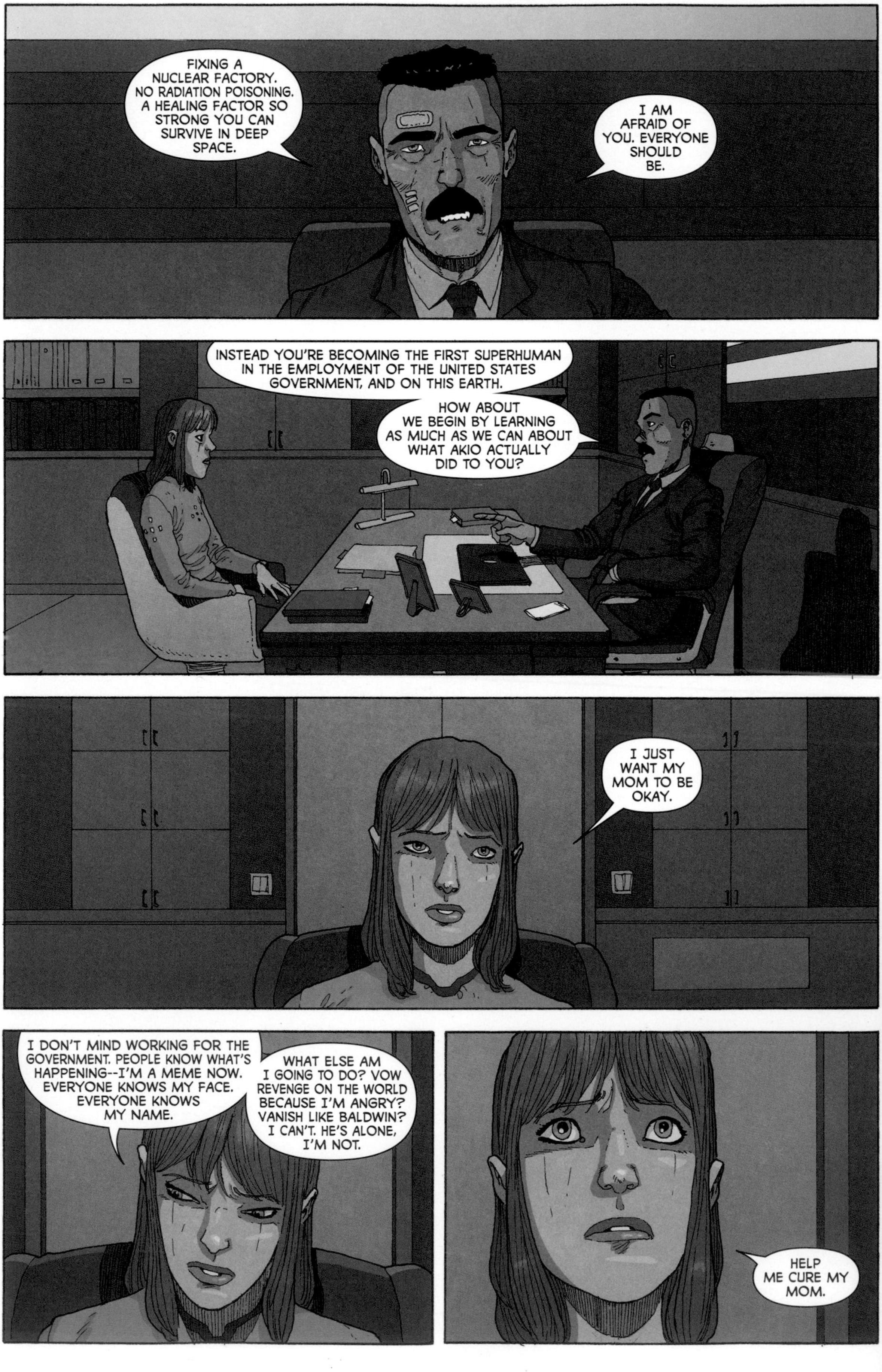
FIXING A NUCLEAR FACTORY. NO RADIATION POISONING. A HEALING FACTOR SO STRONG YOU CAN SURVIVE IN DEEP SPACE.
I AM AFRAID OF YOU. EVERYONE SHOULD BE.
INSTEAD YOU'RE BECOMING THE FIRST SUPERHUMAN IN THE EMPLOYMENT OF THE UNITED STATES GOVERNMENT, AND ON THIS EARTH.
HOW ABOUT WE BEGIN BY LEARNING AS MUCH AS WE CAN ABOUT WHAT AKIO ACTUALLY DID TO YOU?
I JUST WANT MY MOM TO BE OKAY.
I DON'T MIND WORKING FOR THE GOVERNMENT. PEOPLE KNOW WHAT'S HAPPENING--I'M A MEME NOW. EVERYONE KNOWS MY FACE. EVERYONE KNOWS MY NAME.
WHAT ELSE AM I GOING TO DO? VOW REVENGE ON THE WORLD BECAUSE I'M ANGRY? VANISH LIKE BALDWIN? I CAN'T. HE'S ALONE, I'M NOT.
HELP ME CURE MY MOM.

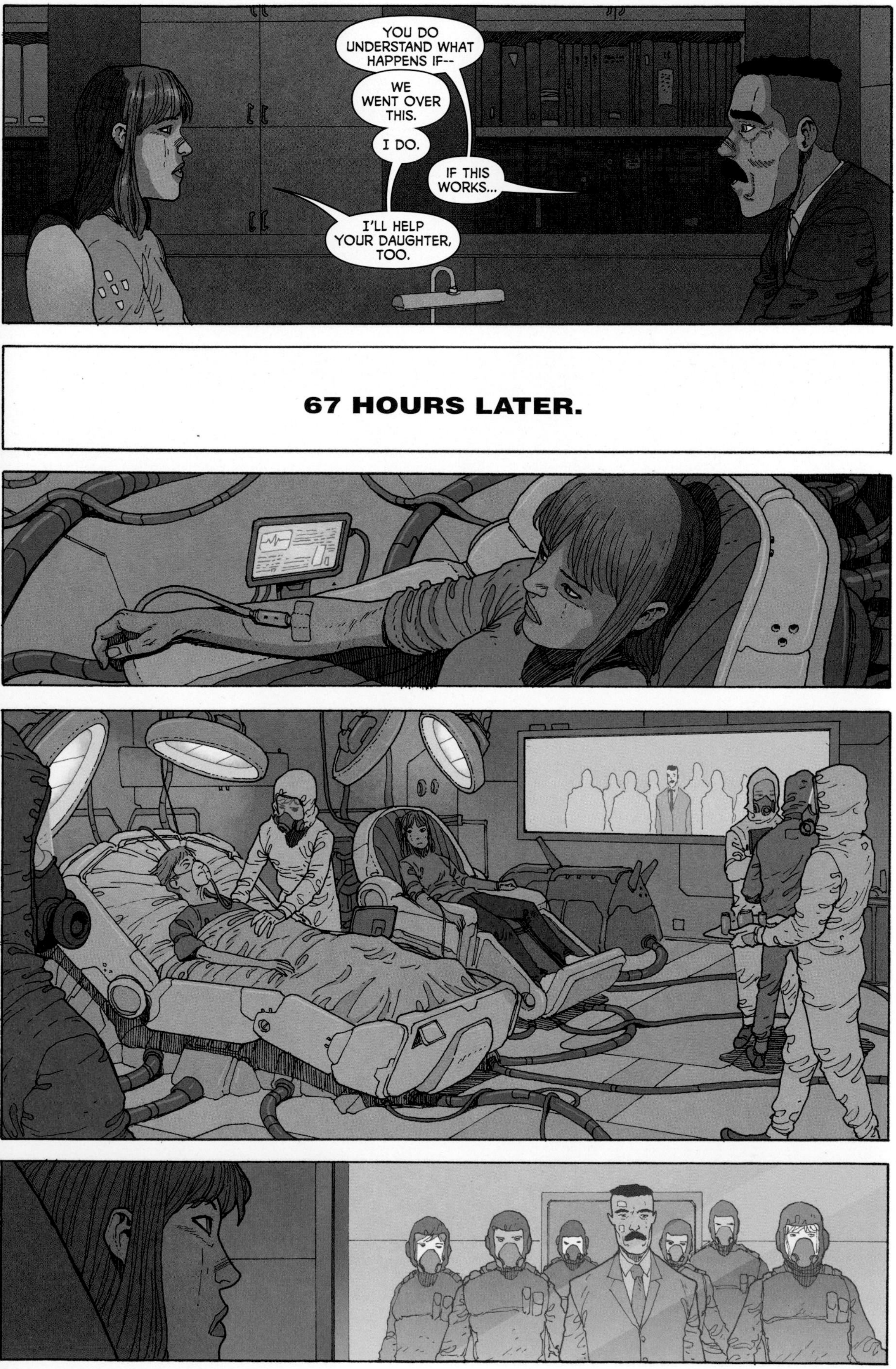
YOU DO UNDERSTAND WHAT HAPPENS IF--
WE WENT OVER THIS.
I DO.
IF THIS WORKS...
I'LL HELP YOUR DAUGHTER, TOO.
67 HOURS LATER.

NEW YORK CITY.
LUSO CASINO

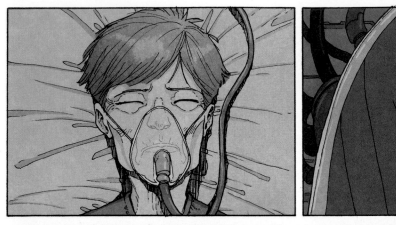

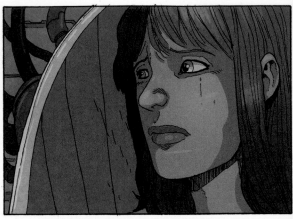

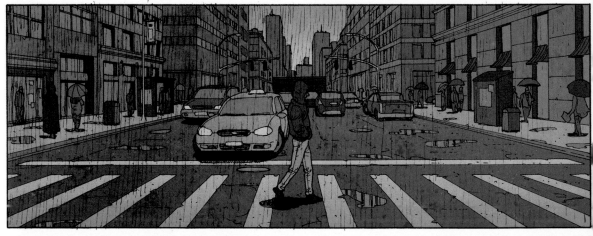

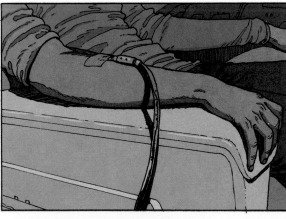

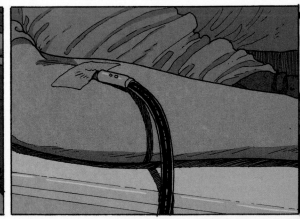

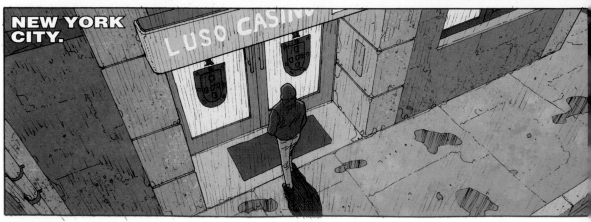

TEN ON RED, TWENTY-TWO.

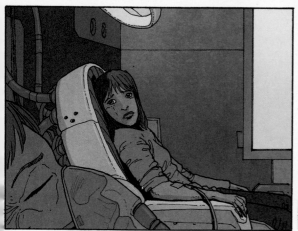

OH GOD, NOT YOU AGAIN.

THE VITALS ARE STEADY. THE PATIENT ISN'T EXHIBITING ANY ABNORMAL SYMPTOMS, WHICH IS STRANGE CONSIDERING THE TEST ADMINISTRATION IS--

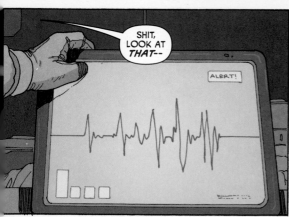

SHIT, LOOK AT *THAT*--

ALERT!

MOM!

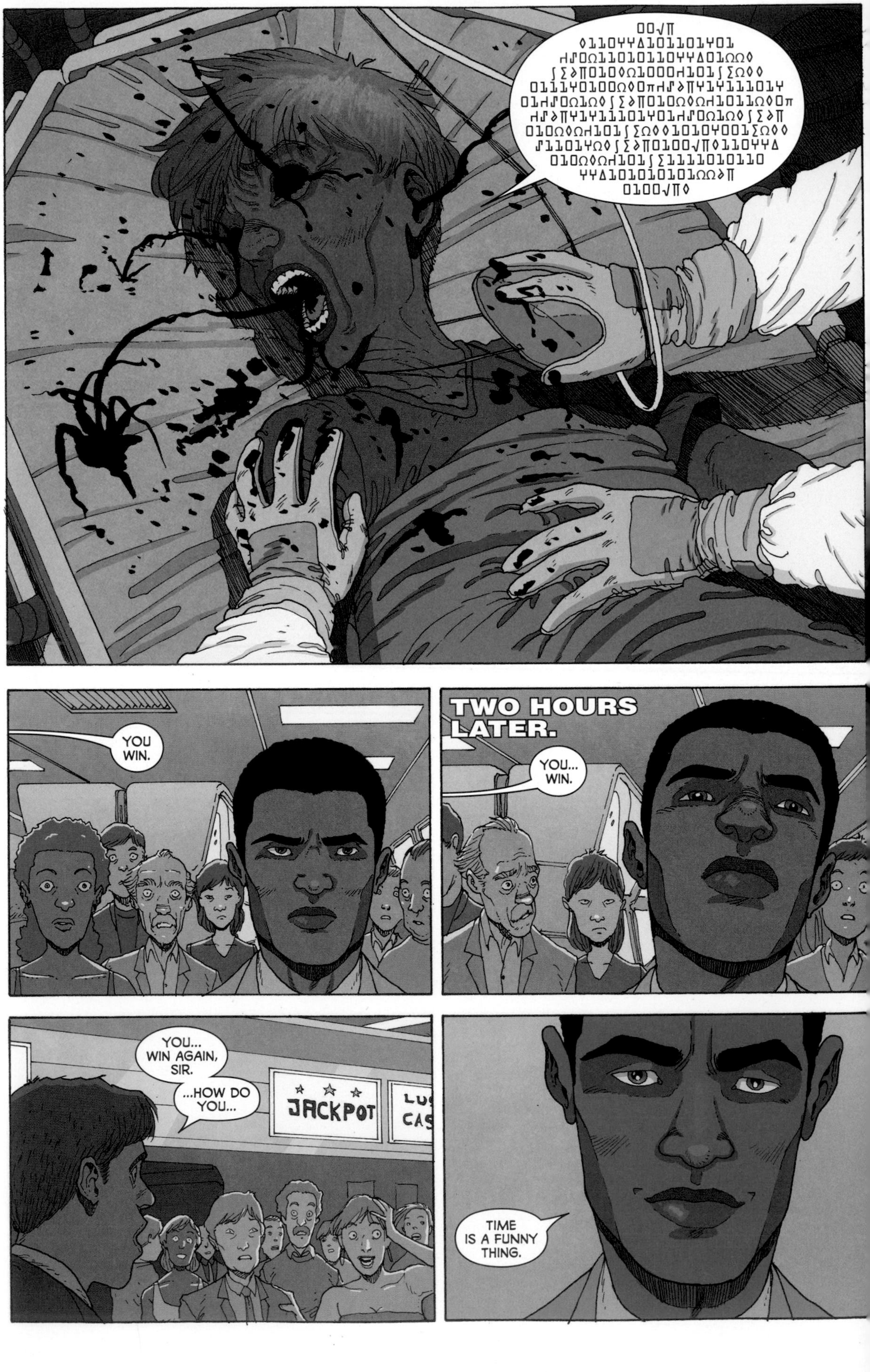
YOU WIN.
TWO HOURS LATER.
YOU... WIN.
YOU... WIN AGAIN, SIR.
...HOW DO YOU...
JACKPOT
TIME IS A FUNNY THING.

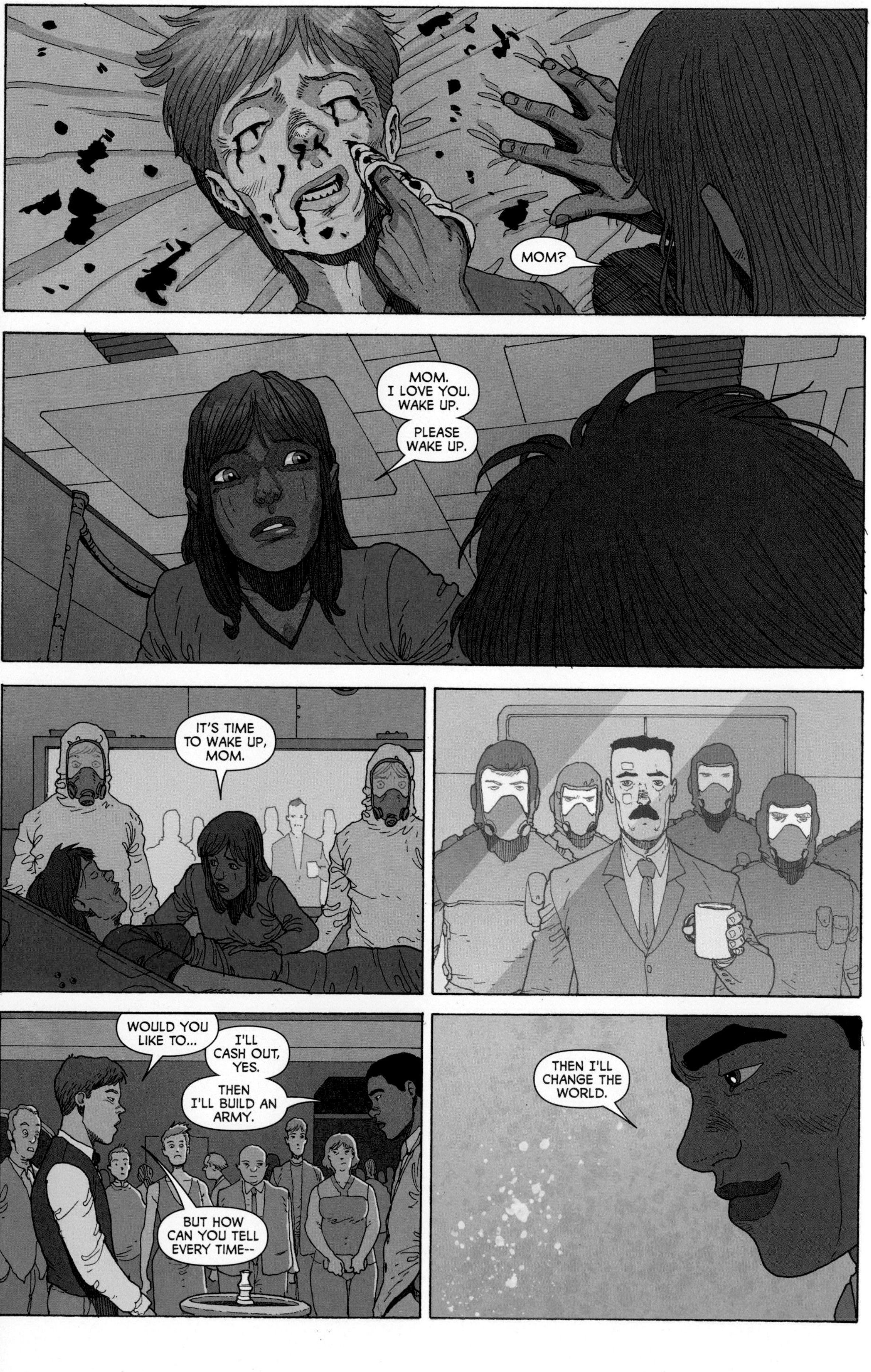
MOM?
MOM. I LOVE YOU. WAKE UP.
PLEASE WAKE UP.
IT'S TIME TO WAKE UP, MOM.
WOULD YOU LIKE TO...
I'LL CASH OUT, YES.
THEN I'LL BUILD AN ARMY.
BUT HOW CAN YOU TELL EVERY TIME--
THEN I'LL CHANGE THE WORLD.

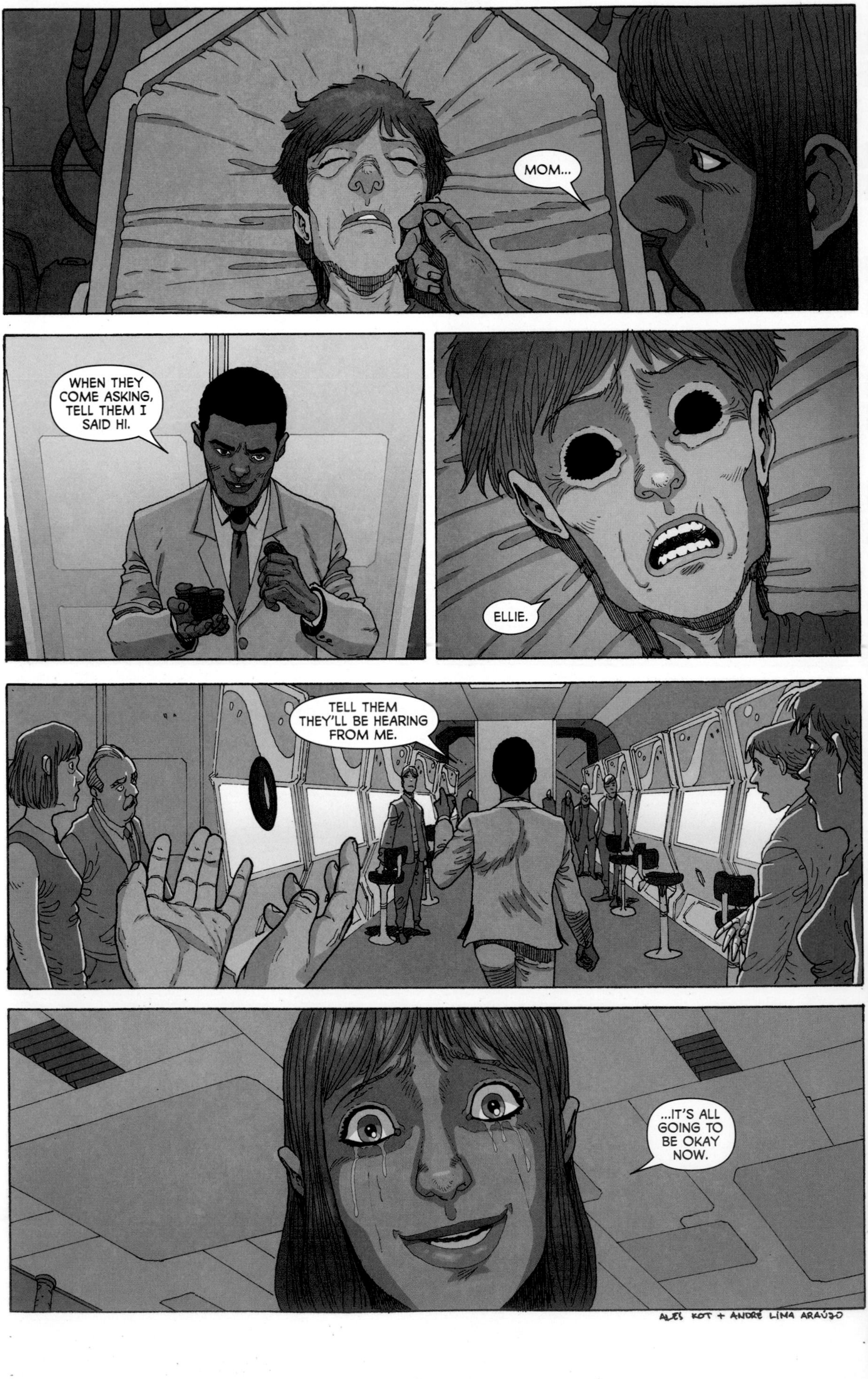
MOM...
WHEN THEY COME ASKING, TELL THEM I SAID HI.
ELLIE.
TELL THEM THEY'LL BE HEARING FROM ME.
...IT'S ALL GOING TO BE OKAY NOW.

ALEŠ KOT + ANDRÉ LIMA ARAÚJO